In the Border Kingdoms

Sefris leaped off the bridge and dashed after *The Black Bouquet*, intent on intercepting it before it slid over the edge. If the old, crumbling book fell to the ground below, the impact could damage it severely.

She dived for the tome at the last possible second, indifferent to the fact that by so doing, she was also flinging herself toward the drop-off. She grabbed the tome, somersaulted to the very brink, and stamped down hard. The action shattered clay tiles, countered her momentum, and kept it from tumbling her off the edge.

The Black Bouquet was hers!

From the mean streets of Faerûn.
From the edge of civilized society.
From the darkest shadows.

The Rogues

The Rogues

The Alabaster Staff
Edward Bolme

The Black Bouquet
Richard Lee Byers

The Crimson Gold
Voronica Whitney-Robinson
December 2003

The Yellow Silk
Don Bassingthwaite
February 2004

Also by
Richard Lee Byers

R.A. Salvatore's War of the Spider Queen
Book I: *Dissolution*

Sembia
The Shattered Mask

The Year of Rogue Dragons
Book I: *The Rage*
2004

Book II: *The Rite*
2005

Book III: *The Ruin*
2006

THE BLACK BOUQUET

RICHARD LEE BYERS

The Rogues

THE BLACK BOUQUET

Distributed in the United States by Holtzbrinck Publishing. Distributed in Canada by Fenn Ltd.

Distributed to the hobby, toy, and comic trade in the United States and Canada by regional distributors.

Distributed worldwide by Wizards of the Coast, Inc. and regional distributors.

Printed in the U.S.A.

Cover art by Mark Zug
Map by Ed Greenwood and Dennis Kauth
First Printing: September 2003
Library of Congress Catalog Card Number: 2003100824

9 8 7 6 5 4 3 2 1

US ISBN: 0-7869-3042-X
UK ISBN: 0-7869-3043-8
620-17996-001-EN

U.S., CANADA,
ASIA, PACIFIC, & LATIN AMERICA
Wizards of the Coast, Inc.
P.O. Box 707
Renton, WA 98057-0707
+1-800-324-6496

EUROPEAN HEADQUARTERS
Wizards of the Coast, Belgium
T Hofveld 6d
1702 Groot-Bijgaarden
Belgium
+322 467 3360

Visit our web site at **www.wizards.com**

DEDICATION

For Fresnel

ACKNOWLEDGMENTS

Thanks to Phil Athans, my editor, and to Ed Greenwood, for sharing his treasure trove of information about the Border Kingdoms.

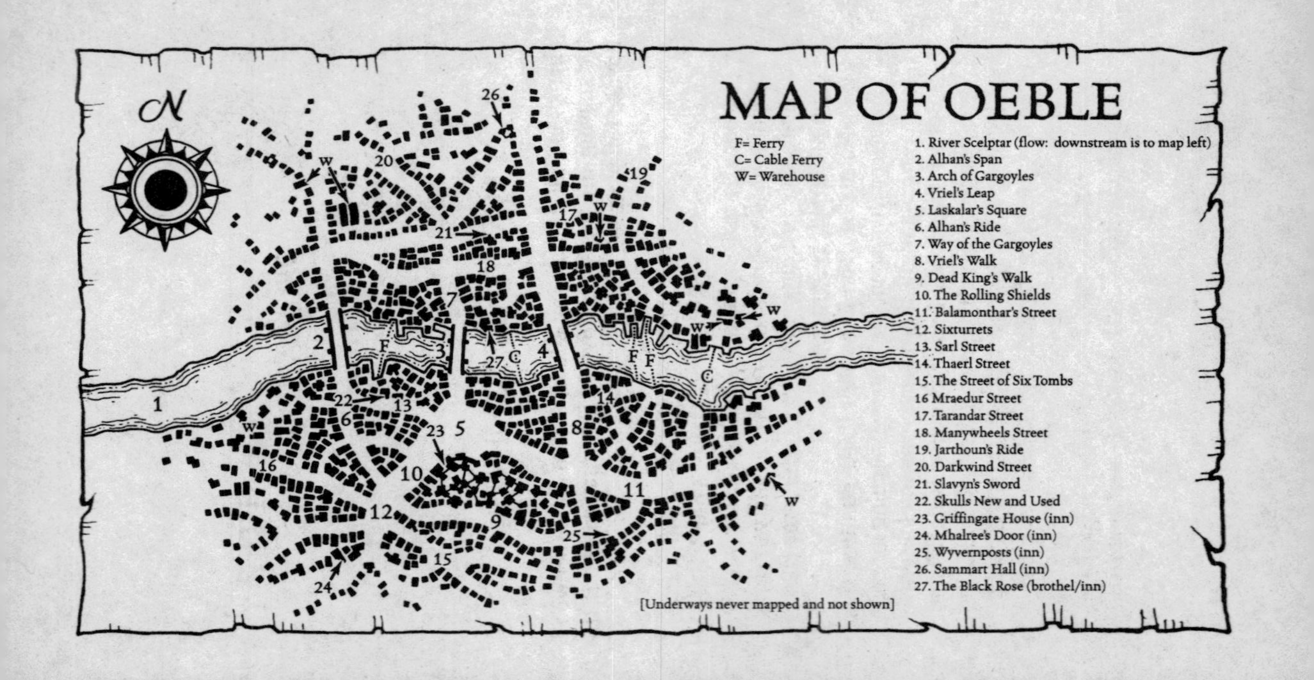
MAP OF OEBLE
F= Ferry
C= Cable Ferry
W= Warehouse
1. River Scelptar (flow: downstream is to map left)
2. Alhan's Span
3. Arch of Gargoyles
4. Vriel's Leap
5. Laskalar's Square
6. Alhan's Ride
7. Way of the Gargoyles
8. Vriel's Walk
9. Dead King's Walk
10. The Rolling Shields
11. Balamonthar's Street
12. Sixturrets
13. Sarl Street
14. Thaerl Street
15. The Street of Six Tombs
16 Mraedur Street
17. Tarandar Street
18. Manywheels Street
19. Jarthoun's Ride
20. Darkwind Street
21. Slavyn's Sword
22. Skulls New and Used
23. Griffingate House (inn)
24. Mhalree's Door (inn)
25. Wyvernposts (inn)
26. Sammart Hall (inn)
27. The Black Rose (brothel/inn)
[Underways never mapped and not shown]

CHAPTER 1

Aeron sar Randal grinned as the caravan came through the gate. He'd spent tendays preparing for that moment, and he could hardly wait to watch the trick unfold.

The travelers' cloaks were brown with dust, and their boots, caked with mud. They looked weary from tendays on the road. Or was it months? Aeron, who'd never in his life ventured more than two days' walk from Oeble, was vague on matters of geography.

No matter. The important thing was that the wayfarers had spent the journey watching for bandits, orcs, and all the other perils infesting the Border Kingdoms, finally swinging wide around Oeble itself, a notorious nest of robbers and slavers in its own right. Having finally reached the Paeraddyn, a walled compound on the southern edge of town that was supposedly the city's only "safe" inn and marketplace, they were starting to relax. It was natural, inevitable, and he could see it in their faces.

Clad in a beggar's rags, vile-looking sores made of tallow and paint mottling his legs, Aeron sat on the ground near one of the horse troughs. From there, he could survey the entire bustling courtyard, and every member of his crew could see him. He turned toward the inn and nodded.

Slouching and scratching, Kerridi came through the door a moment later. She was a big, brawny woman, but pleasant of face, and possessed of a merry, generous nature. Aeron thoroughly enjoyed the occasional nights he spent in her bed.

Beholding her there, though, few would have envied him the experience. The brown stain on her teeth and layers of padding around her middle made her uglier than nature intended, but it was primarily her ferocious scowl that transformed her into the very image of a shrewish wife.

She cast about until she seemingly spotted Gavath sitting at one of the outdoor tables. The scrawny little man had mastered the art of looking like an ass, the better to cheat, swindle, and lift the purses of the unwary, and he'd exercised that peculiar knack to the utmost for the job at hand. His garish, straw-stuffed doublet proclaimed him a would-be fop devoid of any vestige of taste. Pomade plastered strands of black hair across his crown in a ridiculously inadequate attempt to hide his bald patch. Gems of paste and glass twinkled on his fingers. Smirking, he was chatting up a pretty, flaxen-haired serving maid young enough to be his daughter. She was no doubt enduring the clumsy flirtation only for the sake of a generous tip. Gavath had paid the lass a great deal of attention over the course of the past few days, much to his supposed spouse's displeasure, the two of them making sure that everyone staying or working at the Paer noticed.

Thus, few but the newly arrived travelers were particularly startled when Kerridi started screaming invective and abuse. Most of the folk in the courtyard merely grinned and settled back to watch the next scene in the ongoing domestic farce. Kerridi advanced on Gavath, who quailed and goggled in dread. The serving maid scurried for safety.

Gavath attempted to stammer out some sort of excuse, or perhaps simply a plea for mercy. Kerridi lashed him with the back of her hand, a meaty smack that knocked him off his bench. She kicked him until he rolled away and scrambled to his feet. Then, still shrieking, swinging wildly, she chased him about.

Everyone began to laugh, and though the scene truly was comical, that wasn't the entire reason. Dal, who was loitering near the well munching on a pear, deserved some of the credit. Clad in a simple brown laborer's smock and breeches, his nose and cheeks ruddy with broken veins, the old tosspot didn't look like most people's notion of a wizard, but when sober, he was a halfway decent one, able enough to use his magic to influence the emotions of a crowd.

Kerridi connected with another solid buffet, or so it appeared. Gavath hurtled backward and crashed through the side of the pen containing the inn's population of goats, whose flesh and milk served to feed the patrons. At that same instant, Dal, his timing impeccable, surreptitiously cast a spell to alarm the animals. Bleating, they bolted from the enclosure and raced madly about, bumping into people and tables, frightening the horses and ponies, reducing the entire courtyard to chaos and confusion. Except for those unfortunates who were knocked off their feet, drenched in spilled beer, struggling to control fractious mounts, or scrambling to catch the escapees, everyone laughed even harder.

Aeron glanced around. Nobody was looking at him, so he pulled a small pewter vial from inside his shirt and quaffed the bitter, lukewarm contents. It was the last swallow of the potion, and he rather regretted the final expenditure of a resource that had extricated him from several tight spots. But Kesk Turnskull was paying him enough to make using the draught worthwhile.

Sorcerous power tingled through his veins. He could still see his lower body as clearly as before, but from past experience he trusted that he truly had become invisible to the eyes of others. Dodging the scurrying goats, he rose and stalked toward the caravan.

Kesk had told him who to look for, and he spotted her easily enough. She was a female scout or guide, slender, long legged, sun bronzed, clad in leather armor dyed forest green. A broadsword hung at her hip, and she had a bow and quiver of arrows strapped to her saddle. Even with her curly chestnut hair cropped short, she was comely in a stern sort of way. She was smiling at the commotion in the yard but not laughing outright, and didn't look as if she'd entirely relaxed her vigilance.

Well, that was all right. Aeron was confident she wasn't as able a guard as he was a thief. He'd been surprised when Kesk hired him for that particular job. He'd thought the tanarukk still disliked him for his refusal to join the Red Axes. But really, it made perfect sense. The outlaw chieftain knew that no one in his own crude gang of cutthroats possessed the finesse to snatch a prize from within the confines of the Paeraddyn.

Suppressing an idiot impulse to kiss her or tweak her nose, Aeron crept by the ranger. Her head didn't turn, reassuring proof that she didn't hear or otherwise sense him. He examined the baggage lashed to her sorrel mare.

She had a couple scuffed old saddlebags, but only one that, from the distended shape of it, looked to contain a box like the one he was seeking. He started to unbuckle the flap, and everything went wrong.

The saddlebag shrieked like a thousand teakettles sounding at once. Green light pulsed around Aeron's limbs, outlining them. He was sure the radiance was plainly visible to others as well, that he was a phantom no longer. The guide spun around and started to draw her sword.

One disadvantage of such a long blade was that it took a moment to clear the scabbard. Like many folk in Oeble, Aeron was a knife fighter, and could have used that second to throw one of his hidden daggers of fine Arthyn steel.

But he didn't. Though adept with a knife, he had little taste for bloodshed. It was one reason he'd always committed his thefts by dint of trickery, and perhaps it was why he tore the screeching saddlebag free and risked a desperate lunge forward.

He reached the woman in green a bare instant before she would have readied the broadsword. He punched at her jaw. The impact stabbed pain through his knuckles, but she fell backward. He kicked her in the head in hopes of keeping her down.

Aeron whirled and sprinted for the open gate. Spears leveled, two of the Paeraddyn's own guards scrambled to block his path. Another, stationed atop the wall-walk with its merlons, cocked a crossbow. Dal's enchantment had disposed the warriors to mirth, but only within limits. The deafening scream of the saddlebag sufficed to recall them to their duty.

Aeron cast frantically about for another way out, even though he knew none existed within easy reach. He wasn't supposed to need one. If the theft had gone as planned, he, in his guise as a humble beggar, would have limped out the front entrance before anyone realized aught was amiss.

The crossbowman pulled the trigger. Aeron twisted aside, and the quarrel just missed him. Half a dozen of the ranger's fellow wayfarers glided toward him, fanning out to flank him as they came.

Then two of them swayed and crumpled to the ground. Aeron surmised that Dal had surreptitiously thrown a spell of slumber. But why had the magic only affected a pair of them? Apparently they were seasoned warriors, strong in spirit, or else they carried talismans of protection. Either way, it was discouraging.

Aeron still had nowhere to run. He gave ground, trying to keep skittish goats, horses, and pack mules, all thoroughly spooked by the keening saddlebag, between himself and his pursuers. Meanwhile, he prayed for more magical assistance, a brilliant plan, or something that could extricate him from his fix, and he snatched a long, heavy, single-edged "Arthyn fang" from its sheath.

His prize finally stopped screaming, though his ears still rang from the clamor it had raised. The green light died, too, but it didn't matter. Fighting, even if it was just a punch and a kick, had ended his invisibility. That was the way the cursed potion worked. Why, only mages knew.

An instant later, he discerned that he'd run out of animals to interpose between his pursuers and himself, which meant it no longer mattered that he didn't like slicing and stabbing people. There was nothing to do but crouch and await the assault. He took a deep, slow breath to steady himself. Some of the Paer's servants and patrons shouted encouragement to his foes.

The outlander in the lead swung his sword in a vicious head cut. Aeron twisted aside and sprang forward in a single motion, bringing himself so far inside his opponent's reach that the long blade ceased to be a threat. The range, however, was exactly right for a knife, and he sent the traveler reeling backward with a slashed belly.

That was one man out of the fight, but Aeron had to keep moving, spinning, dodging, for if he faltered for even a heartbeat, one of the other three would kill him for certain. Most likely they would anyway, but at least he'd make them work for it. Glimpsing movement at the corner of his vision, he pivoted and snapped the knife across his torso in a lateral parry. Fortunately, the Arthyn fang was heavy enough to brush aside even the thrust of a spear.

But for all its virtues, it couldn't block out two attacks at the same time, and when he saw a bushy-bearded guard in scale armor hacking at him, he felt a surge of terror. Remarkably, though, the stroke wobbled and flew wide, and the warrior collapsed. Kerridi had buried a falchion in his back. Gavath came running up behind her with his own fighting knife in hand.

Aeron was pleasantly surprised at their recklessness, and Dal's, too, come to that, though the latter was still doing his level best to make sure no one noticed he was the one casting spells, relying on magic that didn't burn any sort of trail on the air. Up until that point, no one had known they were Aeron's accomplices. They could have allowed him to fight and die alone, and had a good chance of stealing away unhindered, but evidently they were too fond of him to abandon him. Or else they were hungry enough for the payment Kesk had promised that they were willing to take a considerable risk to get it. Either way, Aeron was grateful for their aid.

The spearman started to pull his lance back for another jab. Aeron cut him across the face, then kicked him in the knee. Bone crunched, and the guard fell.

Aeron whirled to fight alongside his partners. Armed men rushed in at them, too many, but then three of them staggered and tripped as though sick or blind, victims of Dal's wizardry.

Aeron, Kerridi, and Gavath stood fast against the foes who did reach them. Steel flashed and rang, the thieves hurled the next wave of guards back, and for an instant, Aeron dared to hope that somehow they might all escape. Then, across the courtyard, the willowy scout dragged herself to her feet.

She lifted her fingers to her lips and gave a piercing whistle, and even though it was wide eyed with terror, the sorrel mare heeded the call. The steed trotted to her, and she snatched her yew bow from the saddle.

Aeron was sure that meant trouble, but another guard lunged at him, and that kept him from even trying to do anything about it. As he and his opponent shifted and feinted, he saw the ranger whip an arrow from her quiver, then stumble. Dal, bless him, had evidently assailed her with a spell.

Unfortunately, she didn't fall down. Shaking off the effect of the magic, she caught her balance and pivoted in the wizard's direction. Despite his efforts at stealth, she'd discerned he was the source of the unseen attacks that kept hindering her allies.

Dal babbled and slashed his hands through a mystic pattern, not caring who saw anymore, just trying to throw the next spell quickly. Even so, he was too slow. The woman in green nocked her arrow, pulled the gray goose-feather fletching to her ear, and let fly. The shaft slammed into Dal's chest. He blinked as if puzzled, and his knees buckled, dumping him down in the dirt.

Aeron felt shocked. Astonished. He'd seen plenty of men die violent deaths. Indeed, Oeble yielded such a steady crop of slaughtered corpses that the Faceless Master, ruler of the city, employed the freakish "gnarlbones" Hulm Draeridge to drive the Dead Cart through the streets every morning and collect them. But that was Dal!

Perhaps sensing Aeron's horror, his current opponent cut viciously at his flank. Fortunately, the thief's reflexes sufficed to twitch back out of range. Then, before the swordsman could swing his weapon back into position for another chop, Aeron sprang in and stabbed him. The warrior fell.

Aeron peered around. More guards were charging toward the outlaws, or rushing out of the Paeraddyn's market to see what the fuss was about. The ranger strode through the milling horses and goats, plainly seeking a clear shot at the remaining thieves. A gash bisected Gavath's bald spot, and blood stained his face and ridiculous puffed doublet.

Aeron realized he and his comrades had no hope of escape, not without Dal's magic to aid them or a clever idea presenting itself in the next couple of heartbeats. He cast about once more, and finally, it came to him.

The sandstone walls enclosing the compound were high, but not impregnable-citadel high, only about twenty feet. Assuming a man could make it to the top, he might have a chance of surviving a jump.

"Come on!" he shouted.

He and his partners fell back, defending themselves as they retreated. They reached the patch of cool shadow at the foot of the wall, flung their current assailants back, and Aeron led them scrambling up a flight of stairs. Gavath was in the middle, and Kerridi brought up the rear.

Unfortunately, their frantic ascent gave all the bowmen clear shots at them.

"Surrender!" the guide shouted.

Had she been talking to some other scoundrel, Aeron might have laughed. Perhaps, since she was an outlander, she truly believed that a man in his situation might improve his circumstances by giving up, but he knew the sort of unpleasantness awaiting any prisoner who'd tried to commit a robbery in the Paer, particularly if he'd carved up a guard or two in the process. A quick demise was much to be preferred.

Crossbows clacked almost before she finished speaking. It was hard to dodge on the narrow steps, but Aeron flung himself down, and luck was with him. No shaft touched him, though they smashed into the stonework all around.

"Oh, sheltering shadows of Mask," Gavath whimpered.

Aeron looked back. The small man had a quarrel and one of the scout's gray-fletched arrows protruding from his torso. His throat rattled, and he slumped motionless.

"Keep moving!" Kerridi snapped.

She reared up as if she didn't realize she had a crossbow bolt sticking in her too, then swayed, fell over backward, and tumbled down the stairs, knocking into the pursuers who'd started up after her.

Aeron sprinted on. There was nothing else to do. For the next few seconds, he had little to fear from the crossbowmen who'd just discharged their weapons. It took them some time to cock and load. The scout, however, was a different matter. She was already pulling back her bow.

He wondered how many arrows she could loose before he made it up to the wall-walk. Too many, he suspected, for him to dodge them all. Given her manifest competence, he wondered if he could even evade the next one.

Her bow jumped, straightening itself, but the arrow didn't streak at him. It simply dropped at her feet. For an instant, he didn't understand, then he realized the string had broken.

He dashed on, fast as he'd ever moved in his life. A swordsman met him at the top of the steps. He dodged the fellow's blade, then slashed him across the wrist. The guard dropped his weapon, his eyes and mouth gaped open wide, and Aeron bulled him out of the way.

He glanced back. The ranger already had her bow restrung and another arrow drawn back.

He dived over the crenellations, and the ground rushed up at him. He told himself to roll, but he smashed down so hard that afterward he wasn't sure if he'd actually done it or not. Time skipped, and he was sprawled on his back.

He heaved himself to his feet. Evidently the desperate leap hadn't broken any bones. He hurt all over, but that didn't matter any more than the fatigue implicit in his pounding heart and gasping lungs. He had to run before someone took another shot at him from the ramparts, or other foes came streaming out of the gate.

He dashed north, toward the heart of the city with its leaning ramshackle towers, seeking to lose himself in the maze of twisting alleyways. Eventually he found a thin, unmarked flight of stairs at the end of a narrow cul-de-sac, and after descending into the earth, permitted himself to hunker down, utterly spent, and rest. His eyes stung, and he knuckled them angrily.

Bow in hand, guiding the sorrel mare with her knees, Miri Buckman forced her way down the congested lane until it became clear that the thief had outdistanced her.

Could she track him, then? Through a forest or across a moor, almost certainly. But in the city, creaking carts, drawn by oxen and mules, rolled up and down the avenues to erase whatever sign her quarry might have left. Pedestrians milled pointlessly about to complete the obliteration, and moreover, some of the wider thoroughfares were cobbled.

She cursed under her breath. She wasn't fond of cities in general with their crowds, dirt, and stink, and crumbling Oeble seemed a particularly obnoxious one.

By the Hornblade, she thought, the spires look as if they might collapse at any second.

Every other person on the street seemed either to slink furtively or to affect a bravo's strut and sneer. Indeed, every third passerby was a pig-faced, olive-skinned orc or some sort of goblin-kin. She would have had no trouble believing the town was as foul a nest of villains as rumor maintained even if she hadn't suffered an overt demonstration of its lawlessness.

She wheeled the mare and cantered back to the Paeraddyn, where someone had already found a couple healers to tend the injured warriors. It didn't look as if the outlaws had actually killed more than a couple of her warriors. She supposed that was good, though in her present humor, she was half inclined to cut down a few of them herself. Stupid, incompetent—

She took a deep breath and let it out slowly, controlling the anger, or at least redirecting it toward the proper target. She had no business scorning the mercenaries for failing to protect the treasure. Ultimately, it had been her responsibility and, maddeningly, her failure, just a few scant minutes before she might have divested herself of her charge.

Hostegym Longstride hobbled up to her with a faltering gait that belied his surname. Not seeing any blood on the burly, azure-cloaked mercenary, Miri surmised that one of the thieves had scored on him with a shrewd kick to the knee, a stamp to the foot, or some such.

"Most of our lads should survive," he rumbled. "Most of the inn's guards, too, if you care."

"How about the three thieves who didn't get away?" she replied, swinging herself down off her horse. The motion made the top of her head throb where the fraudulent beggar had kicked her.

"All dead," the mercenary captain said. "The arrows and crossbow bolts killed the men outright, and it looks like the big wench broke her neck bouncing down the steps."

"Piss and dung," Miri swore. She'd hoped to question one of them.

A hostler, a pimply, gangling youth, scurried up to her.

"Madame . . . m-madame ranger?" he stammered, as if uncertain of the proper way to address her, or else simply afraid she might take out her frustrations on him. "A gentleman inside the inn wants to talk to you."

"I'm sure he does. Take care of my mount." She handed the boy the reins, then glanced at Hostegym and added, "You might as well come along, too."

They headed into the common room of the inn. Judging by the babble, the dozen or so voices shouting for the taverner's or a serving maid's attention, the excitement of the robbery and brawl had engendered quite a thirst in those who'd simply stood and watched the show. A white, soft-looking hand beckoned through a curtain of yellow glass beads. The scout and mercenary passed through the glittering strands and down a little passage lined with private chambers. The door to the last one on the left was ajar. They stepped through and seated themselves on the opposite side of a scarred, rectangular table from the man they'd come to meet. The small window was closed and shuttered, and the dim, confined space was stuffy with the trapped heat of a warm autumn afternoon.

Catching a first glimpse of that clean, well-tended hand, Miri had immediately guessed it had never performed any task more strenuous than guiding a quill across a piece of parchment. Seeing its owner up close reinforced the impression. Plump, clad in an unpretentious yet well-tailored tunic and breeches, dove gray with brown accents, he had the look of a chief clerk or steward, a highly placed functionary who spent his days assigning work to other people. Yet the set of his fleshy jaw bespoke a certain resolution, and his brown eyes, a wry intelligence, that persuaded her to defer the contempt she generally felt for such citified parasites.

"So," he said.

"You are . . . ?" Miri prompted.

"The man you were supposed to meet," he said. "The fellow who would have examined the item, then gone and fetched the coin and letters of credit if everything was in order. We don't need to throw names around. Certainly not now."

"I thought this Paeraddyn place was supposed to be safe," Hostegym grumbled.

"My master's house is safe," the Oeble man replied, a thin edge of anger in his mild, reasonable baritone voice, "but your employer insisted we make the exchange on neutral ground, no doubt so I'd have difficulty simply seizing the item and refusing to pay the balance due."

"The folk of Oeble," Miri said, "even the more reputable ones, enjoy a certain notoriety."

"And sometimes," the pudgy man said, "a man spends so much effort looking over his shoulder for dragons that he walks right up on a bear. But I suppose it will do no good to debate what we ought to have done."

"I assume," Miri said, "that even Oeble has some sort of watch, or constables."

The man across the table nodded and said, "The Gray Blades, and I daresay they'll make a genuine effort to find a robber who committed an outrage in the Paer. Indeed, my patron can take measures to encourage them to do their utmost. But let's not tell them what the rogue stole."

"Surely if they knew how valuable it—"

"Within a day, every scoundrel in town would know it, too, and that might be less than helpful. We can still reclaim our property if and when the Gray Blades actually recover it."

Miri scowled and said, "You don't seem confident they will."

"They're competent, some are even halfway honest, but they only number about thirty. Oeble is a big place and, I must concede, a rogue's haven, where every day dozens of new crimes compete for the law's attention. We'll just have to hope for the best."

"That's not good enough," Miri said. The warm, stale air was oppressive, and made her head pound. She irritably tugged at her green leather armor, pulling it away from her neck to help her breathe. "We'll find the wretch ourselves."

Hostegym grunted and said, "I wonder if that's a practical idea."

"I'm a scout," she said. "A tracker and hunter. It's what I do."

"It's what you do out in the woods," the mercenary leader replied. "What makes you think you'll have the same kind of luck in a warren like this?"

"Your friend may have a point," the functionary said. "I don't mean to discourage you. As I understand it, your employer has his own problems, and urgently needs the rest of his coin. To say the least, it's in everyone's best interests that we recover the item and complete our transaction. But it won't help anybody if you, Mistress Buckman, merely wind up getting tossed on the Dead Cart."

Miri made a spitting sound and said, "You must be joking. It's only one man who got away."

"If you truly mean to do this," the functionary said, "you'd better get that notion right out of your head. Oeble is full of knaves who'll resent strangers asking questions about one of their own, or about anything, really."

"Fine, point taken. But surely they're no match for a band of trained warriors."

The Oeble man arched an eyebrow.

"All right," she said, "I admit, the four rogues made us look like idiots, but only because they had magic and luck on their side. The wizard's dead now, and the whoreson who jumped off the wall has surely run through all the good fortune the Lady Who Smiles was willing to grant him."

"That's as may be," Hostegym said, shifting uncomfortably in his chair, "but I have to tell you, Miri, if you go ahead with this, you won't have that 'band of trained warriors' watching your back. The lads and me, we're done."

"What?" she cried.

"Now, don't glare like that. We signed on to get your mysterious saddlebag to Oeble, and we did. We fulfilled the letter of the contract."

She laughed and replied, "Do you honestly expect me to see it that way, and meekly hand over the rest of *your* coin? I couldn't even if I were willing. I was supposed to pay you out of what our contact here was going to give me."

The beefy warrior frowned.

"Ouch," he said. "That's bad news."

"So I take it we're still in this together?"

Hostegym sat pondering for a heartbeat or two, then finally shook his head and answered, "No, I don't think so. You know what the boys and I are good at. That's why you hired us. We understand fighting on horseback, watching for bandits and trolls in open country. We're not thief takers, and I don't think we'd fare well playing at it in a place as tricky as Oeble. Fortunately, caravans leave from here all the time, and I reckon the smart way for us to make more coin is to take another job as guards. Come with us if you like. We'd be glad to have you."

She glared at him and said, "You miserable, treacherous coward . . ."

"Call me all the names you like. It won't change anything. The fact is, the 'item' is lost because *you* made a mistake. When the thieves were on the steps, you could have shot the fellow with the saddlebag first, before your bowstring broke."

He was right, of course. It had been the only sensible thing to do. Yet she hadn't, and didn't quite know why. Perhaps it was because she'd recognized that, a minute or two earlier, the bogus beggar could easily have killed her, yet had contented himself with knocking her down and kicking her. Thus, she'd felt obliged to give him one last chance to surrender.

Seeing she had no answer, Hostegym heaved himself to his feet, wincing as his bad leg took his weight.

"I guess we'll stay here at the inn until we land another job," he said. "If you see reason, come find us."
He nodded to the plump man, then limped out the door.
"Does this change your mind?" the functionary asked.
"No," Miri said. "In my guildhouse, they teach us to honor our commitments. I'll recover the item by myself."
"Do you have any idea how?"
"Well, at least I got a look at the thief." The wretch had been lean and fit, with green eyes and keen, intelligent features. Given his agility, she assumed the sores on his legs were fake. Perhaps his goatee was, also. "But beyond that . . ."
She shrugged.
"Well, I know my master will want me to give you all the help I can," the functionary said. "Unfortunately, we don't have many contacts among the gangs and other outlaws. No matter what outsiders may believe, Oeble does have some citizens who don't work hand-in-glove with the robbers and smugglers. But at the very least, I can provide some general information."
Miri nodded and said, "Tell me."

CHAPTER 2

Aeron skulked up the twisting stairs with the saddlebag tucked under one arm, keeping an eye out for anyone who might be lurking there. The risers, a number of which were soft with dry rot or broken outright, would have creaked and groaned beneath most people's feet, but were silent under his. He knew where and how to step.

As usual, he reached his own door without incident. Considering that his father was a cripple, some might think it ridiculous that after all those years they still lived on the uppermost floor of a dilapidated tower. But it was marginally safer. The average housebreaker wouldn't climb so high just to break into such humble lodgings. And in any case, Nicos sar Randal refused to move. He liked the view.

In fact, once Aeron stepped inside the small, sparsely furnished room, locking and barring the door behind himself with reflexive caution, he saw that his father was enjoying the vista even then. The older man sprawled in a chair on the sagging balcony with its broken railing, looking out over the River Scelptar. The sunset stained the water red and burnished the three bridges arching over the flow. The floods carried the spans away every spring, and Oeble rebuilt them every summer. At the moment, they were likely the only spanking new structures in all the ancient city.

Nicos was gaunt, and no longer young, but younger than his frailty made him appear. His scars, the creases on his face and skinny limbs and the noose-mark around his neck, looked as purple as plums in the failing light.

"Come watch the sun go down," he rasped.

Once upon a time, he'd possessed a voice as rich as a bard's, but the rope had taken it.

"In a minute," Aeron replied.

Glum as he felt, he would have preferred solitude, but didn't have the heart to say so. He peeled off his beggar's rags, tossed them on the floor, poured water from the porcelain pitcher into the cracked bowl, and scrubbed the bogus sores off his legs and the brown dye from his coppery hair, eyebrows, and beard. That accomplished, he pulled on one of the slate-gray borato shirts he favored, found a bottle of white wine in the little wrought iron rack, and carried it and the saddlebag out onto the balcony.

He opened the sour vintage with a corkscrew, and he and his father passed the green glass container back and forth until the scarlet rim of the sun cut the hills to the west.

Nicos said, "What's wrong?"

"What makes you think anything's wrong?"

"I know you, don't I? I can read it in your face and the way you carry yourself."

Aeron sighed. He sometimes tried to avoid telling his

father about his various jobs, because it made him fret. But somehow he generally wound up confiding in him anyway.

"I stole something this afternoon."

"I assumed you didn't buy the pouch," Nicos replied, "or what's inside it."

"No. It was a complicated kind of job. I needed help, and things went awry."

Nicos nodded somberly. Probably he was remembering times when his own thefts didn't go as planned.

"I take it one of your helpers came to grief."

"Not one. All three. Kerridi, Gavath, and Dal."

"Damn. I'm sorry." Nicos took a slug of wine, then passed the bottle and asked, "Are they dead, or did the Gray Blades take them alive?"

"I think they're all three dead."

"Well, that's sad, but likely best for you and them both."

"I know. It's just . . . I had to dry Dal out to make him fit to work. I had to buy him new powders, trinkets, and whatnot to cast his spells. I felt smug—proud of myself for being a true friend and helping him out that way. Now it turns out what I was really doing was digging his grave."

"You can't blame yourself. He knew the risks. They all did."

"I suppose."

Nicos hesitated, then said, "You needn't feel guilty, but you can learn from what happened. Rethink the path you've—"

"Please," Aeron snapped, "let's not argue about that all over again. I relish stealing as much as you did in your day, I'm just as good at it, and I can't think of any honest work I could do that would bring in enough to pay for all your poultices and medicines."

Nicos spat, "Don't put it on me. I never asked you to risk your neck just to ease my aches and pains."

"You didn't have to."

"Anyway, if you're such a clever thief, why did your plan turn to dung?"

"Because I dared to steal something inside the walls of the Paeraddyn, I suppose."

Nicos blinked and said, "You're joking."

"No. Kesk Turnskull hired me to do it."

"The tanarukk? You're even madder than I dreamed. I'd better have the story quickly, before you take it into your head to jump off the balcony, just to find out if you can fly."

And so, as the sky blackened, the stars twinkled into view, and the fishermen plying the river in their skiffs lit the colored lanterns hanging fore and aft, Aeron told the tale. Nicos hunched forward, intent, fascinated despite himself. He might worry about his only son's manner of living, but he enjoyed hearing about his escapades. Aeron knew he remained a thief at heart, and would still be robbing folk himself if only his broken body would allow.

Perhaps it was his father's grudging admiration, or simply the wine warming his belly, but as he related the events of the afternoon, Aeron's sorrow receded somewhat, making way for a swelling of pride. Because, though he'd paid a heavy price for his boldness, he'd taken loot from within the Paeraddyn, and in all Oeble, what other knave could say the same?

The story and the wine finished together. He set the empty bottle down carefully. Put one in the wrong spot, and it would topple over and roll off the slanted platform, perhaps to brain some luckless soul passing in the street below.

His scars and infirmity veiled in darkness, Nicos sat quietly for a few more seconds, evidently pondering, then asked, "If you'd known, would you still have tried?"

"Known which?"

"That someone cast spells of warding on the saddlebag. That it had so many able warriors looking after it."

Aeron shrugged and said, "Probably. If we'd known about them, maybe Dal could have neutralized the other mage's enchantments. Then, using the potion, I could have stolen the prize without anyone noticing, and it wouldn't have mattered how many guards were hanging around. But of course, we didn't know. If Kesk had any notion how well protected the prize would be, he didn't see fit to warn me."

"Maybe for fear you'd pass on the job."

"Maybe," said Aeron. "I certainly wouldn't put it past the ugly bastard to withhold vital information."

Aeron pulled open the mouth of the scuffed old saddlebag, slipped out the steel lockbox inside, and hefted it in his hands. It weighed several pounds, and didn't clink or rattle when shaken. Almost any sort of treasure might rest inside.

He rose and fetched his pigskin pouch of picks and probes.

Nicos gave a disapproving grunt and asked, "Do you think Kesk would like you opening the box?"

"Since he specifically told me not to, I doubt it, but I want to see what my partners died for."

"Well, if you must do it, at least make sure you don't break the lock, or—"

"Or leave any telltale scratches around it. I know."

Though he wasn't as adept at teasing open locks as some thieves, Aeron thought he could manage it.

As soon as he inserted a fine steel rod in the keyhole, however, a thunderclap boomed. The blast of sound jolted pain through his bones, kicked the strongbox out of his lap, and sent him tumbling backward in his rickety old chair. Worse, it set the whole balcony bouncing up and down. Aeron lay perfectly still, terrified, certain that the platform was about to tear free of its moorings at last.

Gradually, though, the oscillation subsided, and he lifted his head. Nicos's seat had remained upright, but scooted to the very brink of the balcony, where luckily the older man had fetched up against an intact section of railing, which sufficed to keep him from falling over. Aeron scrambled forward and hauled his wide-eyed parent back from the edge.

Then he thought to look for the case. It had slid to the brink as well, and he felt a sudden impulse to kick it off. Naturally, though, he picked it up instead.

Nicos spoke to him, but he couldn't make out the words through the ringing in his ears. The day had been hard on his hearing. A few more such magical mishaps, and he'd likely be deaf.

"Say it again," he requested.

"I said, another ward," the scarred man repeated. "Wards on the bag and the coffer, too."

"Do you think that was the last of them?"

"I'm not a wizard. How would I know? I wouldn't count on it."

"You're right," said Aeron. "I'll leave off trying to open it. But damn it, the thing got Kerridi, Dal, and Gavath killed, and now it almost did the same to us. To be so well defended, it must be incredibly valuable." He smiled slowly. "Too valuable to hand over for a single bag of gold, even a big one."

"Don't talk crazy. Nobody crosses the Red Axes."

Aeron smiled and said, "I won't. Kesk can have the booty. But first he's going to have to renegotiate our deal."

Sefris Uuthrakt sensed that something was abroad in the night, something, perhaps, spawned in the famously abomination-haunted Qurth Forest to the northeast, but no matter how she tried, she couldn't yet pinpoint its location. Perhaps she would have had better luck if she stood still, but that she was unwilling to do. A task awaited her in the city ahead, and one didn't dawdle when the Lady of Loss called her to serve.

So, trusting in the skills she'd worked so hard to master to protect her if necessary, her legs tirelessly eating up the miles, she simply jogged on down the trail that wound across the hilly grasslands. Her one concession to prudence was to pull a cestus, a leather strap loaded with iron pellets, onto the knuckles of each hand. She was supposed to look like a meek and inoffensive traveler, a pilgrim, perhaps, seeking a shrine of the Morninglord, the Binder of What is Known, or some other weak and contemptible deity, and the enchanted weapons rather spoiled the illusion. But at the moment, she had no companions to remark on them, and in any case, certain creatures existed that even the naked fists of a monastic couldn't damage.

She was passing a stand of twisted elms when something cracked like a whip. She pivoted, dropped into a fighting stance, and peered, using the periphery of her vision. At first, she saw nothing. She was an initiate of the night, yet human, and despite her training, darkness could still hinder her to a degree. Finally, though, she spotted the source of the noise. For an instant, it looked like a long strip of black cloth caught in the branches. Then, however, she realized she was looking at a living creature crouched on its perch, its wings spread and poised to flap.

The flyer's round eyes glared, and it bared its fangs. Come on, Sefris thought, either attack or clear off. You're wasting my time. Then she felt something rushing at her back.

She spun to the side, and a second creature, its foaming jaws gaping wide to bite, hurtled through the space where she'd just been standing. The tip of one furry, beating wing brushed her cowl back, half exposing the shaven scalp beneath. Seen up close, the beasts resembled the huge bats that sometimes lived in the biggest, deepest caverns, but with a hint of submerged humanity in the shape of the head and torso and the over development of its bandy legs. For one attacker to distract her while the other sneaked up at her back bespoke more than animal intelligence, and she thought she understood what manner of brute she faced. The cesti had been a sound idea, even if they were of no use at that moment. The werebat soared up out of range before she could throw a punch.

The chakrams she carried concealed about her person, sacred to the Lady of Loss though they were, didn't carry the same sort of sorcerous enhancement, and thus were apt to prove ineffectual against shapechangers. Such creatures possessed a degree of resistance to mundane sources of injury. But initiates of Sefris's order mastered not one lethal discipline but two, and thus she still possessed ways of attacking the werebats at range. She snatched a pinch of sand from a hidden pocket, tossed it in the air, and breathed words of power.

As sometimes happened, her magic made the darkness shift and whisper around her. The werebat that had just swooped aloft lurched in the air, then plummeted, fast asleep. It smashed into the ground with a bone-shattering crunch, and the corpse began to flow, the wings shrinking as it reverted to its alternate form.

The other shapeshifter shot out of the twisted tree. Perhaps its companion's death had enraged it, or maybe it simply wanted to deny the sorceress the opportunity to cast another spell. In any case, it plainly intended a furious assault.

Had she not schooled her features to resist such random impulses, Sefris might have smiled. She'd done her best to unlearn all emotion save for the spite and bitterness befitting a servant of her goddess, but in truth, she'd never quite managed to quash the joy she took in killing. And though striking someone dead with magic was satisfying in its own way, nothing matched the exhilaration of destroying an opponent with her hands.

The werebat swooped at her. She sidestepped the gnashing fangs and punched at the creature's chest, seeking to smash right through the ribs and into the vital organs beneath.

The blow slammed home, shattered bone, and the shapechanger shrieked, the cry pitched so high that it was more a stabbing pain in her ears than an actual sound. Its outstretched wing swatted her.

She yielded to the impact, permitting it to fling her to the ground, and instantly somersaulted to her feet. The werebat flew upward, but in a jerking, labored manner that revealed she'd hurt it badly. Perhaps it would flee without delaying her any further. Despite the pleasure she would take in its demise, she supposed that would be for the best.

It didn't flee. It wheeled high above, likely out of range of any of her spells, until a couple more vague black shadows joined it. Sefris couldn't tell precisely how many there were, but evidently an entire flock—if that was what one called a family of werebats—had gone hunting across the hills that night, and the wounded one had called them all in to deal with her.

Good. If she killed them all there and then, she wouldn't have to worry about another ambuscade later.

The werebats dived at her. It took long enough to give her time for another bit of sorcery. She rattled off a sibilant couplet, flung out her arm in a cabalistic gesture, and a jagged shaft of darkness leaped from her fingertips. It struck the creature in the lead. The lycanthrope's wings flailed crazily, out of time with one another, and it veered off course.

Then its fellows were right over her head, or nearly so. Fortunately, their size precluded their attacking all at exactly the same time, lest they foul each other's wings. She blocked with her forearm, bashing a set of foaming jaws out of line, then whipped the blade of her hand against the werebat's neck. She grabbed hold of its loose hide, yanked it out of the air, and smashed it down on the ground.

She nearly followed up with a stamp kick before remembering that her sandal-clad foot likely wouldn't hit hard enough to overwhelm a lycanthrope's mystical defenses. Unfortunately, she didn't have time to drop to one knee and continue bashing the brute with her hands. The next shapechanger was already hurtling at her.

She killed that one cleanly with a spear-hand strike to the chest, then leaped clear before its body could flop down on top of her. Another plummeted at her, saw that she was ready for it, and swooped high again.

Something rustled in the grass. She glanced down. Apparently when she'd hit the one werebat in the throat, she'd injured it in a way that prevented its taking to the air again. But it was still game; it was scuttling at her.

She sprang back from it and swept her hand through a mystic pass. The shadow of a nearby sapling reared from the ground and lashed itself around the lycanthrope. The creature flailed helplessly inside the inky coils.

Sefris knew that when she'd focused on the grounded brute, its fellow had surely dived, and by then was nearly in striking range. Peering upward, she whirled, and there it was, its glistening fangs mere inches from piercing her flesh. One such bite, assuming it didn't kill her outright, could change her into a creature like itself. The prospect didn't horrify her as it might have many another person, but neither was it anything to be desired. She was already the instrument the Dark Goddess intended her to be.

She grabbed the werebat by the neck to hold its teeth at bay. Her weight dragged it out of the air, and locked together, they tumbled over the grass. She kept hold of its throat and squeezed, the cesti lending the choke hold an efficacy it might otherwise have lacked.

The werebat struggled frantically, but only for a few heartbeats. Then its spine snapped.

Sefris sprang to her feet. Nothing else was wheeling against the stars or streaking down at her. If any shape-changers remained aloft, they'd evidently decided to leave their comrades unavenged and seek easier prey.

That just left the bodies on the ground, some of which had reverted almost entirely to human, and the shape-shifter still tangled in the shadow tentacle.

When it saw her looking at it, it stopped squirming and abased itself. Despite its bestial features, the enormous, pointed ears and wrinkled snout, she could tell it was begging for mercy. Perhaps offering itself as her slave if only she would spare its life.

Maybe it truly imagined that she might. Maybe it hoped she'd recognize some degree of kinship between them—both killers, both haunters of the dark.

If so, it had mistaken her nature. Sefris had never been particularly prone to sympathy, and her training had purged every trace of it from her soul. Insofar as her limited mortal mind permitted, she strove to emulate her goddess's hatred of all things, whether good or evil, fair or foul, human or monstrous. Killing gave her joy, but she labored not to seek or wallow in the pleasure, but rather to slaughter as an expression of a pure, cold will to destroy.

Such being the case, she wouldn't play with the werebat, wouldn't torture it or savor its desperation. She lunged forward and drove her fist into the center of its low forehead, shattering its skull.

She took a deep breath, and without a backward glance, she trotted on, carrying retribution and ruin to Oeble as her Dark Father had commanded.

CHAPTER 3

Miri found the stairs at the end of a short, strangely quiet passage off the busy Sixturrets intersection, where her contact, the plump man, had said they would be. As she regarded the steps twisting down into the ground, she felt an uncharacteristic pang of doubt. Maybe Hostegym was right; perhaps it was a bad idea. If she was out of her element in the streets and alleys of Oeble, it could only be worse in the city's Underways, supposedly a labyrinth of tunnels where the Gray Blades never ventured, and rogues of every stripe did precisely as they pleased.

But for that very reason, it seemed the best place to seek news of the green-eyed thief and the stolen treasure. Mielikki knew, Miri certainly hadn't had any luck above ground. So she scowled her misgiving away, loosened her sword and dagger in their sheaths, and adjusted the small steel buckler strapped to her wrist. She didn't much like the latter. The weight didn't bother

her, but the armor made her feel awkward when shooting. Still, she thought that in the cramped confines of a subterranean warren, she might find a shield more useful than the bow she nonetheless carried strung and ready in her hand.

She crept down the steps, disturbing a rat that squealed and scuttled on ahead of her. She passed beyond the light leaking down from above into total darkness. Her pulse ticked a little faster.

Then, to her relief, a dim glow blossomed ahead. She stepped off the stairs into an arched tunnel which was neither as wet nor as malodorous as she'd expected. She'd imagined that "Underways" was a fancy way of saying "sewers," and in fact, a faint stench of noisome waste wafted in from somewhere, but there was no stream of muck flowing sluggishly down the center of the passage. Evidently the two systems were separate, at least to some degree.

The tunnel was essentially dark, no hindrance to orcs, goblins, and other creatures that could see in such conditions. Patches of pale sheen smeared the earthen walls in a couple of places, evidently to accommodate those who could not. Miri couldn't tell if they were some species of luminous mold or splashes of a man-made pigment.

Trying to look as if she truly knew where she was headed, as if she belonged down there, she marched away from the stairs. Around the first bend, she came upon two men huddled together, who eyed her speculatively and left off their whispering until she passed by. Not far beyond them, the corpse of a chubby halfling lay facedown. The victim, no bigger than a half-grown human child, bore more than a dozen wounds and had left a trail of blood like a snail. Evidently he'd crawled several yards on his belly while his assailants hacked and stabbed him.

The passage twisted repeatedly, and branching tunnels snaked away into blackness. Miri's sense of direction never failed her in the wild, but she had the unpleasant feeling that, even so, she could lose herself down there. She was glad her first destination was only supposed to be a short walk from the stairs she'd descended, and gladder still when the lamp-lit doorway came into view.

According to the information she'd received, Melder's Door was the only true inn in the Underways, and marginally safer than either of the taverns found "below." It seemed a reasonable place to continue her inquiries.

She pulled open the heavy door and stepped into a surprisingly spacious common room whose walls were lined with stone. The air was damp and chilly, and the glows of the few hanging lanterns, half occluded behind their hinged black iron hoods.

Still, after the gloom outside, she might almost have found the place welcoming, if not for the way all the surly-looking patrons—humans, orcs, towering, dog-faced gnolls, and horned, scaly, diminutive kobolds—turned to stare at her. It was disheartening. An inn, by definition, catered to wayfarers. To strangers. Yet even there, something about the way she looked or carried herself instantly branded her an outsider.

Well, to Fury's Heart with it. She'd be damned if she'd let a pack of ruffians make her feel self-conscious just for looking like a righteous, law-abiding person. She returned sneer for sneer, then strode toward an empty table.

Until something flitted across her field of vision, then hovered in front of her face. She found herself nose to snout with a tiny dragon or wyvern, its wings shimmering, beating fast as a hummingbird's, its skinny body only a trifle longer than her middle finger. Startled, she recoiled, and the onlookers laughed at her discomfiture.

Their mirth made her flush with anger, and the miniature dragon's scrutiny made her wary. It scarcely seemed large enough to pose a threat, yet it might possess a nasty bite or sting or even the capacity to puff flame or poison into her eyes.

She lifted her hand to swat it away, and a bass voice rapped, "Don't."

She froze, the winged reptile whirled past her and away, and she looked around. A handsome man was smiling back at her. His barbered hair and eyes were black, and his skin was dark in a way that owed nothing to the touch of the sun. His purple velvet breeches and tunic were cut tight, the better, perhaps, to flatter his slender frame, save for exceptionally baggy sleeves that hung all the way down over his knuckles. Looking more like a child's toy than an actual weapon, a dainty hand crossbow dangled from a double-looped scarlet belt with a gold buckle.

More tiny dragons fluttered all around him, as if they were bees, and he, a particularly succulent flower. Miri experienced a sudden, unpleasant mental image of all the creatures swarming on a victim simultaneously. How could any one person defend against such an assault, no matter how adroit an archer or fencer she might be?

"Please don't hit my eye," the dark man continued. "You wouldn't like it if I hit you in one of yours."

"I won't," Miri answered. "The beast surprised me is all."

"No harm done." He sketched a bow, elegant and perfunctory at the same time. "I'm Melder. Welcome to the Door." He grinned and added, "My instincts tell me you haven't come in search of accommodations."

"No," she said, "just beer."

"Ah. We have a good ale brewed hereabouts, a fine dark lager from Theymarsh, and—"

"The local stuff will do. Perhaps you'll lift a tankard with me."

"You honor me. Please be seated, and I'll return in a trice."

She did as he'd bade her, then divided her attention between watching her fellow patrons, who were gradually returning to the murmured conversations her arrival had interrupted, and the little reptiles flying about. They wandered wherever they wished, and even the drunkest and most brutish-looking guests resisted the impulse to slap them away.

Melder sat two foaming leather jacks on the table, then sat down across from her.

"My small friends interest you," he said.

"They're beautiful," she replied.

"They're certainly the prettiest things in this dank old place, or were until a few moments ago," he said with a smile. "They keep the bugs and rats down, too. I believe I introduced myself, but I didn't catch your name."

"Miri Buckman."

"A lovely name. It fits you. And what, dear Miri, brings you below? You have a sensible look about you. Tell me you aren't simply indulging your curiosity, that you aren't one of those fools who think no visit to wicked Oeble complete without an excursion into the Underways."

She sipped her ale. He was right, it was good, the flavor hearty and not too bitter.

"Suppose I came down here to do some business," she said. "Could you point me to the right person?"

He chuckled.

Miri felt a pang of irritation and asked, "What's funny about that?"

"Please, forgive me," Melder said. "It's just that one doesn't rush these conversations. The parties generally sample a drink or three, chatting of nothing in particular, acquiring a sense of one another, before anyone broaches the actual point of the discussion. I suspect you know better, you tried to play the game, but your impatience betrayed you."

She knew what he meant. Out in the wild, she would have been more circumspect. She'd once reveled with a tribe of centaurs for three days and nights, satisfying all their elaborate rituals of hospitality, before so much as mentioning the reason for her visit to their camp. But Oeble, and her current dilemma, made her twitchy.

"I haven't much time," she said, "or at least I fear I haven't."

"I understand," he said. "For all you know, the precious saddlebag has already left town."

Miri glared at him and said, "You knew who I was from the start."

Melder shrugged. "I didn't know your name, but people are naturally talking about a robbery inside the Paeraddyn and the ranger tramping around town trying to trace the surviving thief. What was in the pouch, anyway?"

"I don't know, myself."

He grinned, his teeth a flash of white in his swarthy face. A tiny green dragon settled on his shoulder for a moment, almost as if whispering in his ear, then flew away.

"You're a bad liar," he said, "probably because you haven't learned to enjoy it. If I knew what you're looking for, perhaps I could help you find it."

And maybe, she thought, you'd covet it for yourself.

Miri asked, "Are you willing to help me?"

"Well, it all depends. I make a tolerable living from the Door, and as you can imagine, my guests don't rest their heads here because I have a reputation for tattling. Still, it's conceivable you could persuade me to be of some assistance, comely as you are. Grubby from the road, of course, but a bath would fix that."

She made a spitting sound then said, "Apparently you haven't known many rangers, at least not of my guild. We don't pay for anything that way."

"A pity. If you exploited them properly, like a sensible lass, your charms could be a mightier weapon than that bow."

"Forget it. I am willing to pay a hundred Sembian nobles if you furnish information that leads me to what I seek."

"Perhaps some gold up front would serve to jog my memory or sharpen my wits."

"Ever since I started poking around," said Miri, "folk have been hinting they can help me, then they ask for coin in advance. Had I heeded them, my purse would be empty already. I'll pay you when I recover what was in the saddlebag, not before."

"And how, sweet Miri, do I know that I can trust you?"

"Because I swear it by Our Lady of the Forest."

He laughed and said, "Your vow. Delightful."

She glowered at him then asked, "Can you help me or not?"

"I assume you took a good look at the three thieves who died."

"Yes."

"Describe them."

She did, and based on his expression asked, "You recognize them?"

"I believe so, though I didn't know them well. Their names were Gavath, Kerridi, and Dal."

She felt a thrill of excitement.

"What gang did they belong to?" she asked.

Melder shook his head and answered, "None. They were petty operators, really, gleaning what the gangs don't bother to take."

"I don't see how four such little fish, working strictly by themselves, could have conceived an elaborate plan to steal the saddlebag as soon as it reached Oeble. They wouldn't even have known it was coming. Somebody must have hired them to seize it."

"That would be my guess," Melder said. "Have you any notion who that person might have been?"

Someone with a spy in place, Miri thought, either here or in Ormath, to report on what was supposed to have been a secret transaction.

Beyond that, she couldn't say. She spread her hands.

"Whoever it was," Melder said, "he has plenty of coin, or at least convinced the thieves he did. He wouldn't have tried to rob the Paer without a substantial fee in the offing."

"Did the dead outlaws have a particular comrade with whom they often worked? Someone thin, bearded, and around my age, green-eyed and skilled with a knife?"

"I fear I can't tell you. As I said, I didn't know them personally, and we have so many ne'er-do-wells skulking about Oeble—new ones every day. The river barges float them in, and the Dead Cart rolls them out."

"Well, presumably somebody knew them," Miri replied. "At least you've given me a place to start, and I thank you."

She gulped down the rest of her beer, laid a silver coin on the table, rose, and headed for the door.

Melder sat and watched the scout stride away. He generally liked his women with a little more meat on their bones and considerably more concerned with presenting a well-groomed and feminine appearance. But even clad in her dirty woods-runner's armor, breeches, and boots, she was a pleasant sight.

Vlint appeared at his elbow and gave a disapproving snort, a mode of expression admirably suited to his bulbous blue nose, though incongruously prissy for a hobgoblin. Melder sighed and turned his head to meet the hulking, shaggy bravo's sallow eyes.

"I take it you were eavesdropping," the human said, "and think me too garrulous."

"It's not for me to say," said Vlint, in a tone that conveyed his opinion with utter clarity. None of the Door's other guards would have expressed disapproval, but he'd been in his master's employ for a long while, ever since the days when Melder had been a thief in his own right instead of a quasi-respectable innkeeper, and was thus inclined to take liberties.

"I didn't give up any of our patrons," he said.

Something tickled Melder's wrist, and forked tongue flickering, a gray, wedge-shaped head slid out from under the cuff of his long, floppy sleeve. He caressed the restless viper with his fingertip, then coaxed it to slither back where it belonged.

"Come to that," Melder added, "I didn't even give up anyone alive."

"Still," said the bouncer and ruffian-for-hire, "it wasn't the kind of thing you generally do."

"Most thief takers aren't as pretty as that one, and it should serve to keep her wandering around here below."

Vlint scratched at his thick, flea-bitten neck and said, "You think that so long as she's nearby, she might decide to warm your bed after all?"

"Alas, no. The ranger's guilds shouldn't admit women. You let a wench worship a goddess who takes the form of a unicorn, and she's bound to place an exaggerated value on her chastity."

"Then you want to make a play for the saddlebag yourself."

"No. Those days are behind us. Though if it simply fell into my lap. . . . What I think is that as pretty Miri blunders about, someone will decide to make some coin from her, and likely sooner rather than later. Put the word out to the slavers that if anybody catches her, I might be interested in buying. Or at least renting for a day or two."

As befitted his status as chieftain of the Red Axes, Kesk Turnskull lived with a certain style, in an expansive, albeit decaying, house on the river. In better times, the place had likely belonged to a prosperous merchant, who'd built both street entrances and a water gate to facilitate the passage of goods in and out. More recently, diggers had connected the cellars to the Underways.

Thus, Aeron thought, surveying the structure from the Arch of Gargoyles, centermost of the three bridges, he had his choice of ways in. The problem was making sure of a way out. Because it was one thing to resolve to gouge a higher payment out of Kesk and his pack of ruffians, and something else actually to accomplish it. He had to manage the discussion in a manner that would preclude the tanarukk's simply taking him prisoner and torturing him until he divulged the current location of the strongbox.

He pondered the problem for a time, while the reflections of Selûne and her Tears sparkled on the black water rippling below the bridge, and the stone imps squatting atop the piles seemed to brood along with him. At length, when he decided on his approach, he trotted back toward shore. New though they were, the planks bounced and shifted under his feet. The folk of Oeble replaced them every year, but not with any extraordinary care or craftsmanship. Why should they, when the Scelptar was destined to devour them in any case?

Keeping an eye on the sprawling mansion ahead, fieldstone on the ground level and timber above, Aeron skulked along the docks where, in one of his occasional flirtations with honest toil, he'd loaded and unloaded galleys and flatboats. Nobody called out to him. He would have been chagrined if anyone had. Unlike some thieves of his acquaintance, he had no use for flowing cloaks and masklike cowls of midnight black. Those posturing fools who did might as well have worn placards proclaiming themselves nefarious outlaws. But his inconspicuous clothes of dark gray and brown permitted him to blend into the dark with equal facility.

He stepped out onto a deserted pier, considered removing his tunic and boots, and decided against it. Even if he could be sure of returning to that very spot, somebody was likely to walk away with them before he did, Oeble being what it was. He sat down on the edge of the dock, then lowered himself into the water.

Oeblaun fishermen liked to swap stories of pike and freshwater eels huge enough to gobble a man with a single snap of their jaws, but the creatures, if in fact they existed, were evidently either sated just then or hunting elsewhere. He wasn't an exceptionally good swimmer, but the water was still reasonably warm, the current gentle, and he had little difficulty stroking and kicking his way to the sprawling house's river gate.

The gate resembled the mouth of a half-flooded tunnel protected by a portcullis, which, unfortunately, was down. Aeron dived beneath the surface. There, the white light of the moon, and the tail of sparkling motes that people called her Tears, failed him, and he had to grope his way along the steel grille, seeking a breach. He didn't find one.

When he could stay submerged no longer, he came up and sucked in a breath. He knew he couldn't keep diving and searching for long, or one of the sentries would spot him. As best he could judge, that left him only one recourse.

The portcullis would keep out any boat. The spacing of certain of the bars, however, might permit a swimmer to wriggle through, if he was thin and had studied the art of squeezing through tight places. Aeron had. It was a valuable knack to possess if you dabbled in housebreaking.

He slipped beneath the surface, located one of the larger holes in the grillwork, and started to squirm through headfirst.

Shadows of Mask, it was close!

Closer than it had seemed when he was simply gauging its width with his hands. Close enough to scrape patches of his skin raw. So close that down there, in the wet and the black, it seemed to clench around his chest like a clutching fist.

Aeron had gotten stuck before, in windows and chimneys, but never underwater, where if he couldn't free himself within a minute or so, he'd drown. He felt a surge of panic and struggled to quash it. Without a clear head, he had no hope whatsoever of liberating himself.

He gripped a bar to either side of him and tried to haul himself clear. No good. He drew one of his knives and sawed at his shirt and overtunic, trying to strip away the layers of cloth between his flesh and the metal that held him fast. He managed to yank some tatters out, but was still trapped.

He wondered suddenly, with a fresh shock of terror, if the portcullis was magical. The trader who'd originally built the mansion had obviously been wealthy enough to commission an enchanted defense. So was Kesk, as far as that was concerned. Maybe the cursed thing really was squeezing Aeron like a crayfish's pincers.

No. It wasn't. That was just the fear talking, and he wouldn't listen. He strained to drag himself backward rather than forward, only to find retreat as impossible as advancing. Meanwhile, his chest began to ache with the urge to take a fresh breath. Soon his air would run out.

His air. If he emptied his lungs, his chest would be narrower, wouldn't it? Maybe narrow enough to allow him to writhe his way free.

Even though he knew it was his only chance, it took an effort of will to exhale. He forced himself, and the air was gone beyond recall.

He made what would surely be his final effort to pull himself forward. At first, nothing happened, then his chest popped clear like a cork from a bottle of that sweet white sparkling Saelmurian wine poor Kerridi had so enjoyed. He surged forward, only to jerk to a halt an instant later.

He told himself the grillwork hadn't really clamped shut around his ankles. His feet had simply caught on a crossbar. Resisting panic, the impulse to flail wildly, crazily, he tried to untangle himself from the obstruction, and succeeded. He struggled upward.

Desperate for air as he was, it was only at the last second that he remembered he couldn't surface amid a great splashing and floundering, or else one of the Red Axes would notice him. He took care to complete his ascent circumspectly, then breaststroked his way into the shadowy, shielded space between two moored boats.

Clutching at the side of a vessel for support, he sucked in air. It took all the strength he had left simply to make himself inhale and exhale quietly, and he knew that if anyone spotted him before he caught his breath, he'd be helpless to defend himself. Luckily, no one did, and when he recovered, he took a stealthy look around.

The river gate terminated in a stone platform at the far end, where an arched door led farther into the mansion. A walkway ran along either wall. Half a dozen boats floated in the water, tied up until someone should want them. Four were commonplace vessels for transporting passengers and cargo, the fifth a sleek galley equipped with a small ballista in the bow as well as other features useful to river pirates, and the sixth a gilded and ornately carved pleasure barge, aboard which Kesk sometimes chose to pursue his less unsavory amusements.

Two guards slouched on camp stools near the doorway, playing a game of cards for low stakes. The muscular bugbear with its hairy yellow hide was smirking, exposing stained, crooked fangs, and had most of the copper pennies heaped in front of it. The human wore a peeved expression that seemed at home on his pinched and sour face.

Neither one looked particularly alert. Evidently they trusted the portcullis to keep intruders out. Even so, it was going to be tricky.

Aeron drew himself up onto the walkway behind the bugbear's back. He readied the sturdy oaken cudgel he'd brought with him, then skulked forward.

He fancied that few people could have approached the sentries unheard, not clad in soaked garments that wanted to slap and squelch with every step. Fortunately, there was an art to moving silently under even the most adverse conditions, and he'd mastered that one, too.

Yet soft footfalls could only protect a fellow up to a point. He was still a few paces away from the gamblers when the human threw down his creased, greasy hand of cards in disgust, lifted his head, and looked straight at him. The Red Axe's eyes opened wide.

Aeron charged. The bugbear twisted around, and he clubbed at the hulking creature's square, brutish head. The blow cracked home, and the goblinoid jerked at the impact.

By then the human guard was on his feet and had his dagger out. Aeron dodged a thrust, grabbed hold of the little folding camp table that held the game, and flipped it upward. Cards and coins flew everywhere, the coppers clinking on the platform. The tabletop bashed the Red Axe in his face, slamming him backward.

Aeron whirled back around toward the bugbear. Its low forehead bleeding, the burly creature, taller than almost any human its attacker had ever seen, lurched to its feet, snatched its scimitar from its scabbard, and raised it high. Its sleeve slipped down its hairy forearm, revealing the ruddy axe brand Aeron had once declined to wear.

Sidestepping out from under the threat of the curved sword, he lashed the bugbear across the ribs and kicked it in the knee. It stumbled, and that brought its head low enough for him to bash it a second time, and a third. The goblinoid collapsed unconscious.

Aeron pounced atop the bugbear and poised an Arthyn fang at its throat. The human Red Axe, who was lunging forward, hesitated.

"Stay back," Aeron panted, "or I'll kill it."

The guard spat, "I never liked him anyway. I think he cheats."

"If you're such a dunce that a bugbear can trick you," Aeron shot back, "you deserve to lose your coin. Now, you may not like the brute, but I'll bet your chief finds it useful. Useful enough that he wouldn't appreciate you throwing away its life when it can be avoided."

"Maybe. What do you want?"

Aeron nodded toward the windlass and said, "First, raise the portcullis."

He had no intention of squirming through the bars again when it was time to leave.

The guard grumbled, "That's a two-man job."

"The damn thing has a counterweight," Aeron said. "Just put your back into it."

Grunting with effort, or the petulant pretense of it, the Red Axe managed to do as instructed. The chain clanked as it wound around the reel.

"Now what?" the guard asked.

"Now you go into the house and tell Kesk to come out alone for a private talk. Tell him that if he doesn't show himself in the next five minutes, the cardsharp here dies, and he can forget about ever taking possession of the saddlebag."

The sentry stood and stared at him.

"What are you waiting for? Go!"

The Red Axe disappeared through the door, slamming it behind him, and after that, Aeron had nothing to do but listen for approaching footsteps, at least until the bugbear stirred. He pressed the keen edge of his knife against his captive's throat, drawing the goblin-kin's attention to it.

"Don't move," he said, "or you're dead."

"Don't matter," the bugbear said, its bestial voice slurred. Evidently it was still dazed from the beating it had taken.

"You don't care if I kill you?"

"Don't matter you didn't do . . . what you was told. You're still going to die."

Still? What did that mean, precisely? Aeron would have asked, but at that moment, Kesk Turnskull stalked through the door.

If ever a creature was born to rule a company of cutthroats, Kesk was surely the bully in question. Short and stooped as he was, his muscular body looked nearly as thick as it was tall. Patches of coarse hair bristled from his leathery gray hide, and with its truncated snout and jutting tusks, his face resembled that of a wild boar. Despite the oil lamp burning beside the door, the interior of the water gate was dark enough to reveal the faint luminescence of his scarlet eyes, which smoldered like coals beneath a low, ridged brow.

Aeron had heard that tanarukks hadn't always existed, that the race had emerged only in recent times as the result of crossbreeding between orcs and demons. He himself had no firsthand knowledge of such esoterica, but thought that anyone who laid eyes on Kesk would have no difficulty crediting the story.

As always, the founder and master of Oeble's most vicious gang carried a heavy, double-bitted battle-axe in his hand. Supposedly, he'd plundered the enchanted weapon from the body of a fallen foe, a gold dwarf champion who'd believed the axe, a cherished family heirloom, would only serve a pure-hearted warrior of his own race. Kesk liked to tell the story of how he'd proved the fool wrong by using it to slaughter the dwarf's own kin.

The tanarukk regarded Aeron and the bugbear. It was difficult to read the expression on that swinish face, with its protruding lower jaw, but he seemed to be sneering.

"What's the point of this?" Kesk growled. "Why didn't you come to the house through the Underways, as I told you to?"

"If I had, would I be dead already? Did you have some of your murderers lying in wait for me?"

Kesk's red eyes narrowed and he asked, "What are you talking about?"

"According to the bugbear, you meant to kill me."

"You can't club Tharag over the head and expect him to talk sense. He doesn't do much of that at the best of times. Now, if he's smart, he'll shut his hole and let the two of us palaver."

"You expect me to forget what he said?"

"Just use your own head, will you?" Kesk replied. "Why would I hire a man to do a job, then kill him? To get out of paying? I buy stolen and smuggled goods all the time, and a gang chief has to deal fairly. If I picked up a reputation for cheating, no one would do business with me."

When Kesk put it that way, it did seem to make sense, yet Aeron found he wasn't ready to let the topic go.

"You'd betray a hireling in the blink of an eye if it was worth your while, particularly if you thought you could make him disappear with no one the wiser."

"We agreed on a nice fee for your work, but hardly large enough to beggar me, or make me go to the trouble to play you false. I don't see the saddlebag. Where is it?"

"Somewhere safe."

"It's like that, is it?"

"I lost three friends stealing that box."

"Which means you don't have to split up the coin," said the tanarukk. "You can keep it all, and wind up four times richer than you expected. Be satisfied with that. Don't think you can grind me for more."

"You knew to send us after the box, so maybe you knew how well protected it was. But you didn't warn me."

Kesk snorted—a wet, ugly sound like a pig oinking—and said, "I thought you knew the game, redbeard. I thought you were a man. When a job gets bloody, a man doesn't weep and whine about it."

"Right. A man hits back when someone sets him up for a fall."

The tanarukk glared and said, "Why wouldn't I tell you everything I knew about the . . . the box? I wanted you to get away with it, didn't I?"

"Maybe you feared that if I knew what I was getting into, I wouldn't take the job. Or maybe you hoped some of my crew would get killed. That would save you Red Axes the trouble of slaughtering us all yourselves."

"I told you, we weren't planning to kill you. Maybe we still won't, provided you come to your senses. The War Leader knows, you've got a death coming for this harebrained stunt here tonight, but I've got other meat to chew. Now, where's the lockbox?"

"What's it worth to you, really?"

Kesk quivered, quite possibly with the urge to charge and attack.

"Curse you, human," the gang leader said, "we had a deal, and no one goes back on a bargain with me!"

"I'm not reneging, exactly," said Aeron. "It's just that I charge extra for every lie and lost partner."

"You don't know what you're getting into. If you've got any brains at all, you understand I can't let folk cross me and live to brag about it, or else I'm finished in this town. But even that isn't the whole of it."

"You're starting to bore me, Kesk. Perhaps someone else will pay a fair price for the coffer."

The tanarukk shuddered, and the corner of his mouth twitched and drooled around the jutting tusk and fangs.

"All right," Kesk said. "I'll give you five times as much as we agreed on."

"Ten, and we'll make the trade at a place and time of my—"

The flame in the oil lamp flared, momentarily illuminating the shadowy gate as brightly as the noonday sun. Aeron had the misfortune to be looking in the general direction of the blaze, and it dazzled him.

He didn't know how Kesk had accomplished the trick. Maybe it was some innate capacity derived from his demonic heritage. But he didn't even need to hear the pounding footsteps to comprehend why the tanarukk had manipulated the flame. Kesk had had his back to the lamp, so he hadn't been blinded, and he was charging in to attack his startled, crippled foe.

Aeron flung himself to the side. Something whizzed past his head, just missing, judging from the breeze. He assumed it was Kesk's battle-axe.

Tharag roared something in the uncouth language of his kind, reminding Aeron that he had two foes, not just one.

Damn it!

He should have taken a split second to knife the bugbear before rolling clear, but had been too rattled to think of it.

He couldn't battle both of them, not when all he could see was spots and blobs swimming before his eyes. Truth to tell, he wouldn't have bet on his ability to outfight Kesk under any conditions. He had to get out of there.

Aeron sensed something lunging at him. He jumped backward, with a sick certainty that it wasn't enough to save him, then heard two bodies smack together and Kesk bellow in frustrated rage. Evidently he and the bugbear had rushed Aeron at the same instant, and on the fairly narrow platform, had gotten in each other's way.

Aeron knew it had only bought him a second, time he needed to use to leap back down into the water, where his foes' axe and scimitar couldn't reach him. But which way was it? Blind as he was, disoriented from dodging, he was no longer sure.

All he could do was take his best guess. He ran—one stride, a second—and pitched into empty space. He felt a split second of elation, then he crashed down on a solid surface.

For an instant, stunned, Aeron couldn't grasp what had gone wrong, let alone what to do next. Finally it came to him that he'd landed inside one of the boats. The craft bounced as someone else jumped in with him.

Aeron scrambled backward, bumped into the gunwale, and swung himself over the side. His maneuver tipped the craft, and Kesk cursed as he struggled to keep his balance.

Aeron plunged into the water, then struck out in what he prayed was the direction of the river. A missile of some sort, a thrown dagger, perhaps, splashed down beside him. Finally his vision began to clear, and he saw he was headed the right way.

As he reached the mouth of the gate, he glanced backward, and felt a jolt of terror. Kesk held his battle-axe poised for a swing at the chain that held the portcullis in the raised position. The weapon's edge glowed scarlet as he activated some magic bound in the steel.

Aeron hurled himself forward. Metal clashed, chain clattered, and the grille dropped just behind him, kicking up a little wave that carried him a few feet farther out into the Scelptar.

The trick then was to make it safely ashore. Aeron thought Kesk would send the Red Axes to prowl along the riverside, but if he kept on swimming as fast as he could, he reckoned he'd be able to make it onto dry land before the tanarukk could organize the search.

CHAPTER 4

The dirty, dark-haired boy cowered in the corner, for Sefris had hurt him until the pain burned all the resistance out of him. She'd needed a deft touch to avoid marking him. It was all right that he already carried a street urchin's usual collection of bruises and scrapes, but he wouldn't be deemed acceptable if she herself spilled so much as a drop of his blood before the ceremony started. That was just the way it worked.

Thanks to his terrified passivity, she didn't need to worry about his trying to bolt through the door. She could sit by the window and watch the moon sink toward the horizon. She couldn't start until the Dark Goddess's twin sister and greatest foe exited the sky.

Sefris had found the skinny, ragged child begging at a busy intersection. Perhaps he stole as well, when the opportunity arose. Representing herself as a simple traveler and devout worshiper of Ilmater, god of pity, she feigned horror at the discovery of a child so young reduced to such wretched circumstances. She insisted on spiriting him away for a hot supper, a bath, and a new suit of clothes.

At first, wary, he'd been reluctant to go, but with gentle persistence, she persuaded him. Evidently feeling at ease, he started to prattle merrily as they strolled along, but the words caught in his throat as soon as she ushered him into the cramped little flat where, supposedly, her brother and his wife were putting her up.

Upon reaching Oeble, she'd known she needed a private place in which to sleep and perform her rituals, so she'd cleared one out. The broken corpses of the previous tenants sprawled where they'd fallen. The boy froze and gawked at them, which made it easy to relieve him of his knife, immobilize him, and administer as much punishment as required.

Eventually Selûne hid below the horizon like a pale ghost creeping back into its grave. Sefris rose and advanced on the beggar.

"Don't struggle," she said. "It will only make it worse."

Actually, she doubted it could get much worse, but he presumably didn't know that.

Something in her expression or the way she moved must have alerted him, however, because he finally made a scramble for the door. It didn't matter. She pounced on him, paralyzed him by applying pressure to the proper part of the spine, and laid him on the table she'd cleared to serve as a makeshift altar. She chanted the first invocation as she tore his clothes away.

Most sacrifices required scalpels, lancets, and such to pick apart the offering in just the proper way. Sefris took a cold satisfaction in the fact that her fingers were strong and skillful enough for her to achieve the same sort of excruciating precision barehanded. As a result, life lingered until she performed the final mutilation, drawing forth the glistening intestines and looping them to form a mystic sigil on the victim's chest. The boy flopped once like a fish out of water then expired—gratefully, more than likely.

At the same instant, purple light and a wave of chill pulsed across the room. Unsurprised, for it was the desired result of the ritual, Sefris turned. Before her stood what appeared to be a gaunt human male with the long-eared head of a jackal. Its voluminous robes were black, and its body was outlined by a hazy sheath of flickering violet flame that somehow burned cold instead of hot. The garment and fire together made the arcanaloth a living emblem of the Lady of Loss for those with the wit to understand.

The fiend took a disdainful glance around the hovel, with the untidy litter of corpses, then turned its dark eyes back on Sefris. Few mortals could have abided that gaze, freighted as it was with a malice as deep and as wide as the ocean, but it didn't faze the monastic. Indeed, she respected it as essentially the same attitude she herself had striven so diligently to cultivate.

"Dark Sister," the arcanaloth said, acknowledging her, a hint of a canine yip in its tenor voice, "what do you want?"

In Sefris's experience, arcanaloths—the scribes and mystics of their infernal race—were generally direct to the point of rudeness. In and of itself, it didn't bother her. She shared that trait with them as well.

"Do you know why my Dark Father sent me to Oeble?"

The jackal-headed fiend wrinkled its muzzle in a sneer. "I know," it said. "Mortal foolishness."

"Neither one," Sefris replied. "When my order assigns me a task, it's because the deity whom you and I both serve wishes it done."

"I have my own essential tasks awaiting me in Shadow."

Sefris reminded herself that while hatred was a virtue, impatience was not, and she took a breath to steady herself.

"Was the offering acceptable, or not?"

The arcanaloth shrugged and replied, "It was all right."

"Then I've paid your price, and you'll either help me or suffer the consequences of your refusal."

The fiend rolled its eyes and asked, "What help do you require?"

"I've never been to Oeble before. I'm confident I can kill whoever currently holds *The Black Bouquet*, but less sure of my ability to find it. That's where you come in. Your magic is more versatile than mine, so you're gong to cast a divination."

"Very well."

The spirit waved its hand, and a long oval mirror in a golden frame appeared on the wall. It was so highly polished that it almost seemed to glow with its own inner light and so manifestly valuable as to appear grossly incongruous in such humble surroundings. Sefris assumed the fiend had summoned the looking glass from its own extradimensional realm.

The arcanaloth used its claws to tear loose a scrap of the offering's flesh, which it then ate. Sefris had the feeling that wasn't part of the conjuring. The fiend was simply peckish. When it was done nibbling, it dipped its forefinger into one of the boy's wounds, coating the digit with blood that it employed to write arcane signs along the curved edge of the mirror. The runes burned with the same purple flame that surrounded the creature's body.

After that, the arcanaloth stared intently into the mirror. Peering past it, Sefris could no longer see anything coherent in the glass, not even their own reflections, just formless shadows that oozed, merged, and divided. But then, she wasn't the scryer. She assumed the fiend was making more sense of the rippling blackness than she could.

Or at least she did until the arcanaloth abruptly barked an incantation in some demonic language and swept its arms through a complex mystic pass. At that moment, its annoyance was unmistakable. The bloody sigils burned brighter, but the vague shapes flowing inside the glass became no clearer.

"What's the matter?" Sefris asked.

"The Dark Goddess's enemies warded their plunder against attempts at divination. They must have anticipated that someone would try to take it back."

Well, Sefris thought, at least that means they can't use magic to find it either, but the notion was precious little consolation.

"Surely you can do something," she said.

"Not necessarily, and the effort would take a great deal out of me. I told you, I have my own responsibilities to—"

"Do it."

The arcanaloth bared its fangs and said, "We may meet again someday, on my own plane, perhaps, in circumstances where I hold the whip. If so, you might be glad you didn't push me too hard."

"Do as I command you, or I'll speak the words of torment," Sefris replied. "By darkness impenetrable and empty—"

"All right! I can't see the treasure itself, but perhaps I can make out something that connects to it in the great web of fate. That might give you a clue to its whereabouts."

The fiend snarled another incantation, and resumed its peering.

Finally, it said, "There."

"What have you found?" Sefris asked.

"The future is never certain," the arcanaloth said. "But find this woman, and chances are good she'll lead you to your goal."

It gestured, and a face took shape amid the drifting shadows.

Once Aeron waded ashore, he followed a circuitous route, sometimes descending to the Underways, sometimes proceeding at street level, and periodically climbing to the Rainspans, a rickety network of bridges connecting the roofs and balconies of certain of the city's towers. By custom, the aerial paths were open to the public even where they linked one private residence or business to another, and a good many folk traversed them daily in blithe disregard of the manner in which they groaned, shuddered, and swayed. At that, it was arguably safer to walk over them than underneath. Every rogue in Oeble knew the 'spans afforded any number of excellent locations from which to throw knives at or drop heavy objects on a victim.

Aeron glanced around frequently, making sure no Red Axe was creeping up on him. Perhaps he was so intent on spotting Kesk's cutthroats that it blinded him to other dangers. Or maybe Selûne's departure from the sky, and the deeper darkness she'd left in her wake, were to blame. In any event, he was crossing a Rainspan, one that wound among the decaying spires bordering Laskalar's Square, when two Gray Blades and a goblin seemed to pop up out of nowhere just a few paces ahead of him.

Luckily, the lawmen, one human and one who, judging from his slender frame and pointed ears, might have some elf blood, were too busy questioning the stunted, flat-faced creature they'd accosted to notice Aeron's approach. He turned to slink back the way he'd come, but then he heard the half-elf mention the Paeraddyn. The Blades were asking questions about the robbery.

If Aeron was wise, maybe that should be all the more reason to slip away quickly as he could. But he thought in the long run it might pay him to listen to what the Gray Blades had to say. So he crouched motionless, trusting the darkness to hide him.

As the interrogation proceeded, the lawmen slapped the shrilly protesting goblin around and even threatened to toss it off the bridge. Aeron didn't know the runty, bandy-legged creature. Apparently its tormentors had accosted it at random, simply because it looked shifty. From that fact, and the general tenor of their questions, he inferred that they didn't know who they were looking for.

They had a description, however, flawed but still potentially useful, and they were plainly working hard to track him down. That wasn't good.

The Gray Blades had questioned Aeron on more than one occasion, and thus he knew how to recognize when such a session was winding down. As usual, it ended with a few final threats: if the lawmen found out the goblin had lied to them, they'd make it wish it had never been born, and other remarks in the same vein.

Aeron had nearly lingered too long. If he tried to scurry off quickly, the Rainspan would surely creak and bounce, giving his presence away. Instead, he swung himself over the railing and to the underside of the bridge, where he hung by his hands forty feet above the street.

The Blades released the goblin and proceeded on their way, tramping over the spot where Aeron clung. If some folk deemed the Rainspans unsafe, they should have seen that one from his present vantage point. The lawmen's passage shook loose a veritable shower of scraps of rotten wood. The filthy stuff streamed down over Aeron, a goodly portion slipping inside his collar.

First the river and now this, he thought.

Aeron feared his clothes were ruined. It made him glad that, unlike most of the honest jobs for which he qualified, thieving paid well enough that he owned several other outfits.

He waited until the Gray Blades' voices faded away, then pulled himself back up onto the walkway. He skulked on, and in a few more minutes, he reached his home.

As he'd expected, his father had waited up for him. Nicos sat struggling to pluck the strains of a ribald tavern song about a priest and a dancing girl from the strings of his mandolin. He had no real aptitude for the instrument, but with his voice ruined, it was the only music he could make.

He looked Aeron up and down and asked, "What in the name of the black mask happened to you?"

"What didn't?" Aeron replied, stripping off his shirt and tunic.

It gave him a twinge, the result of the two falls he'd taken that day, which had likewise mottled his torso with a livid assortment of bruises.

"Did you talk the tanarukk into a higher price?" his father asked.

"Not exactly."

Aeron poured water from the pitcher into the bowl, picked up the wash rag, and scrubbed the itchy grit from his skin. It felt odd to wash twice in a single day. Some people said too often was unhealthy. He hoped they were wrong.

"What did happen, then?"

"Well . . ."

He toweled himself dry, sat down opposite his father, dragged off his wet boots, and told the tale.

When he finished, Nicos glowered at him.

"Blood and bone, boy, are you trying to die?"

Aeron grinned and said, "When have the Gray Blades ever come close to catching me?"

"When did they try this hard? Why did you have to steal your cursed box inside the Paeraddyn?"

"Because I thought that no one would expect it to happen there, and I was right about that much, anyway. Besides, if the place had been standing in your day, you would have wanted to rob it, too, just to prove you could."

"Perhaps," Nicos sighed. "That wouldn't have made it the smart thing to do."

"Actually, I wonder if the law is hunting me with such zeal only because it was the Paer. Maybe the person who owned the box is pushing them."

"That would mean you robbed somebody rich, powerful, or both."

"Of something he valued highly," added Aeron.

"Making it even more dangerous."

Aeron shifted in his chair, trying to make himself more comfortable, and in so doing, discovered he was already stiffening up. He stretched and twisted in what would probably prove a futile attempt to forestall the process. His spine popped.

"Ordinarily," he said, "I wouldn't sweat over the Gray Blades. If they were my only problem, I could dodge them until they moved on to other matters. But avoiding them and the Red Axes at the same time . . . well, at least I won't be bored."

"That's what's important," said his father with heavy sarcasm. "Still, it's a shame you couldn't reach an understanding with Kesk, though it's no wonder, after you sneaked onto his home ground and kicked two of his bravos around."

"I only sneaked in a little way, and I imagine he thinks guards who let themselves get taken by surprise deserve their bruises. But you're right, more or less. Once Tharag let it slip that Kesk planned to kill my crew and me from the start, that pretty much wrecked any hope of us making a new bargain. I didn't really even want to. Deep down, I was too angry. He must have sensed it and thought the only way he was ever going to see the lockbox was to take me prisoner and force me to cough it up. Or else kill me and pay a necromancer to wring the location out of my ghost. People say that kind of magic is possible, and Kesk wouldn't balk at it if it is."

"You're positive the bugbear told the truth?"

"Yes," Aeron replied. "I could feel it. If you'd been there talking to it, and Kesk, you would have, too."

"Mask forbid that I ever come anywhere near that demon-spawn. Say he did want to murder you. Do you think it's just because you turned down his offer to join the Red Axes all those years ago?"

"That's probably part of it. He really seemed to want me after I stole that barge-load of spices. It plainly offended him when I said no, and he's the kind to hold a grudge. But I reckon there's more to it."

"What is it, then?"

Aeron frowned, pondering, until an idea came to him.

"You said it yourself," he said. "I robbed someone rich, powerful, or both—so much so that even Kesk Turnskull is leery of his wrath. So instead of using members of his own gang to grab the loot, he hires a freelance operator he hates and plans to kill him and his partners when their work is done. That way, nobody can trace the swag to the Red Axes."

Nicos nodded and said, "That makes sense. What are you going to do now?"

"Sell the prize to somebody else. Imrys Skaltahar, maybe. They say he keeps plenty of gold on hand, enough to buy even the most valuable loot without the thief needing to wait on his coin. I think it may be wisest to dispose of the lockbox quickly, and I wouldn't sell it to Kesk even if I could figure out a way to make him deal fairly. I'm not so suicidal as to seek to kill him, but I can keep him from getting what he wants. That'll be at least a little revenge for Kerridi, Gavath, and Dal."

"Skaltahar isn't going to buy the coffer just because you promise that what's inside is valuable."

"You're right," Aeron agreed. "That's the difficulty. Warding spells or no, I have to get the cursed thing open."

Wherever he went, Kesk liked to stride arrogantly, his head bare and sneering tanarukk face on display, his battle-axe in his hand, and several of his henchmen swaggering along behind him. He enjoyed watching the common herd blanch and scurry to get out of the way, relished it when even Gray Blades chose to give him a wide berth.

By the same token, he disliked creeping about muffled in a shabby cloak and hood, and he positively despised rapping on the little twin-paneled door at the rear of the great house, as if he was some sort of tinker, peddler, or beggar.

No one answered right away, which blackened his mood still further, if that was possible. He felt a growing urge to chop down the door with his axe, which he never relinquished even on those rare occasions when he found it necessary to wear a disguise. But then the portal cracked open. A human, only half dressed, his feet bare and his tawny hair uncombed, peered down at what he likely thought a peculiar shrouded figure, taller and even thicker built than a dwarf, but shorter than an elf, waiting in the alley.

"Yes?" the servant yawned.

Scowling, Kesk lifted his head, pushed back his cowl, and finally had the satisfaction of seeing someone flinch. Since it was the only pleasurable moment he was likely to experience on his visit there, he tried to savor it.

"His nibs is expecting me," he said.

The human gave a shaky nod and replied, "Yes. Please, come with me."

At first, they traversed the service areas of the mansion. It was late enough that the servants and slaves had extinguished most of the lamps and candles, and with only a couple exceptions, they lay snoring on their cots and pallets. Kesk knew they'd rise with the dawn to resume their labors, and he experienced a swell of contempt for anyone trapped in such a dreary life. Truly, as he'd often thought, most people were no better than sheep and deserved whatever the wolves of the world cared to do to them.

Eventually his guide conducted him into the section of the house where the master spent his days. The furnishings had a fussy, delicate, pastel quality that made Kesk's skin crawl. He understood that many folk would have considered them "elegant" or "beautiful," but to the extent that he cared about such effete matters at all, he preferred clashing primary colors and bold, simple designs, a taste he shared with his orc ancestors.

The servant tapped on a door.

"Come in," a reedy voice replied, whereupon the flunky ushered Kesk into a lavishly appointed library and workroom.

The décor was of a piece with that seen elsewhere in the house. Carved crystal flowers stood in milky porcelain vases, and a fabulously expensive blackwood clock with golden hands and numerals hung on the wall, its gilded weights dangling beneath it.

Dressed in a tasseled nightcap, slippers, and a quilted satin dressing gown, the owner of all that luxury lounged on a plush velvet divan, a scroll in his lap and a glass of pale wine on the stand beside him. Though well into the afternoon of his life, the smallish human had a boyish, apple-cheeked face that flashed a smile when he saw who'd come to call on him.

"Kesk!" he said. "My dear fellow. I was just about to give up on you for the night."

"Do you have to use my name in front of the help?" Kesk growled.

The servant flinched as if he expected Kesk to reclaim his anonymity by butchering him on the spot. Actually, the idea did have something to recommend it.

"It's a little late to worry about concealing your identity," said the man on the couch. "As far as I know, you're the only tanarukk in Oeble. In any case, Cohis is discreet. Aren't you, Cohis? He'll prove it by running along before he's even asked."

The lackey hastily withdrew and the man said, "Show it to me."

Kesk felt awkward. Almost embarrassed. He wasn't used to such feelings, and it made him angry.

"We hit a snag," he said.

The human arched his eyebrows and asked, "How so? I know one of your minions made off with the prize. It's the talk of the town."

"That's the problem," said Kesk. "He wasn't exactly one of mine. He was someone I hired."

"I was under the impression that you had your own little army of ruffians to attend to such chores. Why would you seek help elsewhere?"

"Different reasons. The thing is, the bastard hasn't handed over the box yet."

"Whyever not?"

"He wants more gold than we agreed on."

"Perhaps you'd better give it to him."

"I can't let a little rat like him change the terms of a deal on me," Kesk said. "It would make me look weak."

"Forgive my selfishness, but I can't help feeling more concerned with my objectives than your reputation."

"You'll get your cursed treasure."

"Will I? I hope so, but I have the disquieting feeling there are things you're not telling me."

How right he was. But he might not appreciate hearing that Kesk had complicated the plan by scheming to seize the prize and settle an old score at the same time. Or that the tanarukk had lost his temper at exactly the wrong moment, lashing out at Aeron and scaring him off when he should have done all he could to allay the trickster's misgivings. Or . . . well, quite a bit of it, really.

"Is it so bad?" Kesk asked. "The way you explained it,

our victim has already squandered a lot of coin and wound up with nothing. You can still ruin him, can't you?"

"Suppose I move prematurely, and he then recovers the *Bouquet*? He'll survive my little coup knowing just what a committed enemy I actually am, which will surely prompt him to retaliate. That's unacceptable. I don't intend to make my play until the box is in my hands and I know for certain he's defenseless. Also, of course, the musty old thing is virtually priceless. You don't want to throw away all the riches it represents, do you?"

"Like I said, I'll get it."

"I never doubted it for an instant. Still, perhaps we can resolve the matter more expeditiously if I take an active role. What's our recalcitrant thief's name?"

"Don't worry about it. I'll deal with him."

"Please, indulge my curiosity."

"Are you going to make me say it outright?" Kesk asked, scowling.

The man on the couch cocked his head and replied, "Apparently so."

"I know I'm not the only knife on your belt. Maybe, if I give you the name, you'll find the thief without any help from me. Then you might figure that just proves you don't need a partner after all."

"What a sour, suspicious turn of mind you have. Of course I need a partner. Can you imagine me traipsing through the Underways, trafficking with your Red Axes and their ilk? Would they trust me or even take me seriously? Not without a great deal of effort on my part, and I have other, more congenial work requiring my attention. Now, please, give me the name. Otherwise, much as it would pain me, I'll have to start questioning your integrity."

"Sorry."

The human heaved a sigh and said, "Oh, very well, have it your way. I was just trying to expedite matters, but . . ."

As he blathered on, his hand slipped toward the pocket of his robe.

Kesk sprang forward. The man in the robe lifted his hand, stray grains of glittering blue powder leaking from his palm. About to fling the stuff, he registered the fact that the outlaw was already poised to swing his battle-axe at his neck, and faltered.

Kesk was so angry that the human's hesitation almost didn't matter.

"You'd cast a spell on me?" the tanarukk demanded.

The rich man opened his fingers and let the colored sand spill harmlessly away.

"It wouldn't have hurt you," he said. "It would merely have inclined you to trust me."

Kesk grinned and said, "Not much hope of that now."

"Come, now. You don't truly wish to hurt me. Think of that rosy future I promised you: the Red Axes doing absolutely anything they please without fear of the Gray Blades, the rest of the underworld either paying homage to you or driven out of Oeble altogether. You'll never achieve that paradise without me."

"Don't be so sure," Kesk said, but he lowered the axe.

The human smiled and rubbed his slender neck as if making sure his head was still attached.

"Thank you for your forbearance."

"No," Kesk spat, "thank you for reminding me you're a wizard. You want to help me find the *Bouquet*? Fine. Let's turn out your drawers and closets and see what kind of talismans you've got."

CHAPTER 5

How much farther?" Miri asked.

Her guide glanced back over his shoulder. The wavering light of his upraised torch stained one side of his smirking face yellow while leaving the other in shadow.

"We're almost there," he replied.

"Almost where?" she demanded. He'd led her into what almost seemed an abandoned section of the Underways. No one else was prowling or loitering about, nor had anybody provided a source of permanent illumination. The stink of sewage was stronger there, and puddles of scummy water filled the low spots on the floor.

"Almost to the hideout of the man you're looking for," her companion said. "The thief who was friends with the drunken mage."

"You'd better be right."

"I am. You'd just better pay me what you promised." He tramped on, and she followed, until, without any warning whatsoever, he dashed the torch in one of the filthy pools, extinguishing it instantly.

Miri had discovered the denizens of the Underways retired to their beds around dawn, at the same time decent people were getting up. She'd reluctantly done the same, catching some fitful slumber at the Paeraddyn, then resuming her search in the afternoon. Eventually it led her to the Talondance, a subterranean tavern catering primarily to goblin-kin, lizard men, and creatures even more feral and less welcome in law-abiding towns. A menu scrawled on a chalkboard offered chops, stews, and kabobs prepared with the flesh of humans, gnomes, and elves, and she was far from certain it was a joke.

Yet even so, a few representatives of her own species had chosen to patronize the place. One of them had claimed he could guide her to the rogue she sought, only to lure her down a quiet tunnel and abruptly take away her light. Most likely he himself possessed a means of seeing in the dark.

Reacting instantly, Miri nocked and loosed an arrow. Even though she was shooting blind, the shaft thunked into something solid. A second later, water splashed.

The senior scouts of Miri's guild studied a limited system of magic in addition to their martial skills and woodcraft. She herself had only commenced that phase of her training a year before and proved to possess no extraordinary aptitude for it. Still, she'd mastered a few spells, and when she'd realized she needed to venture underground, it had been obvious which she ought to prepare for the casting.

She recited a rhyming couplet and swept her hand through a mystic pass. Motes of white light leaped from her fingers like sparks rising from a fire. Glowing without heat, they winked out after a moment or two, as new ones sprang forth to take their places. In the aggregate, they shone about as brightly as a candle.

The light sufficed to reveal her treacherous guide lying dead in the puddle beside the torch. As intended, she'd shot him before he could move off the spot where she'd seen him last. She started to relax, then glimpsed a shifting in the darkness, beyond the point where her light began to fail.

Her heart pounding, Miri thrust her sparking hand out as if it was a torch itself. The glow revealed only the earthen walls of the tunnel. Had she only imagined that something was slinking about?

No. The Forest Queen knew, the odious city and the frustrations of her search were wearing on Miri's nerves. Yet even so, she was no timid tenderfoot to start at shadows. Her guide had lured her toward one or more confederates waiting to waylay her—scoundrels who were lurking still, despite the fact that, for whatever reason, she was having trouble seeing them.

She had no intention of standing still while she tried. With the torch soaked and useless, Miri wanted to reach a place where something else shed light before her spell of illumination ran out of power. Nocking another arrow, she retreated down the tunnel. She pivoted this way and that to keep anyone from sneaking up behind her.

Then she gasped as something alien touched her mind. It was like a bitter chill freezing the inside of her head, or rather, it wasn't, but that was as close as she could come. She'd never felt the repugnant sensation before, and she knew no words to describe it.

She was still trying to shake it off when something hissed in the darkness ahead. A huge black viper, longer than she was tall, slithered into view. It was crawling directly toward her.

She shuddered. Whimpered. Recoiled a step. Her arrow nearly slipped from her fingertips and off the bowstring.

She knew it shouldn't be that way. She'd never been afraid of snakes before. The force that had pierced her mind had poisoned her with an unnatural terror, and she had to resist it.

By sheer force of will, she made herself stop retreating. She controlled her breathing, drew the bowstring back, and let her arrow fly.

The missile drove into the viper's body just behind its head, pinning it to the floor. The serpent lashed madly about, and her fear faded.

When it did, she realized that some other threat could easily have crept up on her while she was so frantically intent on the viper. Reaching for another arrow, she turned, and a cudgel streaked at her head.

Two of her foes had stealthily closed the distance. Unlike the accomplice who'd brought Miri there, neither could have passed for human. The one with the club had a manlike shape but scaly reptilian hide. Its fellow, who wielded a rawhide whip, reared on an ophidian tail instead of legs. Both were the same gray-brown as the dirt walls and floor. Somehow, this chameleonlike ability to change color extended even to their clothing and weapons, and it explained their success at hiding in plain sight.

They were yuan-ti, a race comprising a sinister blend of snake and human. Until that moment, Miri had had the good luck never to encounter the species before, but by all accounts, she could scarcely have blundered into graver peril.

She blocked the cudgel with her buckler. The impact clanged, and it stung her forearm. The whip sliced at her legs, and she tried to parry with her bow. Perhaps she succeeded to a degree, but the flexible braided leather whirled around the length of wood and stung her even so.

The bow was the wrong weapon for close quarters. She dropped it and scrambled backward, meanwhile snatching for the hilt of her broadsword. Hissing, exposing their fangs, her assailants lunged after her. She glimpsed other yuan-ti, no two exactly alike but each a fusion of man and serpent, racing up behind them. The inside of her mind went icy cold, reinfecting her with terror, and she purged it by bellowing a battle cry.

She dodged the whip and parried the club. She backed into the tunnel wall, dislodging a shower of loose grit, and knew she could retreat no farther. Fortunately, at the same instant, her sword cleared the scabbard.

At the sight of the straight, double-edged blade, her foes hesitated. In a moment, they'd spread out to flank her and work together more effectively, except that Miri saw no reason to give them the chance. She sprang at the reptile-man with the club. It swung the weapon, but she discerned the blow was going to miss and simply continued her own attack. The broadsword sheared into the yuan-ti's chest. The creature started to collapse. She yanked the blade free, pivoted—

—and was too slow. The whip lashed her sword arm, the impact painful even through her reinforced leather sleeve, and spun around it. The legless yuan-ti yanked the coils tight and jerked her forward. The creature raised its off hand, which sweated a clear slime, to grab her.

Had Miri been panicked, or simply a less experienced fighter, she might have dug in her heels and resisted. But she knew she didn't have time to play tug-of-war. If she immobilized herself that way, one of her other foes would overwhelm her. So she didn't resist the pull. To the contrary, she scrambled forward as fast as she could, and when the whip slackened, she regained the ability to wield the broadsword.

Unfortunately, by that time, she was in such close proximity to the yuan-ti that the harsh smell of its acidic secretion stung her eyes and nostrils, so near that it was difficult to bring her blade into play. The serpent-man grabbed her shield arm, and her armor started to smolder and hiss. She twisted the limb from its grasp, bashed it in the face with the buckler, then hammered the top of its head with the broadsword's heavy nickel pommel. Bone cracked, and the yuan-ti went down. She frantically freed herself from the coils of the whip and turned to meet her next foes.

At which point, she almost laughed at the futility of all her struggling, because for the first time, she had a sense of just how many of them she was facing. A dozen at least. Conceivably even more.

The yuan-ti surged at her. Poised on guard, she chanted the opening words of her guild's death prayer, beseeching Mielikki to welcome her soul into the House of Nature.

A voice cried out in a sibilant language, presumably the yuan-ti's own. The snake-men halted, though their attitude remained as threatening as before. Some reasserted their ability to blend into the background, which plainly worked best when they weren't moving. It was uncanny how much difficulty Miri had making them out, even knowing they were crouched right in front of her.

"You see how outnumbered you are," said the same voice, but in the common tongue. "You can't win, but we don't want to kill you. If we did, we'd come at you with blades and arrows instead of clubs, nets, and whips."

"What do you want?" Miri asked.

"Someone is smitten with you," said the yuan-ti's spokesman. "So much so that he put out the word, he'll pay well to anyone who arranges a rendezvous."

Miri was accustomed to plain speech, and it took her a moment to puzzle out what had actually been said.

"You're slavers?" she said. "I'm a free woman, no enemy of Oeble, and no outlaw. You have no right to lay hands on me."

Some of the yuan-ti laughed.

"I'm afraid," said their leader, "that down here in the Underways—well, anywhere in Oeble, really—we hunt whom we please, without much worrying what the rules say."

"I came into the tunnels to run an errand for a rich and powerful citizen of Oeble. He'll ransom me."

"That's nice, but in our trade, it pays to do business with folk you already know. Less is likely to go wrong. Now be sensible and throw away your sword."

"No," Miri said. "We don't do that in the Red Hart Guild."

"How brainless, when you have no hope of winning."

"But I do. I'll slay more of you before you take me down, and each of those kills will be a victory. Every one will make the world a little cleaner."

She lunged and cut. The broadsword slashed open the throat of a snake-headed yuan-ti before it even realized the battle had resumed.

She spun just in time to spy another creature—a serpent-woman—puffing on a blowpipe. Miri sidestepped, and the dart, which was no doubt drugged, flew wild. She hacked at the yuan-ti, half severing its scaly hand at the wrist. The slaver shrieked and recoiled. Miri leaped out from under an outflung net with lead weights and fish-hooks attached to the edges, and then stamped on it when it dropped to the ground, thus preventing the brute on the other end from pulling it back for another cast. The slaver let go, and its limbs and torso so flexible it seemed to have no bones, it curled itself into a posture resembling a human wrestler's stance. Acidic jelly smeared itself across its hide, it pounced, and she whirled out of the way, simultaneously slamming the edge of her buckler into its spine. Evidently it had vertebrae after all, because one of them cracked.

Miri knew she'd been fortunate thus far, and that her luck couldn't hold against so many. Sure enough, an instant later, something swept her feet out from underneath her. As she slammed down on her back, she saw it was a long, lashing tail, She tried to scramble up, but the scaly member whipped back around and slashed her across the head.

The impact made everything seem quiet and far away. Dazed, she nonetheless kept struggling to defend herself, but felt she was moving as lazily as a lost feather floating down from the sky. Her foes surrounded her and lifted their weapons. After the carnage she'd wrought, their faces looked so angry that she wondered if they meant to batter her to death.

Perhaps their chief feared the same thing, for it cried, "Remember, we want her alive, and her face unmarked!"

"Fine," said one of the yuan-ti in the circle. Its speech was garbled, as if its forked tongue and long, flexible throat were ill-suited to forming words. "But we have to beat the fight out of her, don't we?"

It lifted its cat-o'-nine-tails, and a spinning steel ring flashed through the air and embedded itself in the back of its hand. Its eyes wide with shock, the serpent-man dropped its weapon.

A second chakram flew an instant later, shearing into a female yuan-ti's serpentine skull. Then a willowy, fair-skinned woman, clad in a nondescript mantle, robe, and sandals, sprang into the midst of the snake-men. It seemed she had no more weapons, not unless the bindings wrapped around her knuckles counted, but the lack didn't trouble her. Whirling, crouching, and leaping, in constant motion, she delivered devastating, bone-shattering attacks with her feet, elbows, fists, the edges of her hands, and even her fingertips. Though Miri had traveled far in her time, she'd never seen anything like it.

Caught by surprise and accordingly rattled, the yuan-ti fell back. The stranger grabbed hold of Miri's arm and hauled her to her feet. She slipped her toes under the scout's fallen broadsword and kicked it up into the air.

Miri blinked free of her half-stupor and caught the weapon by the hilt. She and the newcomer stood back to back, so no foe could take either of them from behind.

Hissing and screeching, the yuan-ti rushed in, and Miri cut and thrust. She realized she might prevail against her foes. The arrival of her newfound ally had given her hope.

Evidently it had altered the yuan-ti leader's expectations as well, because it decided to take a more active role in the battle, declaiming words that somehow made themselves heard despite the clamor of combat. Once again, the creature was speaking a language Miri didn't understand, but from the rhymes and measured cadence, she was certain it was reciting a spell.

Sure enough, a dark vapor abruptly filled the air, its stench so foul that Miri gagged. She felt dizzy, sick to death, while the reptile-men assailing her with whips and cudgels appeared unaffected.

It would have been witless to imagine that, afflicted as she was, she could continue fighting with her customary facility. If she was to endure, it would have to be by trickery. Acting as if she was even sicker than she felt—if such a thing was possible—she swayed and crumpled to her knees. She let the broadsword slip from her fingers.

Her foes took the bait. Confident she was helpless, they lunged in at her. She snatched up her blade and cut, scarcely aiming, the strokes simply as strong and as fast as she could manage.

The ploy worked. Blood spattered, and her mangled adversaries reeled backward. The noxious fumes started to thin, and her nausea and vertigo, to pass.

But it wouldn't matter if the yuan-ti spellcaster kept tossing curses around. Somebody had to stop it. Praying that it had to wave its arms or something to work magic, that its chameleon skin no longer kept it perfectly concealed, she peered about.

There, by the far wall!

It was the largest and least human of any of the yuan-ti, with only a pair of scaly arms to indicate it was anything other than a colossal rearing snake. It carried a bastard sword in one hand and was already crooking the fingers of the other into cabalistic signs.

"Got to move!" Miri gasped.

She scrambled forward. A yuan-ti with hissing serpents sprouting from its shoulders in place of arms sprang into her path. She chopped at its head, jerked the broadsword free, and sprinted on, splashing through one of the scummy pools. She glimpsed other snake-men darting to intercept her, but the stranger was there, too, punching, kicking, holding them back.

The yuan-ti leader saw Miri charging forward, and it left off its conjuring to come on guard. She believed that was good, though from the way it moved, it appeared to know how to manage its weapon.

The bastard sword leaped at her. She brushed it away with the buckler and riposted with a thrust. The yuan-ti's flexible body twisted out of the way.

At once she renewed the attack, trying to score before the serpent-man could raise its heavy weapon for another cut. Unfortunately, she'd momentarily lost sight of the fact that her opponent had other offensive options, one of which it chose to exercise. Its wedge-shaped head shot down at her, jaws spread wide, drops of venom clinging to the points of the long, curved fangs.

Committed to the attack as she was, Miri was in the wrong attitude to parry. Her only hope of avoiding the yuan-ti's bite was to fling herself down on her belly, so she did. The snake-man's snout thumped her between the shoulders like a hammer, but its teeth didn't rip into her body.

They would in an instant, though, if she didn't hold them off. She wrenched herself over and hacked blindly.

By pure luck as much as anything else, the broadsword nearly severed the yuan-ti's head from its trunk, which then flopped down on top of her.

The corpse heaved and writhed as Miri struggled out from under it. After a moment, her ally extended a hand to help her drag herself clear. The stranger's cowl had slipped back to reveal a downy pate she'd obviously shaved within the past couple days. Beyond her lay only the motionless bodies of other yuan-ti. If any of the slavers retained their lives and the use of their limbs, they'd evidently fled the scene. The fight was over.

Sefris hadn't had much trouble locating the scout. A good many folk had taken note of the ranger tramping about the Underways asking questions about the robbery in the Paeraddyn. Once the monastic found her quarry, she'd tailed her, awaiting an opportunity to ingratiate herself. The yuan-ti had provided a splendid one.

After that, however, came the difficult part, far more challenging than slaughtering a gang of serpent-men, formidable though they were. She needed to present herself as the sort of sunny, altruistic soul the guide would be likely to trust, and which she herself particularly detested. She smiled into the face of the Dark Goddess's enemy, the same face she'd seen in the arcanaloth's mirror, and bowed.

At that same instant, as if in outrage at her duplicity, the tunnel went pitch black as the guide's hand stopped shedding its luminous sparks. The ranger quickly recited words of power to renew the spell. It was quite a simple charm, though, paradoxically, one that would forever lie beyond Sefris's grasp. Sorcerers who drew their power from the unholy well called the Shadow Weave were unable to conjure light.

"There," said the ranger, as the white sparks danced anew. "Sorry about that."

Sefris grinned and said, "It's all right. Though we're lucky it didn't happen a minute or two earlier, or the yuan-ti would have defeated us for certain."

"My name is Miri Buckman of the Red Hart Guild. Thank you for saving my life."

"I'm Sefris Uuthrakt of the Broken Ones."

The Broken Ones were a monastic order pledged to the martyr god Ilmater. Though their philosophy and mission differed radically from those of the Dark Moon, their fighting arts were similar, and by pretending to membership in their company, she'd provided a plausible explanation for the unusual skills she'd demonstrated.

"Thank you as well," Sefris continued. "You protected my back as much as I protected yours."

"Maybe," Miri replied, stooping to wipe her bloody broadsword on a dead serpent-man's tunic. "But you didn't have to jump in and help me in the first place."

"Oh, but I did. I have my vows, as I imagine you rangers have yours."

"We have a code." The scout sheathed her sword, then headed toward her fallen bow as she said, "Believe me, I'm not complaining, but what were you doing in these miserable warrens, anyway?"

Sefris tried to judge if her companion was suspicious, and decided she was merely curious.

"We Broken Ones sometimes wander far from our sanctuaries, seeking to learn the lessons only the bustling world can teach. My travels brought me to Oeble, and into the Underways. I heard the sounds of strife, and I rushed to see what was happening. I would have arrived sooner, except that much of the path was dark, and I had to grope my way."

In reality, Sefris had waited to burst onto the scene until Miri truly needed her. Presumably that would ensure the fool was grateful for her intervention. The delay had given the monastic the opportunity to assess the ranger's archery and swordplay. As it turned out, she was reasonably accomplished, though nothing that would inconvenience a daughter of the Dark Moon when the time came.

"Well, bless you for it," Miri said. "I'll make an offering to the Crying God the first chance I get."

"May I ask," Sefris said, "what business brings you 'below,' as the locals say? I would have expected to meet a warrior like you in a forest glade or along a mountain trail, not rubbing shoulders with city orcs, smugglers, and kidnappers."

"I wish you had," Miri said. She picked up her bow, inspected it for signs of damage, and evidently satisfied that it was unscathed, she dangled it casually in her hand. "I've never much liked any town, and this one's the nastiest I've ever seen. But . . ."

She hesitated as if realizing she was speaking too freely.

Sefris inclined her head and replied, "I understand. Your business is your own. I shouldn't have pried."

"Oh, to Fury's Heart with it. It's all right, I trust you. Anyway, by now, everybody else in Oeble knows, or at least part of it. The rangers of my guild hire themselves out, if it's honest work performed for decent folk. I undertook to carry a treasure from Ormath to Oeble, and just as I was about to deliver it, a robber stole it. Obviously, it's my responsibility to get it back. It'll be a great misfortune to any number of people if I don't."

"I understand," Sefris said. "May I help you find it?"

Miri's eyes narrowed and she asked, "Why would you want to do that?"

"I told you, I'm sworn to aid others, and I seek the wisdom that only comes from immersing oneself in worldly affairs."

"It could be dangerous."

"And I confess, I'm scarcely the ablest fighter my order has produced. Others are far more competent. But I did manage to help you against the yuan-ti."

"I can't argue with that," said the ranger.

"Then let me watch your back for a while longer."

"All right, gladly, if you're sure it's what you want. Why not?" Miri smiled crookedly and added, "We can't fare any worse together than I've done nosing about on my own."

"What tactics have you used?"

"I've offered to pay for information, provided it turned out to be true. But as you've just seen, these rogues would rather cheat, rob, or enslave an outsider than earn her coin honestly."

"Perhaps it's time for a different approach," Sefris said. She found one of her chakrams, pulled it from the wound it had inflicted, wiped it clean, and stowed it away in her robe. Later, when she had the leisure, she'd take a hone to the edge. "If you aren't squeamish, we could ask questions in a less gentle fashion."

"Surely the creed of Ilmater doesn't allow for torture," Miri said, peering at her quizzically.

"We Broken Ones are more practical than people give us credit for. Of course, we would never torture a prisoner in the truest sense of the word. We are, however, allowed to intimidate him and cause some brief discomfort, when it's absolutely necessary to further a worthy cause. But perhaps your own code doesn't allow for such tactics."

"It's a gray area. I've never liked it much, but . . . I'm sick of these Oeblaun vermin trying to swindle me and sniggering behind my back. By the Hornblade, this lot are yuan-ti, and they meant to enslave me. I think I could rough up one of them, and live with my conscience afterward."

So, gentle Mielikki's servant had a streak of ruthlessness. The implicit hypocrisy stirred the contempt that was central to Sefris's nature, but she made sure no hint of a sneer showed on her face.

"So be it, then," the monastic said.

"The problem may be," Miri said as she surveyed the fallen reptile-men, "that none of them is capable of answering questions."

Sefris smiled.

"That's one advantage fists have over blades and arrows," she said. "Often, they merely stun instead of kill." To be precise, they stunned when she wanted them to, and in the fight just concluded, intuition had prompted her to leave a couple of the yuan-ti alive. "We just need to wake somebody up."

CHAPTER 6

Aeron met the Dead Cart on Balamonthar's Street. As he would have expected by late afternoon, the mule-drawn wagon carried several corpses, which were starting to smell, and was heading to dump them in the garbage-middens southeast of town.

Hairy and dirty, his limbs twisted out of true by illness or an accident of birth, Hulm Draeridge leered down at Aeron from the seat.

"Hop in the back," he said. "Save me the trouble of lifting you up and chucking you in."

Aeron snorted and said, "I'm not ready to take that ride just yet."

"That's not the way I hear it."

"It doesn't matter if people are looking for me, tanglebones, not as long as my wits are sharper than theirs. It's all part of the sport. Speaking of which, if anybody asks, you haven't seen me."

He tossed the driver a silver bit, and Hulm snatched it from the air.

"I've already forgotten you," the driver said, "as completely as will everyone else ten minutes after you're dead."

Keeping an eye out for Red Axes, Gray Blades, and female rangers, carrying the saddlebag hidden beneath his cape, Aeron strode on into a little cul-de-sac crammed with various commercial endeavors. A tinker's grindstone whined and spewed sparks as he sharpened a hoe. A small-time slave trader cried the virtues of his half dozen shackled human and goblin wares, who sat around his feet in apathetic misery. Hooded falcons stood on their perches, the bells on their feet chiming when they shifted position. The Whistlers, one of the city's smaller and less successful gangs, had stolen the birds at midsummer and were still trying to dispose of them at bargain prices. Unfortunately, the average citizen of Oeble didn't know how to hawk and had no interest in learning.

Aeron, who likewise lacked any experience with the fierce-looking raptors, playthings of noblemen and merchants with lordly pretensions, crept past the perches a little warily, slipped into a tower, and climbed a corkscrew flight of stairs. Somewhere in one of the apartments, a baby cried. In another, bread was baking. The appetizing aroma filled the shaft and made Aeron's mouth water.

Burgell Whitehorn lived on the third floor. Aeron tapped on the gnome's door, then positioned himself in front of the peephole. After a while, three latches clinked in turn as someone unfastened them. The door swung open, and Burgell frowned up at his caller.

Skinny and flaxen-haired, his skin walnut brown and his eyes a startling turquoise, Burgell stood half as tall as Aeron and had to climb up on a stool to look out the peephole. Like most habitations in Oeble, that particular tenement had been built for humans, and smaller residents coped with the resulting awkwardness as best they could.

But at least the relative largeness of the apartment gave Burgell room to pack in all his gnome-sized gear. The front room was his workshop, and it contained a bewildering miscellany of tools: hammers, chisels, saws, lockpicks, tinted lenses, jeweler's loupes, and jars of powdered and shredded ingredients for casting spells. A fat gray cat, the mage's familiar, lay curled atop a grimoire. It opened its eyes, gave Aeron a disdainful yellow stare, then appeared to go back to sleep.

Despite the jolly reputation of his race, Burgell's welcome was no warmer.

"What are you doing wandering about, in broad daylight, no less?"

"Hulm Draeridge more or less asked me the same thing," Aeron said, "but I won't get any business done hiding in some hole. Can I come in?"

"I don't think so. Look what happened to the last wizard who helped you, and that was before you angered the tanarukk."

Aeron sighed and said, "I'm sorry about Dal, but he knew the risks. I'm not asking you to take the same kind of chance. I just want you to do your usual kind of job. You won't even have to leave home."

"Why not do it yourself?"

"Because it's not my specialty, and this particular chore calls for an expert."

Aeron had had enough of discussing his business in the stairwell. He pushed forward, and the little gnome had little choice but to give ground. Aeron shut the door.

"All right," Burgell said. Irritation made his tenor voice shrill. "Do come in by all means. But you know, I don't work cheap."

"So I recall, from all the times you've bled me dry," Aeron replied as he extracted the steel case from the saddle bag. The gray metal gleamed in the sunlight streaming in through the open casement. "Whatever's inside this is valuable. I'll cut you in for one part in twenty."

"One part in five."

"Greed is an ugly thing."

"You'd know."

Aeron grinned and said, "I might at that. One part in ten."

"Done, but I'll need some coin on account. Just in case the box turns out to contain something you can't sell."

"Trust me, whatever it is, I'll find a way to turn it into cash. But if this is what it takes to stop your griping and set you to work . . ."

Aeron opened his belt pouch and extracted several gold coins. In so doing, he nearly exhausted his funds. It was a strange thing. Though no gang chieftain or lieutenant, he was a successful thief by most standards. Yet the profits refused to stick to his fingers, and it wasn't only because his father's pain-killing elixirs and poultices were so expensive. Maybe he spent too many nights carousing in the taverns, bought the house too many rounds, "loaned" too much gold to needy friends who never paid him back. Yet why risk his neck stealing coin if not to enjoy it once he had it? When it ran out, the solution was simply to steal some more.

Burgell bit one of the coins, a Cormyrean dinar, then dumped the clinking lot into the pocket of his shabby dressing gown. He gestured to a stubby-legged work table that, like the rest of the furniture, was sized for little folk, not men.

"Put the box down there," the gnome said, "and tell me what you can."

"It was in this saddlebag when I first laid hands on it. I was invisible at the time, but even so, the pouch screamed a warning and painted me with light."

"Faerie fire."

"Whatever you call it. Anyway, it hasn't done that since, so I guess it was a one-time spell. But when I tried to pick the lock of the coffer itself, it boomed like thunder. The noise actually hurt."

The wizard nodded and muttered, "Layered protections. Never a good thing."

"Truly? Is that your expert opinion?" Aeron teased. "Look, here's where we stand. I don't know if the thunder will sound a second time or what other wards may lie in wait behind that one, but I need you to dissolve them all."

"Any sign of purely mechanical traps? Spring-loaded poison needles, finger-snipping pincers, or the like?"

"I didn't see any, but I wouldn't rule anything out."

"All right," the gnome said. "Stand back."

Taking his own advice, Burgell muttered a cantrip then he pointed his finger at a brass key lying on the workbench. The yellow metal oozed in a way that baffled the eye, as if changing shape and size from one moment to the next. The key floated up into the air and inserted itself in the strongbox's lock. It jerked, trying to turn, but evidently it couldn't shift the tumblers.

Thunder crashed, painfully loud in the confines of the flat. Aeron couldn't help flinching, even though he'd known what to expect. A framed diagram, depicting the interplay of the primal forces of the cosmos or some such gibberish, fell off the wall. The gray cat leaped off the spellbook, dashed for cover, and vanished behind a wooden chest.

"The sonic ward is still active," Burgell said.

"Is that the only way you had of finding out?" Aeron asked. "I could have done that. Come to think of it, I did."

"You're lucky you didn't shatter every bone in your arm. Noise can hit like a mace, if properly focused. That's why you need someone who can manipulate his tools without touching them to do the poking and prodding."

"Just try to poke more quietly."

"Why is it that folk go to the trouble to hire a master,

then insist on telling him how to practice his art? Hush, and let me work."

"Fine."

Aeron sat down on a divan. It was where he customarily sat when consulting Burgell, but as usual, he heeded the impulse to lower himself cautiously and make sure the miniature couch would still bear his weight.

The gnome stuck a jeweler's loupe into his left eye and examined the lockbox from every angle. Eventually he drew himself up straight, slashed his left hand through the air, and rattled off a string of words Aeron couldn't understand.

Magic blared like a dissonant trumpet fanfare. Blue light pulsed through the air in time with the notes. The strongbox jumped, spun like a top, and crashed back down on the table, still closed. The brass key popped out of the lock.

"Shadows of Mask," Aeron swore when the commotion had run its course. "Quietly, I said. What in the name of the Nine Hells is wrong with you today?"

"Nothing. You brought me a special problem. I'll solve it, but it's likely to put up a bit of a fuss in the meantime."

"Then let's at least muffle the ruckus as best we can," Aeron said as he rose and headed for the window.

"I'll have to light the lamps," Burgell said with a frown. "It's a waste of oil."

"One of the coins I gave you will keep you in fuel until spring."

"It still doesn't pay to be a spendthrift. But all right."

The gnome waved his hand, and the various lamps lit themselves. Aeron closed and latched the casement.

After that, the human had nothing to do but return to his seat and watch the mage work. Burgell spent interminable minutes peering at the strongbox through various colored lenses, periodically muttering strings of mystical words at it. To no effect, as far as Aeron could see.

In time, having watched the master cracksman work before, Aeron grew puzzled.

"Aren't you going to use any of your pigments or powders?" he asked.

"If I think it necessary," Burgell said.

"It's just that I remember when you opened that priest's wardrobe for—"

"Do you want to reminisce about old times, or do you want me to crack the box?"

Aeron shook his head, slumped back on the couch, and tried to dismiss the unpleasant feeling gnawing at his nerves. He couldn't believe it was legitimate. He and Burgell had worked together a score of times, and the gnome had always proved trustworthy. Yet, watching the little wizard stare and mumble just then, comparing his ponderous caution to the energy with which he'd attacked other locks, traps, and spells of warding, Aeron couldn't quite shake the suspicion that something was wrong.

He thought maybe he shouldn't be trying to shake it. An outlaw, after all, survived by heeding his instincts. Perhaps he was only striving to ignore them because he'd just lost Dal, Gavath, and Kerridi, and it pained him to think he might lose Burgell in a different but no less final fashion.

"Burg," he finally said, "did someone get to you?"

The gnome blinked and asked, "What nonsense are you talking now?"

His turquoise eyes, brilliant even in the soft lamplight, glanced down and to the left as he spoke. Aeron was fairly certain it was what gamblers called a "tell"—a sign Burgell was lying.

"It occurs to me I've never known you to work with the casement open," said Aeron. "You usually don't want folk peeking in at your business."

"We're on the third floor."

"Someone could spy from one of the upper story apartments in the tower across the way. But let's say you wanted someone to know I'd shown up here. Then the open casement would help you signal."

"Did you see me wave a flag or write a note and fling it out?"

"No, but you triggered the thunderclap, and that kind of clumsiness isn't like you, unless you did it on purpose. You followed that up with more noise and flashing light, and since then, it looks to me like you've just been stalling, waiting for somebody to burst in through the door you didn't bother to relock."

Burgell backed away from the work table and snatched a scrap of ram's horn from his pocket. He lifted it above his head and jabbered words of power.

Aeron leaped up from the couch, charged, dived across the low table, and slammed into Burgell, presumably spoiling his conjuration. He hurled the gnome to the floor, dropped on top of him, and poised an Arthyn fang at this throat. Despite the circumstances, and his own anger, the human felt an irrational flicker of shame for manhandling someone so much smaller than himself.

"Get off me," Burgell panted, "or I'll turn you into a beetle. I'll boil your blood."

"Don't talk nonsense. You're no battle mage, and even if you were, you'd need a demon's luck to get off a spell before I cut your throat. Now, who turned you against me?"

"The Red Axes."

"Well, at least it wasn't the law. Do the Axes have a crew watching the place?" Given that Kesk had all of Oeble to search, and his normal business affairs to manage, that seemed unlikely. "Or just a beggar or streetwalker who'll carry word to the gang?"

If the latter was the case, Aeron might have an extra minute or two in which to make his escape.

"I don't know," answered the gnome. "They didn't tell me."

Aeron's anger clenched tighter inside him.

"Curse you," he said, "why would you do this? I thought we were friends."

"We are," the gnome replied. "That's why I tried to shoo you away from my door, but you wouldn't have it. Once you bulled your way in, I had no choice."

"That's a load of dung."

"No, it's not. I didn't like betraying you, but I have my own neck to worry about. I can't afford to anger Kesk Turnskull. Please," the gnome said, his voice breaking, "anybody would have done the same!"

"And anyone would do what I'm going to do now."

But just as Aeron was about to drive the dagger in, his rage abruptly twisted into sadness and a kind of weary disgust.

"Or not, apparently," Aeron said, "unless you try to get up, call out, or throw another spell."

He rose. Burgell stared at him as if he feared the human was only feigning mercy, toying with his victim before he made the kill.

He shouldn't have worried, if for no other reason than Aeron plainly didn't have time for such an amusement. He stuffed the strongbox back in the saddlebag, then scurried around the workroom, snatching up a selection of Burgell's tools. When he ran out of room in the pouch, he stuck them in his pockets and inside his shirt.

Next he opened the casement and peered outside. He didn't spot any bravos striding through the little marketplace below with obviously hostile intent. That didn't necessarily mean they weren't there, but it was marginally encouraging even so. Above him, the blue sky was unobstructed, which was to say, it didn't have a Rainspan cutting across it, connecting Burgell's spire to another. The only way to effect a departure above ground level would be to crawl across the slanting roofs and leap from one to the next. It would be slow, dangerous, and sure to attract attention in broad daylight.

All things considered, Aeron thought he'd take his chances in the street. He pulled up his hood. Many folk would go without on such a warm, pleasant autumn day, but even so, a covered head would likely be less eye-catching than his red hair.

As he opened the apartment door, it occurred to him to demand his gold back from Burgell. But even if he hadn't been in a hurry, he wouldn't have bothered, wouldn't have wanted to talk to his false friend any more than necessary, and so he simply ran down the steps. The infant had stopped wailing, but the stairwell still smelled of warm, rising bread.

Aeron hoped to reach the exit before any of the Red Axes appeared to block the way, but when he peered over the second floor landing, he saw that he hadn't been that lucky. The door below him opened, and two figures, Tharag the bugbear and the peevish human who'd lost to the hulking goblin-kin at cards, appeared in the bright, sun-lit rectangle. The Red Axes exclaimed at the sight of their quarry and scrambled up the steps.

Aeron retreated to the far end of the landing, drew his largest Arthyn fang, and settled into a fighting crouch. At first, the Red Axes advanced on him with cudgels in their hands. Then they caught sight of the saddlebag tucked under their intended victim's arm, realized they didn't need to take him alive to discover its whereabouts, and readied their own blades.

Aeron waited until they were nearly in striking range. Then he stuck his knife between his teeth, planted his hand on the railing that bordered the landing, and vaulted over.

At least he didn't have as far to fall as when he'd jumped off the parapet at the Paer. The landing jolted him, but he weathered it, and when he looked up, he discovered that his gamble had paid off. The Red Axes weren't so keen to kill him that they were willing to leap after him and risk breaking their own bones. They were scrambling back the way they'd come, which meant Aeron would have no difficulty reaching the door ahead of them.

Grinning, he charged out into the sunlight, only to trip and fall headlong. Something bashed him across the shoulder blades.

He flopped over onto his back. The paunchy, tattooed Whistler who'd been selling falcons stood over him, swinging one of the perches over his head for another blow. It was a clumsy sort of improvised quarterstaff, but it would do to bludgeon a man into submission.

Aeron wondered fleetingly why that particular rogue was meddling in his business. Maybe Kesk had bribed or intimidated the Whistlers into joining the hunt. Or perhaps the wretch was acting on his own initiative. He might want to curry favor with the Red Axes and move up to membership in the more successful gang.

Either way, Aeron had to deal with him quickly, before Tharag and his partner ran back out the door. He tried to twist himself around into position to strike back, but didn't make it in time. The perch hurtled down, and the best defense he could manage was to catch it on his forearms instead of taking it across the face. The blow crashed home with brutal force. Aeron gasped at the pain, and some of the folk in the crowd laughed and cheered the Whistler on. As far as the thief knew, they had no particular reason to favor his assailant over him except that the vendor currently held the upper hand, and the citizens of Oeble tended to enjoy watching a bully administer a good beating.

The perch jerked up into the air. Aeron finished swinging himself around, pulled his knees up to his chest, and lashed out with a double kick. His heels caught the Whistler in the knees, something cracked, and the gang member stumbled back and toppled onto his rump. Aeron hoped he'd crippled the poxy son of a whore.

Alas, he couldn't linger to find out. He had to keep moving. He scrambled to his feet and pivoted this way and that, trying to see what was going on. Squealing, people recoiled from the dagger in his hand, and in so doing, somewhat impeded the advance of the pair of shaggy, long-legged gnolls shambling in his direction.

The hyena-headed Red Axes with their glaring yellow eyes and lolling tongues were blocking the mouth of the cul-de-sac. Aeron had at most a few heartbeats to find another way out of the box. He cast about, looking for a passable alleyway between two of the surrounding spires. He didn't see one.

His only option was to bolt into another of the buildings surrounding the dead end. He dashed toward a doorway, and something smashed down on the top of his head. He collapsed to his knees amid a scatter of clay shards, dry earth, and withered stalks, and he realized someone had leaned out an upper story window and dropped a flower pot on him.

A second such missile shattered beside his right hand and jarred him into action. Shaking off the shock and pain, he scrambled on into the tower.

The building had shops on the ground floor, an ale house to the left and a cobbler to the right. Since their windows opened on the same cul-de-sac he was trying to escape, they were of no use to him. He ran on down a hallway, past the stairs twisting upward and several closed doors that likely led to apartments, seeking a rear exit into the next street over.

Alas, the corridor was a dead end, too. And when he spun back around, the gnolls, Tharag, and the human Red Axe were coming through the entry at the far end.

Aeron tried one of the doors. Locked, and he had no time to pick it or try to break it down. He tested a second.

That one was open. He scrambled through, barred it, and looked around.

As he'd expected, he'd invaded someone's home. The boarder, a haggard-looking, red-eyed woman still dressed in her night clothes, sat at her spinning wheel, performing the labor that likely kept her housed and fed. She gaped at him in fear.

"Sorry," he said, then sprinted toward the one small window.

Behind him, the door rattled, then started banging. The woman gawked for another moment, then she rose and scurried toward the entry. She might not understand what was going on, but she knew she didn't want her door battered down. Aeron almost turned back to restrain her, then he decided his chances would be better if he just kept running.

He squirmed out the window onto a narrow, twisting lane that, like the cul-de-sac, connected to Balamonthar's Street. He dashed to the major thoroughfare, then strode onward through the crowds, no longer running—that would make him too conspicuous—but hurrying. After a few minutes, he permitted himself to believe he'd shaken his pursuers.

He reached under his cowl and gingerly fingered the sore spot where the flower pot had bashed him. He had a lump coming up—it would go nicely with all the bruises he was collecting—but to his relief, his scalp wasn't bloody. Apparently the hood had protected him a little.

So, he'd escaped relatively intact. Outwitted the rest of the world again. He felt the usual surge of exhilaration, the thrill that, as much as the easy coin, accounted for his devotion to the outlaw life.

Yet it wasn't quite as potent as usual. Perhaps Burgell's treachery was to blame. Or the discovery that the Whistlers had joined forces with the Red Axes to hunt him down. Or the way the onlookers had cheered to see him beaten, or the unpleasant surprise of the pot crashing down on his skull. What had that been about?

Shadows of Mask, had all Oeble turned against him?

No, surely not. He just needed to settle this affair of the strongbox, and things would calm down. After a moment's thought, he headed for home, to pick up the lantern he kept there.

CHAPTER 7

With the approach of evening, the Talondance had become more crowded and unruly. The clamor of the customers nearly drowned out the constant reedy music that droned from no visible source, as if ghosts were playing the birdpipes, shaums, and whistlecanes. As she surveyed the assembly of orcs, hobgoblins, bugbears, ogres, lizard men, and humans who appeared equally savage, Miri was glad that she had a comrade to watch her back.

She turned to Sefris and said, "I don't think you'll have to linger here very long to see things you wouldn't see back in the monastery."

"I imagine you're right," Sefris replied. "In fact, here's one of them now. Look sharp."

An orc clad in a shirt of scale armor crowed and leaned forward to rake in its winnings. A lizard man on the opposite side of the table hissed, threw down its cards, grabbed the hooked short sword that lay naked beside its dwindling stakes, and sprang up from its chair. Its lashing tail tripped a garishly painted whore and sent her staggering.

The orc jumped up, and crossing its arms, it reached to draw the daggers it carried sheathed on either hip. Other orcs and lizard men scrambled toward the scene of the confrontation, while those with no interest in choosing a side scurried to distance themselves from it. A human shouted that he'd give two to one on the scaly folk.

Then a massive form, tall as an ogre but even burlier, as well as less human in its proportions, emerged from a shadowy alcove. Armored in yellow-brown chitin, its feelers quivering, it employed its elongated arms with their long, thick claws to knuckle-walk like an ape. It gnashed its huge mandibles once. Everyone jumped at the sharp rasp, turned, then froze when they saw what had made the sound. After a moment, the orcs and lizard men lowered their weapons.

Miri shook her head. She'd seen many strange things in her career as a scout, but few stranger than an umber hulk maintaining order in a tavern. If she could believe her training, the immense subterranean creatures possessed their own kind of intelligence, but not of a sort that disposed them to cooperate with humans or even goblin-kin.

"Amazing," she said as the umber hulk, evidently satisfied that it had cowed the would-be brawlers, turned away.

"The yuan-ti said the owner of the Talondance was a wizard," Sefris replied. "It didn't mention her magic was powerful enough to enslave a brute like that."

"Maybe there's another explanation."

"Possibly."

"Feeling reluctant?" Miri asked.

"No, merely pointing out that we'll need to keep our wits about us."

"Believe it or not, I've been trying to do that right along, even if you couldn't tell it from the way I blundered into the slavers' trap." Miri smiled crookedly, nodded at a female gnoll standing behind a bar, and said, "Let's talk to that one."

As they wended their way through the crowd, a sweaty, musky, half-animal stench, compounded of the individual stinks of unwashed specimens of twenty different races, assailed Miri's nostrils. Its thumb on the scale, a hobgoblin weighed out measures of mordayn powder for eager—in some cases frantic—addicts. Prostitutes pulled down their bodices or lifted their skirts, exposing expanses of pimply, pasty flesh to entice their customers. A potential buyer peered into a slave's ears, and a foppishly dressed, nervous-looking young man dickered with a pair of ruffians, trying to negotiate his uncle's murder.

It was all sordid and repulsive almost beyond belief, and Miri glanced at Sefris to see how she was tolerating it. Somewhat to her surprise, the monastic wore her usual half smile, as if the scene didn't trouble her in the slightest. Evidently the Broken Ones achieved some genuine serenity through their martial exercises and meditations.

"What you want?" snarled the gnoll, a bit of slaver dripping from its canine muzzle. It could speak the common tongue employed by a good many civilized and even barbaric folk across the continent of Faerûn, but not very well.

"We need to speak to Naneetha Dalaeve," Miri said as she laid a silver piece on the bar.

The gnoll failed to pick up the coin.

"Don't know nobody named that," it said. "What you drink?"

"She owns this place," Miri said.

The yuan-ti she and Sefris had interrogated had told them as much, and since the snake-man had feared for its life at the time, she was inclined to believe it.

"Don't know her," the gnoll repeated. "Buy drinks, or get out."

Miri sensed it would do no good to increase the size of the bribe.

"Two jacks of ale," she said.

The shaggy, long-legged gnoll fetched them, one hoped without drooling into them during the process, and the two humans stepped away from the bar.

"What now?" Sefris asked.

"See that doorway in the rear wall?" Miri replied. "It stands to reason that if the owner isn't out here, she's in the back somewhere. The problem will be reaching her. I've already had enough excitement for one day. I'd just as soon pass on fighting an umber hulk and half the goblin-kin in Oeble."

"Suppose I distract everyone?" the monastic asked. "Would you be comfortable bracing a wizard by yourself?"

"Yes," Miri said, "but what are you planning? I don't want you putting yourself in danger."

Sefris's enigmatic smile widened ever so slightly as she said, "Don't worry. Everybody in Oeble loves knife-play, so I'll simply teach them a thing or two about the sport. Wait until everyone is looking my way, then make your move."

The monastic slipped through the throng toward the spot where an orc, a goblin, and a lizard man stood throwing daggers at a human silhouette crudely daubed on the wall. The otherwise black target had its eyes, throat, and heart picked out in red, presumably for bull's-eyes. Some of the Dance's patrons sat just to the sides of the mark, but they didn't look nervous because of it. Either they trusted the competitors' accuracy, or they were too drunk or reckless by nature to mind the blades hurtling past scant inches from their bodies.

Sefris pushed back her cowl. The rogues, goblin-kin, and scaly folk had already marked her as an outsider, but beholding her shaved head, they realized she was a more exotic visitor than they'd initially thought.

"Pitiful," she said. She wasn't shouting, not in any obvious way, but even so, her voice carried across the tavern back to where Miri was standing.

The orc turned. It was missing its left ear, and perhaps as some obscure form of compensation, it wore several jangling golden hoops pierced into the right.

"Are you talking to us?" it asked.

"I'm afraid so," Sefris replied. "All my life, I've heard how deftly folk in Oeble handle knives. I thought when I finally saw it I'd marvel. But the three of you throw like blind, arthritic old grannies."

The orc bristled. Considering that neither it nor its fellow players had missed the painted figure, it was entitled.

"Can you do better?" the humanoid grunted.

"Of course," said Sefris. "Anyone could."

Her movements a fluid blur, she snatched her chakrams from her pockets and threw them one after the other. Miri was impressed. She'd trained hard to learn to nock, draw, and loose her arrows rapidly, but she would have been hard-pressed to send a pair of them flying as fast as that.

The razor-edged rings thunked into the target's torso.

The one-eared orc spat. "That's not as good as my throwing. Last round, I hit both the eyes."

"I needed to warm up," Sefris replied. "I'm ready to play now."

"We already have a game going on," the goblin said.

The small, bandy-legged creature wore a royal-blue velvet cape that was both bloodstained and considerably too large for it. Presumably it had stolen the garment off a corpse.

"Begin a new one," Sefris said. "Unless you're afraid to play against someone who knows how to throw a knife."

"Why should we start over?" asked the orc. "We throw for gold. Have you got any?"

"Not much," Sefris said.

"Then stop wasting our time, before we decide to use you for a target."

"What I do have," the monastic continued, "is myself. If I lose, I'll do the winner's bidding until sunrise. Anything he asks."

The offer shocked Miri and likewise silenced the crowd for a heartbeat or two. Then the onlookers started to laugh and babble.

"You say 'anything,' " said the orc. "It's liable to be just about anything. Anything nasty."

"What do I care about warm-blood females?" growled the lizard man.

"You could rent her out," said the one-eared orc. "The place is full of folk who'd relish a go at a fresh, clean human woman, even if she is bald. Not that you're going to win. I am."

"I take it my wager is acceptable," Sefris said.

"Yes," said the orc, leering. "There's just one thing. You challenged us to a knife-throwing contest, so you'll have to use knives, not those rings."

It pulled a pair of daggers from its boots, tossed them into the air, caught them by the blades, and proffered them hilts first.

If Sefris felt dismay at the substitution, she didn't let it show.

She examined the knives, and then said, "These will do. What are the rules?"

"You throw two times every round," said the orc. "Hit the black, and it's a point. Hit the red, and it's five. Miss the red three turns in a row, and you're out. First one to three hundred wins."

Sefris nodded and asked, "Who starts?"

"Maidens first," the orc said with a grin.

Miri saw that the whole tavern was watching the bout, which meant it was time to sneak away. But she couldn't, not just then. She couldn't bring herself to abandon Sefris until she felt confident that the monastic had at least a reasonable chance of holding her own against the other players.

Sefris threw the daggers as quickly as she'd cast the chakrams. One pierced the target's heart, and the other, its throat. She was equally accurate the following round.

Of course, even if she was victorious, it wouldn't necessarily mean she was out of danger. The losers might resent the humiliation and decide to molest her anyway. But for the moment at least, she was safe. The spectators perceived she had such a good chance that some of them were betting on her, and everyone wanted to see how the contest would turn out.

Miri would do her best to return before the end, so that whatever happened, Sefris would have a comrade to help her escape harm. For surely, wager or no, the monastic had no intention of submitting herself to the brutality of a gang of ruffians and goblin-kin, nor as far as Miri was concerned, did honor require that she should.

The ranger skulked along the wall until she reached the doorway, then slipped through. On the other side was a corridor with chambers opening off to either side. Storerooms held beer barrels and racks of wine. Blocks of ice, an expensive commodity in the Border Kingdoms with their warm climate and lack of mountains, cooled the larder. Rather to Miri's relief, none of the red-and-white hanging carcasses was human, the menu she'd noticed earlier notwithstanding. Inside the steamy kitchen, a fat cook in a stained apron screamed curses and beat a cringing goblin assistant about the head with a ladle.

And that was it. The hallway didn't seem to go anywhere else. Yet the yuan-ti had sworn that the reclusive Naneetha Dalaeve lived somewhere on the premises.

If so, Miri had to find the mage's personal quarters quickly, before someone else stepped into the corridor and spotted her. Knowing that spellcasters sometimes used illusions to hide that which they wished to remain private, she peered closely at the sections of wall around her, and when that failed to yield results, she ran her hands over the brick.

At first that didn't work, either, but then roughness smoothed beneath her fingers. Once her sense of touch defeated the phantasm, her vision pierced it a moment later, and she was looking at an oak door.

She tried the brass handle, and found the panel was unlocked. She slipped warily through into a suite dimly illuminated by the soft greenish light of everlasting candles. The sitting room was lavishly furnished in a frilly, lacy style that set her teeth on edge. It looked like the habitation of a nobleman's pampered daughter, not the lair of a wizard who ran a tavern catering to dastards of every stripe. The books on the shelves were of a piece with the rest of the décor. Instead of tomes of arcane lore, they were ballads and romances, tales of knights slaying dragons for the love of princesses both beautiful and pure.

A small dog yapped, and in response, a feminine voice laughed. Miri followed the sound through the apartment. She crept past one room that manifestly was a wizard's conjuration chamber, with a rather slim grimoire reposing on a lectern, sigils of protection inscribed on the walls, and the memory of bitter incense hanging in the air, then came to the source of the noise. Beyond another doorway, a blond woman in a shimmering blue silk dressing gown tossed a rawhide chew toy for a little fox-red terrier, which bounded after the plaything and fetched it back to her. The dog's mistress sat with her back to the door.

"Mistress Dalaeve," Miri said.

The terrier rounded on her and barked. The blond woman gave a start then, without turning around, swept her hands through what was clearly a cabalistic gesture.

"No spells!" Miri nocked an arrow and drew the fletching back to her ear. "I'm not here to hurt you, but—"

She broke off the threat because Naneetha obviously had no intention of heeding her. Her hands kept moving.

Such stubbornness posed a dilemma. If Miri was prudent, she'd loose the arrow before the wizard could complete the magic. But she wouldn't be able to question Naneetha if she killed her, and common sense told her it was difficult for any marksman, even a wizard, to target a foe while looking in the opposite direction. So she hesitated a heartbeat, and the blond woman pressed her hands to her own face.

As far as Miri could see, nothing happened as a result.

Naneetha uncovered her features and said, "Quiet, Saeval!"

The terrier yipped a final time, then subsided. The wizard turned, revealing a flawlessly beautiful heart-shaped countenance worthy of a heroine in one of the sagas on which she evidently doted.

"Who are you," the woman asked, "and what do you want?"

Miri released the tension on her bow and pointed the arrow at the floor, but kept it on the string.

"My name is Miri Buckman. I'm a guide of the Red Hart Guild. I apologize for bursting in on you this way, but my business is urgent, and your staff didn't want to let me in to see you."

"I like my privacy."

"I won't intrude on it any longer than necessary. I just need you to answer a few questions. A robber stole a strongbox from the courtyard of the Paera—"

"I know. Everyone does. You must be the ranger who lost the prize."

Miri sighed and said, "What everyone doesn't know is the name of the thief, or at least, no one's been willing to tell me. But I've learned he's a friend of yours. He and his three accomplices drank here often."

"As I'm sure you've seen, the Dance is a busy place. Many rogues squander their loot here."

"But sometimes you invited this particular scoundrel, who's young, lean, fit, and wears a goatee, to wander back to your suite and visit you."

"You're mistaken."

"I don't believe you," Miri said, "and I promise, I'll pay for information."

"The Dance brings in all the coin I need," Naneetha said. "Now, please go."

"I'm sorry, it isn't that easy."

"Let's be clear, then," the woman asked. "Are you threatening to shoot me if I refuse to betray a friend?"

Even as frustrated as she was, Miri didn't have the stomach for such callous retribution, but she didn't have to admit as much.

"Why shouldn't I kill you?" she asked. "You provide a haven for the worst kinds of vermin to conduct their business and pursue depraved amusements. That makes you as bad as they are."

"It must be nice out in the wilderness, where everything's so simple . . . good or evil, gold or dung. In Oeble, we live as best we can."

"If your goal is to live, give me the robber's name."

"No," Naneetha said. "I don't have many friends. It's hard to make them when you spend your days in a cellar, and Saeval and my books aren't enough to hold the loneliness at bay. The few companions I do have brighten my days with the stories of their adventures, and the lad you seek has told me some splendid ones."

Miri wondered if Naneetha was an invalid or such a notorious fugitive that she dared not show her face in the city above, for she seemed to be saying she felt unable ever to leave the confines of the Talondance.

"Whatever lies the wretch feeds you," Miri said, "he's a common thief, not a hero out of your storybooks."

The wizard shrugged.

"Look," Miri persisted, "it's nice you have someone to keep you company, but a good many people will suffer if I don't recover the lockbox."

"Why?"

"I'm not at liberty to say, but you have my word that it's the truth."

"Well, you have mine that I'd sooner push a hundred strangers into the Abyss than betray one friend." Naneetha lifted her hands, making a show of poising them for further conjuration, and added, "Now, are we going to fight?"

No, Miri thought bitterly, we aren't.

Naneetha had called her bluff, and that was that. It felt in keeping with the fundamental perversity of Oeble that the first even vaguely honorable person she'd met in the Underways had proved just as unwilling to help her as all the black-hearted scoundrels she'd questioned hitherto.

She was pondering how to make a dignified exit when the dog yapped.

"I see you found her," Sefris said.

Miri glanced over her shoulder. The monastic appeared unscathed and unruffled as usual.

"Thank Mielikki—and Ilmater—that you're all right," Miri said.

"It was no great matter. I won the contest, the orc and goblin took exception to it, and I had to knock each of them senseless. That started a brawl even the umber hulks—it turns out there are two—had some difficulty quelling. In the confusion, I slipped back here to join you."

Once again, Miri was impressed. Logic suggested that when the fight had broken out, Sefris must have been at the very center of it. She'd surely needed almost preternatural powers of stealth and evasion to extricate herself from the fray.

"And what of you?" the monastic continued. "Are you finding the answers you seek?"

"No," Naneetha said, "she isn't. She was just leaving, and I ask you to do the same."

"You don't seem to realize the situation has changed," Sefris said. In the blink of an eye, a chakram appeared in her hand. "The scout and I are both adept at combat. Perhaps your magic could fend off her or me alone, but not the two of us together, and after we've subdued you, we'll make sure you can't give us any more trouble. I never yet met a mage who was much of a threat with broken fingers."

"Nor I a warrior, once she was burned from head to toe," Naneetha replied.

Miri would have sworn the doorway wasn't wide enough to accommodate two women without them squeezing and jostling one another, but Sefris twisted through in one sudden movement, without even brushing her. Once inside the room, she had a clear shot with the chakram, and when she lifted it, the ranger realized she hadn't been bluffing.

Miri snatched frantically and grabbed Sefris's arm.

"No!" she cried.

Her eyes cold, unreadable, Sefris stared at her.

"She knows," he monastic said. "The yuan-ti said so."

"Still. . . ."

Sefris took a breath and let it out slowly.

"As you wish," she said. "It's your errand. I just came along to help as best I can."

"I take it you're leaving," Naneetha said.

"Yes," Miri said. She started to turn away, then yielded to the urge to make one more try. "It's your own people, your own city, that will benefit if I recover the box."

"Such vagaries mean nothing," the wizard said.

At the same time, Sefris murmured something under her breath then sprang past Miri and dashed back down the hall. The ranger turned just in time to see her comrade vanish into the conjuration chamber.

"What's she doing?" Naneetha asked, sounding rattled for the first time.

"I don't know," Miri said.

Sefris strode back into view with the mage's open grimoire. One hand clutched the vellum pages, ready to tear.

"Tell us what we need to know," the monastic said, "or I'll destroy this."

"Is that supposed to frighten me?" Naneetha asked. "I can buy a new spellbook, or scribe one myself if need be."

"Yes," Sefris said, "but in the meantime, you won't have access to your magic. You won't be able to cover your face with a mask of illusion. Everyone will see your scars."

Naneetha stared, swallowed, then said, "I have no idea what you mean."

"Of course you do," Sefris replied. "Is this the page with the disguise spell?" The monastic ripped a leaf in half, crumpled the loose portion, and dropped it to the floor. "Or is it the next?"

"Stop it, or I swear I'll burn you!"

"While I'm holding the grimoire? I doubt it."

She tore a second page.

"Please," the wizard begged, all the defiance running out of her at once, "you're a woman, too. Don't make me be ugly. My friends won't come to see me anymore."

"Then the choice should be easy," Sefris said. "Betray one companion, or lose them all."

It took Naneetha several seconds to force the words out. "His name is Aeron sar Randal."

Miri felt a pang of excitement, undercut by a muddled shame at the manner in which Sefris had extracted the information.

"Where does he live?" the ranger asked.

"I don't know. I don't think many people do. A lot of thieves are wary of letting folk know where they sleep."

"Well, fortunately," Miri said, "the town's not huge. Did this Aeron talk to you about the plot to steal the strongbox?"

"A little. The Red Axes hired him to do it."

"The Red Axes?"

"The biggest gang in Oeble."

"Then by now," said Miri glumly, "he's delivered the coffer to them."

Naneetha hesitated for an instant as if trying to decide whether to risk a lie.

"No," the wizard said. "For some reason, he didn't hand it over, and now they're looking for him, too."

For once, the ranger thought, maybe the Oeblaun propensity for double-dealing would work in her favor.

"Then we have to find him first," said Miri.

CHAPTER 8

Aeron glanced over his shoulder. He didn't have any particular reason to think anyone was shadowing him, but it was an ingrained habit to check. In so doing, he caught sight of Oeble, its towers, some visibly leaning, black against the evening sky. Ordinarily the view would have pleased him, but the tangled spires seemed somehow threatening just then, like the writhing facial tentacles of those green, centipede-like monstrosities that sometimes crawled into the Underways from Mask alone knew where.

He snorted his momentary uneasiness away. Oeble was home, as good a home as an outlaw could want, and if it had treated him harshly those past couple days, that was part of what made life within its environs so exciting. He'd sell the contents of the lockbox, lie low until everyone tired of hunting him, and everything would be all right.

He hiked on into a stand of trees, trying with some success to keep the dry fallen leaves from crunching beneath his feet, enjoying the sharp scent of the pines. Night engulfed the world, but Selûne shed enough silvery glow to guide him. He didn't bother to light his lantern until he reached the glade at the center of the wood, where he and Kerridi had sometimes picnicked.

The benighted clearing was hardly the ideal workspace in which to crack open a magically protected coffer, but Aeron hadn't dared tackle the job in the center of town. If he triggered more thunderclaps, they were likely to lead some of his various and sundry ill-wishers straight to him. Out there in the countryside, that at least ought not to be a problem.

Aeron found a level bit of ground, unrolled the white sheet he'd brought, and set the steel case on top of it. He unpacked the tools he'd taken from Burgell's flat and felt himself tensing, his pulse ticking faster. Aeron willed himself to relax.

Maybe he was no master cracksman like the faithless gnome, certainly no wizard, but he knew the basics of defeating magical traps. He thought that if he was careful, methodical, he could get the box open without killing himself in the process.

He peered at the case through a topaz lens. It didn't reveal anything he hadn't seen already, so he pulled the cork from a glass vial and dusted one side of the strongbox with gray powder. The coarse grains crawled and clumped together, forming letters and geometric figures, covering over and thus revealing the invisible symbols a spellcaster had drawn upon the steel.

So far, so good, he thought, but now comes the tricky part.

Aeron picked up a file and scraped at the glyphs, defacing them. Metal rasped on metal. Though in theory he knew at which angles and junctures he could attack the symbols safely, he kept wanting to flinch as he imagined the magic rousing and striking at him in some devastating fashion.

It didn't, though, not then, and not when he neutralized the sigils on the other faces of the box. He sighed with relief and picked up the brass key, which still appeared in constant flux even though he couldn't feel it changing shape between his thumb and forefinger. He slipped it into the lock and twisted.

Perhaps he felt it stick or shiver. In any event, he sensed he had to let go immediately. He snatched his hand back, and thunder boomed a split second later. The blast slammed him onto his back and brought loose twigs and dead leaves showering down from the branches overhead. Half dazed, he climbed back up onto his haunches, felt a wetness in his mustache, and wiped a smear of it onto his fingertips. His nose was bleeding.

He felt a jab of anger, a regret he'd ever come within a hundred leagues of that wretched box that had killed his friends. He wanted to grab it and fling it into the underbrush, never to be found or trouble anyone again.

But naturally, he didn't really feel that way. No thief truly wanted to cast away his loot. Had he won it at great cost, that was just reason to prize it all the more. He swallowed his frustration and pondered the task at hand.

Maybe the glyphs were only decoys. In any case, spoiling them hadn't silenced the thunder, and he didn't see any other way to attempt it.

But so far, the blast had only sounded when someone inserted a pick or skeleton key in the lock. Maybe he could open the case in another way. He turned it around so he could get at the hinges.

Try as he might, he couldn't loosen the pins. If was as if they weren't merely fastened but frozen, glued, or rusted in place. He assumed another enchantment was to blame.

Well, maybe he had the countermagic for that one. He opened another of Burgell's vials and poured a quantity of viscous blue fluid on each of the hinges. Brewed by one of the outlaw community's more capable alchemists, the oil wasn't merely slippery. Rather, according to the gnome, it embodied the fundamental *idea* of slipperiness. Aeron wasn't sure what that really meant, and he had a hunch it might just be impressive-sounding mumbo jumbo, but he knew from personal experience that the lubricant was slick enough to unstick almost anything.

He resumed his assault on the hinges. The component parts seemed to loosen grudgingly, by infinitesimal degrees, only to tighten back up as soon as he released pressure from them. At first, in the uncertain light, he wasn't sure, but eventually he saw that that was exactly what was happening. Like living creatures, the mechanisms were resisting vivisection, screwing and jamming themselves back together.

Most likely that meant he wouldn't be able to disassemble them. By loosening them, he had, however, temporarily opened a crack between the lid and bottom of the box, which until then had fit perfectly together. In desperation, he drew his largest Arthyn fang, a blade sturdy enough to double as a lever, shoved it into the gap, braced the coffer, and pried with all his strength.

The hinges tore with a screech of tortured steel. The two halves of the strongbox popped apart, and the thrice-damned thunderclap boomed once more, bashing him like a club. He gasped a curse, and when he succeeded in blinking the tears of pain from his vision, perceived that the coffer hadn't yet finished giving him trouble.

A vapor wafted from the interior of the box, swirled, and coalesced into a squat, dark thing. At first glance, it was vaguely toadlike, but then he made out the six stubby arms terminating in four-fingered hands and the three eyes, positioned asymmetrically and shifting around at the ends of flexible lumps. The central mass of it was either all head or all torso, depending on how one cared to look at it, with a bizarre vertical maw that opened it almost all the way down to the sexless crotch when it bared its fangs. It oriented on Aeron and charged, covering ground as fast as a man despite the seeming handicap of its stumpy legs.

Aeron scrambled backward, tried to poise his Arthyn fang to meet the threat, then realized he'd lost hold of it, the largest and most formidable of his weapons, when the final thunderclap boomed. He snatched out a throwing knife, a flat, leaf-shaped blade with a leather-wrapped handle, and hurled it. It pierced the guardian demon's flesh, but the creature kept coming.

Still retreating, Aeron flung a second dagger. Though it put out one of the apparition's eyes, that didn't stop it, either. It suddenly sprinted even faster, leaning forward so its jaws were poised to bite off the legs of its prey.

His heart pounding, Aeron made himself stand still until the last possible instant. That way, the demon would have trouble compensating when he dodged. Unless, of course, he delayed too long, in which case it would simply catch him in its spikelike teeth.

He spun to the side and stabbed with his fourth and next-to-last dagger. The demon's teeth clashed shut, missing him, and the blade rammed deep into its flank. Using his off hand, he bashed it with his cudgel.

Unfortunately, that still didn't slow it down. Pivoting, yanking the hilt of the knife from his grasp, it grabbed at his leg with its broad, stubby-fingered hands, no doubt seeking to hold him fast long enough to bring its jaws to bear. Its talons jabbed through his breeches and the skin beneath. He wrenched himself free, but he lost his balance in so doing. He reeled backward, fell on his rump, and the demon pounced on top of him.

It jaws gaped, reaching for his head. Terrified, he jammed the club between them. It served to hold them open for a moment, but the wood bowed under the pressure. In another second, it would snap.

Aeron whipped his final knife from his boot and plunged it into the demon's side. The creature thrashed, made an ugly gargling sound, and stinking slime geysered up from its maw. Its death throes broke the cudgel in two, and it slumped motionless.

Aeron dragged himself out from underneath the carcass, then sat until he stopped panting and shivering. He was used to fighting people, even if he didn't often enjoy it, but demons were another matter.

Still, he'd bested the vile thing, and it was time to see what his victory had gained him. Trying to brush away the sludge the spirit had puked onto his tunic, he strode back to the sundered halves of the broken strongbox.

His prize lay in the padded bottom section, where it fit snugly. It was a big, old-looking book bound in black.

As he reached for it, it occurred to Aeron that perhaps he still hadn't reached the end of the wards. But shadows of Mask, he'd already contended with the warning screech, the glimmering that neutralized his invisibility, spells of locking, thunderclaps, and a guardian imp. Surely even the most cautious shipper would have deemed those protections sufficient, and in any case, Aeron was simply too impatient to muck around with Burgell's tools and powders any longer. He picked up the book, and nothing disastrous happened as a result.

The tome had a title embossed on the cover and spine with a few flecks of gold leaf still clinging to the letters, but since Aeron couldn't read, that was no help. His father had sometimes encouraged him to learn, but it had always seemed like a lot of effort for a minimal return.

His best guess was that he'd stolen a wizard's grimoire, for what other kind of book could be valuable enough to warrant such elaborate defenses? But he'd handled a couple of those in his time, and when he leafed through it, he didn't find the elaborate pentagrams and illustrations of mystical hand gestures he was expecting.

What he did discover were lines of text, pictures of leaves and flowers, and a hundred smells, many exquisitely sweet, faint yet still perceptible even through the musty, nose-tickling odor of aged, decaying parchment.

The dark street was narrow, and the towers crowded close on either side. Miri found it oppressive. Considering that she was comfortable in even the deepest reaches of primordial forests like the Chondalwood, with gigantic mossy trees looming all around, it was ridiculous, but true nonetheless.

Well, at least she had a patch of open sky above her head once more and hope of completing her mission without the necessity of a return to the claustrophobic confines of the Underways. In fact, if she could only ease her mind on a certain matter, she might feel better than at any time since Aeron sar Randal made off with the saddlebag.

The problem was figuring out how to broach the subject with a comrade who'd been nothing but helpful, who had, indeed, saved her life. As a general rule, Miri believed in directness, yet she had a sense that in that situation, she'd feel like an ingrate if she failed to muster a degree of tact.

"I still can't make out how you knew," she said as they hiked along.

"About Mistress Dalaeve's face?" Sefris replied.

"Yes."

"We Broken Ones can see through illusions sometimes. Open eyes are a benefit of our meditations." As they neared an intersection, Sefris pointed to a frieze of manticores decorating a crumbling wall and said, "This is where our informant told us to turn."

Miri peered around the corner, studying the path ahead. Even up in what was allegedly the law-abiding part of Oeble, it appeared to her that an absurd number of folk were skulking about in the dark, engaged in business that, were it wholly legitimate, they would have conducted by day. But none of them looked like they were lying in wait for outlanders, so she and the monastic proceeded on their way.

"But how did you know she was so worried about keeping her scars hidden that a threat to unmask her would break her will?" the ranger asked.

Sefris shrugged and replied, "It was a guess, based on what we'd heard and seen. Her reclusiveness. The dim lighting and frilly furnishings. Her taste in reading matter, and the fact that the false visage she affected was absolutely perfect, like a statue's face."

"Very clever," said Miri.

His cane tapping and bowl outstretched, a stained strip of linen tied over his eyes, a beggar meandered toward the two women. Reminded of sar Randal's disguise, Miri scowled, and the "blind" mendicant, who evidently saw her forbidding expression perfectly well, veered off.

"Thank you," Sefris said. "Yet I sense you don't wholly approve of my tactics."

"It's not that, exactly. I suppose I'm trained to fight with my hands, not by finding a person's private shame and rubbing salt in the wound. It just felt dirty, somehow."

Sefris arched an eyebrow and said, "I intended to master the wizard through the exercise of our martial skills. You stopped me."

"Because unlike the yuan-ti, who tried to enslave me, she hadn't done anything that made her fair game."

"Operating a haven for the foulest kind of outlaws and goblin-kin doesn't qualify?"

"It seems like it should," Miri said with a sigh, "doesn't it?"

"Yet you pity her." To her surprise, Miri thought she heard a trace of scorn in the monastic's generally calm, mild tone, and she wondered if it was directed at Naneetha or herself. "Consider this, then. Suppose something scarred you. Would you spend the rest of your life hiding in a hole?"

"No. It wouldn't make all that much difference to me, I suppose."

"Nor me, nor anyone who wasn't bloated with vanity to begin with. Whatever distress Mistress Dalaeve experiences is the result of her own stupidity and weakness. You and I are not to blame."

"And your deity is tender Ilmater, god of mercy," said Miri with wry incredulity.

"Whose sympathy and help are given first and foremost to the innocent and those who strive for the right. Like you, my friend, and the good folk who you say will benefit when we recover your stolen treasure. There. That's it, isn't it?"

The scout peered and saw that Sefris was right. Ahead and to the left were the broken foundations of two spires, like decaying stumps in a row of teeth. One tower had evidently fallen sideways, demolishing its neighbor in the course of its collapse. Imagining the catastrophe, Miri winced at the probable loss of life.

But it had happened long ago, and all those unfortunate souls were beyond her power to help. What mattered then was that if her informant, one of Oeble's apothecaries, had told the truth, Aeron sar Randal lived on the top floor of a tower three doors farther down.

Miri and Sefris stalked forward, stepping silently and gliding through the shadows. The ranger spotted a hobgoblin lurking in a recessed doorway, its cloak draped so that it half concealed the crossbow dangling in its hairy hand. She stopped and raised her hand, whereupon Sefris, too, halted instantly. Miri pointed.

"A lookout," she whispered.

"Yes, I see it now. Aeron's sentry, do you think?"

"It's possible, but it feels wrong. At the Paeraddyn, his accomplices were all human, and if I understood Naneetha correctly, he doesn't even belong to a gang himself. He might not have any partners as a general rule."

"Well, whoever it is, it's likely no friend of ours, not unless you have other allies you haven't told me about."

"No," Miri replied.

"I can't fling a chakram that far, but you can surely hit it with an arrow."

Miri reached for a shaft, then left it in the quiver.

"I can't just kill it without knowing for certain who it is or what it's doing," she said. "It might be working with the Gray Blades."

"A hobgoblin?"

"I know it seems unlikely, but Oeble is full of townsfolk the rest of the world disdains as savage marauders. Maybe some of them even spy for the law."

"What should we do, then?" Sefris asked. "Creep around to the back of the tower and look for another way in, one the watcher can't see?"

"I'll do that. You keep an eye on the hobgoblin and this approach, and hoot like an owl if you need to alert me to anything."

Sefris smiled and said, "I remind you, this isn't the wild."

"They must have a few owls," Miri replied. "Anyway, we need some sort of signal."

She started toward the alley that ran between the two buildings, and the door to Aeron's tower opened.

Several ruffians, a couple human, the others not, skulked out onto the street. The one in the lead was a tanarukk, the first of that infamous breed Miri had noticed among Oeble's motley population. Stooped and massive, curved tusks jutting from its lower jaw, it stalked along with a heavy battle-axe in one fist and a lead line in the other.

The trailing end of the rope bound the hands of a human prisoner, who hobbled as best he could with a burlap sack over his head. For a moment, Miri wondered if it was Aeron, then decided it couldn't be. The captive was excruciatingly gaunt, not lean, and carried an assortment of old scars on the exposed portions of his skin.

The hobgoblin lookout emerged from the doorway to join his comrades. Miri laid an arrow across her bow.

Sefris touched her on the arm.

"What are you doing?" she whispered.

Miri was surprised that a Broken One, sworn to help the victims of cruelty, would ask.

"I'm going to shoot an outlaw or two," the ranger replied.

"Why? We don't know this is any of our affair. The toughs and goblin-kin look villainous enough, but perhaps they have some legitimate grievance against this man."

"Then let them go to the law with their complaint. I thought that's what towns are supposed to be good for."

"How many acts of injustice and brutality have you seen since coming to Oeble?" asked Sefris. "How many chained thralls wailing that they were enslaved unlawfully? How many pimps beating their whores and bravos terrorizing shopkeepers for protection? Yet you passed on by, because you're on a mission, and if you deviated from it to right every wrong you stumbled across in this den of scoundrels, you'd never get it done."

"Maybe we don't have to close our eyes every time."

"Something about the plight of this particular wretch has stirred your sympathy, but surely your guild masters taught you that mere emotion is no reason to abandon a strategy."

"I admit, they did, but . . ."

Uncertain, hating Sefris a little but herself more, Miri watched the kidnappers, if that was what they were, lead their captive away.

"All right," Miri said when the street was clear, "let's get this done."

She promised herself that once it was, and she'd delivered the strongbox into the proper hands, she'd depart Oeble within the hour, never to return. Unless it was at the head of an army, to raze the filthy place.

She and Sefris scurried into the tower and on up the shadowy spiral stairs. The risers were soft, treacherous, half rotten, but they managed the climb quietly even so. On the third-floor landing, a door opened, and a halfling in a feathered hat started to emerge. He took one look at the two grim-faced human strangers striding by and retreated back inside.

The door to Aeron sar Randal's garret apartment was standing open. Miri and Sefris ascended the remaining stairs warily, then they peeked beyond the threshold. Someone had torn the flat apart. At first the exercise had likely been a search, but had included simple malicious destruction before it was through. Shards of shattered bottles littered the floor, and the varnished scraps of a broken mandolin lay in the reeking puddle of spilled wine.

No one was inside, though Miri was reasonably certain she'd seen the vandals only minutes before.

"Look," Sefris said, pointing. The light of the garret's one surviving lamp sufficed to reveal the outline of an axe scrawled in crimson chalk on the wall. "The Red Axes signed their work."

"And plainly," Miri said, "it was them we saw coming out of the tower with their prisoner. Otherwise, the coincidence is just too great. Curse us, we should have waylaid them."

"Perhaps so," the monastic replied, "but let's take a moment to think it through. Who do you think they abducted, Aeron's father?"

"Somebody dear to him, at any rate, someone they hope to trade for the box."

"Not a bad idea, and if we take the hostage from them, we can try the same thing."

Miri frowned and said, "We're not kidnappers, to hold a man prisoner and barter his life for treasure."

"Do you think the captive an innocent? My guess is that he's as wicked a knave as Aeron himself, for what bond of affection could exist between such a thief and a righteous man?"

"We can't mistreat him just on the basis of our suspicions."

"No," Sefris sighed. "Of course not. What was I thinking? I think this evil place is corrupting my judg—"

Without warning, she leaped and spun, her heel streaking at Miri's head.

Reacting out of sheer reflex, Miri bounded back out of range, and the monastic's kick missed her by an inch. The scout continued her frantic retreat, meanwhile nocking and drawing an arrow. Sefris landed in a deep crouch, one hand high and open, the other clenched into a fist and cocked at her hip.

"What is this?" Miri demanded. "Why would you attack me?"

"The arcanaloth promised you'd guide me along the path to the *Bouquet*," Sefris replied, "but I think you've done your part. From this point onward, your mawkish scruples and squeamishness would only get in the way. So now I'm going to kill you for daring to set yourself against the Lady of Loss."

Miri didn't understand all of that. She didn't know what an "arcanaloth" was, for example. But it was plain that Sefris was as treacherous a double-dealer as most everyone else she'd met in Oeble, and had been playing her for a fool from the start.

"I'm the one with an arrow aimed at your heart," Miri said. "If you so much as twitch, I'll let it fly. Now, you're no Broken One. Who are you?"

"Perhaps you've heard of the Monks of the Dark Moon."

Sefris's hand leaped toward her pocket and the chakram inside it. Miri released the bowstring.

The arrow flew straight, but the monastic twisted aside. The chakram whirled through the air. Miri simultaneously ducked and flailed at the ring, and by luck as much as skill, she swatted it away with her buckler. Steel clashed against steel.

Sefris pounced, too fast for even the deftest archer to ready another shaft. In desperation, Miri swung her bow like a club. The monastic caught the weapon, twirled it out of Miri's grasp, and cast it aside.

At least that took an instant, which Miri used to scramble backward once more. The retreat took her out onto the balcony, which groaned and dipped alarmingly under her weight. She also had time to snatch out her broadsword and, when Sefris lunged forward again, prompting the platform to creak and lurch, meet her with a stop cut. The robed, shaven-headed woman halted instantly, cleanly, on balance, and the attack fell short.

Smiling ever so slightly, Sefris shifted back and forth, looking for an opening. Miri felt an unaccustomed pang of fear, and struggled to quash it.

I know she's good, she thought, *but the sword gives me the reach on her, and she can't dodge around too much out here. The balcony's too small.*

Miri advanced, feinted to the head, and cut to the flank. Sefris ignored the false attack and swept down her arm to parry the true one. It shouldn't have worked very well. The broadsword should have chopped into her wrist, but the block incorporated a subtle spinning motion that somehow permitted her to fling the blade away and remain unscathed.

She riposted with a spring into the air and a front kick to the face. Miri swayed backward, out of harm's way, and slashed at the other woman's extended leg. She grazed the flapping hem of her robe, but that was all. Sefris touched down, spun, and caught the sword with a crescent kick. The impact tore it from Miri's grasp and sent it flying over the broken railing.

The ranger grabbed for the hilt of the dagger sheathed at her belt. Hands poised for slaughter, Sefris whirled around to face her.

Wood cracked and screamed, and the balcony swung down, the horizontal surface becoming a steep incline. The platform was pulling loose from it anchors.

Sefris turned and, nimble as a cat, clambered up the slope and into the safety of the garret. Miri tried to do the same, but scrabble as she might, she couldn't catch hold of anything to pull herself up. Her boots kicked away rotten fragments of railing, wood cracked and snapped, and she and the balcony plummeted, tumbling through empty space.

CHAPTER 9

As the crash sounded below, Sefris drew a calming breath. She hadn't feared Miri's bow or sword, but she had felt a twinge of alarm when the balcony unexpectedly gave way. The fear proved she still had a way to go before she achieved a perfect, contemptuous indifference to the well-being of all unworthy created things, herself included.

It was something to work on in her meditations, but not just then. She had to recapture the opportunity that was receding beyond her grasp. The monastic retrieved her fallen chakram, she then sprinted back down the spiral stairs.

As Sefris hurtled downward, she cast off—she wished for all time—the habits of speech and expression she'd adopted to impersonate a Broken One. The warmth and compassion of a servant of Ilmater were entirely alien to her own nature. It had taken a constant effort to counterfeit them, and she knew she hadn't managed perfectly. Still, she'd passed muster right up until the end, and that was what mattered.

When she reached ground level, she raced down the street in the direction the kidnappers and their victim had taken. She kept to the shadows as best she could, but stealth was less important than speed, and her sandals pounded the wheel-rutted earth.

Indeed, she'd nearly passed the narrow cul-de-sac before she registered the stairs at the end of it, like a well lined with steps twisting downward into the ground. When she spotted it, however, she stopped cold.

The part of Oeble that knew rain and sunlight did possess some semblance of law and order, no matter how corrupt or ineffectual, so it seemed unlikely that outlaws dragging a prisoner along would opt to continue in the streets when they could descend to the Underways instead. Sefris bounded down the narrow, unrailed steps, indifferent to the possibility of a fall. Her Dark Moon training had honed her sense of balance to such a degree that the rapid descent was no more difficult than sprinting on level ground.

The real challenge came when the stairs deposited her in a twisting tunnel, the inky darkness relieved only by the smears of phosphorescence on the walls. Peering around, she saw nothing to indicate in which direction the Red Axes had gone.

Accordingly, she listened, hoping that, since they'd returned "below," the toughs would start taunting their victim or gloating over their success. In her experience, such mindless, undisciplined behavior was typical of robbers and goblin-kin the world over.

She thought she heard catcalls and laughter echoing faintly from the right, and she hurried in that direction. She judged she was heading more or less toward the river, though the mazelike warrens were already muddling her sense of direction. She rather wished she could cast a spell of tracking or guidance to keep her on the proper course, but the simple fact was that no sorceress could master every conceivable conjuration and enchantment, and such tricks weren't a part of her repertoire.

As it turned out, she didn't need them. She rushed or skulked past various scenes of the sort the Underways provided in such abundance—a burglar selling a silk wedding dress to a dealer in such stolen commodities, ruffians and apprentices squatting in a circle throwing knucklebones, several orcs closing in on a human who'd managed to draw his dagger but looked too drunk to wield it properly—and the kidnappers came into view. Unfortunately, they still had such a lead on Sefris that she wouldn't have spotted them if that length of tunnel hadn't been unusually straight or if a brothel-keeper hadn't hung a scarlet lantern to lure patrons to the doorway of his establishment.

She loped to close the distance, meanwhile pondering the tactical parameters of her situation, not with trepidation, but simply in order to manage the coming slaughter as efficiently as possible. Her foes were many, and she was only one. They had crossbows, which could shoot their quarrels considerably farther than she could fling a chakram. The non-humans could see considerably better in the dark.

She, however, possessed her own advantages. The enemy didn't know she was trailing them. Even more importantly, the Red Axes were simply ruffians, while Sefris was an elite agent of the Lady of Loss, possessed of all the lethal skills a Dark Sister required. A single spell could thin out the toughs in short order.

Unfortunately, the drawback to that approach was that the prisoner was limping along in the midst of the outlaws, and he looked frail enough that any magic potent enough to incapacitate a half dozen bravos was likely to kill him outright. Sefris was still trying to think her way around that aspect of the problem when the folk ahead turned down a side tunnel.

Afraid of losing them, she quickened her pace yet again, but even so, she was too late. When she peeked around the bend, she found that the way dead-ended in a massive oak door reinforced with iron, more like the sallyport of a castle than any entrance to a common residence. Plainly, her quarry had passed through.

She frowned in annoyance, because though killing a group of Red Axes in the Underways would have posed certain problems, invading their fortress was likely to prove far more difficult. Then an alternative occurred to her.

She proceeded to the door. Someone watched her approach. She couldn't see the peephole or hidden sentry box, but she felt the pressure of his gaze. She knocked on the panel.

After several seconds, a gruff voice sounded through the door, "Password."

"I don't know it," she said. "I'm not one of you, but I have business with your chief."

"He's busy."

"Tell him it's about the strongbox Aeron sar Randal stole from the ranger."

For a while, there was no response to that. Then the door opened. The short passage on the other side likewise reminded Sefris of castle architecture, for it resembled a barbican, with murder holes in the ceiling and another stout door at the far end. Two ruffians, one a black-bearded man whose brawny arms writhed with tattoos, the other a naked, crouching meazel, waved her inside. The latter was another of Oeble's surprises. Sefris would have thought the stunted, green-skinned semi-aquatic brutes with their talons and webbed feet too feral and dull-witted to relate to other humanoids as anything but prey, but plainly the leader of the Red Axes had attracted at least one of the brutes into his employ.

"We're going to search you," said the tattooed man. It was the same voice Sefris had heard before.

"Here," she said, removing her chakrams and cesti from her pockets.

The ruffian frisked her anyway, fondling her in the process. It didn't bother her. During her training, her Dark Father and other teachers had systematically subjected her to ordeals compared to which a bit of lascivious groping was meaningless. The important thing was that the sentry failed to discover the various spell components secreted about her person. The confiscation of those would have diminished her capabilities far more than the surrender of her weapons.

But even though the tattooed man's impudence failed to perturb her, she memorized his face for chastisement later on. Her faith virtually required it, for as much as anything, the Lady of Loss was a goddess of revenge.

The toughs escorted her on through cellars crammed with a hodgepodge of no doubt stolen and smuggled goods, then up a flight of stairs into the living areas of what had once been a lavish mansion. In its essence, it still was, but the dirt, dust, scattered garbage, and smell of mildew marred the splendor. Eventually they reached a spacious solar on the second floor. The north wall was essentially one long window, made of genuine glass, and the expensive panes, cracked, smeared, and grimy though they were, provided a panoramic view of the Scelptar, the bridges spanning it, and the moon, her Tears, and the stars sparkling across the night sky.

The leader of the Red Axes apparently used the chamber as a lord would employ his hall, to grant audiences and issue decrees, for, his battle-axe lying across his thighs, the tanarukk lounged in a high-backed, gilded throne at the far end. A dozen of his followers loitered around in attendance, and the prisoner sprawled on the floor. Someone had pulled the sack off his head, revealing haggard, intelligent features, frightened but defiant, and an old scar around his neck.

"Bring her closer," the tanarukk growled.

The meazel gave Sefris a shove, its filthy, likely disease-bearing talons jabbing her but not quite breaking the skin.

She advanced and said, "Kesk Turnskull."

He grunted a swinish grunt and asked, "And who are you?"

"Sefris Uuthrakt."

"What do you know about the lockbox?"

"I won't bore you with the tale of everything that happened in far Ormath months ago," she said. "Let's just say I know what's in it, and I came to Oeble to acquire it."

Kesk grinned around the long, curved spikes of his tusks.

"Then you're out of luck," he said. "It's already spoken for."

"I figured you already had a buyer. I'll pay more. I can lay my hands on three hundred thousand gold pieces' worth of gems. Rubies, emeralds, diamonds, tomb jade, and ghost stones, all of the finest quality."

The lie reduced the hall to astonished, greedy silence for a moment, and then Kesk said, "I don't know you. Why should I believe in this treasure trove?"

Sefris hoped an admixture of truth would make her deception seem more plausible.

"I serve the Lady of Loss," she said. "Like you Red Axes, our temple reaves plenty of wealth from those unable to defend it." She waited a beat. "Would it bother you to deal with us?"

Kesk, leering, said, "Do you know where the race of tanarukks sprang from? I'll trade with anybody, no matter what devil-goddess she worships, so long as I can turn a profit. And I'd guess that the secret strongholds of Shar, wherever they may be, do have plenty of coin. But can you prove you're one of the priestesses, or am I just supposed to take it on faith, like the existence of all these jewels you're going to give us?"

"Have you heard of the Dark Moon?"

Kesk's eyes, red and faintly luminous, like embers, narrowed.

"Of Shar's clergy," he said, "yet not. They're protectors and assassins."

Sefris inclined her head and replied, "Something like that. If you've heard of us, you know we study a certain unarmed fighting style. If I defeat a couple of your men at once, using only my empty hands, will that prove I'm who I claim to be?"

"It might," the tanarukk said, "and if they beat you down instead, well, we were already planning on some torture. We might as well question you and old Nicos at once. He can tell us where his son keeps the coffer, and you can give us the truth about all those gems. Presmer, Sewer Rat—you brought her up here, you deal with her. Orvaega, you help. You can bleed her and break her bones, but try not to kill her."

The tattooed man—Presmer, Sefris assumed—whirled off his short leather cape, dangled it in one hand, and drew his short sword with the other. The meazel—the monastic wondered if Sewer Rat was its actual name, translated into human speech, or just a nickname the other rogues had given it—simply hissed and crouched. Evidently it saw no need for any weapons other than its claws. Orvaega, a female orc, hefted a war club in both hands.

Sefris stood still as her opponents spread out to encircle her. Then, suddenly, she bellowed a battle cry, pivoted, and leaped into the air, kicking at Presmer. Startled, he recoiled, as she'd intended. She touched down, whirled, and Sewer Rat and Orvaega were lunging at her. That, too, was as she desired. She'd turned her back and feinted at Presmer to lure them in. Control what your adversaries did, and when, and you were well on the way to defeating them.

Twisting at the hips, she performed a double-arm block that bounced the war club harmlessly away. She then punched the startled Orvaega in the snout, breaking bone and knocking the orc unconscious, and shoved her into Sewer Rat, which served to knock the runtish meazel backward, spoiling its frenzied attack. Floundering out from under the dead weight of its comrade, the black-eyed creature snarled and spat.

Sefris would have rushed Sewer Rat while the meazel was still off balance and encumbered, except that she knew enough time had passed for Presmer to have returned to the fray. She turned, and he swung his cape at her face, seeking to blind her. And stun her, too, perhaps, it the garment had weights sewn into the hem. She dropped into a squat, letting the cloak fly harmlessly over her head, and she simultaneously hooked his ankle with her foot. Presmer crashed down on his back.

Sefris sensed Sewer Rat pouncing. She turned, grabbed the meazel—immobilizing its raking claws in the process—spun it through the air, and smashed it down on top of Presmer. The impact snapped bones and stunned the both of them, and Sefris's only remaining problem was resisting the impulse to go ahead and make the kills. A long, slow breath served to buttress her self-control. She inclined her head to Kesk.

"There," she said.

He gave a grudging nod. If he had any concern for the welfare of the followers she'd just mauled, she could see no sign of it in his demeanor.

"I guess you probably do belong to the Dark Moon," the tanarukk said. "It still doesn't prove you have a king's ransom in jewels to barter."

"I'll produce them when the time comes. If I don't, simply sell the book to the person who first asked you to steal it."

"The fact of the matter is, he's promised more than coin."

"Do you trust him to keep his pledges," Sefris replied, "once he has the book in hand?"

Kesk spat. The gesture left a strand of saliva, which he didn't bother to wipe away, dangling beside the base of one tusk.

He said, "I don't trust anybody much."

"Rest assured, if it's a guarantee of future help you want, or even a genuine alliance, no one can offer more than the followers of Shar. We often make common cause with others who stand against the witless laws of men."

"I'll think about it," said Kesk. "Tell me how to get in touch with you."

"I'd hoped to stay with you for the time being."

The Red Axe snorted and said, "I still don't know what to make of you, human. Until I do, I don't want you running around my house."

"But you may need me. We may need to work together to take possession of the book."

"I doubt it."

"I take it you're going to try two approaches," Sefris said. "The first will be to hope Aeron's father knows the location of the strongbox and torture the secret out of him."

"Do your worst," the old man rasped. "It won't matter. I don't know where the cursed thing is."

Sefris ignored him to stay focused on Kesk.

"The problem," she continued, "is that, as we can see from all those scars, somebody got to him before you and mangled him severely. He's fragile now, and elderly to boot. If you question him in some crude fashion, his heart is likely to stop. But a child of the Dark Moon understands the human body as a healer understands it. It's part of our secret lore. I can cause a prisoner excruciating pain without doing serious harm."

Kesk shrugged and said, "That could come in handy, I suppose."

"I can make myself just as useful if you need to trade the old man for the book. Because it may not go smoothly. Aeron may decide he'd rather be rich than regain his father. He may try to trick you. Or you may decide to deal falsely with him."

"The wretch broke our deal. I'm no longer obliged to keep any promises I give him."

"I agree, and the point is, I can help you catch him. I have my skills, and he won't know we're working together until it's too late."

The tanarukk, scowling, said, "You're not as special as you think you are, woman. We Red Axes have managed to run Oeble for years now without any help from the likes of you."

"But you haven't managed to catch Aeron sar Randal. He's still running around free with the strongbox, laughing at you."

Kesk glared and trembled. His hands clenched on the haft of his axe. For a second, Sefris wondered if she'd pushed too hard, and would have to defend herself against him and all his henchmen, too. She called the words of a spell to mind.

Then, however, he brought himself under control.

"All right, you can stay for the time being." He waved his hand at Aeron's father and added, "Let me see this light touch of yours."

Sefris smiled without having to feign satisfaction, because she'd accomplished her objective, and her new situation, dangerous though it was, afforded her several advantages. As long as she was working with the Red Axes, she wouldn't have to worry about their somehow laying hands on the book ahead of her. A gang of cutthroats could manage a prisoner more easily than could a lone monastic, and since Oeble was their city, they ought to have less trouble making contact with Aeron. When the time came, it would be challenging to snatch the prize and vanish from their midst, but she was confident of her ability to do so.

She rounded on Nicos, who, his courage notwithstanding, saw something in her manner that made him blanch. She jumped him, found the proper pressure point, and paralyzed him as she had the beggar boy.

⊙

When Aeron slipped through the door of the cramped little shop, Daelric Heldeion was at his desk, whittling a chop from a piece of pine. The paunchy scribe was primarily in the business of writing and reading documents, but he'd made a profitable sideline of providing his illiterate clientele with a means of signing their names, or in the case of the budget-minded, their initials, to a piece of parchment.

Daelric looked up, realized who'd come to call on him, and his gray eyes opened wide. In light of recent events, that was all Aeron needed to see. He whipped out a throwing knife, cocked his arm, and Daelric froze.

"Are the Red Axes watching this place?" Aeron asked. "Are you supposed to give a signal?"

"No!" Daelric said. "But Kesk's ruffians have been around hunting you. The Gray Blades, too, though they don't know who they're looking for. Why in the Binder's name are you still in town?"

"I can dodge the folk who wish me ill. I always have before."

"If you say so. I wish you'd put the knife down."

Aeron returned the weapon to its sheath and said, "You'll see it again up close if you try anything foolish."

"What would I try? I'm a scribe, not one of you cutthroats," Daelric replied. He produced a linen handkerchief and blotted the sweat on his round, pink face. "What's that muck on your tunic? I can smell the stink from over here."

"Demon gore."

Aeron advanced to the desk, its surface littered with quills, inkwells, penknives, pine shavings, a stack of parchment, and lancets for those who insisted on contracts and promissory notes signed in blood. He cleared a space, brought the black book out from under his cloak, and set it down. Daelric goggled at it.

"This is the prize everyone wants so badly?" the scribe asked.

"Yes, and I need you to read enough of it to tell me why."

The scribe rubbed his thumb and fingertips together.

Aeron sighed. He set the rest of his coin atop the desk. Daelric regarded the copper and silver pieces without enthusiasm.

"Is that all you have?" said the scribe. "If the Red Axes find out I helped you, it could mean my life."

"I'll give you more—lots more—once I sell the book. Or, if that's not good enough, I'll find somebody else to read it, and not only will you miss out on the coin, you'll never know what all the fuss was about."

Aeron knew from past dealings that the clerk possessed a healthy streak of curiosity.

"Oh, all right." Daelric ran his finger under the embossed words on the cover. "The title is *The Black Bouquet*. Does that mean anything to you?"

"No."

"Nor to me," Daelric said.

He opened the volume, and sweet fragrances wafted up, combined with the smell of crumbling paper. He started to read. Aeron waited for a couple minutes, until impatience got the better of him.

"Well?" he asked.

"Well," Daelric replied, "it's old."

"I could tell that much."

"The point is, languages, and our way of writing them, change over time."

Aeron frowned and said, "That sounds strange. Why would they?"

"They just do, and as a result, old books are more difficult to read than new ones. I'm having a slow time of it, but I think this one is a formulary."

"A formulary?"

"A recipe book," the scribe explained. "For making perfumes."

"That would explain all the flowery scents clinging to the pages. But . . . magical perfumes?"

"It doesn't seem like it."

"Then what makes it so cursed special?" Aeron asked.

"I may need to read it cover to cover to determine that."

"How long will that take?"

"A couple days, perhaps."

"Thanks anyway." Maybe Daelric was more trustworthy than Burgell—it would be nice to think so—but Aeron couldn't linger that long, nor was he such a fool as to let the book out of his possession. "I'll figure it out some other way. By the way, you haven't seen me."

"I understand," the scribe said.

"For your own sake, I hope so."

Aeron tucked the formulary back under his cloak, opened the door, checked the street for lurking cutthroats and patrolling Gray Blades, then prowled on his way.

Concerned that someone might spot him moving through the open spaces comprising Laskalar's Square, he swung wide around it and reached his own tower a few minutes later. As he climbed the rickety stairs, he was looking forward to telling his father about his adventures. Maybe Nicos had heard of *The Black Bouquet*.

One glimpse of the open door at the top of the steps turned eagerness to anxiety. The old man would never have left it that way. Aeron started to run, realized someone might be lying in wait inside the garret, and forced himself to proceed warily instead. It was as hard as anything he'd ever done in his life.

No one was waiting for him, Nicos included. Intruders had plainly ransacked the apartment and smashed it up as well, and scrawled a crimson battle-axe sign on the wall so he'd know who to blame.

Aeron felt stunned. He hadn't anticipated Kesk's finding his home. No enemy had ever sought it out before, even though a few friends and tradesmen knew where it was. Even if he'd expected it, he wouldn't have thought the Red Axes would hurt Nicos. The old man had done nothing to offend them, and he had in his time been a respected member of the outlaw fraternity. In the Dance, the Door, and the Hungry Haunting, the bards still told tales of his most daring thefts.

Aeron realized that up until then, his rogue's life, though perilous, had always seemed to abide by certain rules. His rivals and the law would try to interfere with him, but only up to a point. Maybe it was just luck, and his own folly, that made it feel that way, or maybe, by stealing *The Black Bouquet* and defying Kesk, he'd spurred his adversaries to new heights of energy and ruthlessness. But either way, he was playing a new game, one where every hand was raised against him, and no tactic was out of bounds.

Everyone was right, he thought. I should have run away when I had the chance.

Unfortunately, it was too late. He couldn't flee and leave Nicos in danger.

He noticed the empty space where the balcony had been. It was hard to imagine that the Red Axes, maliciously destructive as they'd been, had taken the trouble to break the platform loose from its anchors. It had probably fallen on its own, and Nicos had loved to lounge out there and watch the river. What if Kesk's outlaws hadn't kidnapped him after all? What if—Aeron didn't want to finish the thought. He just scrambled to the brink and peered down.

Two stories below, a Rainspan connected the tower to the roof of a small building. The balcony had smashed down on the bridge and shattered. Most of the planks had plummeted to the ground far below, but a few, along with a motionless human figure, littered the elevated pathway.

Aeron raced out of the garret and down the steps. He found the door to the Rainspan and plunged out onto the end. The bridge creaked and shifted under his weight. He couldn't remember a time when it had truly felt secure, but the impact from above had clearly weakened it.

His eyes widened in surprise. The bloody body sprawled on the Rainspan wasn't his father. It was the female ranger from whom he'd stolen the saddlebag. Her broadsword stuck up out of the walkway, so close to her head that it might have sheared a lock of her close-cropped hair. Maybe she'd had it in her hand when the balcony collapsed, and she lost her grip on it. At any rate, he could picture it tumbling on its own and striking the bridge point first a second after her, nearly piercing her face in the process.

He pushed the grisly image out of his head. What mattered was that it wasn't his father lying there. Nicos must really be in Kesk's brutal hands, and Aeron had to find a way to set him free. He started to turn away, but then he hesitated.

He told himself not to be an idiot. The scout deserved whatever misfortune came her way. She'd killed Kerridi, Gavath, and Dal.

Yet she hadn't shot Aeron, and he hadn't knifed her when he'd had the chance. What was the point of sparing her then, only to let her die later? Assuming she wasn't dead already. From where he stood, he couldn't tell.

Maybe she'd watched the Red Axes abduct Nicos. Maybe she could tell Aeron something he needed to know.

His reasons for intervening felt like mere excuses, unconvincing even to himself. Yet, witless though it was, he'd feel base and vile if he simply walked away. He set the book down, and took a cautious step toward her, and the Rainspan squealed and shuddered. He froze.

"Scout," he said, "if you're alive, you have to let me know. Otherwise, I'm not coming out there."

She didn't respond. That was it, then. Maybe she was only unconscious, not dead, but all things considered, it would be stupid to risk his own neck to find out.

Or so he told himself. Then he crept forward anyway.

He moved slowly, setting his feet down as softly as he ever had slinking toward the jewelry box on a lady's vanity with the woman and her husband snoring in bed just a few feet away. Despite his caution, the Rainspan snarled and jerked.

It didn't crumble away beneath him, however, and in time he reached the woman. He stooped, cupped his hand over her nose and mouth, and felt the brush of her exhalation. She was alive.

Aeron guessed that meant he wasn't a complete fool. Maybe three quarters' worth.

"Ranger," he said, "wake up."

He gave her a little shake, then pinched her cheek hard. No matter what he did, she wouldn't stir.

"Wonderful," he said.

He lifted the guide in his arms. The damaged bridge had protested simply at supporting him. The weight of two people concentrated in a single spot made it rasp and buck repeatedly. The jerking grew increasingly violent, and the snapping and grinding, louder.

Aeron's heart hammered. His mouth was dry. He felt an almost ungovernable urge to scramble off the walkway as quickly as he could, but he forced himself to proceed as cautiously as before, until finally he reached the safety of the shelf to which the Rainspan was attached.

He set the archer down, wiped at the sweat on his face, and panted until he caught his breath. Then he searched her.

Her sword was stuck out on the bridge, and her bow presumably lay somewhere in the street below. She still had a dirk, a buckler, and some arrows in her quiver, however, all of which he tossed beyond her reach. She certainly seemed severely injured, but he was no healer. He wanted to make certain she didn't suddenly rouse and stick something sharp in him or brain him with the shield.

Next he went after her coin. Like many folk in Oeble, she carried a few coins in the pigskin purse on her belt, but more in an interior pocket of her leather armor. When he relieved her of her gold and saw just what a tidy sum it was, he grinned. At least he was back in funds again.

He stuffed *The Black Bouquet* under his tunic. Big as it was, it rode uncomfortably there, but he needed both hands. Though someone had once told him an injured person shouldn't be moved any more than necessary, he couldn't leave the ranger there. He had to take her someplace where she could be helped.

He wrapped her in her cloak in what he recognized was a rather pitiable attempt to disguise the nature of the peculiar burden he proposed to carry through the streets. He tugged his hood as far forward as it would go, to shadow his features, then he picked her up, carried her down the stairs, and out of the tower.

He was fit and she was slender, but the past couple days had been strenuous, and his arms and back soon started to ache. He was pondering the advisability of draping her over his shoulder when someone whistled in the darkness up ahead. A moment later, a similar series of shrill notes warbled from behind. Aeron couldn't understand the signals—as far as he knew, no outsider could—but he recognized the distinctive signature of Whistlers calling to one another. The first one trilled again. It sounded closer. The gang member was evidently heading down the street.

Aeron could have dashed for the mouth of an alleyway, but not quickly enough, not encumbered with the ranger. He considered dumping her, but even if no one molested her, there was no guarantee that anybody would help her, either, and he simply couldn't bring himself to do it. He could also try relying on his cowl to conceal his identity, but he doubted it would do the job, not if the Whistler was actually hunting him and passed close by.

That meant his best option was to hide. He carried the scout into a shadowy doorway and hunkered down. He drew a throwing knife in case he did have to fight, and stayed motionless thereafter.

A pair of bravos, both human, came into view. The clean-shaven one swaggered and sneered as, Aeron assumed, bullies the world over were wont to do. The one with the long, drooping mustache looked bored.

They glanced this way and that, plainly searching for someone or something. The man with the mustache peered straight at Aeron, but then turned indifferently away. The fugitive slumped with relief, and the ranger twitched and groaned.

He frantically tried to clap his hand over her mouth. It took him a second to find it inside the muffling cloak. Meanwhile, he waited to see if the Whistlers had heard her.

No, evidently not, for they wandered on down the street. Once they were gone, and his nerves left off jangling, he checked on the guide. She was still unconscious. She'd moaned in her sleep, if "sleep" was the proper word for her condition.

"You're too much trouble," he told her. "I earned every bit of your stinking gold." He wrapped her up again and carried her onward.

The priests of Ilmater maintained a house of healing on the thoroughfare called the Rolling Shields. Someone had painted the god's emblem, a pair of white hands bound with red rope, on the door, where the lamplight illuminated it. A scarlet bell pull hung beside the sigil, but with his hands full, Aeron found it easier simply to kick the panel until a stocky young acolyte with bloodstained sleeves opened it. The smells of astringent soap, incense, and sickness drifted out from inside.

"I have an injured woman here," Aeron said. "I'll pay for a private room and the best care you can give her."

"Everyone receives the best care we can give, no matter the size of the donation," the novice said stiffly.

Still, he led Aeron past the public wards with their double rows of cots to a chamber with a single bed in it. Aeron set the scout down, and the acolyte disappeared. A senior priest, scrawny, pale, and grizzled, appeared a minute later. He gave Aeron a curt nod, then proceeded to examine his patient. Eventually he rested his fingertips against her head and murmured an incantation. Pale light shone around them both, as if they were celestial beings possessed of halos. Bone clicked inside the guide's body. Aeron assumed it was knitting itself back together, but even so, the noise set his teeth on edge.

"How is she?" he asked.

"She was gravely injured," said the priest, "but she'll mend."

"Quickly, I imagine, since you used a spell on her."

"I'll be using more, but even so, it may be tomorrow or even the next day before she regains consciousness."

"Piss and dung," Aeron muttered.

He couldn't wait that long to set about the task of freeing his father, which meant he was likely going to have to proceed without the benefit of whatever information the ranger could give him. Oh, well, he doubted she actually had anything critical to say. He produced a handful of her gold.

"Take good care of her," Aeron told the priest, "and please, don't tell anyone she's here. There are people who want to hurt her."

That last could well be true, if the Red Axes knew she'd been poking around, and had decided they didn't like it.

"What about you?" he priest asked. "You're bruised and battered. You look like you could use a chirurgeon's attention yourself."

It occurred to Aeron that he ought to conserve his coin, but he decided, to the Abyss with it. He definitely could use some relief for his aches and pains, and a safe—well, as safe as anywhere in Oeble—refuge in which to rest. He scooped out more coins.

"You're right," he said. "In fact, I'd like to stay for a while myself. You can drag a cot or pallet in here, and if you can lay hands on a fresh shirt and tunic, I'd be grateful for those as well."

CHAPTER 10

Kesk disliked being awake before mid-afternoon. He disliked Slarvyn's Sword, too, even though the food was good and the décor—an eclectic collection of weapons, suits of armor, and the skulls and preserved carcasses of ferocious beasts—was to his taste. The problem with the dining club was the gauzy-winged sprites flitting about to maintain order. It rankled that the tiny fey, by wielding the slender wands with which the proprietor had equipped them, could paralyze even a tanarukk with a single burst of magic.

So, all in all, Kesk was in a foul mood, which soured still further when Aeron sat down opposite him. He quivered with the urge to leap up and swing his axe. The sprites would never stop him in time. But, unfortunately, such a tactic was unlikely to gain him the book, so he controlled himself.

"You're late," he growled.

"I had to look the place over," Aeron said, "to make sure you came alone."

From his calm demeanor, no one would have guessed he feared for his father's life, but Kesk thought that was a bluff and that the facade would crack soon enough.

"I did as the urchin you sent told me to do," said the tanarukk. "Where's the box?"

"*The Black Bouquet*, you mean."

Kesk sighed and said, "So you got it open."

"Yes, and now I'm ready to sell it. I was thinking Imrys Skaltahar might be interested. He has enough coin to pay a fair price, and he's so well established that he's one of the few people who doesn't need to fear you. Half of your own operations would fall apart if he wasn't involved."

Denied the satisfaction of an axe stroke, Kesk riposted with mockery of his own, "Let's not be hasty. Skaltahar can't give you your father back. Only I can do that, and I will, if we can come to an arrangement. For now, here's a little bit of him, as a show of good faith." He tossed a small bundle onto the tabletop. "Go on, look at it."

His hands trembling almost imperceptibly, Aeron unrolled the bloody rag to reveal the severed finger inside.

"You piece of filth."

"What did you think we were going to do to him," Kesk replied, "after you betrayed me?"

"He had no part in it."

"I couldn't be sure of that until we questioned him. Anyway, I needed a stick to beat you with, and, lucky him, he's it. Really, a chopped finger is the least of it. We've kept him screaming ever since we caught him. Nobody in the house can get any sleep. We're going to go right on torturing him, too, and snipping pieces off, until you hand over the book."

Aeron sat silently for a few heartbeats, then said, "I have to get something out of this."

"You get Nicos back."

"Yes, and that's as it must be. I love him. But . . . he's old and sick. He might not survive much longer in any case.

I've got my whole life in front of me, and if I can live it as a rich man, I'm not going to let the chance slip away. Back in the water gate, we agreed on a new price."

"Back in the water gate, I didn't have Nicos."

"I'm telling you, he's not enough."

It irked Kesk even to give the appearance of yielding, but he felt that, all things considered, further resistance was a waste of time and effort.

"All right, damn you. You'll get the coin and poor old Papa, too."

"And peace thereafter. Give me your vow that you and the Red Axes won't hold a grudge."

"I swear by He Who Never Sleeps," Kesk said with a sneer, "and the Horde Leader that we won't hold this against you. But you'll run afoul of us again, and probably sooner rather than later. When that happens, I'll have your skull to make me a goblet."

"We'll see."

"So we will. Bring the book to my house. You have until sunset, and—"

Aeron snorted, then said, "Do you think I'm stupid enough to walk into the dragon's cave? Call me timid, but I have a hunch I wouldn't come out again. Come midnight, put my father and the coin on board that pleasure barge of yours. Row out under the central span of the Arch of Gargoyles and drop anchor. If I see any of your henchmen on the bridge, or any bows, slings, or javelins on the boat, then you won't see me."

"Agreed."

"Then we're done," Aeron said as he rose.

Kesk leered and said, "You're forgetting the finger. Don't you want it? If not, maybe I'll have the cook fry it up."

The human gave him a level stare, then, plainly thinking better of whatever it was he wanted to do or say, he turned away in a swirl of gray cape. Kesk watched, interested to see how Aeron would exit. Obviously, the thief had chosen the dining club because there were so many ways in and out. It was accessible through the Underways, at street level, and via Rainspans. It would be hard for even the most determined gang to lay a trap along every route.

Kesk hadn't tried. The trap, such as it was, was sitting just a few tables away, sipping tea, her cowl pulled up to cover her shaved scalp.

Kesk didn't know what to make of Dark Sister Sefris. He certainly didn't trust her, any more than he would have trusted anyone who professed allegiance to Shar. Humans and dwarves called his own gods, the deities of the orc pantheon, evil, but in fact, they were simply powers who granted their worshipers strength, plunder, and pleasure, the things every sensible person wanted. In contrast, the Lady of Loss, from what the tanarukk vaguely understood, sought the destruction of the entire world, her own followers included. Only a lunatic would pledge himself to a patron such as that.

Still, Sefris plainly did have useful talents, exactly as she'd claimed, and just as importantly, Aeron had no idea who she was. With luck, she could deal with him, Kesk would deal with her, and he could acquire the fortune in gems—if it even existed—either by trading honestly or cheating. Cheating, most likely. If he murdered the monastic, he could follow through on his deal with his original partner, and make that much more coin. Maybe even one day control all the illegal activity in Oeble, entirely unhindered by the Gray Blades, assuming he could trust the little weasel that far.

When he thought about it that way, it seemed as if a splendid future lay in store, but the complexity of the current situation irked him. It almost made him wish he'd told Aeron the truth from the start. Maybe if he had, the job would be over already.

The funny thing was, he wasn't even sure why he'd withheld so much information. To avoid scaring Aeron off, or shave his fee? Possibly. That was what he'd told himself, but he suspected he'd really done it out of spite, simply because he didn't like the human. If so, the impulse had worked against him. But in general, it was his determination never to forget a slight or injury, to do his foes a bad turn at every opportunity, which had made him the most powerful chieftain in Oeble's underworld, so he supposed it was an acceptable trade off.

Aeron climbed the stairs to the second floor. Unless he was planning to double back down again, he was headed for the Rainspans. Sefris took a final sip of tea, laid a silver piece on her table, and rose to follow.

Sefris knew any number of tricks for tailing a man without being spotted. More valuable than any technique, however, was the instinct that warned her when her quarry was going to look around. When Aeron reached the door, she sensed it was about to happen.

Fortunately, the upper stories of Slarvyn's Sword, like the ground floor, were crammed with decorations selected to please the sensibilities of warriors, adventurers, and those who enjoyed imagining themselves in such roles. She sidestepped behind the stuffed body of a peryton. The trophy was a fine specimen, its aquiline body more than eight feet long, and the antlers curving forward from its purple, staglike head, sprouting eight points each. It smelled faintly of some bitter substance the taxidermist had used to preserve it.

One of the sprites, a blue-skinned grig with the antennae and long, folded legs of a cricket, swooped in front of her and hovered. Evidently it had noticed her ducking into hiding, while she, intent on Aeron, had missed spotting it. It pointed its rune-carved wooden wand at her face.

She was reasonably certain she could swat it out of the air before it could speak the word that triggered the weapon, but perhaps not without attracting the hostile attention of its fellows.

"I'm not going to cause any trouble in here," she said, keeping her voice low. "What happens outside is no concern of yours."

The grig regarded her for another moment, then gave a curt nod and flew away. In other places, the fey had a reputation for fighting "evil," but it seemed that in Oeble, even they thought twice about meddling in affairs that were none of their business.

Sefris stepped from behind the peryton. Aeron was gone. Through the door, presumably, though if he was as wily as his reputation indicated, maybe not. She strode to it and cracked it open.

It was all right. There he was, moving down the Rainspan. It wasn't necessarily the escape route Sefris would have chosen. If someone was chasing you, you could only flee in one direction. But by the same token, you only had to keep an eye out for foes straight ahead or directly behind.

Which meant Sefris couldn't afford to look like an enemy. She let him get a few paces farther ahead, then ambled out into the sunlight, gawking like a rustic to whom the towers and elevated pathways were a marvel.

At best, the pretence would fool Aeron for a little while. If he kept a sharp eye out, started and stopped, and doubled back as she expected him to, he was bound to mark her eventually. Her objective was to close to striking range before that happened, then drop him.

He paused as if to admire the view. She knew it would seem too much of a coincidence if she abruptly did the same, so she kept on strolling. Once she was close enough, her nerves fairly sang with the urge to strike him. Alas, other people were nearby. In all likelihood, it would be easy enough to kill them if they were so foolish as to intervene, but it was more sensible to be patient and wait until she and her prey were alone. She passed on by.

At the end of the bridge, steps twisted up and down around the outside of a spire built of crumbling brick, and a door led into the interior. She had no way to predict which way Aeron would choose, and therefore climbed to the start of another rickety Rainspan a story higher. At least from that vantage point, she could count on seeing where he went.

As he neared the tower, she reflected that she could spin a chakram down and hit him. She had a perfect shot, and the folk with whom they'd shared the bridge were entering Slarvyn's Sword. The only thing that deterred her was that the razor-edged rings were made for maiming and killing, not simply stunning a man helpless. Despite her skill, she might conceivably hurt Aeron so severely that he wouldn't be able to reveal the location of the book.

A spell, however, was a different matter. She plucked a pinch of sand from her pocket, tossed it into the air, and murmured the charm that would put a victim, or even several, to sleep.

A dimness seethed about her, the Shadow Weave manifesting itself even in the midst of the bright sunlight. Power whispered. But Aeron kept right on walking. He had a strong spirit, or was merely lucky, for somehow he'd resisted the spell, probably without ever even realizing he was under magical attack.

Well, she'd get him next time. When he reached the tower, he started down around the outside, in a moment disappearing around the curve of the rounded wall. As she headed after him, she saw a shaggy-headed ruffian skulk from the dining club. She assumed it was her own shadow. Kesk lacked subtlety, but had sense enough to try to ensure that she wouldn't get hold of *The Black Bouquet* and vanish.

The Red Axe—or Whistler, or member of some other gang beholden to the tanarukk—was of no importance at the moment. Sefris would kill or evade him when the time came. She had to keep up with Aeron, and she hurried down the side of the tower, knowing that until he came into view below her, he couldn't see her, either.

The problem was that he never did appear, not on the steps or on the ground underneath, either, and by the time Sefris reached the second story, she realized what was wrong. He'd noticed her magic after all, and was trying to shake her off his trail.

How, though? Had he sprinted to the ground and concealed himself? It was possible, but she hadn't heard his running footsteps slapping on the steps. It seemed more likely that he'd slipped through one of the doors leading into the tower.

She did the same, and found herself on a landing lined with doors. Interior staircases zigzagged up and down. Which way?

She was grimly aware that he could have gone anywhere. But a sorceress learned to heed her intuition, and hers told her he'd scurried upward, doubling back to the Rainspans. She dashed in that direction.

She threw open the door that led to the bridge she'd crossed a minute before. Kesk's minion was in the middle of it.

"Did you see where Aeron went?" she snapped.

He gaped at her, evidently amazed that she'd picked up on who he was and manifestly useless.

She raced on up the inside of the tower and plunged through the exit to the higher of the two Rainspans. Aeron sar Randal was scurrying along it. When he heard the door bang against the wall, he turned, saw her, and likewise looked surprised, in his case surprised that she was still on his track and catching up so quickly. He shouldn't have been. Her training enabled her to run faster than any common thief.

Nobody else was on the bridge to deter her from attacking. She charged, and Aeron threw a dagger at her. It flew straight and true, and without breaking stride, she batted it out of the air.

The thief hurled a second knife. She ducked it. He spun, ran, reached the end of the Rainspan, and sprinted on down the long axis of a clay-tiled gable-and-valley roof, which the builders had made flat to create a narrow walkway. At the far end was the top of a spiral staircase that presumably corkscrewed all the way down to the ground.

Not that it mattered where it ended. Aeron wouldn't make it that far before she overtook him. Evidently he realized it, because he spun around to face her and reached under his cloak. Grabbing for another weapon, she supposed.

But she was wrong. He brought out *The Black Bouquet* itself. He'd carried the volume to his meeting with Kesk, the Dark Goddess alone knew why. He heaved it away, at right angles to the path. It thumped on the tiles and slid on down the steep pitch of the roof.

Sefris leaped off the bridge and dashed after *The Black Bouquet*, intent on intercepting it before it slid over the edge. If the old, crumbling book fell to the ground below, the impact could damage it severely.

She dived for it at the last possible second, indifferent to the fact that by so doing, she was also flinging herself toward the drop-off. She grabbed the tome, somersaulted to the very brink, and stamped down hard. The action shattered clay tiles, countered her momentum, and kept it from tumbling her off the edge.

She felt a swell of satisfaction, which ended abruptly when she took a good look at her prize. Viewed up close, it was a little too small and didn't have a title embossed on the front cover. It wasn't the perfumer's formulary after all, just a decoy Aeron had procured in case he needed a diversion.

She spun around. The ridge walkway was clear. The thief had disappeared, but where?

As before, Sefris could think of several possibilities, but she knew that at that point, in Aeron's place, she would have tried to reach the ground as quickly as possible, which meant he'd bolted down the stairs. She could use them herself, but despite her skills, would waste precious seconds clambering back up the slanted roof. It would be far quicker to descend via the controlled plummet she'd learned during her training.

She swung herself off the brink and dropped, grabbing at protrusions and depressions, the merest unevenness sometimes, in the timber wall with its flaking white paint. Many of these handholds could never have borne her full weight, but even so, the fleeting contacts served to slow her down a little.

She landed in a snowy flurry of dislodged paint chips, executed a shoulder roll, and vaulted to her feet uninjured. The gable-and-valley configuration of the roof existed at street level as well, which was to say the whole building was cross-shaped, and positioned behind one of the projecting arms, she could no longer see the spiral steps.

She dashed around the structure until they came into view. Her quarry didn't. Assuming she'd correctly guessed his intentions, he'd already made it down to the teeming street, where a good many humans, orcs, goblins, halflings, and gnomes were bustling about.

She pivoted, peering into the crowd, and abruptly spotted a flash of copper in the bright, warm autumn sunlight. Aeron had pulled up his cowl to cover his red hair, but when he glanced back, no doubt checking to see if she was still on his trail, it didn't quite hide his goatee. The thief was striding toward a staircase that, at first glance, looked like it led down into someone's cellar, but which she suspected was actually an entrance to the Underways.

She didn't want him to reach the steps. He probably could elude her down in the tunnels. She couldn't hit him with a chakram, not with so many people milling around between them, but her magic might work, and at that point, she didn't care who saw. If anyone took exception to her actions, she'd deal with him.

She gestured, and the shadow of a brown-and-white horse standing in the traces of a parked hay wagon lengthened and deformed into a tentacle, which then reared from the ground. The animal whinnied and shied, and people nearby cried out in alarm. Aeron turned, saw the length of darkness lashing in his direction, and tried to dodge. He wasn't quite quick enough. The tentacle spun around him and held him fast. He thrashed, struggling to squirm free. Agile as he was, with that skinny frame, he might actually do it, but it wouldn't save him. By that time, Sefris would have closed to striking distance. She raced forward.

Broadsword in hand, a Gray Blade scrambled out of the crowd to bar her path. With his slender frame, ivory skin, and vivid green eyes, he looked as if he might possess some elf blood.

"Hold it!" he said. "I saw you ca—"

Sefris drove her stiffened fingers at the half-elf's solar plexus. He had excellent reflexes. He jumped back in time and brought his round target shield up to block. His sword leaped in a head cut. She shifted in so close that the stroke fell harmlessly behind her. Sefris rammed the heel of her palm into his jaw, snapped his neck, and raced on toward Aeron.

Maddeningly, a second Gray Blade—middle-aged, stocky, and entirely human—lunged at her. Apparently he'd been hurrying toward Aeron and the tentacle, but had spied his partner's fate and turned back around to avenge him. His sword point streaked at her face. She sought to deflect it with a press, and avoiding the block, it dipped down to threaten her midsection. She had to retreat a step and twist at the hips to keep it from piercing her guts.

She gave him a roundhouse kick to the knee. Bone snapped, and he fell down. She stamped on his chest, breaking ribs and rupturing his heart.

She ran on. People scurried to get out of her way, which afforded her a good view of the conjured tentacle. It writhed and shifted from side to side, clenching and unclenching, its coils empty. The Gray Blades had delayed her long enough for Aeron to wriggle free.

She dashed down the steps into the Underways, cast uselessly about, chose a direction at random, and sprinted that way. After she passed a couple intersections, she realized further pursuit was futile. The thief had escaped her for the time being.

But not forever. She'd eavesdropped on Aeron's conversation with Kesk, and was convinced that the tanarukk was right about his fellow rogue: The redheaded thief would keep on trying to liberate his father. That meant she'd have another chance to catch him, and surely he couldn't be so lucky twice in a row.

Miri woke feeling sore, yet drowsily contented. Judging from the warm covers and medicinal smells, her comrades had carried her to the healers' tent, and she was going to be all right. She could feel it, and in any case, the important thing was that she hadn't disgraced herself.

Standing behind the bramble barricades with the senior rangers and their allies, waiting for her first battle to begin, she'd been frightened she wouldn't be able to bear it, that she'd throw down her bow and run away. And when the enemy—orcs, ogres, and huge, shapeless, crawling masses of mold—appeared among the trees, it was as terrifying as she'd imagined. But somehow she'd stood her ground, loosing arrow after arrow until the foe overran her position, then frantically hacking with her broadsword. She cut down two orcs, turned, and saw an ogre swinging its club at her. The world went dark.

Evidently her side had won the fight. Otherwise, she wouldn't be lying in a clean, soft bed. She realized her throat was dry, opened her eyes fully, and looked about to see if one of the priests had left her some water.

She wasn't in a tent but a small, sparsely furnished candlelit room with bare whitewashed walls. A thin young man with a red beard sat watching her. The sight of him made her snatch for the sword that no longer hung at her side, even as it pierced her confusion.

It wasn't an ogre that had wounded her—that had happened years ago, in the Winterwood—it was a collapsing balcony in Oeble, after which, what? Had Aeron sar Randal found her and decided to make her his prisoner?

As if by magic, a long, heavy fighting knife appeared in the thief's hand.

"Calm down!" he said. "I don't mean to hurt you. If I had, I wouldn't have carried you to Ilmater's house for healing."

She sneered and replied, "Yet you pull a dagger on me, even though I'm injured and unarmed."

"According to the healer who attended you, you're only a little bit hurt at this point." He smiled crookedly and added, "Besides, this afternoon I found out just how tough an unarmed outlander woman could be."

"You met Sefris."

"I did if she shaves her head and moves like . . . I don't know what. A cat? Lightning? Flowing water? Whatever you liken it to, it was scary."

"That's her."

"Who in the Nine Hells is she? How do you know her?"

"How do you? What happened?"

"I'm the one with the knife," said Aeron, "so I'm going to ask the questions."

She glanced surreptitiously around. Her weapons were nowhere in evidence, nor was there anything much she could grab and use for self-defense. Even the pewter candlestick was out of reach. Still, perhaps her plight wasn't all that desperate.

"If this truly is a house of healing," she said, "all I need do is shout, and someone will rush to my aid."

"Faster than I can stick an Arthyn fang between your ribs?" he countered. "Don't count on it."

"Are you ruthless enough? I don't see it in your eyes."

He sighed like a man with a headache and said, "I already said I don't want to do it. I'm just hoping you can tell me something to help me get my father back."

She felt a reluctant twinge of sympathy for him. She remembered how it had felt to lose her own parents, when the white fever took them both within a tenday of one another.

"I saw a gang of ruffians march him away with a sack over his head," she said. "One of them was a tanarukk."

"Right, the Red Axes. I know who kidnapped him, but did you overhear them say anything about exactly where in the house they're holding him, or how he's restrained, or guarded? Anything like that?"

"No. I'm sorry."

"Curse it. Really, I don't even know what I thought you might be able to tell me, but I prayed there'd be something. What were you doing in my garret?"

"Looking for you and the strongbox."

"You can say '*The Black Bouquet*.' I know what I've got. Sort of. Were you up there questioning my father when the Red Axes showed up?"

"No," Miri replied. "Sefris and I were just approaching the tower when the Red Axes and your father came out."

His eyes narrowed.

"Then you," he said, "this Sefris woman, and Kesk are all working together?"

"No. I mean, Sefris and I aren't on the same side anymore. It's complicated," Miri answered. She blinked when she absorbed the implications of what he'd just said. "Are you telling me Sefris has joined forces with the Red Axes?"

He frowned, considering, then said, "I assumed so at the time, but now that you ask, I guess I can't be absolutely sure. Anyway, I told you I'll ask the questions, and I think we're going to have to start at the beginning and go step by step for me to make sense of the answers. What is *The Black Bouquet*? A perfume maker's cookbook, I know that much, but what makes it so valuable? A secret message hidden somewhere inside?"

She hesitated, then decided that, since he knew so much already, it wouldn't hurt to tell him. In the course of interrogating her, he was likely to reveal things that she wished to know as well.

"No," she said, "it's just a formulary, but the formulary of Courynn Dulsaer."

Aeron looked blank.

"Until I got involved in this affair," Miri admitted, "I'd never heard of him, either, but evidently he's famous if you care about perfume. In fact, he was the most famous perfumer who ever lived. His concoctions weren't magical, but they might as well have been, for they delighted anyone who got a whiff. These days, when some lucky soul discovers an unopened bottle, it sells for thousands of gold pieces."

"Because nobody knows how to make any more."

"Right. Courynn never took on an apprentice, or taught anybody else his secrets, and *The Black Bouquet* disappeared mysteriously at the time of his death. That was three hundred years ago, and everyone thought the book lost forever. Recently, however, in Ormath on the Shining Plains, Lord Quwen's agents uncovered and destroyed a temple of Shar. They found *The Black Bouquet* with the rest of the cult's treasure."

"And it's truly valuable," Aeron said.

Plainly, the thief was still trying to wrap his head around the idea that anyone cared so much about perfume. Miri had had the same reaction when she'd first heard the story.

"I'm no merchant—thank the Forest Queen!—but I'm told that if the right person used the book to set up a perfume manufactory, he'd probably wind up as rich as a prince," the ranger continued. "Anyway, Ormath has had its problems recently. It's had to cope with three bad harvests in a row, fend off raiders, and fight an actual war or two with its neighbors. For that reason and others, Lord Quwen was more interested in selling the book and turning a profit quickly than going into the perfume trade himself. He put out the word that he had it . . ."

"And a rich merchant here in Oeble arranged to buy it," Aeron finished for her. "Which one?"

"That, I can't tell you."

He scowled and said, "Ranger . . ."

"Threats won't move me. Come at me if you want, and we'll find out if an unarmed scout of the Red Hart Guild can defeat a common cutpurse waving a knife."

"Oh, calm down," said Aeron. "Maybe it doesn't matter who wanted it, or maybe we'll come back to that point later. For now, go on with your story."

"At the buyer's insistence," she continued with a nod, "the negotiations were conducted in secret, Lord Quwen dickering with the merchant's factor in Ormath. Finally they struck a deal. The buyer made a down payment, the balance due when he took delivery of the book. Quwen undertook to get the volume to Oeble. Since that too was supposed to happen secretly, he didn't want to use his own troops to move it. Instead, he applied to my guild for an experienced guide—me—and I in turn hired a company of mercenaries. In addition, Quwen's court wizard cast spells of warding on the strongbox and saddlebag intended to hold the *Bouquet*."

Miri sighed and added, "You know the rest of the story better than I do. The sellswords and I carried the formulary all the way here, and you stole it mere minutes before I could hand it over. Because, plainly, the expedition wasn't a secret. How did you know we were coming?"

"Only because Kesk hired me to steal the coffer. My guess is, he knew because somebody asked him to get it. Kesk's a power to be reckoned with here in Oeble, but I doubt he has spies in faraway cities. Though he might have one in a rich man's household here in town."

"I take it he's the most dangerous scoundrel hereabouts."

Aeron shrugged and said, "One of them."

"I'm surprised you dared defy him."

"He held back information that might have kept my friends alive," Aeron replied. "It made me angry. Though why I turned on him, then saved you who actually killed Dal and Gavath with your own hands, is a puzzle."

"I killed them in a fair fight you outlaws started."

"Does that make them any less dead?"

"No, and if you feel the need to avenge them, come ahead."

"Maybe we'll get to that," Aeron said. "Tell me about Sefris."

"What do you know about the followers of Shar?"

Aeron frowned and replied, "Just what everybody knows. They're vicious, mad, and worship an evil goddess."

"I don't know a great deal more myself, but I have heard of a cult within the cult. Or that watches over the main cult. Something like that. They're called the Monks of the Dark Moon, and they learn a special, highly effective style of fighting. Sefris claims to be one of them, and I believe her. Evidently her order sent her here to recover the treasure Quwen plundered from their goddess."

Aeron cocked his head and asked, "So what were you doing wandering around with her?"

Miri felt her face grow warm.

"At first," she said, "I didn't know who she was. She tricked me into accepting her as my comrade. For some reason, she must have thought she'd have better luck getting her hands on the *Bouquet* if we hunted it together. In the end, she turned on me, because I wouldn't agree to help her take your father from the Red Axes and hold him hostage ourselves, and that was when she told me who she really is. We fought until your balcony collapsed beneath us. She managed to scramble off, but I didn't. It's a miracle I'm not dead."

"You didn't fall all the way to the ground," said Aeron. "You landed on a Rainspan partway down. If Sefris wants to take the book back to the cult, and Kesk wants it for some other reason, how could they work together?"

"I don't know. You're fairly certain they are?"

"I palavered with Kesk today. Sefris stalked me when I left and tried to capture me. How did she know to find me there unless that pig-faced bastard told her?"

"If she tried to catch you, you were lucky to get away. As lucky as I am to still be alive."

"I realize that. The first time she threw a spell at me, it didn't take, but I felt a kind of tickle in my head. I glanced around and spotted a woman standing in a wriggling blot of shadow, or twilight, in the middle of the sunshine. It only lasted a second. If I'd looked a heartbeat later, I wouldn't have seen anything funny. I might have decided the tickle was just my imagination, and not known I was in danger until it was too late."

Miri stared at him and asked, "Sefris threw a spell?"

"Yes. You didn't even know she was a sorceress? Shadows of Mask, you are thick."

"She didn't cast any spells when we were together. Magic must be the secret weapon she likes to hold in reserve."

"Maybe."

"I assume Kesk offered to ransom your father for the formulary?" Miri asked.

"Yes."

"Are you going to do it?"

"I don't see how I can. I figured that if I tried, he'd play me false. Seize the book, take me prisoner, and kill both my father and me. He's like that: mean, treacherous, and vengeful. But I wasn't sure of it, so I arranged a meeting in Slarvyn's Sword to feel him out. After what happened, I'm positive I can't trust him. Though maybe if I'm clever enough, I can set up the exchange in such a way that he has no choice but to keep his word."

"You sound doubtful," Miri said, "as well you should."

She decided she was tired of sitting up in bed like an invalid, so she pushed back the covers, and swung her bare feet to the floor. Someone had dressed her in a white linen shift sufficient for modesty.

"Why don't we do the sensible thing?" she asked.

He arched an eyebrow.

"Go to the authorities," she continued, "and report that the Red Axes abducted your father. If you have the kind of reputation I suspect, they might not take your word for it, but the Red Hart Guild is known far and wide as an honorable fraternity, and I'll back you up. I won't even tell them you're the thief who committed the outrage in the Paeraddyn and escaped to tell the tale, and in exchange for my help and forbearance, you'll return *The Black Bouquet*."

Aeron chuckled grimly and said, "I don't think so."

"Why not?"

"First off, I'd have to trust you, and all I know about you is that you killed my friends, and stood and watched as the Red Axes kidnapped a sick old man. I didn't think 'honorable' rangers were supposed to behave like that."

The barb evoked a rush of shame in Miri, which she did her best to hide.

"I've seen a hundred cruel and depraved acts since I came to this cesspool of a city," the ranger said. "I couldn't interfere with all of them. Anyway, who are you, a miserable thief, to lecture me on my duty?"

He shrugged and said, "Nobody, obviously, in your eyes. Anyway, there are other reasons I don't want to go to the Gray Blades. I wouldn't be surprised if some of them are in Kesk's pay, or beholden to the person who hired him to get the book. Even if they're not, they're as leery of the Red Axes as the gang is of them. They wouldn't want to break into Kesk's stronghold just on our say-so. They do know I'm an outlaw even if they've never been able to hang anything on me, and while your guild may be known the world over as honest and true, you're still an outlander, which means you don't count for much."

"The rightful owner of the book does. If I can convince him to speak up. . . ."

"It's still not a sure thing. Look, my father was a notable robber in his time. The law hasn't forgotten, and it doesn't love him, either. But let's say we could convince the Gray Blades to raid Kesk's mansion. Do you think they'd find my father alive? The house surely has secret rooms, and sits on the river to boot."

"So the only answer is to out-trick Kesk?" Miri asked. "And his henchmen? And Sefris?"

"I imagine."

"In that case, let me help you, and when your father is safe, you'll return *The Black Bouquet* to me."

"Right," Aeron said with a snort, "and as soon as I turn my back, you knock me over the head, tie me up, and torture the location of the book out of me. Or hand me over to the law and let them do it."

"I swear by the Hornblade that I won't."

"Oh, well, that changes everything."

Miri felt a surge of anger, and quashed it as best she could. In his world, perhaps it wasn't a deadly insult to doubt the sanctity of another person's oath.

"Look," she said, "neither you nor I are a match for Sefris and the Red Axes by ourselves. But if we work together, we might have a chance."

Frowning, he thought it over for a moment.

"At the end," he said, "when I turn over the book, I want a reward."

"We're talking about your father's life."

"Even so," the thief replied. "Think of it as wergild for my friends."

"All right. I can arrange it. Where are my clothes and weapons?"

"Your clothes and armor are in the chest at the foot of the bed. We'll have to buy you a new sword and bow."

CHAPTER 11

The night was overcast and dark. Still, peering down from the Rainspan, Aeron could make out some detail inside the shadowy enclosure off Dead King's Walk. From the looks of her, Miri could, too. In fact, from the way she fingered her new longbow, he could tell she was thinking she could hit the guard who periodically emerged from his sentry box to amble around checking on the merchandise, and never mind that she'd complained of the poor quality of the weapon compared to the one she'd lost.

She was a dangerous woman for certain, one who'd already killed some of Aeron's friends, and he was trusting her simply because, when she'd promised to deal fairly with him, she'd seemed to be speaking honestly, and even if not, so long as she didn't know where he'd stashed *The Black Bouquet*, she might well hesitate to attack him. For what if matters went awry, and he either escaped her or wound up dead?

In any case, he had to run the risk of working with her, because she was right. For the time being, he did need her. His truest friends were dead, and Kesk had demonstrated his ability to turn the rest of Oeble against him.

"What do you think?" he asked.

"I can make the shot," Miri replied. A cool breeze, moist with the promise of rain before morning, shifted a lock of her close-cropped hair. "And I don't like slavers. But the trade is legal in Oeble, isn't it?"

"Thank Mask I'm just a 'miserable thief,' " he said. "Such concerns don't matter to me. Yes, a slave emporium is legal in and of itself, even if an outlaw like Kesk owns it. But if it makes you feel any better, I'd wager a wagon full of gold that he didn't come by all his stock in a lawful manner."

"That does make it better. Still, I'd rather not murder a man unnecessarily." She glowered and added, "If that makes me a squeamish fool in your eyes, so be it."

"It doesn't," he admitted. "If you remember, I tried to steal *The Black Bouquet* without anybody getting hurt. We'll use the other plan."

Keeping an eye out for those who were scouring the city hunting him, they stalked to the end of the bridge, entered a squat octagonal tower, and descended to ground level via the stairs inside. Aeron cracked open the matchboarded external door, peeked out, and frowned. Dead King's Walk was one of Oeble's primary thoroughfares, and despite the lateness of the hour, that particular section was both better lit and busier than he would have liked. He and Miri would just have to cope.

They sauntered to the slave market entrance. Aeron figured he had just a moment or two to make an assessment. If he took any longer, someone might conclude that he and his companion were loitering suspiciously.

The gate had a sturdy, well-made lock. Burgell could have opened it with a perfunctory mystical whisper, but it was likely to take Aeron a while. The high fence had long nails driven all the way through to catch and pierce a climber's flesh. He thought he could swarm over unscathed, but had no idea whether Miri could do as well.

All things considered, he felt the third option was the best. He positioned himself against the fence, where someone opening the gate wouldn't see him, then Miri took hold of the rope hanging from the brass bell and rang.

She had to clang it twice more before a surly voice replied from the other side, "We're closed. Come back tomorrow."

"I'm traveling at first light," she said, "and I need thralls to tend the pack animals. I'll pay well."

The guard opened the gate a notch to peer out at what appeared to be a lone woman in a non-threatening stance, no blade in her hand or arrow on her bowstring. Squeaking a little, the hinges in need of oil, the portal swung wider.

Aeron threw his shoulder against it and slammed it all the way open, staggering the half-orc watchman in the process. He lunged onward and hammered his new cudgel against the guard's temple. The half-breed collapsed, and Miri closed the gate. The whole thing had only taken a second, and with luck, no one outside the fence had observed it.

Miri gave Aeron a nod of approval, and a second attendant, a human, stepped onto the stoop of the shack at the rear of the fenced-in yard. He'd plainly heard the bell, too, and come to see what was going on. He goggled, then whirled to run back inside.

Aeron grabbed an Arthyn fang and threw it. The blade plunged into the target's back at the same instant as Miri's arrow. The man stumbled, made a ghastly little gargling sound, and fell on his face, the top half of him over the threshold and the rest still stretched across the little porch.

Aeron sighed. They'd hoped to do their job without killing, but it simply hadn't worked out that way. They couldn't let the wretch raise an alarm. Anyway, the dead man was a Red Axe, wasn't he, or as good as. Aeron shoved the matter out of his mind.

The slaves slept in what amounted to lean-tos in the middle of the yard, with buckets provided for sanitation. Evidently no one had emptied them in a while, and the stink made Aeron's eyes water. The thralls stared at him and Miri apprehensively.

"It's all right," the ranger said. "We're here to free you. Where do the overseers keep the tools?"

An underfed, half-naked hobgoblin, its back and shoulders striped with whip marks, pointed at the shack. Miri stepped over the corpse in the doorway, then reappeared with mallets and chisels. Some of the slaves clamored for them.

"Keep quiet!" she hissed.

Once they obeyed, she passed out the tools, and they started striking off their leg irons.

"Kesk will puke blood when he finds out all this coin has grown wings and flown away," Aeron said with a grin.

"Coin?" Miri repeated. "Is that all they are to you? I suppose if it was practical, you wouldn't free them, but simply steal them to sell yourself."

"You're wrong," Aeron said. He didn't know why he should care about her opinion of him, but her scorn was starting to rankle. "In my time I've stolen copper ingots, bales of silk, pots of jam, and as it turns out, a formulary. Why not? They're just things. What difference does it make whose pocket they wind up in? But I've never tried my hand at slaving—or kidnapping, or killing for hire. I don't have the stomach for any of that."

"But you do hurt people, in the course of committing your outrages. You and your accomplices killed some of my mercenaries."

"At least killing isn't the very heart of our trade. Unlike yours. A ranger's a warrior and manhunter, right? I don't suppose you would have joined your Red Hart Guild unless you liked shooting people."

"I like defending the innocent. Sometimes that re—"

"This is madness!" one of the thralls, a rather pretty blond woman with an upturned nose, suddenly wailed. "We can't escape! They'll only punish us, maybe kill us, if we try."

"Not if you're smart," Aeron said. "If you were enslaved illegally and can prove it, run to your families or the Gray Blades. The rest of you, sneak out of town before dawn, stay off the roads, and head for the Barony of the Great Oak. It's not far, and they don't traffic in slaves there. They won't send you back." He opened his belt pouch and handed one of the slaves a few coins. Miri probably suspected the funds he was spending were the same coins she'd been carrying before her fall, but so far, she hadn't made an issue of it. "This will buy food, or pay a bribe if need be."

"It won't help," the blond thrall said.

"You gutless bitch," snarled the hobgoblin with all the lash scars. "Always whining, or tattling on the rest of us."

The hobgoblin had already freed itself, and it lunged at her, swinging a length of broken chain like a morning star.

Aeron and Miri sprang forward and grabbed the goblin-kin, which, biting and thrashing, struggled madly to break free. It was surprisingly strong despite the mistreatment it had endured.

"Easy!" Aeron said. "Take it easy!"

So intent was he on restraining the creature that when the other thralls cried out, it took a split second for the warning to register.

When it did, Aeron looked over his shoulder, just in time to see the Red Axes pull the triggers of their crossbows. The weapons clacked, and he dived forward with all his strength, bulling Miri and the hobgoblin down to the ground.

The goblin-kin grunted as one of the bolts pierced its body. Aeron was unscathed. He hoped Miri was, too, but didn't have time to check on her. It was more important to assess the threat. He scrambled around to orient on the marksmen.

He saw five Red Axes, three human, one long-legged, hyena-faced gnoll, and an orc. Perhaps they'd been prowling around the city hunting him, or else some other business had called them forth from the mansion on the river. Either way, they must have heard the clank of the thralls breaking their fetters and come to investigate, entering through the gate Miri had closed but neglected to relock.

A couple ruffians reached for their quivers.

A big man with a boil on his neck shouted, "Don't shoot! That's him, Aeron sar Randal. Take him alive."

His companions obediently dropped the crossbows and readied their cudgels.

Aeron was glad of that, at least. Their reluctance to kill the one person who could lead them to *The Black Bouquet* was the only advantage he had. As he scrambled up, he plucked a throwing knife from his boot. He faked a cast at the gnoll, whose eyes widened in alarm, then he pivoted and flung the dagger at a human wearing a foppish slashed doublet and fancy sash instead. The knife plunged into the bravo's chest, and he reeled backward.

At the same moment, however, the orc lifted a tiny metal bottle, threw back its head, and gulped the contents. The man with the boil tossed what looked like a little brass toy to the ground. It scuttled forward under its own power, and as it advanced, it grew larger, swelling into a clattering metal preying mantis two heads taller than Aeron himself.

The slaves kept on screaming. He didn't blame them.

Aeron couldn't imagine a throwing blade damaging the enchanted apparatus, so retreating, he reached for his heavy fighting knife instead. That wasn't likely to do much good either, but if was the best weapon he had.

Miri shot the mantis twice. The first arrow glanced off its long, thin body. The second stuck for a second, then drooped and fell away, leaving a shallow pock mark in the brass. She nocked a third shaft, registered the foes of flesh and blood rushing in at her, pivoted, and let fly at them instead. The arrow plunged so deeply into the torso of a human Red Axe that half of it popped out of his back. The outlaw dropped.

Her next arrow flew at the orc, whose flesh emitted a sickly greenish light—a product, no doubt, of the potion it had consumed. The shaft hit the creature squarely in the neck, but simply snapped in two without even slowing its target.

The orc had figured out that the Red Axes didn't need to take anyone but Aeron alive. It still carried a long club in its left hand, but had drawn its scimitar with its right, and as it scrambled into the distance, it slashed at Miri's knee. She retreated, avoiding the cut, tossed the longbow away, and snatched for the hilt of her new broadsword.

Aeron watched it all from the corner of his eye, directing most of his attention to the metal insect mincing toward him, graceful despite its size and the clanking that attended its every move.

The mantis leaped, its long hind legs straightening explosively and hurling it through the air.

Even though Aeron had his eye on it, the move caught him by surprise. If the mechanism landed on him, the shock would break bone, and the sheer weight of it would pin him to the ground even if it didn't crush him outright. He sprang desperately backward.

Even so, the mantis crashed down right in front of him, the impact jolting the ground. Up close, it smelled of oil. Long serrated pincers opened to snatch him up.

He dodged one set of claws and riposted with a stab. The Arthyn fang grated along brass, merely scratching it. The other forelimb leaped at him, and a hand shoved him out of the way. The pincers snapped shut on empty air.

He glanced at his rescuer. It was the gaunt hobgoblin with the whip marks. The creature had a crossbow quarrel sticking in its left shoulder, but apparently wasn't too badly wounded to fight. It lashed the mantis with its chain. The construct twisted its head, evidently considering the thrall through its bulbous faceted eyes, then it returned its attention to Aeron.

It chased him across the yard, snatching for him relentlessly, occasionally dipping its head lower in an effort to seize him in its mandibles. The other slaves scurried to stay clear. Aeron thrust and hacked with the knife when he could, which wasn't often. It was hard enough just to stay out of the construct's clutches and keep it from cornering him against the fence. He supposed the lack of offense didn't much matter. As predicted, the blade wasn't doing the device any real damage, any more than was the hobgoblin still gamely flailing away at its flank.

When Aeron was facing in the right direction, he caught glimpses of Miri and her opponents, who'd spread out to attack her from two sides. The orc pressed her hard, trusting the magical elixir it had consumed to keep her blade from penetrating its flesh. For the most part, the gnoll fought more defensively, hanging back a little until it judged that its comrade had her distracted, then attacking furiously. So far, neither of them had succeeded in penetrating her guard, but her manifest skill notwithstanding, Aeron was sure she was in trouble.

She was in no more trouble than he was in himself, but the hobgoblin's attempts to save him weren't helping. It was possible the slave could aid Miri, however, so he gasped in the air to shout and tell it to go to her.

But before he could get the words out, the goblin-kin left off battering the mantis and grabbed one of its middle legs. The thrall was either trying to tear it off, use it to heave the mechanism onto its side, or simply immobilize the thing. Aeron couldn't tell which.

Whatever the hobgoblin intended, the maneuver finally served to distract the mantis. Pausing in its pursuit of Aeron, it jerked its leg, shook the slave loose, pivoted, and snatched it up in its pincers. It gave the thrall a shake, then flipped it across the yard to slam into the front of the shack, after which the hobgoblin sprawled motionless.

Though the goblin-kin's effort had failed, perhaps it had given Aeron a chance. While the mantis was concentrating on its other foe, he dashed around to the back of it, the end it typically carried so low it nearly brushed the ground. Without hesitation, he clambered straight up its narrow body, the years he'd spent scaling sheer walls and traversing treacherous ledges and rooftops allowing him to maintain balance and traction on the slippery, rounded surface.

He straddled its neck like a rider sitting a horse. While he stayed there, he hoped, it couldn't reach him with either its claws or mandibles. Looking down, he saw a gap where the head connected to the body. He jammed his knife into the crack, and when that had no appreciable effect, he threw his weight against the blade, prying as if it were a lever.

The mantis pitched sideways, and he realized that if he remained where he was, it was going to roll on him. He leaped clear, and landed hard. Metal crashed. Numb, half stunned, he forced himself to his feet, and the apparatus did, too.

Flinging itself to the ground had damaged it. One side was dented, and its left forelimb protruded at an angle. Still, it pounced at Aeron as agilely as before.

As once again he fled before it, he struggled not to give way to outright panic and despair. There had to be a way to stop it. Once Nicos had resigned himself to the fact that his son meant to follow in his footsteps, he'd taught him that if only a thief kept his head, he could think his way around any danger.

And so, dodging, panting, gasping for breath, his heart pounding, Aeron strained to think, and eventually something struck him. Two Red Axes were dead. The orc and gnoll were fighting Miri.

Where is the fifth one, Aeron thought, the heavyset man with the boil? Why isn't he battling alongside his comrades and the mantis?

Once Aeron looked, it was easy enough to spot the fellow, even though he was standing well back from the action. The ruffian was simply gazing fixedly at his quarry's struggle with the metal insect . . . because he was controlling the contraption with his mind? Aeron had spent enough time with Dal and Burgell to know it was possible.

It was a long dagger cast to the Red Axe, but he doubted the mantis would let him get much closer. He dodged its next attack and snatched out a throwing knife. The brass insect pivoted, cutting off Aeron's view of his target, so he sprinted to bring the man with the boil back into sight.

Thanks to the delay, the Red Axe had plainly spotted the new weapon, for he stood poised to duck or dodge. Aeron cocked his arm and flicked his wrist, faking a cast to make Kesk's henchman move. The bravo jumped to the left, and Aeron truly threw the blade, leading the target slightly. The man with the boil was committed to his useless evasive action. He couldn't arrest or change it, and the flat, leaf-shaped Arthyn fang plunged into his chest right up to the handle.

Aeron sensed motion above him. He looked up at a pair of grasping claws and jumped back just in time to avoid them. Pincers clashing and gnashing, the mantis lunged after him, and sick with terror and hopelessness, Aeron thought he'd guessed wrong. It didn't matter that he'd killed the outlaw with the blemish. The apparatus would keep attacking on its own.

Then, however, he saw that it was hesitating between advances and attacks—slowing down—until, after a few more seconds, it froze into immobility with a final metallic groan.

Aeron would have liked nothing better than to stand still and catch his breath, but when he glanced around, he saw that Miri's plight was as difficult as before. Accordingly, he transferred the big Arthyn fang back into his primary hand and charged across the yard. He bellowed to draw the attention of the orc and gnoll. Or rather, he tried. The sound came out as more of a bleat.

Still, it worked. The Red Axes faltered in their attack and glanced around. Miri tried to take advantage of the opportunity that afforded her. She lunged, her arm straight, the broadsword extended to pierce the towering gnoll's guts. She almost scored, too, but the canine-headed creature must have glimpsed the motion from the corner of its eye. It wrenched itself back around just in time to parry with the sturdy brass-headed cane in its off hand, then it chopped at her head with a falchion. She turned the stroke with her steel buckler. Metal rang.

Foam flying from its muzzle, the gnoll snarled something in its own yipping language. Aeron couldn't understand it, but the orc must have, because it immediately turned to face him. The sheen of its warty flesh made his eyes ache and his stomach queasy. It reminded him of the way he felt on those rare occasions when he drank enough to make the world spin around.

The orc feinted a cudgel jab at his face, and when he lifted his arm to block, it swung its scimitar at his leg. Evidently it trusted that it could cripple him without killing him outright. Caught by surprise, Aeron still managed to recoil in time. Then, before the Red Axe could come back on guard, he sprang in close and thrust the Arthyn fang at its ribs.

The blade screeched and glanced away, tearing the orc's tunic and shirt, but not the skin underneath. The Red Axe threw its arms around him and clasped him in a bear hug, meanwhile gouging at his throat and face with the tusks jutting upward from its lower jaw. For some reason, it trusted that wouldn't kill him, either, or else in its excitement, it had forgotten the object was to take him alive.

Whatever it had in mind, Aeron was sure he had only seconds to break free before it blinded him or flensed the flesh off his skull. He wrestled frantically, holding its boar-like teeth away, trying to loosen its grip, grimly certain that most of the tricks he might ordinarily have tried in such a predicament—a head butt, biting, a knee to the groin—wouldn't deter the magically armored orc. It strained to fling him down beneath it onto the ground. Aeron could feel his balance going, and with a last frenzied effort, he tore himself away from it.

They both came back on guard at the same time. The orc whipped the club at his head. He ducked, stabbed the underside of its wrist, and failed to break the skin. As before, by committing to an attack, he'd merely opened himself up for the Red Axe's riposte. He had to snatch his foot back to keep the scimitar from chopping it in two.

Aeron groped for another idea. He wasn't confident of the one that came to him, but it was all he had. He ducked, dodged, parried, and gave ground while he waited for the chance to try it. He knew a few obscene taunts in the orc tongue, and gasped them out in hopes of further angering his adversary and so undermining the creature's judgment.

The Red Axe charged and swung the cudgel. Aeron lunged in close, avoiding the stroke in the process. He didn't bother to thrust out the knife in another futile attack. Instead, he dropped it to free up his hands. He shifted behind the orc and kicked it in the knee.

The assault likely would have lamed an ordinary foe. He was sure it hadn't hurt the Red Axe, but it did cost the creature its balance. The orc stumbled, and Aeron threw himself on its back and bore it to the ground.

Using his weight, Aeron fought to hold the orc down. He grabbed its neck and squeezed. It heaved and thrashed, trying to buck him off.

Once or twice, it nearly succeeded, but then its struggles grew weaker. As he'd hoped, though the potion's magic kept its flesh from being pierced or pulped, it couldn't stop Aeron from pressing its windpipe closed and cutting off its air.

Eventually the Red Axe stopped squirming. Aeron choked the orc for a few more seconds, just to be sure, then he let go. His hands ached.

"Are you all right?" Miri asked.

He turned. At some point in the last minute or so, she'd disposed of the gnoll, which lay on the ground behind her with a deep cut on the left side of its chest.

"Yes," Aeron replied, panting, "and from the looks of it, you are, too."

He rose and hurried to the fallen hobgoblin. Miri followed.

To Aeron's relief, the slave was still breathing, and though he was no healer, speaking to it and patting its hairy, big-nosed faced sufficed to restore it to consciousness.

"How are you?" Aeron asked.

The hobgoblin sat up and rubbed its head.

"I've had worse," it said. "My people are hard to kill."

"I reckon so," Aeron replied. He took out some gold and pressed it into the goblin-kin's hand. "Plainly, you have more grit than these others. Can you make sure they get to the Barony of the Great Oak before you strike out on your own?"

"I can if you get this crossbow bolt out of my shoulder."

"I'm no chirurgeon," Miri said, kneeling down beside it and drawing her knife, "but I've done this a time or two, when none was available. Let me."

It made Aeron wince to watch her cut the quarrel out. The hobgoblin, however, bore it stoically. Only its clenched jaw revealed how much it was hurting. Once Miri bandaged the puncture as best she could with strips of cloth, the former slave gave the two humans a nod, then hauled itself to its feet and appropriated the strangled orc's scimitar.

It glared at its fellow thralls and said, "What are you all standing around for? Loot the bodies and the shack. We want weapons, coin, and any clothes that aren't blood-stained. You've got three minutes. Move!"

Aeron turned to Miri and asked, "Do you feel up to wrecking another of Kesk's operations?"

"Why not?" She sniffed the breeze and said, "We've still got a while before it rains. Let's salvage my arrows, leave your mark on the wall, and move on."

Sometimes the Red Axes struck or spat on Nicos as they passed by the chair to which he was tied, but no one had made a serious, sustained effort to torture him since they'd decided he really didn't know where Aeron was hiding or where he'd stashed the strongbox. Still, it hardly mattered. His body screamed with the memory of the agony Sefris Uuthrakt had inflicted on him.

He'd thought he understood pain. It had, after all, been his constant companion since the night the master of a caravan from Innarlith caught him trying to steal a cartload of valuable rugs. Instead of turning him over to the Gray Blades, the merchant decided to mete out his own form of justice. His guards beat Nicos, then hanged him.

Miraculously, the noose didn't kill him. He dangled for hours, slowly strangling yet enduring, until friends found him and cut him down, to suffer, hobble, and silently curse his infirmities forever after. Or rather, until just then. Nicos thought that after the torment Sefris had inflicted on him, if he somehow managed to escape Kesk's mansion alive, he'd never, even in the privacy of his own thoughts, complain of his everyday afflictions again.

He must have passed out for a while, because suddenly, or so it seemed to him, the long row of windows shone with the soft silver light of a rainy morning. Despite the grime on the panes, to say nothing of his own distress, the cloudy sky and rippling river were lovely, and lifted his spirits for just a moment.

Then, her garments wet and dripping, Sefris stalked into the solar, and any semblance of peace or ease in Nicos's soul died in a spasm of terror. He hated himself for feeling so afraid, but after what she'd put him through, he couldn't help it. Toward the end, had it been possible, he might even have betrayed Aeron to make it stop.

To his relief, the monastic ignored him to focus on Kesk, slouched in his golden chair with his battle-axe across his knees and a half-eaten sausage in his fist.

"Well?" the tanarukk snapped through a mouthful of meat.

"I haven't found him yet," Sefris replied.

She ought to have been feeling a chill, but if so, Nicos saw no sign of it in her manner.

"Well, he found us," Kesk said. "He stole some of my slaves, and killed the Red Axes who tried to stop him. Hurt and robbed two more whose job it was to collect protection coin along the docks. Burned a wine shop I operated onboard a barge. Didn't even try to steal the till, just destroyed the place."

"He's sending you a message," Sefris said.

Kesk trembled, and his eyes shone red.

"That I have his father, but he can hurt me, too, by interfering with my business," said the tanarukk. "I understand. I'm not a fool. The question is what to do about it."

"The same thing we have been doing. Hunt."

"We've already seen how pitiful you are at that."

If the taunt nettled Sefris, Nicos couldn't tell that, either. She remained as calm as ever, as composed as she'd been throughout the torture and the amputation of his finger.

"Aeron only escaped me by a fluke," she said. "It won't happen again."

"So you say. I never should have trusted an outsider."

"I'm better able to handle this chore than are your underlings. You may recall that I proved that by defeating three of them at once. In any case, you still want the jewels, don't you? If so, let me break my fast and sleep for an hour or two, then I'll return to the search. I imagine we'll have Aeron in hand before we see another sunrise."

"I don't want you relaxing just yet. Have another go at the old man."

Nicos cringed, straining against his bonds. His chair rocked and bumped against the floor.

"If he had anything to tell us," Sefris said, "we would have heard it already. His only use is as bait."

Nicos prayed Kesk would believe her and relent. But everything he'd seen or heard about the outlaw chieftain suggested otherwise.

And sure enough: "I don't care if he's got nothing to say. I want to hear him squeal. I promised Aeron we'd make the father pay for the son's treachery, and so we will."

The monastic inclined her head.

"As you wish," she said as she advanced on Nicos.

Nicos fought the urge to squinch his eyes shut or twist his head away. Her fingertips wandered about his body, pressing here and there. She didn't seem to be straining or exerting any extraordinary force, yet the sensation was excruciating. Nicos prayed for her to ask some questions. That would stop the pain for at least a moment. When she didn't bother, he still cried out the lies he hoped would satisfy her. They didn't, though, and before long, he was screaming wordlessly instead.

He didn't know how long the torture continued. Long enough for him to shriek his throat raw and reduce his already ruined voice to the thinnest of whispers. In his disorientation, he didn't know precisely when it stopped, just eventually realized that at some point, for some reason, it had. He sucked in a ragged breath, blinked the tears from his eyes, and peered about. Sefris was backing away from him. By the looks of it, she meant to take up a position with a couple of the Red Axes who were loitering around.

Nicos didn't understand it. Kesk didn't, either. He glowered at the slender monastic in her robe and hood, his stare demanding an explanation.

Sefris provided one, in an ambiguous sort of way. She touched a finger to her lips, then pointed at the door.

Kesk looked where she'd bade him. For a moment, there was nothing to see, and he almost seemed to swell with impatience, then a small figure sauntered into view. The newcomer wore a dark green camlet mantle, lightweight but voluminous, and a hood like the one Sefris used to shadow her features and cover her shaved scalp. He'd wrapped a knit lemister scarf around the lower part of his face.

A law-abiding person might have thought the stranger a menacing figure, but Nicos had spent his life among folk who wore masks of one sort or another. To his eye, the newcomer, who didn't carry himself like a warrior or bravo, was, except for himself, the least fearsome person in the room. But Kesk and Sefris eyed the stranger as if they knew something their prisoner didn't, as if leery of the gold-knobbed blackwood stick in his clean, soft-looking hand. Maybe it was just a long cane, but it might also be a magician's staff. Indeed, as Nicos peered closer, the fact that the small man was entirely dry argued for the latter.

"Shall I show my face," the newcomer said, "or do you know me?"

He spoke like an educated man. Nicos didn't recognize the voice.

"I know you," Kesk growled, "and I told you to stay away. I'll handle this."

"As I recall," the stranger said, "you didn't want me to look for your rebellious hireling all by myself, for fear I'd find him, then decide to cut you out of the profits. It occurred to me, however, that if we locate him together, you won't have cause for concern. So here I am."

"What if somebody saw you come?"

"I'm wearing a disguise, and I left home stealthily, through the exercise of my Art. The same way I entered here, without the bother of persuading your guards to admit me. It will all be fine, and even if it's not, it's my worry more than yours."

"If something happens to you," said Kesk, "you won't be able to pay me."

"Nor will I should we fail to recover the prize. In that case, there won't be anything to pay for."

Nicos was still in so much pain that it was difficult to follow the conversation. Yet even so, he gradually figured out that the stranger with the cane was the rich man who'd hired Kesk to steal the coffer.

"I told you," said Kesk, "I'll find it."

"Will you? My sources inform me you can't lay hands on our quarry even when he's robbing one of your own enterprises."

Having figured out who the small man was, Nicos could think of one reason why Kesk wanted to get rid of him, and why Sefris had concealed herself among the common ruffians: The two of them had conspired against the stranger, and didn't want to give him the chance to find out.

The tanarukk looked as if the newcomer's last observation had so irked him that he scarcely cared any longer. He shuddered, and chucked away the remains of the sausage to grip his axe with both fists.

"Are you mocking me?" he demanded.

"Of course not," the stranger said, his mild, cultured voice steady. He seemed almost as unflappable as Sefris. "I'm simply pointing out that now, even more than before, it's in your best interests to let me assist you. I can think of several reasons why you'd be reluctant, but . . ."

As the man with the cane nattered on, Nicos had a sudden horrifying inspiration. He could ruin Kesk and Sefris's deception simply by speaking up.

The idea terrified him. After what he'd already suffered at their hands, the last thing he wanted to do was attract their renewed attention, let alone infuriate them.

Yet he despised himself for his dread. He yearned to defy it.

Would it do any good, though? He didn't understand enough to foresee the consequences of such an action.

He did, however, have good reason to fear that if matters continued as they were, Aeron was doomed. Apparently his son had enjoyed remarkable success in evading the Red Axes, then taking the fight to them, but it wouldn't last. A lone thief, no matter how cunning or deft with a knife, couldn't oppose Oeble's most powerful gang for long. But maybe, if Nicos sabotaged relations among the boy's enemies, his chances would somehow improve.

If so, he had to try, not only because he loved Aeron, but because it was his fault the lad was in danger. Oh, conceivably, Aeron might have become an outlaw anyway. He'd always had a taste for excitement and the tawdry life of the gutter and the Underways. Still, Nicos thought he'd sealed his son's fate by getting himself crippled. From that point onward, Aeron had become his family's sole support, and there had been no honest way for a boy so young to earn as much coin as was required.

Nicos screwed up his courage, then cried out to the man with the cane. Or rather, he tried. His throat was still so dry and raw, his voice so feeble, that it was inaudible even to him.

He swallowed and tried again. This time, he heard the frail little croak, but no one else paid any attention. In desperation, he thrashed, and the legs of his chair, bumping and squeaking against the floor, finally made some significant noise.

The other people in the room regarded him with some surprise. He understood why. Once ruffians bound, tortured, and seemingly broke a man down, they didn't expect him to do anything to assert himself thereafter. Such mistreatment typically left a victim as cowed and passive as a piece of furniture.

"Who's this?" asked the small man.

"Just someone who crossed me," Kesk said.

He didn't seem too upset that Nicos had stirred. He must not have any notion of what his hostage intended to do.

"Wizard," Nicos rasped, "if that's what you are, you have to listen to me."

"Do I?" The small man shrugged and said, "Then I'd better move closer. As it is, I can barely hear you."

Kesk's smoldering eyes narrowed. Perhaps he felt a

sudden uneasiness, an inkling that Nicos could cause him some actual inconvenience.

"Surely," the tanarukk growled, "you don't need to hear the wretch grovel for his life. I'll have somebody shut him up so we can palaver in peace."

"Don't be hasty," the stranger replied. The ferule of his walking stick clicked on the floor as he ambled in Nicos's direction. "Perhaps it would be worthwhile to hear what he has to say."

"It will be for you," Nicos said. "Kesk has sold you out. I overheard the whole thing."

The tanarukk sprang up from his seat and brandished his battle-axe at his captive.

"By the War Maker," he said, "hold your lying tongue, or I'll split your skull here and now!"

"Is it a lie?" said the man with the cane.

"Of course it is!" Kesk snarled. "Who would I sell you out to? Your rival? Why? He couldn't afford to give me as much as you promised. He definitely wouldn't pledge to make the Red Axes supreme over all other gangs in Oeble and keep the Gray Blades from troubling us ever again."

Sefris shifted just inside Nicos's field of vision, stepping so stealthily that the small man probably hadn't even noticed. Her change of expression was just as subtle. Her calm, inscrutable expression was essentially just the same as ever, yet something in her steady gaze conveyed the promise of hideous retribution if he continued on his present course.

It nearly intimidated him, but not quite. It felt too good to strike back at his tormentors, no matter what the eventual cost.

"Kesk is conspiring with that woman there." Nicos indicated Sefris with a nod and continued, "She's a Shar worshiper, a monk . . . or nun . . . whatever you call the women . . . of the Dark Moon. I imagine you know your treasure was plunder taken from one of the cult's hidden temples. They sent her to get it back."

"Liar," said Kesk. "She's just another Red Axe."

"Fair enough," said the man in the green cloak. "I suppose, then, that she wears your brand?"

"She just joined," the tanarukk said. "We haven't gotten around to it."

The stranger reached into one of the pockets of his mantle, produced a copper piece, and made it vanish and reappear like a mountebank performing on a street corner. He murmured an incantation behind his scarf, and magic sighed through the air.

"Well, now," the wizard muttered.

"What?" Kesk asked.

"I'm listening to other people's thoughts. The prisoner's. Hers. Yours."

The tanarukk jerked, as did his axe, and he said, "How dare you . . ."

"Oh, calm down. I'm the one with a legitimate grievance, because it's all true. Dark Sister Sefris is an agent of the Dark Moon, and you and she have been plotting behind my back. The only reason I'm not more upset is that you haven't yet decided which of us you truly mean to betray. I'm afraid the time has come to choose. I can't continue our arrangement until I'm sure I can trust you."

"If I decide against you, merchant, you won't leave this house alive."

"I assumed as much. You could have killed me back in my study, and you were alone then. I'm certain you, your henchmen, and the Dark Sister working together can manage the job. But I'm still willing to press the issue to see it resolved."

"So be it," Sefris said. "Kesk, I've told you what I offer. A fortune in gems, and the guarantee of future aid from a secret society feared the world over for its power and guile."

"Show me the jewels," the tanarukk said. "Show me just one of them."

"I don't have any of them on my person," Sefris said, "but they're real enough, I assure you."

"She's lying," the wizard said. "I can see it in her mind."

Kesk snorted, a nasty, porcine sound. Slobber, brown from the sausage, dripped down his chin.

"What else would you say," the tanarukk challenged, "when you're trying to turn me against her?"

"Well," said the mage, "consider this, then. I may be a scoundrel by some people's standards, but I'm not lunatic enough to worship the Dark Goddess. She is. Which of us is likely to prove more dependable?"

"I sought power," Sefris said to Kesk, "and took it where I found it. I don't believe we're so different in that regard."

"Maybe not," the tanarukk admitted.

"You differ in at least one way," said the man with the cane. "She's an outlander. She came to Oeble for *The Black Bouquet*, and when she has it, she'll leave. At that point, what becomes of any promises she made you? Why should she keep them, or spare you another thought? I, on the other hand, am like you. I live in this city. I've built something here, and will bide here the rest of my days to enjoy and protect it. That means it's in my best interests to deal fairly with you. If I don't, you can always find me to retaliate."

"That makes sense," said Kesk. "But this is twice you've tried to muck around inside my head with magic. I didn't like it either time, and I do like emeralds and ghost stones."

Leering, he lifted his axe, then suddenly pivoted and struck at Sefris.

She skipped back out of range, and the weapon whizzed harmlessly passed her. Her foot snapped out and caught Kesk in the chest. Despite the squat massiveness of him, the attack slammed him staggering backward.

"Get her!" the tanarukk roared.

The Red Axes snatched out their knives and swords and rushed in.

Nicos wouldn't have imagined that anyone could survive such an onslaught, but Sefris dodged and sidestepped unpredictably. When the Red Axes veered to compensate, they stumbled into one another's way. Somehow her hands and forearms deflected sharp steel without being cut, while her punches, elbow strikes, and kicks thudded home to stun or injure one orc, bugbear, or human assailant after another. As she fought, she gradually retreated toward the row of windows. In her place, Nicos would have done the same. It was the best escape route available.

She was nearly there when the small man reached inside his mantle, produced a silver dirk, brandished it, and chanted words of power. Another knife, this one made of blue light, shimmered into existence, floating in the air before him. At first it was so vague and ghostly that Nicos could hardly make out what it was supposed to be, but it became more clearly defined, somehow more real, by the second. Nicos surmised that in another instant, when it was substantial enough, it would fly at Sefris and attack her.

The monastic simultaneously ducked the swing of a scimitar, rattled off a rhyme, and swirled her hand through a mystic pass. The floating knife blinked out of existence like a puffed-out candle flame.

She then shifted in close to the Red Axe with the scimitar, grabbed him by the sword arm, pivoted, and flung him at the row of windows. The outlaw crashed through one of the panes and plummeted out of sight.

Kesk had been maneuvering frantically, trying to bull his way past his own men and get at Sefris. When she tossed the swordsman through the glass, she finally cleared a path. The tanarukk charged in and swung his axe. Nicos was sure that if the weapon connected, it would kill her, her sorcerous and combat skills notwithstanding. Even a warrior in plate armor couldn't have withstood that mighty chop.

Her expression as calm as ever, Sefris swayed backward like a reed in a breeze, and the stroke missed. She hooked Kesk's ankle with her foot and jerked his leg out from under him, staggering him for a moment. She used the time to scurry to the broken window, where a few triangular shards of glass still hung around the frame. She dived through the opening headfirst. Nicos assumed that, agile as she was, she managed a safe plunge into the river below.

For a second, the Red Axes and the wizard in green simply stared at the shattered window as if unable to believe Sefris had truly succeeded in escaping.

Kesk roared, "Useless! Useless, the lot of you!"

Spit flew from his mouth. His men quailed before his anger—or rather, most of them did. Sefris had kicked one skinny fellow in the head early on, after which he'd lain insensible on the floor. That one lifted himself up on one elbow and rubbed his temple.

"What?" he mumbled, drooling a little. "What happened?"

"You let her get away!" Kesk replied. "Just like Aeron! Just like *everybody!*"

He charged. The battle-axe hurtled down and split the human's pinched, petulant-looking face from scalp to chin.

The tanarukk wrenched the weapon free, spattering blood and brains in the process.

"Find them!" the tanarukk commanded. "Aeron sar Randal and that monk-bitch, too!"

Most of the Red Axes, even those still dazed or in pain from Sefris's attacks, hastily exited the room.

"It's unfortunate the monastic escaped," said the man in green, "but the important thing is that we kept our partnership from foundering."

Kesk spun around to face him and grumbled, "You miserable . . . You're supposed to be a wizard, but you were just as worthless as the rest of them."

"I'm sorry about that, but I'm not a battle mage. Just a dilettante, when you get right down to it. I don't have any experience fighting other spellcasters, whereas Sefris manifestly does. She dispelled my sending before I could, ah, *send* it. If need be, I'll do better next time. Meanwhile, we mustn't lose sight of the fact that our objective is still to lay hands on the *Bouquet*, not chase a Shar worshiper around town."

"I wish I'd never heard of the cursed book. Or you."

"You won't say that when it makes you the richest, most powerful outlaw in the Border Kingdoms. Sefris's gems were just a fantasy, but the joyous tomorrow you and I are going to share is quite real."

"It had better be." Short and burly as he was, the tanarukk only had to stoop a little to stick his wild-boar face close to Nicos's. "Now, old man, you're going to learn a lesson about speaking out of turn. What Sefris put you through is nothing compared to what I'm going to do."

Nicos was pleasantly surprised to discover that, for whatever reason, he wasn't frightened.

He sneered back at his captor, "Go ahead. It's like the Shar cultist told you. I won't have to endure it for long. My heart will give out under the strain."

Kesk backhanded Nicos across the face. But only once, then he wrenched himself away.

CHAPTER 12

I keep worrying about the hobgoblin," Miri said.

Aeron asked, "How's that?"

He scanned the crowd in the street ahead. Many folk had covered up their heads against the drizzle, which made the task of spotting Kesk's henchmen more difficult. Still, it appeared that all the people in the immediate vicinity were law-abiding sorts scurrying off to their jobs, and that made sense. Most of Oeble's outlaws slept in the morning. In fact, Aeron looked forward to doing the same, but he and Miri had one more stop to make first.

"Will the creature really help the other slaves run away," she said, "or will it betray them? It is goblin-kin, after all. I'm sure it has no love for the civilized races."

Miri had stayed awake as long and worked as hard as Aeron, but she still seemed relatively fresh. It was as if the rising of the sun, which generally made him yawn, had infused her with fresh vitality.

He snorted and said, "Goblin-kin. Of course. I bet your fingers were just itching to shoot the creature, and never mind that it risked its neck to help me fight the mantis."

"I didn't say it was inconceivable that it would keep its word. Nor do I relish killing, whatever you think. I certainly took no joy in shooting your friends."

"I'm sure you didn't," he said sardonically.

They swung around a mule-drawn wagon heaped with bags of flour, the product of one of the mills upriver.

"I didn't," she insisted, "and . . . I'm sorry I didn't try to rescue your father when the Red Axes were kidnapping him. I shouldn't have let Sefris talk me out of it. It's this place. It makes me doubt my instincts. It even makes it hard to know right from wrong."

He shook his head in puzzlement and asked, "Is Oeble truly so much fouler than other towns?"

"You've never visited another?"

"Not a big one, just little villages hereabouts."

Miri took a long stride to avoid stepping in a puddle.

"Well," she said, "Oeble is the worst I've seen. I'll admit, though, I've never visited a city that didn't make my skin crawl. They all have their dirt, crowds, and stenches. That's why I'm a scout."

"Because cities spook you?"

"Because as a ranger, you spend most of your time in the parts of the world that are worth living in: forests, mountains, rivers, the prairies, and the sea."

He grinned and said, "Without a soft bed or a mug of beer to be had for leagues in any direction."

She smiled back.

"You don't miss easy living once you lose the habit," she said. "Not that I ever had it much, growing up on a little farm on the edge of the wilderness. Haven't you ever wanted to roam, and see wonders you could never even have imagined?"

"Everything I want is right here in Oeble."

It was true, but just for a moment, Aeron wondered whether he might discover something more to desire if only he opened up his eyes.

Ombert Blackdale's thick-built brownstone drum of a tower came into view around the next bend, and the sight banished the peculiar, wistful thought from his mind.

"That's it," he said, pointing.

Miri peered at it and said, "I don't see any sentries."

"I don't either, yet, but Ombert will have somebody keeping an eye out. He always does. Not that it matters."

"True, considering that we're proposing to serve ourselves up to him on a platter."

"You know," Aeron said, "you don't need to come inside. I can do this by myself."

"I'll stick with you."

"To help me fight my way out again if necessary?"

"That, and to keep you from deciding our alliance is a mistake, and skipping out the back door."

He chuckled and said, "You're finally learning to think like somebody who belongs in Oeble."

"That's an insult, but I'll let it pass."

They headed for the tower and climbed the three steps to the entrance, a high, arched oaken panel with a smaller door, scarcely taller than waist high, inset in the larger one. Aeron clanked the wrought iron knocker up and down, and they waited.

After a time, Miri said, "Maybe they decided they don't want any part of our problems."

"Or maybe," Aeron replied, "they need a couple minutes to ready their trap."

She scowled and said, "If you actually think th—"

The full door swung open, and a stocky man with waxed, upturned mustachios frowned out.

"Get inside," he grunted

Aeron stepped through, and Miri followed. Beyond the threshold was a gloomy, windowless anteroom.

"Now give me your weapons," the stocky man said.

"I'm here to see Ombert Blackdale," Aeron replied. "He knows me. We've pulled jobs together."

"He knows who's come calling," said the tough, "and he told me either to collect your blades or send you on your way."

Aeron sighed. He hadn't expected to win that particular argument, but it had been worth a try. He handed over all his Arthyn fangs except for one throwing knife he was currently carrying strapped to his forearm beneath his sleeve. By itself, it was a slim defense, but better than nothing.

Glowering, plainly not liking it one little bit, Miri surrendered her sword, bow, quiver, and dirk. The ruffian hung everything on a pegboard, then led the visitors deeper into the tower. His heart pounding, Aeron waited for other outlaws to rush out at them.

They didn't.

The inhabitants of the well-kept, lavishly furnished spire eyed the newcomers speculatively, but made no effort to interfere with them. Most of the folk who were still awake were smaller even than gnomes like Burgell, smaller than many human children, and that was as Aeron expected. The Lynxes were notorious for being Oeble's preeminent halfling gang, though they did occasionally recruit a representative of another race. Like Kesk, they'd invited Aeron once upon a time, but unlike the tanarukk, hadn't taken offense when he declined.

The stocky ruffian led the visitors up a flight of stairs. The climb felt awkward, because the risers were too low and shallow for long human legs and feet. Still, Aeron managed the ascent without stumbling. At the top, they found the leader of the Lynxes seated at a halfling-sized table tucking into a breakfast substantial enough for a giant.

Ombert Blackdale had the straight, shiny raven hair, luxuriant sideburns, and pleasant features characteristic of his kind. In his case, a round face and a sprinkle of freckles contributed to the general appearance of amiability. Despite the short sword lying ready to hand among his silverware and fine porcelain crockery, he scarcely looked the part of an outlaw chieftain, but anyone familiar with Oeble's criminal element could attest to the fact that he was almost as dangerous a felon as Kesk, though he lacked the latter's instinct for sheer viciousness.

"Good morning, Aeron!" the halfling called. "Who's your friend?"

"Miri Buckman of the Red Hart Guild," the ranger replied.

Ombert frowned and asked, "The same guide who killed Kerridi and the others?"

"Yes," Aeron said, "but I can't afford to care about that right now."

"If you say so," Ombert said with a shrug. "They were your friends. Welcome to the both of you, then. Will you join me? I like a good breakfast before I turn in, and I think Cook made enough for a couple more plates."

The twinkle in his blue eyes said he understood very well that the kitchen had prepared enough eggs, toast, ham, bacon, and slices of apple and melon to feed a dozen.

Aeron hadn't eaten since the start of the previous night, and the steaming food both looked and smelled appetizing. He opened his mouth to accept the invitation, and it occurred to him: What if something was drugged? That would explain why the Lynxes hadn't tried to overwhelm him and Miri by force of arms. They knew an easier way to take them prisoner.

Yet he'd decided to gamble on Ombert. Otherwise, he and Miri wouldn't be there at all. It made no sense to go that far, then risk offending the halfling by declining his hospitality.

Accordingly, Aeron said, "Thanks, we could use a meal. I'm afraid these cloaks are wet . . ."

"Toss them anywhere," Ombert said. "Someone will come around to clean up after us."

The little chairs were hopeless for full-grown humans. Aeron realized that he and Miri would do better sitting or kneeling on the floor. She looked entirely comfortable in that attitude. He supposed scouts were used to taking their meals without the benefit of any sort of furniture.

The food was delicious, and nourishment seemed to push back his weariness a little. That was good. He wanted his wits sharp for the conversation to come.

Ombert let his guests eat in peace for a while, with only the clink of their forks on their plates to break the silence.

Eventually he said, "Well, my friend, it seems you're the most popular man in Oeble. Everyone is looking for you."

"Including the Lynxes?" Aeron asked

"Of course," Ombert said, his voice as serious as could be. "When I clap my hands, a net will fall from the ceiling." Miri glanced upward, and the halfling grinned. "I'm joking. The tanarukk is offering a considerable bounty, enough to tempt most anyone, but I'm inclined to let the Red Axes do their own dirty work."

Aeron said, "I was hoping you still hated him."

Ombert smiled, but his eyes were cold.

"Hate's such an ugly word," said the halfling. "Let's just say that he and I have been trying to pick many of the same plums for quite a while now."

"As I recall, he made a couple attempts to kill you."

"I survived, and sent a warning. It's old news now. Let's talk about your adventures. What was in the lockbox you stole?"

Aeron saw no point in giving that particular piece of information away.

"I don't know," he said. "It's warded, and I haven't been able to crack it."

"If you don't even know what it is, then why didn't you hand it over to Kesk as agreed? It's not like you to break a deal."

"Kesk knew the box would be well protected. He didn't warn me, and Kerridi, Dal, and Gavath died. What's more, the Red Axes were planning to murder whichever of us survived the job."

"So no one could trace the coffer to them. Fair enough, that certainly relieves you of any obligation. Though it doesn't explain why you're running around with the same guard you robbed in the Paeraddyn."

"Kesk took my father hostage," Aeron said.

Ombert frowned and said, "That's a breach of the code, as I see it. Nicos was one of us in his time, and always dealt fairly with his fellow thieves. He earned the right to live safely in his retirement."

"When has Kesk ever truly cared about the code?"

"You have a point."

"Anyway, Miri offered to help me rescue my father. In return, I'll give the strongbox back to her."

Shifting his gaze to the scout, Ombert arched an eyebrow.

"Wouldn't it be easier just to knock this rascal over the head when he isn't looking," the halfling asked Miri, "tie him up, then torture the location of the coffer out of him?"

Miri glared at him and said, "I gave my oath."

"Of course," Ombert said. "Forgive me, I meant no offense. So, it's the two of you against the Red Axes and all the lesser gangs who truckle to them. I'm afraid you're still facing some long odds."

"You Lynxes could improve them," Miri said, "by joining forces with us."

"Why," said the halfling, "would we do that?"

"If you hate Kesk," she replied, "this is a chance to spite or maybe even kill him."

"Outlaws don't prosper by indulging such passions,"

said the halfling. "The successful ones concentrate on gold and silver."

"If that's the case," Miri said, "the man to whom the lockbox rightfully belongs will reward you."

"How much will he pay?" Ombert asked. "Enough to warrant risking my entire operation in another blood feud with the strongest gang in Oeble? It seems unlikely."

Miri drew a deep breath, evidently to calm herself, then said, "Look. You spoke of following a code. Well, if the coffer doesn't reach its proper destination, a good many innocent folk will suffer. Lord Quwen and the people of Ormath need the gold the sale of it will bring."

Ombert poured himself some tea from a silver pot.

"I've never been to Ormath," he said, "but I've heard tell of the place. The proudest, most warlike city on the Shining Plains, ready to attack its neighbors at the twitch of a cat's tail. If they're currently enduring hardship, perhaps they brought it on themselves."

Miri blinked. Plainly, Ombert's knowledge of faraway lands had taken her by surprise.

She pressed on: "Let's talk about Oeble, then. I can't tell you what's in the strongbox. It's not my secret to give away. I will say that in the right hands, it can bring prosperity to a good many folk."

Ombert waved his hand in a vague gesture that took in the spacious room, the gleaming table setting with its bounty of food, the thick carpets adorning the hardwood floor, and the vivid tapestries on the walls.

"Oeble's prosperous already," he said.

"For you reavers," Miri answered. "But how many other folk suffer as a result of your killing, stealing, and slaving? How many rot in poverty because they're too honest to join one of the gangs? It doesn't have to be that way. Given the proper opportunity, Oeble could make its gold lawfully."

"Which doesn't sound like nearly as much fun," Ombert said, and he shot Aeron a wink.

"It would be healthier," Miri said. "The rest of the Border Kingdoms scorn Oeble for the nest of robbers it is. Someday, one of your neighbors is going to clean it up. In other words, conquer, rule, and exploit you to suit themselves. Unless you mend your ways."

Ombert added milk and sugar to his tea.

"Mistress ranger," he said, "you have some interesting notions. But I must tell you, I don't aspire to be a god or even the Faceless Master, and I'm not prepared to take responsibility for the welfare of every wretch in Oeble. I have enough to do just looking after my own followers. And as for the threat of someone marching into town and taking over, well, I'll deal with it when and if it happens. The Gray Blades have never managed to stamp out the Lynxes, and I doubt that an outlander garrison would fare any better."

Miri scowled and said, "Then you won't fight alongside us."

"No," Ombert said, "certainly not. Aeron should have known better, even if you didn't."

"I did," Aeron said.

The halfling eyed him quizzically and asked, "Then why did you come to see me? Surely this isn't just a social visit."

"Naturally," Aeron said, "you aren't going to wage open war against Kesk simply for my sake, or my father's. It's not in your interest." To his surprise, Aeron felt angry at Ombert, as if Miri's extravagant fancies about duty and honor had infected his own practical thinking. He strained to quash the irrational feeling. "But there is a way you can help us and yourself, too."

"I'm listening."

"Miri and I have been raiding Kesk's various operations," said Aeron. "You can do the same. Steal his profits and destroy ventures that compete with your own. Kill the Red Axes responsible for controlling particular pieces of territory, then move in yourself. You won't ruin Kesk, but you'll weaken him, and improve your own position."

"How does that differ from declaring all-out war?"

"It's different if you make it seem like I'm the one doing all the damage," Aeron replied. "That way, it doesn't come back on you."

"No, but rather on you," said the halfling. "However this business with the coffer turns out, Kesk will never forgive you."

"It's already too late to worry about that. I just need him driven crazy, and all the Red Axes running around town hunting me even more frantically than they already are."

Ombert shrugged and said, "In that case, I agree to your proposal, and I pray the Master of All Thieves will receive your spirit kindly when the half-demon sends it into Shadow."

By midday, the rain had stopped, and the sun had broken through the clouds. As she prowled the streets, Sefris rather wished it were otherwise. A good many people were wandering around enjoying the warm golden light, and it would be inconvenient if someone recognized her as the same woman who'd killed two Gray Blades and worked dark magic in the vicinity of Slarvyn's Sword.

She suspected she might have done as well to stay in her hideout until dusk, for after all, her quarry had likely gone to ground. Yet once she'd slept for a couple hours, she found it impossible to linger. She was too impatient to take up her errand once again. Her seeming lack of progress evoked an unaccustomed feeling of frustration.

As the arcanaloth had promised, Miri had led her to Kesk, who had in turn brought her into contact with Aeron. Then, however, everything had gone wrong. The thief had eluded her, the wizard in green had subsequently turned the Red Axes against her, and as a result, she was more or less right back where she'd started.

But obviously she couldn't let it rest there, couldn't fail the Lady of Loss and the Dark Moon. Born a slave in Mulhorand, Sefris had suffered the abuses of a master and mistress who used her cruelly. Finally she escaped their household, only to discover a life in the streets—picking through rotting garbage in search of edible scraps, freezing on cold nights, selling herself for coppers—that was equally terrifying and degrading. It was then that she truly learned to hate the world, to recognize all its bright promises of freedom and happiness for the lies they were.

When the order of the Dark Moon recruited her, it rescued her from want and squalor, and cured her of fear by teaching her to kill. But even more importantly, the Lady of Loss gave her disciples the assurance that the vileness of creation would one day dissolve into the purity of oblivion, and it was that knowledge that truly sustained Sefris. She thought that without it, she might have lost her mind.

She knew that every errand she completed brought universal obliteration a small step closer, albeit generally in a way no mere mortal could comprehend. Such being the case, she'd never allowed herself to fail, and never would.

But how was she to proceed? She'd considered summoning the arcanaloth again, but experience had taught her it was generally pointless to seek a second such consultation on the same problem. The spirit likely wouldn't have anything new to tell her.

She could stand watch over one of the markets full of smuggled and stolen goods, brothels, gambling halls, mordayn dens, counterfeiter's lairs, or other enterprises the Red Axes still had running. Kesk had given her a list.

But the odds of intercepting Aeron at any given one of them were slim. He simply had too many to choose from, and wasn't likely to strike before nightfall anyway. In the meantime, one of the Red Axe sentries might spot her lurking about. Ordinarily, she would have pitted her trained aptitude for stealth against their vigilance without hesitation, but she didn't know what magical devices the wizard might have supplied to heighten their natural abilities.

After some consideration, a vague instinct prompted her to visit those locations Aeron had already raided. She didn't know what she might discover there, but thought it would be easy enough to find out. Spread thin, the Red Axes were unlikely to mount much of a guard over a place the red-bearded thief had already attacked.

She hadn't learned anything at the blackened ruin of the floating wine shop. The place had burned down to the waterline. She could only hope the slave market off Dead King's Walk would prove more instructive. As she made her approach, she scanned the busy street for signs that someone was keeping an eye on the place. If so, she couldn't tell it from outside the high fence all a-bristle with nails.

She marched up to the entrance as if she had every right in the world to do so, and no one paid her any mind. The gate was locked, so she whispered a charm of opening. For a split second, she stood in cool shadow, as if a cloud has passed before the sun. The latch clacked, yielding to the magic.

She slipped through the gate and pushed it shut behind her. The hinges squeaked a little. Before her, the enclosure was deserted. Peaceful. At first glance, only the splashes of dried blood and discharged crossbow bolts on the muddy ground gave evidence of the violence that had erupted there the night before.

Well, those and the taunting "A" chalked in bold white strokes on the roof of one of the low, unwalled slave kennels. Sefris surmised that Aeron sar Randal didn't know how to write his name, but could manage his initial.

Once satisfied that none of Kesk's minions was going to leap out and attack her, Sefris prowled around examining the ground. She found the broken fetters and the hammers and chisels the thralls had used to strike them off. On the ground nearby were the distinctive tracks the brass mantis had made as it hopped and scuttled about. The rest of the scene was a muddled confusion that only a ranger might have deciphered.

Sefris felt irritated with herself for even trying. Suppose she could read the tracks. Suppose she could follow the course of the battle from the first flight of quarrels to the final knife thrust. What difference would it make? This was all just a waste of time.

She started to turn to go, and a pang of intuition spun her back around, just in time to glimpse movement inside the window of the tumbledown shack at the back of the yard. Somebody had peeked out at her, then ducked back down under cover, but not quite quickly enough.

Probably just a Red Axe with the good sense to be leery of tackling Sefris by himself. That meant he was no threat at present, but since she and the gang were overt enemies, she saw no point in leaving him alive to get in the way later on. Sefris extracted a chakram from its pocket, charged the shed, and sprang through the doorway, hands poised to deflect a missile or blade.

But it wasn't a weapon that assailed her. Rather, a shrill scream pierced her ears. Huddled on the floor in the far corner, a young woman with an upturned nose and straw-colored hair squinched her eyes shut and shrieked again and again.

The blonde seemed to be rather comely, though it was hard to tell with her features contorted, tears streaming down her cheeks, and snot glistening on her upper lip. She had shackle galls on her ankles, but otherwise appeared relatively free of bruises, scars, or other signs of abuse. She looked well fed, too. Sefris knew what tender young female slaves had to do to earn soft treatment, and felt a surge of contempt directed in equal measure at the wretch before her and the child she herself had been.

The feeling was a distraction, and she stifled it with practiced ease. Viewed properly, the blonde was despicable, but no more so than any other created thing. Which was to say, she was of no importance except as a potential resource to further Sefris's mission.

Assuming the thrall knew something of significance, how best to extract it? Ordinarily, Sefris would have opted for threats and torture, but the blonde was already frightened beyond the point of hysteria. It seemed unlikely that heightening her terror would render her any more coherent. So, distasteful though it was, the monastic rearranged her features into the same sympathetic simper she'd worn while drifting about with Miri.

She tucked the chakram away, crossed the grubby one-room shack with its few sticks of rickety furniture, and kneeled beside the slave. The blonde cringed away from her gentle touch.

"Easy," Sefris said, "I'm not going to hurt you."

The thrall sobbed.

"Really," Sefris added. She took the blonde's chin between her thumb and forefinger and turned her averted face until they were eye to eye, compelling the other woman to take note of her own compassionate expression. "I'd never hurt a slave. I was a slave myself, once upon a time."

"I'm not a runaway!" wailed the thrall.

"It's all right. I'm not a slave catcher, and I'm not interested in returning you to your master."

The blonde said, "I have to go back. What else can I do? But they'll blame me. They'll whip me to death."

She was afraid to seize the opportunity Aeron had given her and even try to be free. The realization gave Sefris another twinge of disdain, even though she knew that, ultimately, liberty was as foul as bondage or any other condition or thing to which one could put a name.

In any case, if all the thrall cared about was escaping punishment, then that was the lever Sefris would use to pry some sense out of her.

"If you mean to return to your master," the monastic said, "then maybe I can put in a good word for you. Help you convince him it wasn't your fault."

The blonde snuffled, "You'd do that?"

"I follow the Broken God, and he teaches us to help those in need. The only thing is, I won't be able to persuade another of your innocence until I myself understand exactly what happened. I mean, you say you didn't want to run away, but you did strike off your leg irons."

"All the other slaves were doing it. I was afraid they'd hurt me if I didn't let them break my chains, too. I went off with them for the same reason, but sneaked away as soon as I could. By the time I got back, though, some more of the masters were already here, loading the dead bodies into a wagon. They'd seen everyone was gone, me included, so I was scared to approach them. I hid until they drove away, then came into the shed to try and figure out what to do."

"Well, that explains it to some extent," said Sefris, "but you'd better tell me the whole story from the beginning. How did the red-bearded man get inside?"

"He rang the bell. Or she did, the woman who was with him. When Master Durth went to answer, the man shoved through and clubbed him."

Sefris nodded. Durth, the half-orc Aeron had knocked unconscious but left alive, had only a cloudy memory of the attack, but thought he recalled a woman. The ruffians the thief had ambushed along the docks likewise had a vague impression that Aeron hadn't acted alone, and it certainly seemed unlikely that he'd defeated five Red Axes and an enchanted construct unaided. Sefris had already concluded that he'd found an accomplice foolhardy enough to stand with him against the gang.

"Master Evendur came out to see what was going on," the thrall continued, "and the man and woman killed him. Afterward, they fetched the tools to strike the chains off, and told us to run away. I said it was madness, but nobody would listen to me."

"Then the other Red Axes—the masters with the big metal insect—came to investigate the noise?"

"Yes. I thought that then, everything would be all right. I didn't have my shackles off yet, so they wouldn't punish me. But the man, the woman, and Yagan—a hobgoblin, one of us thralls—killed the masters. The man threw knives. The woman shot arrows, then fought with a broadsword and buckler. Yag—"

"Hold on," Sefris interrupted. A sudden suspicion took hold of her. It was ridiculous, of course. The world was full of archers, and even if it wasn't, no one but a magician or highly trained monk could have survived the fall from the top story of Aeron's tower. Still, she had to ask. "This woman. Was she a good shot?"

The blonde cocked her head as if puzzled by the question, but answered willingly enough, "She never missed."

"Describe her."

"Tall and slim, with curly brown hair chopped off short. She had on leather armor, and when she went into the shed, and the lamplight caught her, I saw it was dyed green."

Sefris felt astonished. She'd never been more certain of a kill, yet she had no doubt it was Miri the thrall had seen. Somehow, the guide was still alive and had joined forces with Aeron. If Sefris had examined the Red Axe corpses and recognized the arrow punctures for what they were, she might have suspected sooner.

Yet what sense did it make? She assumed Aeron's goal was to put so much pressure on Kesk that the tanarukk would be willing to undertake a fair exchange of Nicos for *The Black Bouquet* in order to put an end to the harassment. Miri presumably still wanted to deliver the formulary to whoever had bought it from Lord Quwen. How, then, could they possibly work together?

When the answer came to Sefris, she couldn't help smiling a fleeting but genuine smile, because it solved her problem. She didn't need to scour the city looking for Aeron. She knew where he'd turn up sooner or later.

Her companion cringed from the momentary change in her expression.

"What is it?" whimpered the thrall.

"It's fine." Sefris rose. "You told me what I needed to hear."

"Are you leaving?" asked the blonde. "You said you'd help me. Please, take pity on me."

"No," Sefris said. "Shar teaches that nothing in the world deserves our pity, neither others nor ourselves."

Still, what she was about to do would be mercy, the only true mercy any being ever received. It was the thrall's good fortune that her deliverer didn't want her repeating their conversation to the Red Axes.

All it took was a simple front snap kick. The ball of Sefris's foot slammed into the blonde's delicate chin, breaking her neck. She was dead before her yellow-haired head touched the floor.

Despite the ease with which she'd managed it, Sefris found the kill particularly satisfying. She wasn't sure why.

CHAPTER 13

Aeron peered at the crack between the wide double doors, then lightly pressed one of them with his palm.

"Can you open it?" Miri whispered.

She looked odd, and it wasn't the olive pigment they'd both smeared on their skin to make themselves resemble half-orcs. He couldn't see the color amid the darkness of the narrow cul-de-sac. Rather, it was the absence of a bow, quiver, and her distinctively dyed armor, which had seemed as much a part of her as her hands and feet.

"No," he said. "It doesn't have a lock for me to pick, just a bar on the other side. However, the place does have a skylight."

He prowled along the warehouse wall, looking at a spot where the brick was cracked and pitted enough to provide some decent handholds. When he found it, he swarmed upward onto the slanted roof, where a night breeze wafted. The cool air felt strange on his newly shaved chin.

It was easy to work a knife between the skylight and frame and pop the latch. The hard part would come after he slipped through. It was a thirty-foot drop to the floor. He'd had good luck lately surviving long falls relatively unscathed—it was about the only good fortune he'd enjoyed—but it would be mad to risk another unnecessarily.

In other circumstances, he would have lowered a rope, but even if he'd had one, he wouldn't have been able to leave it hanging down for someone to discover. So he gripped the protruding underside of a rafter. Clinging by the sheer strength of his fingers, Aeron inched along it until he could swing himself over the railing onto the loft that ran around the walls.

He found the long hooked pole used to manipulate the skylight and swung it closed then skulked down the stairs. The warehouse was more empty than otherwise, a testimony to Imrys Skaltahar's ability to move stolen goods quickly, but stacks of crates sat here and there, providing places to hide.

Aeron unbarred the door, and resecured it once Miri slipped inside.

"How in Fury's Heart does this Skaltahar scoundrel get in and out?" she asked, peering warily around the interior of the building.

"I imagine he has a private tunnel connecting the warehouse to the Hungry Haunting."

She considered a pile of boxes shrouded with a drop cloth, then gave him an inquiring glance. He nodded, and they crouched down behind it. After that, they had nothing to do but wait.

It wore on his nerves, and maybe on hers as well, because eventually she whispered, "Nothing's happening."

"It will. Here in Oeble, thieves move loot through the Underways whenever possible, but some things are just too big and heavy to drag around below ground. They have to go through the streets, and the Red Axes make a delivery to Imrys around this time every fifth day."

"How do you know?"

Aeron just grinned.

"All right," she said, "but are you certain they won't postpone it? After all, they're looking for you, and trying to protect all their various enterprises, too. If the halflings are raiding them as promised, they should be feeling all the more inclined to pull in and stay safe."

"You'd think. But a gang chieftain like Kesk has to keep his operation running and the coin flowing, if only because otherwise it would make him look weak. He can't afford that. He's got rival organizations, the Gray Blades, and ambitious underlings all eager to strike at him if they think they see an opening."

"That makes sense, I suppose." She was silent for a time then said, "Was I completely foolish, hoping Ombert would help us just because it's the right thing to do? He said you rogues have a code."

"It's not the same kind your guild evidently holds to. It doesn't say you have to put your own hand on the chopping block to help out somebody else. It just says outlaws are supposed to deal fairly with one another." He smiled ruefully and added, "Even so, we break the rules when it suits us."

"I'd be ashamed to tell people my name if I were content to live like that."

He wasn't sure she'd aimed the barb specifically at him, but even so, it stung.

"You're so sure you know right from wrong," he said, "but you work for this Lord Quwen, and according to Ombert, the bastard loves war. Maybe he's going to use the gold he makes off the *Bouquet* to launch another campaign against his neighbors."

"He's not! He told me himself, it's to provide food and shelter for folk in need, just as, here in Oeble, the book will give a good many laborers a chance to live both comfortably and honestly."

He grinned and asked, "Do you believe everything people tell you?"

She glared, but before she could retort, a hitherto concealed trapdoor in the plank floor swung upward, and she had the good sense to fall absolutely silent.

A lantern in one hand and a scimitar hanging at his hip, Imrys Skaltahar climbed into view and closed the hatch. Oeble's preeminent receiver of stolen goods was a square-built man with dark, watchful eyes. Time had stolen much of his hair, etched lines in his face, and begun to tug the flesh under his jaw into dewlaps, but he still had the lithe tread of the young bravo he'd started out as. He was simply but well dressed in an indigo buffin tunic and leather breeches.

Imrys started drifting about, idly contemplating this heap of plunder or that, pulling the lid off a crate to look at the ivory tusks inside. Aeron's mouth went dry. Somehow, when he'd conceived the plan, it hadn't occurred to him that the fence might simply wander through the warehouse until he inevitably stumbled upon the intruders.

Aeron assumed that together, he and Miri could overpower Imrys, but that wasn't the point. Any confrontation would ruin the plan, and even if matters were otherwise, he had no desire to raise his hand to a man who'd always treated him relatively well.

Fortunately, before it could come to that, someone rapped on the door. Imrys unbarred it, and a wagon, drawn by a white horse and a black one, rolled inside. Tharag the bugbear held the reins, and an orc cradling a crossbow served as guard.

Imrys shut the door behind them. After the three exchanged a few words, the Red Axes hopped down and unloaded some barrels from the back of the cart. From the ease with which they accomplished the task, it was plain the kegs were empty.

They had to shift them, however, to more easily raise a hidden hatch of their own. The wagon bed was hollow, deeper than it looked, and held the actual shipment: cloth bundles that clanked or clattered when they lifted them out and set them on the floor.

Imrys crouched to unwrap one, and a pungent scent of oil filled the air. Inside were gleaming sword blades. Evidently nobody had sharpened them yet, for he had no difficulty flexing one without cutting his hand. Poking with his index finger and muttering under his breath, he counted them, then turned his attention to the next bale, which proved to contain spear shafts.

Tharag and the orc looked on as Imrys conducted his inspection, responding, as best they were able, to the fence's shrewd observations regarding short counts and deficiencies in workmanship. Aeron was grateful to the older man for keeping the Red Axes occupied. It was the only reason his plan, which, since the moment had come to try it, looked harebrained even to Aeron, had even the slightest chance of working.

He gave Miri a nod, and they glided forward, keeping low, using every available bit of cover. He was glad she moved as silently as any burglar he'd ever known. He supposed rangers had to master stealth to stalk game and goblin-kin through the woods.

Imrys liked to cook for the patrons of his tavern, and was renowned for his tangy stews. Aeron's path led him nearly within arm's reach of the fence, so close that the scent of spice clinging to Imrys's hands and clothes tickled his nose, and for a moment, he was afraid he was going to sneeze. He didn't, though, and he and Miri reached the wagon without anyone looking up. Nor did the draught horses, stolid beasts of burden that they were, do anything to give them away.

Aeron managed to crawl into the cramped interior of the wagon bed without making noise. Miri did almost as well, though once, when she'd squirmed most of the way in, the tip of her scabbard softly thumped the wood. Aeron winced, but Imrys and the Axes didn't react.

Aeron and Miri lay in the claustrophobic space like corpses in a coffin built for two, and he wondered how they could defend themselves if discovered. He'd just about concluded it would be impossible when Imrys completed his inventory and declared exactly how much he was willing to pay.

Tharag objected in a desultory fashion, even invoked the threat of Kesk's displeasure, but then accepted the offer. The fact was, even the Red Axes found Imrys too useful to risk alienating him over an everyday sort of transaction.

And to a thief operating outside the gangs, the fence's good will was all but indispensable. If Imrys ever found out Aeron had used him as an unwitting tool in a quarrel with Kesk, the consequences could be severe. Yet with his father's life in jeopardy, and schemes for rescuing him in short supply, he hadn't seen another choice.

Tharag laboriously counted Imrys's coin, and the orc slammed the hatch shut without looking inside. The boards above Aeron's face groaned a little as the Red Axes reloaded the empty casks. Then, axles creaking, the wagon began to roll. The wood was hard against the thief's back, and felt harder still when the cart's progress bounced him up and down.

Miri's voice murmured from the darkness, softly enough that the Red Axes wouldn't hear it over the noise made by their horses and conveyance, "Suppose they don't bother to unload the barrels when they get back to the mansion. How are we supposed to climb out of here without jostling them around and making a lot of noise?"

"I don't know," Aeron answered. "I knew about the trick wagon, but I kind of forgot about the kegs."

"How clever of you."

"We'll manage, all right? If you don't like this idea, what was your cunning plan?"

She was quiet for a moment, then said, "I'm sorry. You're right. Barrels or no, this is a better scheme than any I was able to devise, and I shouldn't find fault."

"Well, I'm glad I didn't have to attempt it alone, and glad you know how to creep. You have the makings of an able cutpurse or housebreaker."

She snorted and said, "Thanks so much. I imagine someone could make a passable woodsman of you. If you were willing to stop depending on all those little knives and invest the time and effort to learn to use real weapons."

"I guess if I learned to draw a bow, I could kill people from a long way off, when they had no way of fighting back."

"I told you, I took no joy in shooting your friends."

"I know," he said with a sigh. "You were only doing your job, and they knew the risks. I just miss them, is all."

"I understand. I've lost my share of comrades."

"Who knows, maybe I've already lost my father, too. He's frail. If Kesk tortured him the way he said, he may have killed him without even meaning to."

Groping in the blackness, Miri found his shoulder and gave it a squeeze.

"Don't dwell on such thoughts," she said. "Focus on practical matters: how to accomplish the task at hand, and what to do after."

"Right. Once we get him out, he'll probably need a healer. We can take him to Ilmater's house, but I don't think he or I should spend another night there. When someone's after you, it's often safer to keep moving around. I have one more person I trust. Her name is Naneetha Dalaeve, and—"

"And she owns the Talondance," finished Miri, in the tone of one reluctantly delivering bad news. "She gave up your name to Sefris. It was how we traced you to your garret."

"Shadows of Mask, why would she do that?"

"It's not important. What matters is that your friendship is no great secret, and if someone could make her betray you once, the same thing could happen again. If I were you, I'd find somewhere else to hide, or another way to be safe. Let me help you with that, too."

"You mean, you'll ask the same rich bastard I robbed in the first place to protect me?"

"By all accounts, he's an honorable per—"

" 'By all accounts,' " Aeron broke in. "You've never even met him, have you?"

"Well, no, only his representatives, but . . ."

"Thanks, anyway, but Father and I will take our chances on our own. You just keep your mouth shut about exactly who stole the *Bouquet*, or helped you recover it, for that matter."

After that, the conversation lagged, and Aeron felt a black mood coming on. Even sweet, unworldly Naneetha, who doted on tales of chivalrous heroes and pure damsels faithful unto death, had sold him out. It was even more of a shock than Burgell's treachery.

But Miri was right, it was not the time to brood about it. He struggled to shake off the hurt and concentrate on his immediate concerns, on how he and the scout would locate Nicos, then escape Kesk's stronghold alive.

The wagon accelerated and slowed, turned periodically. Aeron found it impossible to judge how much time had passed or how far the conveyance had traveled since the Red Axes drove it out of the warehouse. His discomfort and trepidation made it feel like hours. Finally, though, the cart rumbled to a stop. He listened as, judging from what he could hear, Tharag and the orc climbed down from their seat and unhitched the horses. After that, everything was quiet.

"Now?" Miri breathed.

"A little longer," he replied.

He counted off twenty heartbeats, then squirmed around until he could reach the catch that held the hidden panel down.

Even working blind, it was child's play to pop it open. When he raised the hatch, however, the barrels on top slid, toppled, and clunked hollowly together. He'd expected it, but scowled at the noise even so.

He'd only raised the panel a few inches. Plainly, if he shoved it all the way back, the casks would fall and bang around even more.

"Hold this," he said.

Aeron dragged himself out through the narrow gap. When he got his feet under him and looked around, he discovered he was in Kesk's stable. Horses and mules eyed him from their stalls, but no Red Axes were in view. Evidently the kegs hadn't made enough of a racket to attract attention.

He held the hatch for Miri while she wriggled free. She pointed to a door that apparently led to the main body of the mansion. He gave her a nod.

The interior of the sprawling house was gloomy. Only a few of the lamps were burning, and due to the mild autumn weather, most of the hearths were cold. Still, enough light shone for even human eyes to make out the dirt and other signs of neglect, and naturally, the dimness did nothing to cover up the smell of mildew.

Neither Aeron nor his father was much of a housekeeper. That had been his mother's province until she passed away unexpectedly in her sleep, worn out, perhaps, by worrying over her son's embrace of the outlaw life and her husband's infirmities. But then again, he'd never lived anywhere fancy, and his own slovenly habits notwithstanding, he still felt a twinge of disgust at Kesk for letting such a palace gradually crumble into ruin.

But what mattered was that the mansion was quiet. Aeron knew it wasn't deserted. The tanarukk wouldn't have left his coffers of gold and stores of loot and contraband entirely unguarded. But from the sound of it, most of the Red Axes were off hunting Aeron, or standing watch over their various interests throughout the city, and that meant his scheme might actually work.

"Which way?" Miri whispered.

He shook his head and replied, "I've never been inside here before. They could be keeping my father anywhere. We'll just have to look."

They skulked on, keeping to the shadows, cracking open doors to check the rooms on the other side. The damp river air had warped some of them, making them stick in their frames, and the intruders had to force them open. The resulting squeaks and rasps jangled Aeron's nerves.

They didn't raise an alarm, however, and as the minutes passed without calamity, Aeron started to feel the old familiar thrill. He was still frightened for Nicos, and for himself, come to that, but it was nonetheless a delight to outwit his opponents in the game a burglar played, to trespass where he wasn't allowed and do what wasn't permitted.

In time, he and Miri found a staircase leading down to the cellars.

"Maybe the Red Axes have their own little dungeon," the scout suggested.

Aeron thought about it for a second, listening to the same instincts that had led him to many a hidden cubbyhole or closet filled with valuables.

"It's possible," he said, "but they wouldn't need to lock my father in a cell to keep him under control. Feeble as he is, a bit of rope would do the job, and I reckon Kesk would prefer to keep him close by. That way, he could hurt him whenever he felt the urge, without the bother of tramping up and down stairs."

"So we need to find where Kesk spends the majority of his time."

"Which will be the most lavish part of the house."

They prowled on, and in time caught sight of a wide marble staircase sweeping upward. Partway up, a bravo sat on one of the steps picking something out of his shaggy, tangled beard. At the top, tall double doors, inlaid with a stylized scene of a river, boats, leaping fish, and spindly-legged wading birds, stood open.

Aeron and Miri retreated back into the shadows before the Red Axe could spot them.

"That looks like it could be it," the ranger said. "If you'd let me keep my bow. . . ."

Perhaps he should have, but it was too uncommon a weapon in Oeble. It had marked her almost as well as her green leather armor.

"You still couldn't count on picking that fellow off without him making some noise," Aeron said. "Maybe we can find a back way in. A big room in a rich man's house is likely to have at least two doors, one for the masters and one for the flunkies."

She gave him a nod and said, "Lead on."

It didn't take long to find the servants' stairs, spiraling up and down in a claustrophobic shaft. The risers were narrow, the way all but lightless, and the trapped air was stale. Aeron wondered how many maids and valets had taken a nasty tumble back when the house was young. He caught his first glimpse of the chamber at the top, and it drove such casual speculations from his mind.

The long hall was a solar, one wall a continuous row of windows intended to admit sunlight and provide a panoramic view of the Scelptar. Nicos sat tied in a chair, his eyes closed and his head lolling. His chest rose and fell, reassuring proof that he was only unconscious, not dead. In fact, apart from the mutilation of his hand, he didn't look as badly injured as Aeron had expected.

Unfortunately, the prisoner wasn't alone. The big gilded chair in which Kesk no doubt liked to sit was currently vacant, but Tharag, the orc who'd accompanied the bugbear to Imrys's warehouse, and a human outlaw were hanging around. Moreover, one of the glass panes had shattered, and a small man with a wool scarf masking the lower portion of his face stood before the breach, evidently because it afforded a clearer view than the cracked, filthy windows that remained intact. Gazing through a brass astrolabe, he alternately scrutinized the night sky and scratched his observations on a slate. A green mantle and gold-knobbed blackwood cane rested on a little table beside him.

Aeron wondered if the astrologer was also a magician, and had supplied the Red Axes with the metal mantis and potion of invulnerability that had nearly cost him and Miri their lives. If so, he was likely to prove more clever and dangerous than the common ruffians.

Miri tugged on Aeron's arm, and they sneaked back down the steps a little way, where they could whisper without fear of being overheard.

"How fast can you throw your knives?" she asked.

"Not fast enough to kill four men before one of them yells for help. I think it's time to test these disguises."

She stared at him as if he'd gone mad. Maybe he had.

"I figured that at best, they'd only work at a distance," the ranger said. "I mean, I've seen half-orcs. We don't look right."

"Close enough, maybe, if no one peers too closely," Aeron replied. "A disguise is half attitude and the way you carry yourself. We have the advantage that the Red Axes never expected us to sneak in here. I'm sure of that much. Besides, if they recognize us, and we wind up having to fight, it won't be any worse than if we started out that way."

"Yes, it will. We'll have lost the advantage of surprise." She frowned and continued, "Still, Nicos is your father, and it was your tactics that got us this far. If you're sure you want to try it this way, I'll follow your lead."

"Thanks. Let me do the talking."

They climbed back up the stairs, making no particular effort to do so quietly. The risers creaked.

When the Red Axes glanced in his direction, Aeron felt a split second of panic, of certainty that the greenish pigment on his skin, the black dye in his hair, and the absence of his goatee wouldn't fool anyone. He slouched on into the room anyway, praying that his cowl cast his features into shadow. Kesk's operation was large and varied enough to make it unlikely that all his minions knew one another well, but it was possible they'd all laid eyes on one another at least a time or two.

Aeron grunted one of the orc greetings he'd picked up over the years then ambled to Nicos with Miri following along behind. He crouched beside his father's chair and started untying him. The old man came awake with a start.

"Hey!" Tharag said. "What are you doing?"

"What's it look like?" Aeron replied in his best imitation of a surly goblin-kin voice.

He kept his head bowed over his work.

"It looks like you're undoing the rope," Tharag said.

"I knew you could figure it out if you strained hard enough," Aeron replied. "Look, Kesk's sick of having the old man up here all the time. He wants us to stick him somewhere else. You don't think we're going to carry him and the chair, too, do you? Not as long as he can walk."

The hulking bugbear blinked its green, red-pupiled eyes and asked, "Kesk's back?"

"He couldn't give orders if he wasn't, now could be? He said he'll be up here in a minute, soon as he checks something that came in through the Underways."

The last knot yielded, and Aeron jerked Nicos to his feet. Miri grabbed hold of the hostage's forearm, and they wrenched him around toward the servants' door.

For a couple of steps, no one protested, and Aeron felt a surge of exultation that he and Miri were actually getting away with it.

Then a mild baritone voice said, "Please, hold on for just a moment."

It had to be the astrologer. No one else in the room would speak in that educated accent. For want of a better idea, Aeron and Miri ignored him and kept on moving.

"Excuse me," said the man in the scarf, raising his voice a little.

Brilliant white light blazed through the room. Startled, the Red Axes shouted and cursed. The intruders spun around, only to discover they didn't need to defend themselves. The flare of light had been simply that, not a sign they were under mystical assault. Not yet. It had been a warning the wizard could attack them if they refused to heed him.

"What?" Aeron growled.

"Do any of you fellows know these two?" the small man asked. "Look closely."

At some point over the course of the past couple minutes, he'd tossed his cloak over his shoulders and picked up his cane.

"We rob travelers along the river," Miri said, making her voice coarse. "We don't get into town much."

"That may be," said the magician, "but I'm going to ask the same thing of you that I did of Dark Sister Sefris. Show me your brands."

Aeron pulled back his sleeve to display the false scar he'd shaped from crimson candle wax.

"Nice," the wizard chuckled through his lemister scarf, "but not quite convincing enough. You're the man himself, aren't you? Aeron sar Randal, even bolder than your reputation led me to believe. I thi—"

Aeron whipped an Arthyn fang from its sheath and hurled it at the arcanist's chest. The knife hit the target, but clanked and rebounded. The small man had some magical protection in place that kept it from penetrating.

A crossbow bolt streaked at Miri. She shielded herself with her buckler, then turned to face the human Red Axe, who was charging her with a dagger in either hand. He drew her broadsword and cut in a single motion, ripping open the outlaw's belly. His knees buckled, and he dropped.

"If you Red Axes have any of my talismans or elixirs," the astrologer shouted, "use them!"

He backed away, putting distance between himself and the intruders.

It was evidence the whoreson wasn't entirely impervious to harm, but Aeron was more interested in getting away than in trying to hurt him. He considered a leap out the broken window, but feared Nicos wouldn't survive the fall into the river, and that even if he did, he couldn't manage the frantic swim for safety afterward.

He shouted, "Down the stairs, Father! We'll follow."

Nicos spat an obscenity. Plainly, frail as he was, it still irked him to flee while other folk risked their lives to cover his retreat. But he tottered backward as quickly as his weakness allowed.

No doubt drawn by the commotion, the Red Axe with the long, matted beard appeared in the doorway at the far end of the hall. Half concealed behind Tharag, the wizard chanted, and swept whatever it was he held between thumb and forefinger through a mystic pass. Standing closest to Aeron, Miri, and Nicos, the bugbear and orc gulped the contents of tiny bottles.

Aeron threw a knife at Tharag. The creature wrenched himself sideways, and the blade pierced his forearm instead of his chest. A painful wound, perhaps, but it wouldn't stop the creature. An instant later, Tharag's body swelled, becoming bigger and likely stronger than an ogre's. His clothing and gear grew with him, though for some reason, Aeron's dagger didn't. The process of enlargement shoved it out of the wound to fall and clank on the floor. Tharag raised his cudgel, bellowed a battle cry, and rushed the human who'd hurt him.

Huge as the bugbear was, his head nearly brushing the high ceiling, he seemed as terrible an opponent as the brass mantis. Aeron was sure he lacked the strength to parry a blow from the heavy club, so he dodged the first vicious stroke instead. He told himself it was just possible that, by drinking the potion, Tharag had outsmarted himself. At his present size, the Red Axe wouldn't be able to pursue his foes down the servants' stairs.

Nicos cried out in dismay. Hard-pressed though he was, Aeron risked a glance over his shoulder. A mesh of slimy gray cables, sticky enough to adhere to the walls, floor, and ceiling, sealed the entrance to the narrow steps, as if a gigantic spider had spun a web there. Obviously, the man with the blackwood cane had conjured the strands to cut off the intruders' retreat.

Miri and the orc circled one another near Kesk's throne. The Red Axe opened its mouth wide and seemingly spat out its own tongue. The pink flesh flew through the air, meanwhile stretching into a cord a dozen feet long. It slapped and whirled around the startled ranger's legs, yanking her off balance and binding her to the heavy chair. The orc sprang at her with its short sword leveled to pierce her belly.

Aeron wanted to rush to her aid, but it was impossible. He didn't dare ignore his own opponent. He hastily faced forward, and Tharag swung the cudgel down like a man splitting wood. Aeron dodged. The weapon clashed against the floor.

Maybe Aeron could hamstring the goblin-kin before he could lift the stick for another stroke. He sprang in close, only to find that Tharag had anticipated the move. The bugbear's boot lashed out at him.

Aeron tried to dodge, but the brutal kick still struck him a glancing blow. That was enough to smash the breath from his lungs and send him staggering. As he did, he caught a glimpse of Miri, still alive but still bound as well. The orc was trying to stab her from behind, and she was only barely able to twist around far enough to fend him off.

Snowballs pelted her. Plainly, it was another conjuration, one that looked almost comical, though it was evident from the way she jerked that the white barrage inflicted actual pain. The orc lunged, and once again she managed to turn its blade with her buckler. Her riposte, however, was a feeble, fumbling action easily avoided. In fact, it looked like she almost lost her grip on her broadsword.

Nicos had picked up a bronze cuspidor to use as a makeshift bludgeon, then limped to intercept the Red Axe with the unkempt whiskers. The old man had been a formidable brawler in his day, but it was obvious from the way Nicos moved that, without sufficient strength or agility to back them up, his rusty skills no longer posed a threat. The Red Axe thought so, too. Leering, he advanced with his guard lowered, daring Nicos to strike at him.

Two more ruffians appeared in the far doorway.

Tharag rushed in. Aeron flailed his arms and recovered his balance just in time to dodge the next sweep of the bugbear's cudgel. It was hard to imagine it mattered. He, his father, and Miri might last a little while longer, but the Red Axes were inevitably going to prevail.

CHAPTER 14

Perched atop a gabled slate roof overlooking Kesk's mansion, Sefris peered down, watching for Aeron and Miri while munching on a cold toasted roll with a greasy sausage-and-apple filling. She'd brought food and a canteen because she'd known she might have to remain at her post for hours before the red-bearded thief made his play. Indeed, it was possible that Aeron wouldn't try to rescue Nicos at all, but Sefris considered that unlikely. He'd be eager to retrieve the old man before the Red Axes snipped off any more pieces.

She was certain that, after confusing the gang with raids throughout the city, Aeron meant to invade their stronghold. No other plan would give Miri a reason to work with him. The difficulty was predicting how the pair would try to enter a building theoretically accessible from the Scelptar, at ground level, and via the Underways.

After some thought, Sefris had ruled out the river. Kesk had found and patched the breach in the portcullis defending the water gate, and anyway, it was unlikely that Aeron would attempt the same approach twice. The Underways also seemed an implausible choice. She'd seen that the passage connecting the cellars to the lawless tunnels was well fortified, and Aeron surely had some inkling of that. That left advancing up the street and across the yard. Kesk undoubtedly had a sentry on watch, and kept his doors and windows locked. But Aeron would trust in his ability to avoid detection by the former and tease open the latter, for after all, it was his trade.

The lawns and gardens surrounding the mansion were overgrown and weed infested. Slinking about just after sunset, Sefris had cast spells of warning on the best hiding places. If a second intruder used those choice bits of cover to sneak up on the house, she'd sense it. Then she climbed up on top of a neighboring building to wait.

In time, another watcher's attention might have wandered, but her teachers had trained her to suppress boredom as efficiently as any other emotion. She gazed down at Kesk's residence as patiently as a python hanging in a tree waiting for prey to happen along beneath.

Yet even so, she almost missed the light, for it was just a momentary flicker at the periphery of her vision. By the time her head snapped around toward the north and the river, it was already gone.

She wondered what the pale radiance had been. The moon, peeking momentarily from behind a cloud? No. The sky was clear that night, and Selûne, her Tears, and the stars had shone brightly right along. It must have been magical, then. Firelight wouldn't be so white, nor could it blaze and die so quickly.

Maybe a priest or sorcerer out sailing, or on the far shore, had cast a spell that kindled a momentary glow. But she wondered about Kesk's employer. The last time she'd seen the wretch, it had been in the solar on the opposite side of the house. Suppose he lingered there still, and his magic had produced the flare. The light could have pulsed out the long row of windows and reflected off the surface of the river.

Maybe, but even if the masked wizard had used his art, it didn't have to be because he was engaged in a confrontation with Aeron sar Randal. Sefris strained, listening for shouting, the clash of blades against shields, or some other sign of strife. All she heard was the constant murmur of the city around her.

Still, over the course of the next minute or so, she felt a growing certainty that somehow Aeron and Miri had slipped past her and into the house. Either they'd free Nicos and make their escape, or more likely, the Red Axes would kill the scout and take their fellow outlaw prisoner. However it worked out, it could result in *The Black Bouquet* passing beyond Sefris's grasp forever.

That was unacceptable. She'd hoped to capture Aeron before he had a chance to enter the mansion, not make another foray into a place she'd fled with some difficulty the night before, but she saw no alternative. She sprang off the edge of the roof, snatching and releasing the irregularities in the wall to slow her plummeting descent.

When she hit the ground, the impact jolted her but did no real harm. She rolled to her feet and charged the house. Given a choice, she would once again have skulked up in hopes of remaining undetected, but she felt speed was more important.

Nobody shouted or sent a quarrel or sling stone flying in her direction. She was certain Kesk routinely posted a sentry, but if she was right, if something was happening inside the house, perhaps it had already diverted the guard's attention.

The primary entrance was a pair of massive double doors. Neither their solid weight nor the intricacy of the lock would have hindered her spell of opening, but she begrudged even the moment it would take to stop and recite the incantation. She raced up the wide steps, leaped into the air, and thrust-kicked at the juncture of the panels, attacking it as if her entire body was a battering ram.

The doors bucked in the frame, and something crunched. Sefris rebounded and fell onto the porch. She scrambled to her feet and kicked a second time. The two leaves flew apart.

As she sprinted on, she heard the clamor that had been inaudible from outside. Sure enough, it was coming from upstairs. She smiled slightly to know she'd guessed correctly, and two ruffians scrambled out of a doorway up ahead. Evidently they were rushing toward the noise as well, but faltered when they spotted her.

While a tolerated guest, Sefris had taken the trouble to learn the floor plan of the mansion. Thus, she knew the bravos were blocking the shortest route to the solar, and likewise knew she needed to clear them from her path. Considering that they were still several yards away, magic might have been the safest way to go about it, but she'd already wasted a measure of her power creating the alarms her quarry had somehow bypassed, and she wanted to save the rest to address more serious threats. So she simply charged.

One Red Axe threw a dagger at her. He had a good eye, and it would have plunged into her heart if she hadn't slapped it spinning off course. She responded in kind with a backhand flip of a chakram. The razor-edged ring sheared into his neck, and he fell. Blood spurted from the wound to spatter his companion.

The second outlaw winced but stood his ground, a slim needle of a thrusting sword cocked back in one hand and a parrying dagger extended in the other. Maybe he fancied himself a duelist, for his stance, spine straight and knees flexed, bespoke some formal training in the fencer's science. Sefris kept on charging, one cestus-wrapped fist raised and threatening a punch. Confident that proper timing and the length of his blade would protect him, he'd almost certainly respond to her seemingly reckless advance with a stop hit.

He did. He stepped backward, and his point leaped at her breast. She dropped underneath it, smacked down on the floor, and still carried along by her momentum, slid at him feet first. She kicked at the proper moment, bone cracked, and the duelist went down with a shattered ankle.

It was unlikely he'd give her any more trouble, but Sefris saw no reason to chance it, not when it would take only a split second to finish him off. She scrambled onto his chest, crushed his windpipe with a jab of her stiffened fingers, leaped up, retrieved her chakram, and ran onward.

Nobody was on the marble staircase. Judging from the muddled racket issuing from the top, all the other Red Axes who'd remained in the house had already reached the solar. When she charged up the steps and peered into the hall, she saw that the situation was just about as inconvenient as it could be.

Along with Miri and Nicos, Aeron was at the far end of the room, up by Kesk's chair. The only way to keep him out of the Red Axes' hands and wring the location of *The Black Bouquet* out of him herself was to kill her way through a dozen or so gang members and the wizard in the green cloak, too.

So be it, then. At least Kesk's henchmen were all facing away from the door. That would give her a brief initial advantage. She sprang into the solar and punched, breaking a hobgoblin's spine. The tall, hairy creature needed to fall first to give her a clear toss at the small man. She'd already concluded he was no seasoned combat wizard—he was too hesitant and miserly with his magic in a fight—but he was still the most dangerous opponent in the room.

She was just about to fling a chakram when she glimpsed movement at the edge of her vision. She pivoted. Sewer Rat rushed her, clawed hands extended to rake. After the trouncing she'd already given it, the stunted, green-skinned savage should have known better, but maybe it ached to avenge its earlier humiliation.

She sidestepped out of the meazel's way, cracked its skull with an elbow strike as it blundered past, and returned her attention to the wizard. He'd spotted her and was jabbering a spell at her. Futilely. He wouldn't finish in time.

She hurled the chakram. It hit the mage in the forehead and bounced away. He bore an enchantment to shield him from missiles.

Even so, the mere fact of a blow to the face would have startled many a spellcaster into botching his conjuration. The small man, however, maintained his focus. He spoke the final word, and a ragged fan-shaped distortion, like hot air rippling over pavement on a torrid summer day, shot from the head of his cane.

Sefris tried to dodge, and nearly made it. The edge of the magic grazed her, however.

It didn't make her feel any different, and for a second imagined it hadn't affected her at all. Then she perceived that the wizard was backing away with an implausible quickness. In fact, everything—Aeron's battle with a gigantic bugbear, Miri's clash with an orc, the other Red Axes maneuvering to close with one foe or another—was scuttling and jerking around more rapidly than before.

Sefris realized that wasn't actually so. It just looked that way to her. The man with the cane hadn't sped the rest of the world up. He'd slowed her down.

Had the enemy allowed her a moment, she probably could have dissolved the enchantment with a counter-spell, but suddenly, or so it seemed to her, other Red Axes were rushing her. A dagger slashed at her eyes. From her perspective, the blade came in as fast as if one of her teachers was wielding it, and she nearly failed to duck. She riposted with a punch to the jaw, and the outlaw jerked out of the way.

She flowed into one of the combinations her instructors had drilled into her, following up with a blow to the ribs. The Red Axe didn't dodge that one. Her knuckles smashed bone. He stumbled backward and fell on his rump.

But already two more Red Axes, one human, the other a slavering, hyena-headed gnoll, were spreading out to flank her. She realized that, in her present condition, she could no longer count on simple trained reflex to snatch her out of harm's way. She had to read their stances and predict how and where each attack would come.

It looked like the gnoll would cut to the head and the human would try a low-line thrust, and when they pounced at her, it was so. She evaded both attacks and retaliated with a snap kick to the knee that crippled the goblin-kin. Unfortunately, that gave the remaining cut-throat time for a second stab, and she couldn't pivot fast enough for a clean, fully effective block. She kept the dagger out of her lung, but it pierced her forearm, grating on bone before ripping free.

It didn't hurt, not yet, and wouldn't until she allowed it to. Mere force of will, however, wouldn't stop the bleeding or the weakness it would eventually produce. She realized she was genuinely in trouble.

Aeron crouched before Tharag, and when the enormous bugbear swung its club, the rogue lunged forward, safely inside the arc of the blow, and swept his Arthyn fang in an overhand stab at the creature's stomach. The point plunged through magically thickened layers of tanned horsehide armor and clothing to pierce the Red Axe's flesh.

Tharag roared in rage and snatched at Aeron with his off hand. Aeron ducked and stabbed a second time. The bugbear lunged forward, trying, apparently, to knock his foe down and trample him. Aeron sprang aside, and Tharag lurched past.

In the instant it took the Red Axe to spin back around, Aeron had his first chance to survey the entire room in . . . he realized he had no idea how long. He'd lost all track of time trying to contend with Tharag.

Miri was still alive. Indeed, she was faring better than the last time he'd taken note of her situation. She looked as if she'd shaken off the shock of the snowballs, and at some point had managed to chop through the coil of pink flesh that had bound her legs to the chair. She stood facing both the orc and the bravo with the matted beard, who'd already finished with Nicos. Aeron felt a pang of fear and rage to see his father sprawled motionless on the floor.

A second tongue-rope lay twitching on the floor. Evidently the wizard's elixir enabled the orc to spit more than one. But the second such attack had failed to take its target by surprise, and Miri managed to dodge.

Aeron was surprised to see that Sefris Uuthrakt had appeared at the far end of the room. Something was wrong with the way she was moving, though he couldn't make out precisely what. Still, the wizard and the rest of the Red Axes had turned to engage her. Apparently they weren't all on the same side anymore.

Aeron realized that could be his salvation. It was possible that he, Nicos, and Miri could make their escape while the gang was busy battling the agent of the Dark Moon. First, however, they'd have to dispose of their current opponents, and that wouldn't be easy. It was plain from the way Tharag turned, quick and surefooted as before, that the Arthyn fang might have jabbed his skin, but hadn't reached his guts. Aeron felt as if he might as well have pricked the towering brute with a pin.

Then he thought of a ploy that might enable him to do some actual damage. Another idiot idea, perhaps, but the only one he had. He retreated toward Miri, and Tharag lumbered after him.

The problem was that he couldn't simply tell the scout what he had in mind, or Tharag would hear, too. He could only hint at it, praying she'd understand and the bugbear wouldn't.

Aeron said, "If we could trip him. . . ."

"Right," Miri panted.

A few heartbeats later, the man with the tangled whiskers feinted a cut to the leg, then lunged at Miri in earnest. She caught the true attack—a head cut—on her buckler, but to all appearances, the impact staggered her.

Aeron could only assume she was faking. He hopped backward, and Tharag compensated by taking a stride forward, into what ought to be the proper position.

Hoping to take advantage of Miri's seeming incapacity, the orc spat a third extending tendril of flesh. The guide wrenched herself out of the way. The wet, meaty strand flew past her and lashed itself around Tharag's ankles. The bugbear pitched off balance, but didn't fall.

Aeron threw his shoulder against Tharag's leg. That brought the giant crashing to the floor, and he scrambled toward its neck, where no armor protected it, and a major artery throbbed just beneath the skin.

Tharag flailed at him but missed, then was in position. He slashed, a torrent of blood sprayed, and the bugbear thrashed in its death throes.

Aeron jumped up and rushed in on the orc's flank. The pig-faced creature pivoted and parried his knife with its short sword, but in the instant it was distracted, Miri cut into its chest. It whimpered, and its legs gave way.

That left Aeron and Miri confronting the man with the beard. Aeron just had time for an instant of savage satisfaction that for once, it was the foe who found himself outnumbered.

Miri said, "Deal with him."

She turned, and dashed away.

Aeron and the Red Axe shifted in and out of the distance, feinting, striking, and parrying, neither, in those first moments, able to score. Something shattered, then warmth and a wavering yellow light flowered at Aeron's back. He surmised that Miri had smashed an oil lamp to set something on fire. The blaze alarmed his opponent, who started shouting for help.

If the Red Axe kept on yelling, some of his comrades just might heed him, too, even though, so far, Sefris was holding her own against them. Desperate to shut him up, Aeron lunged forward, inviting a stop cut. When it came, he blocked with the knife in his off hand and simultaneously drove his largest Arthyn fang into the Red Axe's chest.

It took the ruffian a moment to drop, and by that time, Aeron could feel the hot pain burning in his shoulder. His knife had been too light a weapon, or his defense not deft enough, to stop the heavy sword entirely. His parry had robbed the stroke of some of its force, but the blade still gashed his flesh.

Aeron knew he had no time to stop and examine the wound. Instead, he pivoted toward Miri and the fire. She'd set the mesh sealing off the servants' stairs alight, and the gluey cables were burning away.

"I learned to clear spider web in the Thornwood," she said, flashing him a grin. "Help me with your father."

As they dashed toward Nicos, a couple more Red Axes started in their direction.

Fine, Aeron thought. If it was a race, he and Miri would just have to win it.

He caught sight of the wizard. Standing by the windows at a reasonably safe distance from any of the intruders, the mage had also oriented on the thief and the ranger. Holding a spell focus—Aeron couldn't make out precisely what the small object was—high above his head, he recited a rhyme.

A dark blue vapor billowed up around Aeron's feet, so thickly that he could no longer see any farther than his hand could reach. Even worse, the fumes had a vile, rotten smell that instantly turned his stomach. Stricken with a nausea as intense as any he'd ever experienced, Aeron swallowed to keep from puking.

"Run!" cried Miri from somewhere in the mist.

The strain in her tone made it obvious that she too was struggling not to be sick.

"My father!" Aeron called back.

"We can't . . . find him . . . in this murk," Miri replied between coughs, "and we're too ill . . . to carry him off . . . if we could. It's over . . . for tonight."

He hated her for it, but she was right. Silently vowing that he'd come back for Nicos somehow, he tried to turn around toward the servants' stairs, only to realize he no longer knew where they were. He was so sick it made him dizzy.

He nearly panicked, then spotted a smudge of brightness that could only be the firelight. He staggered forward into the center of it. Curling wisps of burning web seared him as he brushed by.

At the moment, it didn't matter. The fog hadn't penetrated far beyond the doorway, and as soon as he clambered down out of it, his nausea abated. The relief of that rendered the sting of his blisters insignificant.

Miri stood below him on the steps. She beckoned impatiently, and they ran on down to the first floor, then onward through the house. When they reached the stairs leading down to the cellars, he swiped some blood from his shoulder wound and smeared it on the banister.

CHAPTER 15

Sefris had suffered a second wound, a gash just above the knee, by the time the fire started and the ruffian at the far end of the hall started bawling for help. A couple of the other Red Axes left off attacking her to answer the call.

She dodged a dagger thrust, grabbed her assailant, and spun him at a goblin armed with a spiky-headed mace. The outlaws fell in a tangle, and finally, for the first time since the man with the cane had snared her in his enchantment, she had time to rattle off a spell of her own.

She snatched a handful of black ribbons from one of her pockets, recited the words of power, and snapped the lengths of silk as if they were a cat-o'-nine-tails. Tatters of shadow exploded from a point on the floor to engulf the nearest Red Axes, who cried out at the insubstantial but somehow repulsive contact. They stood dazed and shaken for a few moments, and their incapacity bought Sefris even more time.

Time to dissolve the unnatural sluggishness with which the wizard had afflicted her. Crooking her fingers through the proper signs, she began the counterspell. Gloom crawled around her, the Shadow Weave responding to her call.

At the same time, she took note of the blue fog filling the opposite end of the room. Thanks to her own magical expertise, she knew what the conjured mist was. No doubt it was intended to drop Aeron and Miri in their tracks, make them too nauseated to do anything but retch, but it evidently hadn't. Sefris could hear them calling to one another inside the cloud. If they could resist the vapor long enough, they were going to flee through the far doorway.

Sefris wouldn't be able to follow without fighting her way past more Red Axes and subjecting herself to the debilitating queasiness engendered by the fog. She thought she'd be better off trying something else instead.

She spoke the final word of power. The air around her sizzled like meat frying in a pan as her own magic burned the small man's hindering spell away. She whirled, dashed out the door, and bounded down the wide marble steps.

As she ran, her wounded leg throbbed, the pain begging her to favor it. She blocked the discomfort from her mind. If she allowed herself to limp, she might not be fast enough to intercept Aeron on the ground floor.

It turned out that she wasn't anyway. When she saw the bloody mark on the banister of the cellar stairs, she realized he and Miri had scurried down them to escape through the Underways. She continued the chase through the labyrinth of storerooms and piled crates until she found her way to the exit.

It was still locked. And bolted. Even if Aeron knew a burglar's trick that would allow him to secure it fully from the other side, it was unlikely he would have taken the time. He and Miri had actually fled the house at ground level.

Which was to say the handprint had been a trick to make a pursuer believe the fugitives had gone that way. It had worked well, too. It would be futile to race back upstairs and try to pick up Aeron's trail. Even if it didn't result in another useless encounter with the Red Axes, and further delay, he'd gained too long a lead.

Sefris simply opened the inner door, then the outer one, and departed via the tunnels herself. She felt herself seething with anger, and worked to quash the feeling. Her frustration and injured pride in her own competence didn't matter, nor the pain of her wounds—only patience, resolution, and the success they would bring did.

Yet deep down, she hoped with a bitter fervor that, in the course of accomplishing her mission, she'd have the chance to slaughter Aeron, Miri, Kesk, the wizard with the blackwood cane, and everyone else who'd gotten in her way. Perhaps it was a prayer that even a deity as cold and unyielding as the Lady of Loss would grant.

A couple blocks from Kesk's mansion, Miri and Aeron climbed a rusty wrought iron ladder, the rungs tangled in ivy, that ran up a tower wall. At the top was a Rainspan. From there, they could watch for signs of pursuit. Thus far, she hadn't seen any.

She and the outlaw leaned on the railing and panted for a time, catching their breaths and waiting for their stomachs to settle. The night breeze was mild, but her clothes were so sweat-soaked that it chilled her even so.

When Miri felt able, she said, "Better let me take a look at that shoulder."

"All right."

For once, Aeron's voice was dull, not the energetic, sometimes humorous tone to which she'd become accustomed.

She ripped the rent in his bloodstained sleeve wider to get a better look at the gash.

"You're lucky," said the ranger. "It's shallow. If you think it's unsafe to go back to Ilmater's house, some salve from an apothecary and a bandage will probably take care of it. If need be, I can put a couple stitches in."

"Lucky. . . ."

From the bitterness in his voice, Miri realized he wasn't talking about the cut.

"I'm sorry the plan didn't work," she said. "It nearly did. If the wizard hadn't been there . . ."

"Even though he was," Aeron said, "we almost saved my father. Another couple paces, and I would have picked him up in my arms. Then the fog came, and it panicked us. We turned tail and left him lying there."

"We didn't have a choice."

"You can't be sure of that. Maybe we still could have gotten him out. We'll never know, because you said we had to run, and I listened."

She stared at him, then said, "So it's all the fault of my cowardice that things didn't work out."

"I didn't say that."

"Not in so many words, but . . . Listen, when we fight your fellow cutthroats, all they do is try to club you unconscious, or cut a leg out from under you. They're out to *kill* me. So I'll be damned if I understand where you find the gall to question my courage."

"I said we both panicked. I didn't mean to put it all off on you."

"I'm a scout of the Red Hart Guild," Miri replied. "I have honor. You're a common sneak thief. You don't. Be thankful I'm willing to dirty my . . ."

She felt the clench in her muscles and heard the shrillness in her voice. She took a long breath.

"Never mind," Miri continued. "I shouldn't have said that. I'm frustrated, too."

For a few heartbeats, Aeron just stared out at the night as if struggling to swallow his own anger.

Eventually he said, "For all we know, he could be dead now."

"I don't think the mist would kill him," Miri replied, "and I didn't see any fresh blood on him when he was lying on the floor. I think the one Red Axe just knocked him out with the flat of his blade, or his fist."

"That could have been enough to kill him, sickly as he is. Or maybe, after what happened, the Axes decided I'm never going to trade the book, and they stuck a knife in him."

"I doubt the wizard would let them do anything rash," said the ranger. "He strikes me as too canny."

She reached out to give Aeron a reassuring pat on the shoulder, but he irritably twisted away from her touch.

"You don't know that, either," he said. "All we do know is that we wasted our one chance to sneak into Kesk's house. We'll never get inside a second time."

"Then it's time to try it my way, isn't it? Seek help from the *Bouquet*'s rightful owner, and the authorities."

Aeron scowled and said, "I explained to you why that wouldn't work."

Despite herself, Miri felt her own hostility welling up anew.

"While painting our faces green like clowns in a pageant works brilliantly," she said. "I think you won't turn to the law just because it *is* the law. It would tarnish this notion you have of yourself as some sort of master rogue, and you couldn't bear that. You'd rather let your father die."

"That isn't true. It just wouldn't help."

"What is the answer, then?"

"I don't know," he said. "Shut your mouth for a while, and maybe something will come to me."

⊙

Kesk's mood was already sour from several fruitless hours of hunting Aeron through the Underways, and it curdled into cold fury as soon as he tramped into the solar and saw his henchmen. It was obvious from the way they quailed from his gaze, as much as their fresh splints and bandages and the sooty fire damage around the far doorway, that some new fiasco had occurred in his absence.

Ambling closer, his cane tapping the floor, the wizard took it upon himself to explain how Aeron and a female accomplice had entered the house in disguise to spirit Nicos away.

"We would have captured them," the wizard added, "except that Dark Sister Sefris burst in to snatch them away. Evidently she'd been tracking them or something. While we all fought over Master sar Randal and his ally, they escaped. It's rather ironic when you think about it."

Kesk trembled. At that moment, he would dearly have loved to split the rich man's masked face with his axe.

"You think it's funny, do you?" the tanarukk asked.

"Mildly," the wizard replied. "Now, don't glare at me like that. Aeron didn't rescue his father, which means that except for a few casualties, which you, with your horde of underlings, can readily afford, we're no worse off than before."

"And no better."

What truly infuriated Kesk wasn't the wear and tear on his henchmen. Those too weak to defend themselves deserved whatever they got. What nettled him was that, by arranging the raids on his various enterprises, Aeron had successfully concealed his true intentions. In other words, made a fool of him. Kesk wondered which of his other foes or rivals were actually responsible for the harassment his operation had suffered earlier in the evening, at the same time the redheaded thief was invading his home. He vowed to find out, and pay them back triple, but supposed it would have to wait until he settled the maddening business with the black book.

"If," the wizard said, "Aeron could be convinced we'll make a fair trade, give him Nicos and a reasonable amount of coin, too, and not come after either of them later, don't you think he'd agree to it?"

Across the room, bound to his chair, Nicos laughed feebly until an orc silenced him with a slap.

"I suppose that is the proper response to my suggestion," sighed the small man. "Aeron would have to be mad to trust us at this point. Your malice and bungling saw to that."

Kesk glared.

"Get it straight once and for all," the tanarukk grumbled. "I'm not your lackey, and I don't take orders from you. I did what I thought best."

"And look how far it got us."

"As far as your fumble-fingered wizardry and magical toys."

" 'Toys' you extorted from me after I spent years collecting them," the mage countered. "I wouldn't care if it had done some good. But even equipped with enchanted gear, your Red Axes can't lay their hands on one lone-wolf cutpurse. Instead, he's made you look like a dunce in front of the entire city."

Kesk had been thinking something similar himself, which only made the magician's taunt rankle all the more. For a second, he was so angry that it choked off the words in his throat, and the merchant saw something in his face that made the eyes above the lemister scarf widen in alarm.

"Well," gritted Kesk when he was able, "I'm not going to look foolish for much longer. Tomorrow I'm going to put an end to this business."

"How?"

"My people will spread the word that if Aeron doesn't hand over what I want by midnight, I'll chop his father's head off and dump the sundered pieces in Laskalar's Square."

The wizard shrugged and said, "You've been threatening Nicos's welfare right along. How will this be any different?"

"Because of the deadline, my promise to display the corpse to the whole city, and the fact that my men will repeat it to every robber, slaver, and whore they can find. Aeron will know I have to follow through. Otherwise, I'll lose respect."

The magician cocked his head and asked, "You mean, if things don't work out as planned, you actually mean to do it?"

"Yes."

"Then we lose our hold on Aeron, don't we? With Nicos slain, what's to stop him from fleeing Oeble with *The Black Bouquet* still in his possession?"

"Nothing, I guess. At least I'll be rid of him," Kesk replied, "and you."

"Without me for a partner, you'll never rise any higher than you have already."

Kesk sneered and said, "Maybe it doesn't look like it to you, but since the day I first came to Oeble, with nothing but this axe to help me carve out a life, I've climbed pretty high already. If I never go any farther, that will be all right."

"You don't mean that."

"Oh, yes, I do, and you can't talk me out of it. So why don't you turn that twisty mind to yours to the task of laying a trap that Aeron can't possibly escape?"

Aeron kept quickening his pace despite the fact that even under normal circumstances, it could be dangerous to race headlong through the Underways. You could blunder into a strong-arm robber lying in wait for easy prey or intrude on plotters willing to kill to keep their palavering a secret.

Thus, whenever he caught himself, he forced himself to slow down, but it was hard. After fleeing Kesk's mansion, he and Miri had slept aboard an unattended skiff moored at one of the docks. Restless, anguished over their failure to rescue Nicos, he woke first and rose to prowl the streets. It was then that he overheard a team of thieves, two pickpockets, a bag man, and a lookout, discussing Kesk's well-publicized threat to murder his hostage at midnight unless Aeron gave him what he wanted. Since then, he'd felt a seething urgency that made him want to hurry every instant, whether it was sensible or not.

"Do you really think," said Miri, striding along beside him with her bow slung over her shoulder, "our allies are likely to do more than they have already?"

"We won't know until we ask."

"Actually," said the scout, "I already did ask, when we talked to Om—their chief the first time. If you recall, he said he'd snipe at the Red Axes on the sly, but not risk open war."

Squinting against the darkness, Aeron peered down the passage. Three people stood murmuring to one another at the next intersection. He recognized one of them, and once more had to quash the impulse to rush.

"Then I'll just have to change his mind," the thief said.

"I tell you, visiting him again is just a waste of precious time. Let's go to my employer."

"We had this talk already."

The trio ahead were good at their trade. They didn't even glance up as Aeron and Miri drew nearer.

"We had it hours ago," said the scout, "and you promised to come up with a new strategy. This desperate notion won't do, and if it's all you can think of, then we need to try things my way. Fury's Heart, try behaving like a decent, law-abiding person for once in your life. You might like it."

"I might like it all the way up the gallows steps."

The loiterers were just a couple paces away. Aeron's heartbeat quickened.

"I swear by the Forest Queen," said Miri, "I'll make sure you aren't punished. My employer doesn't care about you. He only wants his property retur—"

Aeron pivoted and threw a punch.

Miri must have seen him swing, for she reacted with the quickness of a trained warrior. She dodged, and he only struck her a glancing blow.

She sprang back and reached for the hilt of her broadsword. The problem was that, by retreating from Aeron, she'd merely shifted closer to his three confederates. The largest of them, a half-orc with a broken nose, lashed its cudgel against her back. The blow slapped her leather armor, and she lurched forward.

The other two ruffians lunged at her, bludgeons flailing. She swept her buckler in a backhand stroke that held them off long enough for her sword to clear the scabbard. She cut, the half-orc recoiled, and her blade missed its torso by a finger-length. A passerby who'd stopped to watch the show cried out in excitement.

Aeron edged in on her flank, then faked a leap into the distance. She turned and thrust, and that gave the half-orc a chance to give her another blow from behind. It knocked her to one knee, and the creature's human partners swarmed over her. Her sword was useless at such close quarters. After a few moments of frantic struggling, they pummeled her into submission, then lashed her hands behind her back with rawhide.

"When I said you were learning to think like an Oeblaun native," Aeron said to her, "I gave you too much credit. You told me how one fellow led you into a trap here in the tunnels, and now you've let exactly the same thing happen again. I don't think Sefris will save you this time around."

Miri glared up at him. Blood trickled from her split lip. "Why are you doing this?" she asked.

"You can't help me rescue my father. Maybe if you had the rest of your precious guild behind you, but not by yourself. I gave you your chance, but you aren't skilled or brave enough."

"Shall we get her moving?" asked the half-orc.

"Yes," Aeron said.

His confederates hauled Miri to her feet and relieved her of her belt pouch and remaining weapons. The half-orc shoved her to set her stumbling in the right direction.

"I'm a better fighter than you," she said, still focused on Aeron. "I still don't see the point of this."

"It's simple enough. I can't trust Kesk to hold to any deal we make. You and I alone can't fight all the Red Axes, or sneak into their lair a second time. So I've decided to save my father with gold. I'll bribe one of the gang to smuggle him out."

"Maybe that would work," she said, "but . . ."

The half-orc gave her another push.

"Unfortunately," Aeron said, "the Axes are all afraid of their chief, and they live pretty well already. That means it's going to take a lot of coin to tempt one of them. More than I've got, and more than I can steal in the time remaining. I wouldn't be able to sell *The Black Bouquet* quickly enough, either, or use the book itself as a bribe. Kesk's cutthroats wouldn't understand what it is or why it's valuable any more than I did until you explained it to me."

"But you decided what you could do," Miri said, "is sell me."

Aeron grinned and replied, "I found out who wanted all

those yuan-ti to capture you, then asked him if he was still interested. It turned out he is, so we arranged the details."

"Listen to me," she said. "You don't have to do this. If you want to try bribery, I can get the gold from my employer. I won't even have to mention your name."

He shook his head and told her, "I feel safer dealing with my own kind."

"Curse you for a liar and a traitor! You have rat's blood in your veins!"

"What did you expect?" Aeron asked. "You're the one who said I'm just a common thief, with no notion what honor means."

"I didn't truly want to believe that."

"Well, believe this," he said. "Folk like you and me are natural enemies, you killed my friends, and even if none of that was true, I'd sell out you and a hundred like you to save my father. Look, it's your new home."

They marched her onward, through the entrance to Melder's Door.

Even at that hour, when so many of Oeble's rogues were snoring in their beds, the stone-walled common room held a motley assortment of travelers and waiters, and as usual, tiny dragons flitted everywhere. Most everyone, whether human, goblin-kin, or reptile, eyed Miri with curiosity, some with malicious amusement, and none, so far as Aeron could judge, with sympathy.

Smiling, handsomely clad in a red silk shirt and a black suede jerkin laced with scarlet cord, Melder sauntered up to inspect his prize. Miri spat at him, and a dozen of the little wyrms hurtled at her like bees defending a violated hive.

Melder raised a swarthy hand, and the dragons veered off.

"Please," he said to Miri. "It can all be quite pleasant, if you'll only allow it to be."

"I'll kill you for this," she said, "and even if I fail, the Red Hart Guild will avenge me."

"As your own experience demonstrates," Melder said, "your friends had better stick to their forests and mountains. Oeble will eat them alive." He looked at the half-orc. "Why don't you lock her away, then I'll pay you?"

The creature and its fellow kidnappers manhandled Miri across the common room. She struggled every step of the way, but with her hands bound, to no avail. She and her captors disappeared through a doorway.

"I'd like to get paid, too," Aeron said.

"Surely," Melder said. "Vlint?"

A hobgoblin appeared at his elbow with a clinking pigskin purse in hand.

Aeron untied the laces, lifted the flap, and stirred the coins inside with his fingertip, which afforded him a glimpse of the ones at the bottom.

"Thanks," Aeron breathed.

"I realize," Melder said, "that these days you have to be careful about lingering too long in any one place. But will you have a glass of something before you go?"

Aeron smiled a crooked smile and said, "I suppose I might as well celebrate. This was the first plan that's gone off without a hitch since before I robbed the Paer."

Sefris heard voices echoing down the tunnel, and though she couldn't make out the muttered words, instinct warned her she had cause for caution. She cast about and spotted a notch in the wall, containing a steep flight of steps that probably linked that section of the Underways to somebody's cellar. She silently hurried partway up the steps, above the eye level of anyone likely to pass below then crouched motionless in the narrow, unlit space.

Sure enough, two Red Axes tramped by. She recognized them from the time she'd spent among the gang, and assumed they were scouting the tunnels near Melder's Door for the same reason she was. They'd heard the gossip that Aeron sar Randal had visited the inn to sell his former ally to the proprietor.

It seemed unlikely that Aeron was still lingering in the area, but it also seemed inexplicable that he'd made such a conspicuous display of himself in Melder's establishment in the first place. In any case, Sefris didn't know where else to look for him, so there she was.

She crept down the stairs and onward through the darkness, in the opposite direction from Kesk's henchmen. She encountered other ruffians, some of whom eyed her speculatively. But when she returned their stares, making it clear she registered their interest without the slightest flicker of alarm, they allowed her to continue on her way unmolested.

It was difficult to keep track of time underground. Eventually, though, she became convinced she'd been searching for quite a while. Certainly she was retracing her steps through sections of tunnel she'd traversed before. Maybe, she thought, she should return to her sanctuary and consult the arcanaloth after all. Then, some distance ahead, a lanky figure stepped from a doorway. He froze for a moment as if startled to see her, which gave her a decent look at his face. Though the gloom dulled the bright copper of his hair to a nondescript gray, Sefris recognized the man she'd come to find.

She sprinted toward him. She'd tended the wounds she'd received the night before, and though her thigh ached, she was able to run as fast as ever. She snatched a chakram from her pocket and broke stride for the split second required to fling it spinning ahead of her, skimming low to maim Aeron's leg.

The ring flew as true as any cast she'd ever made. Unfortunately, however, it was a long throw, which gave

Aeron time to dodge. He scrambled onto the first riser of a staircase and on up out of sight.

When she followed him onto the steps, she realized from the wan trace of sunlight leaking down from overhead that they connected the tunnel with the outdoors. If Aeron reached the top, it might give him the chance to flee in more than one direction, or lose himself in a crowd. Resolved to catch him while he was still inside the stairwell, she ran even harder.

From above her came a sudden clatter. She was still peering, trying to figure out what the sound meant, when her sandal landed on something small, hard, and round. The objects rolled, and despite all her training, threw her off balance. She fell, caught herself, and at the same time realized that Aeron had tossed a quantity of marbles bouncing down the steps.

A good trick, but the fall hadn't injured her, nor delayed her for more than an instant. She could still catch him. She raced on.

As she neared the top of the steps, the daylight dazzled her. She squinted against it, but still missed seeing the cord her quarry had stretched at ankle level. She tripped and fell a second time.

Her wounded leg throbbed, and she suspected she'd torn open the cut. He still hadn't stopped her, though, nor saved himself. He'd simply annoyed her, which meant it was going to be even more satisfying to hurt him.

She scrambled up into a little unpaved cul-de-sac. Towers rose around her, with Rainspans linking the upper stories. To her right, a door slammed. She dashed to it and grabbed the black wrought iron handle. It turned, the latch disengaged, but the panel wouldn't push open. She had to kick it twice to dislodge the wooden wedge her quarry had used to jam it shut.

Judging by the look and stink of the interior, the spire was another of Oeble's squalid tenements, with hordes of paupers living, breeding, and dying in its tiny rooms. Aeron's footsteps thudded on the stairs zigzagging away into shadow overhead. Sefris raced after him.

She thought he'd bolt out onto one of the elevated bridges, but he surprised her. He ran all the way to the top floor, then scrambled up a ladder and through a trapdoor.

She expected him to lie in wait by the hatch, poised to knife her, and when she swarmed up the ladder, she was ready to defend herself. It wasn't necessary. What he'd actually done was retreat to the very edge of the square, flat roof, then hop up on the low parapet that ran along it.

It had to be another trick, didn't it? She looked at him and all around, but couldn't spot the hidden threat.

"You're fine," he panted. "I'm the one who's in danger. If I lose my balance, if anything jostles me, I'll fall to my death."

"What does this mean?" she asked.

"You don't think I just happened to be carrying a bag of marbles, a trip cord, and a wedge around with me, do you?" he replied with a grin. "I wanted to talk to you, so I let people see me in the Door. I figured you'd hear about it and come sniffing around. I spotted you, let you do the same to me, then used my tricks to slow you down while you chased me. I couldn't let you catch up until I led you here. You won't throw a spell or one of those rings at me now, will you?"

"What I will do is take hold of you and pull you down," she said, then started forward.

"Don't try!" Aeron called. "I'll jump, and you'll never find out where I hid *The Black Bouquet*."

She didn't believe him, but she wasn't absolutely sure she was right, and thus she hesitated. Maybe it would be safer to hear him out first, and call his bluff later if need be. It wasn't as if he could evade her. He'd backed himself into a corner.

"I don't think you want to die and leave your father in the tanarukk's hands," said Sefris.

"You're right, but I know I can't save him by myself—or working with Miri, for that matter. That's why I sold her to Melder."

Sefris frowned, trying to follow his train of thought.

"What do you mean?" she asked. "What did betraying Miri accomplish?"

"Well, I told people it was to raise the coin to bribe one of the Red Axes, but that's not practical, considering that none of them is any more trustworthy than Kesk himself. I just wanted folk to think it was the reason, so they wouldn't figure out I was getting rid of her to clear the way for you."

"Clear the way for me?"

"Yes. I can't very well work with you and Miri both, considering that you'd both demand the black book in payment, and you're the one I need. You fight better than anyone I've ever seen, and you're a sorceress on top of it. Her talents are nothing compared to yours."

"So you're offering me the *Bouquet* in exchange for my help in rescuing your father."

"And peace between you and me afterward."

"I agree."

Aeron smiled and said, "Good, except that I don't believe you yet. Maybe it's because I'm such a faithless liar myself, but it strikes me that you might promise anything to lure me into your clutches, with no intention of keeping your word."

"I swear by Shar that I will."

Some deities might object to their worshipers making false vows in their names, but the Lady of Loss wasn't one of them. She wanted her work done by any means necessary. Indeed, she relished treachery and oath-breaking to the extent that she could be said to savor anything in the vile stew that was creation.

"That's wonderful," Aeron said, an ironic edge in his voice, "but even so, I want to ask you something. How did my father hold up under torture?"

"Fairly well," she admitted.

In truth, Nicos had borne up remarkably well. After what he'd suffered, he should have been too cowed to utter a word unbidden, yet instead he'd exposed her identity to the mage with the blackwood cane.

"Remember," Aeron said, "he's old and sick. I'm young, healthy, and my father's son. I could hold out even longer. I could sit on the location of the book until it's too late. Until the cursed thing's destroyed."

She felt a thrill of dismay, and asked, "Destroyed . . . how?"

"If I told you, it might help you figure out where it is. Just take my word for it. If I don't fetch it from its current hiding place by sunrise tomorrow, that will be the end of it. Your only hope of getting it is for me to hand it over voluntarily."

"I understand," she said, and it was so.

Evidently she did have to play along for the time being, and that was all right. Eventually a moment would come when he no longer held the formulary hostage, and at that moment, she'd repay him in full for all the trouble he'd caused her.

"Good."

Aeron stepped down off the parapet. He was trying to appear confident, and it would have fooled most people, but she could read the tension in his lean frame, the fear that she was going to lunge at him. It made her wish she could.

He said, "Here's what I think we should do . . ."

CHAPTER 16

Aeron noticed a patch of fresh blood staining the skirt of his new ally's robe.

"You're bleeding," he said.

"It's nothing."

Leaning against the weather-beaten railing with its flaking paint, Sefris peered down from the Rainspan at the street fifteen feet below. Aeron hoped that to a casual observer they looked like two innocent loiterers idly chatting and watching the traffic pass under the bridge. He knew, however, that no one who took a close look at Sefris would dismiss her so lightly. In her eyes he discerned a terrifying contradiction, calmness and calculation overlying a deeper madness. Or maybe he only thought he saw it because she made him nervous.

Which in turn made him want to engage her in conversation, perhaps in hopes of uncovering human feeling in someone who superficially seemed as cold as the brass mantis, and he supposed he might as well indulge the impulse. Maybe he'd find out something useful.

"I'm surprised your cult even cares about *The Black Bouquet*. I mean, if it was a grimoire full of evil magic, I could see it, but it's just a tool for making perfume."

She glanced over at him and replied, "It's not my place to question the tasks my Dark Father sets me."

"But you must at least think about them. I can tell you're not stupid."

It took her a moment to decide if she wanted to answer.

"It takes wealth to wage war," she said finally, "and we're the Dark Goddess's army in the struggle against everyone and everything."

"So you need a lot of wealth."

"Also, when Quwen sacked our temple in Ormath, it was a defeat and an affront to our Lady. We couldn't let it stand. In time, we'll erase it fully. Wash it away with his lordship's blood."

Aeron was sure Sefris wouldn't have divulged such a thing if she thought he might live to repeat it. That simply confirmed what he'd already concluded, but he felt a chill nonetheless.

"In that case," he said, "I'm glad I'm not him."

"It has occurred to me," Sefris said, her unblinking stare becoming a shade less piercing, her tone a bit more introspective, "that it's fitting for my order to lay claim to this particular treasure. Because of the title."

Aeron cocked his head and replied, "I don't follow."

"The Lady of Loss teaches that the whole world is like a black bouquet. Parts of it are pretty, to lure the foolish, but all the flowers are poison."

Though her statement was unsettling, he forced a grin. He said, "That's a cheery point of view."

"You of all people should see the truth of it. You live in Oeble, where the folk prey on one another like starving rats, and friend betrays friend for a copper bit."

He snorted and said, "I guess we must be pretty bad at that, if our habits make a Shar worshiper squeamish."

"My point is, the rest of the world is no different. It's just that in Oeble, no one tries to cover up the essential foulness."

"Does that mean that in the big bouquet, we're stems as opposed to blossoms?"

"Mock Shar's wisdom if you want," she said. "Your opinion means nothing."

"I wasn't mocking, exactly . . ."

She pointed and said, "Look."

A few steps below street level, the door to the mordayn den opened, and three Red Axes, a pair of humans and a gnoll, emerged blinking into the sunlight. Aeron was disappointed, but not surprised. He'd assumed that none of Kesk's henchmen would roam around the city alone. The Lynxes had probably stopped raiding their competition—Ombert was shrewd enough to know he couldn't continue the harassment for long without his rivals discovering who was responsible—but the Axes couldn't be certain it was over.

"Loan me a couple of your knives," Sefris said.

"That's not the plan," Aeron answered as he started toward the end of the bridge.

She followed, saying, "If I hide, and throw daggers instead of chakrams, no one will realize I'm helping you. They'll think you made the kills."

"Just do it my way, all right?" Aeron said. "Stay well back unless I need you."

He almost wondered himself why he didn't take her up on her offer. Those past few days, his hands had run red with blood. It was probably stupid to scruple at spilling any more, particularly if it belonged to the cutthroats who were holding his father prisoner. Mask knew, Aeron had come to hate the bastards. Yet even so, given the choice, he'd manage the last part of his scheme without murder.

He slipped down the stairs that connected the Rainspan to the street, then started to shadow Kesk's men. Fortunately, the street was busy enough that he had a fair chance of going unnoticed. As he skulked along, he took inventory of his enemies' weapons. The gnoll bore a crossbow that was already cocked and loaded. Since it could strike fast and at a distance, Aeron needed to be particularly wary of it.

Alas, he had no way of telling what the Axes might be carrying in the way of potions, figurines that grew and came to life, or other magical creations. He'd just have to try to incapacitate them so quickly that they wouldn't have time to use such tricks even if they possessed them.

The Red Axes cut across the avenue toward the mouth of an alley. One of the human cutthroats, a beefy youth with a florid complexion and blond hair that stuck up in unruly tufts, kicked a beggar child who was too slow scurrying out of the way.

When he reached the start of it, Aeron saw that the alleyway wasn't nearly as busy as the street. Without dozens of pedestrians wandering every which way, he had a clear throw at his targets. He stooped, picked up a pair of round, heavy stones, and hurled them one after the other.

He wasn't as accurate with rocks as he was with daggers. He hadn't practiced as much. Still, the first stone cracked against the back of the gnoll's canine head, and the creature pitched forward. The second one hurtled past the blond lad's skull, missing by an inch.

The human Red Axes cried out in surprise and lurched around. By then, Aeron had another rock in his hand. He threw that one at the yellow-haired cutthroat's face, but his target jerked up his arm to shield himself. The resulting impact must have stung, maybe even chipped bone, but wasn't enough to put him down.

"That's Aeron sar Randal!" said the remaining bravo.

Stocky and middle-aged, he dressed all in blue, wore an abundance of cheap silver ornaments, and possessed a shrill, almost girlish voice. He and the blond youth snatched out their blades and charged.

Aeron was at least pleased that they hadn't pulled out any obviously enchanted weapons, and the gnoll appeared to be entirely unconscious. Still, the confrontation had become considerably riskier than Aeron wanted it to be.

He judged he had time for one more throw, so he grabbed a stone and faked a cast at the young Red Axe, who flinched. Aeron pivoted and flung the missile at the man in blue instead. The rock clipped his temple, and he stumbled to a halt. Looking shocked, his scimitar dangling at his side, he fingered the bloody graze.

The blond youth must have realized his comrade had stopped running, because he, too, balked. It gave Aeron a chance to put his hand on yet another stone. When he grabbed it, though, the Red Axe started rushing in again. He must have decided that even a fair fight, one against one and knife against knife, was preferable to standing off and letting a foe pelt him with rocks.

Aeron threw the stone. It smacked the youth in the chest but didn't stop him. He pounced, slashed, and Aeron, his hands empty, could only defend by springing frantically backward.

The Red Axe pursued him. Aeron had to dodge two more attacks before he could ready his own weapons, his largest Arthyn fang in one hand and his cudgel in the other.

He feinted a stab to the stomach with the knife, then lashed the club at the blond youth's face. Undeceived, the Red Axe simultaneously ducked the true attack and slashed at Aeron's wrist. The knife tore the underside of his forearm.

Aeron thought, hoped, the wound was shallow. He couldn't stop and check. He retreated to a safe distance, fought defensively for a few heartbeats, then flowed into the same combination he'd tried before, a low feint with the knife and a strike to the head with the cudgel. He made the actions just big and slow enough that his opponent was sure to understand them.

Naturally, the youth responded with the same counterattack as before. Why not, it had worked the first time. When his dagger flashed at Aeron's arm, the redheaded outlaw spun the club, trapped the blade, and carried it safely aside. At once he stepped in and hammered the heavy pommel of his own knife into the center of the Red Axe's forehead. The lad's eyes rolled up in his head, and his knees buckled.

Aeron felt a momentary satisfaction, cut short when he sensed a presence at his back. He leaped aside, and a scimitar whizzed through the space he'd just vacated. One profile smeared with blood, the cutthroat in blue had shaken off the shock of his superficial injury and crept up on the person responsible.

Aeron parried the next cut with his cudgel. It worked, it kept the blade out of his guts, but the force of the stroke knocked the club from his grip, leaving only his own blades with which to defend himself.

The Red Axe hacked at him repeatedly, and whenever Aeron could, he used a variation of the blond boy's counter. He ducked or dodged his opponent's blade and slashed or thrust at his extended arm. Before long, the man in blue became accustomed to the pattern, to an adversary who fought as he did, with a single weapon, and that was when Aeron surreptitiously slipped a second knife into his off hand.

He flourished the big Arthyn fang, locking the Red Axe's attention on it, then threw the smaller dagger. The knife plunged into the older man's throat. He made a gargling sound, pawed at the hilt for a second, and collapsed.

The Red Axe's death left Aeron feeling vaguely disgusted, but it was not the time to dwell on it. He inspected the gash on his forearm. He'd guessed right, it wasn't bad enough to require expert attention, not immediately, anyway. Employing his fingers and teeth, he knotted a kerchief into a makeshift bandage, then crouched to check the yellow-haired lad.

It occurred to him that it would be just his luck if he'd accidentally killed all three Red Axes, but in fact, the boy was breathing. He gripped him under the arms and dragged him into a recessed doorway, which might at least hide them from the casual notice of passersby. He kneeled down in front of his prisoner, then slapped and pinched him, trying to rouse him.

It took a while—long enough for a couple of garishly painted whores to wander down the alley, discover the corpse of the man in blue and the still-unconscious gnoll, and steal their purses and other valuables. Finally, though, the blond lad moaned, and his eyes fluttered open. Aeron poised an Arthyn fang at his throat, and he cringed.

"Don't fight, stay quiet, and I won't hurt you," Aeron said. "Otherwise, I'll stick you and talk to somebody else."

"You're crazy," said the youth, sounding more indignant than frightened. "Attacking us in broad daylight in the middle of the street? What if the Gray Blades had come along?"

"In case you haven't noticed, recently the law has been the least of my problems. At the moment, it's the least of yours, too."

"I'm not giving you any trouble, am I? What do you want?"

"For you to carry a message to Kesk. We're going to make the exchange, the treasure for my father."

"Good, let me walk you to the house. That will stop any other Red Axes trying to kill you."

Aeron grinned and said, "How kind. But I'm not going back into your stronghold. We'll make the trade in Laskalar's Square an hour after sunset."

"Out in the open, with people wandering all around?"

"You just said yourself, witnesses tend to discourage us outlaws from slaughtering one another. Not always, but some of the time."

"Kesk won't like it."

"Or my next requirement, either. He's to bring my father by himself. If I spot any other Red Axes—or magicians in scarves—you won't see me."

The blond lad sneered, "If you don't show up, your father dies."

"Better him than the both of us," Aeron replied. "And we both die if I let Kesk make the rules."

"Well, he won't let you make them."

"Deliver the message," Aeron said, "and we'll see."

Aeron rose and edged away. The Red Axe clambered to his feet and hurried off with many a wary backward glance. He hesitated over the gnoll as if pondering the advisability of trying to help the long-legged creature, then left it where it lay.

"That was sloppy," Sefris murmured, "letting him cut you."

Startled, Aeron jerked around. The willowy monastic in her cowl and robe was standing right beside him.

"I told you to hang back," he said.

"The Red Axes didn't see me," she replied, "and I didn't want you to think you had the option of slipping away from me. If I had to chase you down again, it would only be a waste of our time and energy."

"Why would I run when I need you? When I went to so much trouble to make contact with you in the first place?"

"Now that you've seen me close up, spoken with me, maybe you have second thoughts."

"No."

He'd finished those long ago—he supposed he'd reached his tenth or eleventh thoughts. But with only a few hours left before Kesk carried out his threat, he didn't have time to slip away from her, go into hiding, and hatch a more sensible plan.

Sefris asked, "Do you think Kesk will follow your instructions?"

"He'll come to Laskalar's Square, but not alone," Aeron replied with a grin. "His underlings will be lurking around, waiting to move in on my father and me as soon as the trade is done. Fortunately, they won't know you're sneaking around, too."

"You realize the tanarukk won't want to free Nicos until he has *The Black Bouquet* in his hands. But I can't allow you to give it to him."

"Don't worry, I won't even carry it to the meeting. If I did, you might be tempted to forget our bargain and take it away from me on the spot."

"Then how will you get Nicos out of Kesk's clutches, and even if you do, how can a lame old man hobble away quickly enough to keep the Red Axes from capturing him again?"

"Trickery," Aeron answered. "Tell me all the spells you can cast, and we'll figure it out from there."

Hulm had presumably finished his rounds before nightfall, but when Aeron passed from the Rolling Shields into Laskalar's Square, the Dead Cart was parked in front of Griffingate House. The gnarlbones presumably had personal business somewhere in the vicinity. The utilitarian wagon stood out in obscurely ominous contrast to the opulent gargoyle-encrusted facade of Oeble's most expensive inn. Aeron supposed a priest or philosopher of the proper persuasion could draw some sort of moral lesson from the scene. For his part, he only hoped it wasn't an omen of his own impending demise.

Dotted with trees and the occasional pigeon-spattered bit of statuary, the square itself was as busy as he'd expected. The shops and kiosks were doing a brisk business. Storytellers, minstrels, jugglers, and tumblers vied for the attention of the crowd, and the aromas of frying sausage and fresh-baked sweet buns scented the air. Aeron knew that under other circumstances, the smells would have made his mouth water. He hadn't eaten since leaving Melder's Door that morning. But at the moment, he was too edgy to think about food.

As he drifted around, he tried to spot Kesk's minions without their realizing he was looking. He marked one hobgoblin reaver pretending to watch a lewd puppet show and a human ruffian seemingly examining a leatherworker's wares, but not the rest, not yet. It didn't bother him too much that he couldn't pick out all the Red Axes. It was more troubling that he couldn't find the wizard, who was surely hanging around as well.

Oh, well, he thought, if everything goes as planned, I'll flush the whoreson out of hiding.

If not, the magician was still likely to make his presence obvious soon enough, in one inconvenient fashion or another.

It was on the north side of the grassy rectangle that Aeron finally caught sight of Nicos and Kesk. The Red Axes had cleaned the old man up, probably so it wouldn't be obvious to any casual observer that he was in distress. Thus, he wasn't bound or leashed, and of course didn't need to be. The tanarukk could fell him in an instant if he tried to make any trouble.

Like Aeron himself, Kesk wore a cowl to obscure his identity, and in the dark, some folk could have mistaken him for an unusually short and burly orc if they failed to notice the crimson smolder of his devilish eyes. No doubt he carried his battle-axe concealed beneath his cloak. As he stalked along, the set of his enormous shoulders hinted at his anger and impatience.

Aeron took a deep, steadying breath and called, "I'm here."

Kesk and Nicos turned. The hostage gave his head an almost imperceptible shake. Aeron knew it was his father's way of warning him to flee while he still could. He wished he could somehow make Nicos understand that he realized Kesk intended to cheat, and had planned a ploy of his own. But if he attempted any sort of signal, the tanarukk might see it, too.

"Let's do this," said Kesk.

"Not quite yet," Aeron answered. "Follow me, but don't try to catch up until I stop."

He led Kesk and Nicos back in the general direction of the two Red Axes he'd already spotted. They'd likely remain where they were, but others might skulk after him so they'd be close enough to strike as soon as the trade was finished. That would give him a final chance to pick them out.

He noticed one outlaw trailing him with a javelin clutched in either grubby, tattooed hand, and marked something else, two Gray Blades buying battered tin tankards of ale from a rawboned woman who ladled the brew out of an open keg. A few more mugs lay in the wheelbarrow behind her. Probably she'd used the conveyance to haul the cask to the patch of ground she rented from whatever gang currently controlled that portion of the square.

Aeron hesitated for an instant. He hadn't included any Gray Blades in his scheme, and supposed that when trouble erupted, they were just about as likely to interfere with him as they were with the Red Axes. Yet they certainly had the potential to add to the general chaos, and he thought he might as well trust his hunches and his luck. If they failed him, he and Nicos were doomed anyway.

So he stopped just a few feet away from the officers, beneath the boughs of a chestnut tree. His feet rustled the dry fallen leaves on the ground. He held up his hand to halt Kesk when the gang chieftain and Nicos were still a couple paces away, which was to say, while Aeron was still beyond the reach of his enemy's axe. The tanarukk glowered at the Blades, then spat. They didn't notice.

"I'm not fond of them, either," Aeron said, "but maybe having them close by will help you remember to behave yourself."

"Give me the book," said Kesk.

"First set my father free."

The tanarukk laughed and said, "Don't be stupid. Hand it over before I lose my patience, butcher you and the old man, too, and simply take it. I don't know why I haven't done that already."

Aeron grinned and replied, "I imagine because you gave your solemn promise. Also, you'd hate to send me to the Lord of Shadows prematurely, then find out you haven't really gotten your hands on *The Black Bouquet* after all."

Kesk's snout twitched, and saliva trickled around one of his tusks. It made Aeron want to take a step back, but he controlled himself.

"Show me the cursed book," the half-demon growled. "We'll start with that."

"That, I'm willing to do."

Aeron brought Miri's scuffed old saddlebag out from beneath his cape, unbuckled it, and pulled the steel strongbox out.

Kesk stared. For a second, he seemed less wrathful than perplexed.

"You locked it back in the coffer?" the tanarukk asked.

Aeron shrugged and said, "I was worried the Gray Blades were looking for a thief in possession of an old black tome full of perfumer's formulae. The box is less distinctive. Merchants and couriers use similar ones all the time."

"Well, open it."

"I can't," Aeron replied. "Not without my tools. Not without hunkering down over it for several minutes and making it obvious to anybody walking by that I'm having to crack it. At that, I'd be leery of triggering the wards again. One makes a boom so loud the entire square would hear it. I assumed you could open it without any problem, seeing as how I was supposed to give it to you in the first place."

"Set it on the ground," Kesk growled.

Aeron obeyed, and Kesk brought his axe out from under his mantle. The edges glowed red as he activated the same enchantment that had enabled him to chop through the heavy chain so easily. Aeron caught an acrid whiff of hot metal, reminiscent of a forge.

"Are you just going to bash it open?" he asked. "You might spoil the book, it's crumbling as it is, and the box truly is liable to thunder and break your arm. Maybe you should send for Burgell Whitehorn, now that he's on your side."

"Just shut your hole."

Kesk waved his massive gray hand with its coarse nails and patches of bristle. After a moment's hesitation, a slender figure approached. To all appearances, he was an elf, short as Kesk, ivory-skinned, green-eyed, and clad in sturdy traveler's attire. When he spoke, however, it was in the cultured tones of the anonymous wizard. He'd masked himself with illusion instead of a scarf. Aeron suspected the yew bow in his hand was actually the blackwood cane.

"I thought we agreed," the magician said, "that I'd keep my distance."

"I'm settling this business now," Kesk said, "without another second of delay, and that means I need you to open this." He gave the strongbox a little kick. "Get to it."

"Very well," the wizard said. He dropped to one knee, inspected the coffer, and muttered a charm under his breath. "The wards are gone."

Kesk gave Aeron a suspicious scowl. The human outlaw shrugged.

"I'm no arcanist," the rogue said. "How could I be sure of that?"

"I suppose the important thing," said the wizard, "is what's inside."

He removed a silver key from his pocket. The metal shimmered subtly in a manner that made Aeron suspect it was enchanted, like Burgell's skeleton key. He slipped it in the lock, twisted it, and the box popped open. The magician raised the lid completely and lifted out the musty black volume inside.

It wasn't *The Black Bouquet*, just another old, similarly colored volume Aeron had pilfered from the shop of a used book dealer. But neither Kesk nor his employer had ever laid eyes on the original, and shouldn't be able to tell until they looked inside. For the moment, they gazed raptly at what they took to be the prize they'd worked so hard to win. Anyone would have done the same.

Excitement, however, didn't turn Kesk completely stupid. He never could have schemed and murdered his way to ascendancy in Oeble's underworld if he was that easy a mark. He still kept a wary eye on Aeron, but unfortunately for the tanarukk, Aeron wasn't the one who was about to attack him. The redheaded outlaw simply eased a step backward, out of what was supposed to be the area of effect of Sefris's spell. Her timing was perfect. A split second later, tatters of shadow exploded from a central point in the air like the petals of some hellish flower blooming all in an instant. Caught in the silent blast, Kesk and his employer thrashed as if some fierce beast had seized them in its jaws.

It was possible that Aeron could have killed them both in that moment of near paralysis, but he still would have had to contend with the other outlaws, and the two Gray Blades who, alarmed by the murky burst of magic, were pivoting in his direction. All things considered, he deemed it best to get Nicos moving away while everyone was still startled. The spell had stunned the old man, too. When, taking care not to touch the rippling corona of shadow, Aeron grabbed him by the arm and hustled him away from his captors, reflex kept him shuffling along until his senses cleared.

Aeron peered desperately around, looking for all the Red Axes who were no doubt rushing to attack him. The plan called for Sefris to throw at least one follow-up spell at Kesk and the wizard, Aeron's two closest and most dangerous enemies, to keep them from chasing right after him, which meant that for a second at least, he was on his own when it came to dealing with the common ruffians.

The man with the tattooed hands threw a javelin. Either he didn't guess Aeron still hadn't surrendered the *Bouquet*, he was too excited and full of bloodlust to care, or maybe Kesk had ordered his henchmen to kill the pest and be done with it no matter how the meeting turned out. Aeron jerked his father out of the way. The second spear flew wild, almost striking a curly-headed goodwife carrying a wicker shopping basket on her arm. She squealed. Other people started shouting and shrieking, too.

A bugbear charged with a mace in either hand. Aeron lifted a throwing knife, but then one of the Gray Blades scrambled into the creature's path. He almost certainly had no clear idea of what was really going on, but recognized murderous intent when he saw it. The Red Axe tried to smash him out of its way, and he parried the first blow with his broadsword.

A crossbow bolt streaked past Aeron's head. He didn't know precisely where it had come from, and was simply glad it would take the marksman a few moments to reload. He glimpsed motion and pivoted. A Red Axe was drawing his bow. Aeron poised himself to spring aside and pull Nicos out of harm's way as well. He would have succeeded, too, except that the arrow must have been another enchanted weapon, for in flight, it multiplied into three.

One of them struck Aeron in the forearm. Denying the shock that might otherwise have made him slow and stupid, he snapped the shaft off short so it wouldn't hinder his movements.

"Are you hit?" he asked his father.

"No," Nicos panted, "but you are. You have to leave me. I'm slowing you down too much."

"After I went to all this trouble? To the Nine Hells with that. Just watch my back."

A Red Axe armed with a short sword charged them. Aeron threw an Arthyn fang, and the snapping motion triggered the first flare of pain from the arrowhead still embedded in his muscle. Still, the knife flew straight, and caught the bravo in the chest.

An orc wearing leather gloves studded with copper rivets thrust out its hands like a wizard casting a spell. Aeron didn't know what to expect, but instinct prompted him to hurl Nicos and himself to the ground. A dazzling white flare of lightning crackled over their heads. He rolled to one knee and tossed a dagger. His aim was too low, and the blade only pierced the orc's thigh. Still, the Red Axe faltered, gaping at the protruding hilt in seeming disbelief, as folk sometimes did when they took a wound.

Maybe the orc would retire from the fight and take its magical gloves with it, but even if so, would it matter?

Aeron was hurt, and it seemed as if Kesk had brought his entire band of cutthroats to the square.

What was Sefris doing?

If she was dead, or simply too busy with Kesk and the wizard to cast the spell Aeron was awaiting, he and Nicos were as good as dead.

CHAPTER 17

Following the burst of shadow, Sefris regarded Kesk and the wizard with cold satisfaction. Her ambuscade had taken them entirely by surprise, and they stood dazed and all but helpless. Only for a moment, but that gave her time for another spell, one with an excellent chance of killing them outright, or failing that, so crippling them that she'd have no trouble finishing them off with her hands. Then she'd help Aeron and Nicos escape the rest of the Red Axes, which would probably provide her the chance to slaughter a goodly number of them. Afterward, the lone-wolf thief would give her *The Black Bouquet*, and as soon as she had it, she'd complete her work by butchering him and the old man, too. In a world where everything was dung, and all prospect of pleasure bitter and hollow, it would nonetheless be about as rewarding an evening as a servant of Shar could wish for.

She plucked a pellet of guano and sulfur from one of her pockets and swept it through a cabalistic pass, meanwhile whispering a rhyme. Ordinarily she much preferred spells of shadow and darkness to any that conjured fire, but she was pragmatist enough to use the most effective tool for the task at hand.

A male voice, shrill with excitement, shouted, "Stop that!"

She turned her head. One of the Gray Blades, a muscular young man who'd tried with scant success to grow a beard, had spotted her and pointed a crossbow in her direction. She'd thought Aeron an imbecile to conduct his business in the lawmen's vicinity, and there was the proof.

As soon as he saw her face, the Gray Blade shot his quarrel. Something in her expression must have panicked him. She slapped the missile aside, but in so doing, spoiled her mystical gesturing and thus her spell.

The young man's eyes widened in amazement when she deflected the bolt, but he was game. With a rasp of metal on metal, he pulled his broadsword from its scabbard and charged. She spun a chakram at him and caught him in the throat. He staggered two more steps, then fell.

It had only taken a moment to deal with him. Yet she suspected it was a moment too long, and when she wheeled back around, it was clear that she was right. Kesk and the wizard had shaken off the effect of the shadow blast and scrambled out of the ragged bulb of darkness. The edges of his battle-axe shining red as magma, the tanarukk charged her. The magician wasn't doing much of anything yet. He didn't react as quickly as his partner, but given a chance, he'd start conjuring soon enough.

She sidestepped, thus interposing Kesk between the wizard and herself, and snap-kicked at the gang chieftain's massive knob of a knee. To her surprise, he managed to jerk his leg aside, and the ball of her foot only grazed him. The axe plunged at her, a powerful yet subtle stroke she had to spring backward to avoid.

Kesk leered at her and said, "Did you think you were better than me, bitch? You surprised me the first time, but now I understand how you fight."

Sefris did think she was his superior. She was confident she could defeat him and the wizard, too, but that alone wouldn't be good enough. She needed to do it fast, so she could proceed to the next part of the plan before Aeron and Nicos were overwhelmed. She launched herself at Kesk, attacking furiously, whirling, leaping, punching, and kicking.

Despite his bravado, Kesk gave ground, chopping at her as he backed away. He was fighting defensively, playing for time. She landed her share of strikes even so, but his thick hide seemed to blunt the force of her blows. Meanwhile the wizard maneuvered at a safe distance from the melee, obviously trying to reach a position from which he could target her without fear of accidentally hitting the half-demon with his magic.

She risked dividing her attention to rattle off an incantation and thrust her arm at the arcanist in his elf disguise. Jagged lances of darkness leaped from her palm to plunge into his chest without tearing his garments or breaking the skin. He reeled, but didn't fall, and his riposte came a moment later. Darts of blue light hurtled from his fingertips to pierce her own body in that same bloodless but still injurious manner. The cold pain was intense. Perhaps hoping the shock of the attack had paralyzed her, Kesk drove in hard, swinging the axe at her chest. She knocked it aside with both forearms, then followed up with a backhand strike that snapped one of his tusks and knocked him staggering backward.

At that moment, he was vulnerable. She could have lunged after him and delivered the death blow, except that she felt a sort of charge in the air that could only be the wizard's power enfolding her. Her sorceress's intuition told her it was the same spell of sluggishness that had so hindered her before. She focused her will, resisting the magic, and felt it dissolve without catching hold of her. Unfortunately, that gave Kesk time to come back on guard.

Precious seconds were racing by, and she still hadn't found the moment she needed to save Aeron. Her foes were pressing her too hard. She had to dispose of at least one of them without further delay, and unfortunately, she wasn't certain that any single attack at her disposal would suffice to cripple or kill.

But maybe she could rid herself of the wizard another way. He didn't want folk to know who Kesk's partner was, and with luck, his nerves were still shaky from the shadow burst. It generally had such a lingering effect. Once again seeking to cast a spell and evade the relentless axe at the same time, dodging the deadly strokes by inches, she recited the incantation and swept her cestus-wrapped hand through the proper pattern.

Just as when she'd negated the sluggishness, her magic broke the wizard's enchantment of disguise. The appearance of an elf wayfarer melted away, revealing a small man with a round-cheeked, boyish face, elegant silk and velvet clothes, and a long blackwood cane. He stared down at himself in astonishment, then pulled up a fold of his cloak to shield his face. He turned and ran. As Sefris had hoped, he truly was a wizard, which was to say, the kind of arcanist who needed to prepare his spells in advance. He didn't have another charm of illusion ready for the casting, and thus had no choice but to flee if he didn't want scores of onlookers to witness him fighting in concert with the Red Axes.

"Curse you!" Kesk bellowed. "Come back!" He glared at Sefris. "It doesn't matter. I'll still ki—"

She smashed a roundhouse kick into the side of his head, shattering some of his fangs and knocking him stumbling off balance. As she whirled with the attack, she spotted Nicos and Aeron. They hadn't made it very far toward the perimeter of the square, the idiot son had a bloody wound in his forearm, and the Red Axes were closing in. If she was to save them, it had to be right away.

She spoke the words of power and made the proper gesture. As before, it only took an instant, yet once again, that was all the time Kesk needed to recover. When she pivoted back in his direction, the axe was already flashing at her body.

Aeron hurled his last throwing knife and pierced a bugbear's chest. That left him only the largest Arthyn fang, the cudgel, and plenty of Red Axes still eager to spill his and Nicos's blood.

His arm throbbing, he offered his father the club. The weapon wouldn't save Nicos, but Aeron knew he'd prefer to go down fighting. The old man reached for it, and the air around them swam and thickened, giving birth to dank coils of thick white mist. In a moment, Aeron could scarcely see past the end of his nose. Elsewhere in the vapor, the Red Axes called out in dismay.

Ever since Nicos and Aeron had broken away from Kesk and the wizard, and despite the distracting business of struggling to stay alive, the younger thief had kept track of his position and orientation in the square, and the location of the objects in his vicinity. Thus he was still able to hurry his father along toward where he wanted him to go.

The Red Axe with the filthy, tattooed hands appeared in the mist, almost seeming to materialize like a phantom. His javelins expended, he clutched a short sword.

Lunging, he shouted, "They're here!"

Aeron parried and thrust in his turn. The bravo hopped backward, out of range. Aeron knew he couldn't afford to linger and fence with the Red Axe, for fear that the wretch's initial outcry would draw other foes to the spot. He threw himself forward, risking a counterattack in order to close the distance.

The reckless dive caught the tattooed man by surprise. Though he did attempt a stab, by then Aeron's Arthyn fang had already pierced his chest. The short sword slipped from spastic fingers, leaving the red-haired thief unscathed.

Aeron had only sprinted two long strides, but when he turned back around, he was, to all appearances, alone.

"Father!" he whispered.

"Here," Nicos answered.

Guided by the sound, Aeron scurried to the old man's side. He had to hope that, despite the interruption of having to fight the Red Axe, he hadn't lost his bearings. He led his father onward.

Elsewhere in the mist, lightning crackled, the vapor diffusing the glare into a softer glow. Somebody screamed. Aeron hoped the victim was a Red Axe and not a noncombatant.

The fugitives scrambled on for what felt like a long time, until Aeron was all but certain he'd lost his way. The trunk of an elm tree swam out of the fog. The bottommost branches hung low to the ground, and despite the season, still clung to most of their leaves.

"Can you climb?" he asked.

"A little, if I have to," Nicos said.

Aeron grabbed him by the belt and lifted him upward.

"And hide?" the rogue asked.

Nicos gripped a limb, and grunting with effort, dragged himself higher, relieving Aeron of his weight.

The old man said, "That should be no problem."

"Then get above eye level and stay still until the Red Axes go home, no matter how long that takes. I don't think they'll find you as long as I draw their attention elsewhere, and without you slowing me down, I can get away."

"Mask protect you," Nicos said.

Aeron strode away. After a few moments, he stumbled on the spot where a tinker in a patched cloak had set up shop. The thief snatched up a copper pot awaiting repair and banged it with the pommel of his fighting knife.

"We're here, you bastards!" he yelled. "Catch us if you can!"

He dropped his makeshift gong and rushed onward.

He wondered how Sefris was faring. Plainly, she'd still been alive when she finally conjured the fog as planned. Having performed that final service, the Red Axes were more than welcome to kill her. But actually, Aeron was sure it wasn't going to be that easy for him, just as he was certain that he and Nicos couldn't evade her for long. He had to dispose of her. He just hoped the last phase of his plan, the part she presumably knew nothing about, would do the job.

He felt more than saw the imposing mass of Griffingate House before him. He stalked along the side of the inn, heading for the alleyway where he was supposed to rendezvous with Sefris, and his luck deserted him again.

Unable to see it in the blinding fog, the small wizard tripped over the guy line of a vendor's tent and fell heavily to the ground. Perhaps the impact knocked the panic out of him, for when he raised his head, he felt better able to think.

Frightened or not, he still had no intention of letting half of Oeble witness him fighting in concert with the city's most infamous outlaws. He had to slip away, but before he did, perhaps he could cast a final spell to help his accomplices deal with Aeron sar Randal.

He hoped that despite the disorienting turmoil of the past couple minutes, including the alarming discovery that Aeron and Sefris were working together, the Red Axes still meant to capture the lone-wolf thief, not kill him. Otherwise, they'd likely lose *The Black Bouquet* forever. Yet even if they did, it would be better than if it somehow reached its rightful owner, and the magician found that, rattled and frustrated as he was, he'd actually come around to Kesk's point of view. It was time to put an end to the business, and to the redheaded nuisance who'd so complicated it, in whatever way it could be accomplished.

Plainly, Aeron and Nicos hoped to sneak away from the square under cover of the mist. If the small man could wash the muck from the air, perhaps Kesk's men could still catch them.

He didn't know whether it was possible. Sefris had dispelled two of his enchantments, whereas he'd never tried to cancel one of hers. It was entirely possible she was the superior spellcaster, for after all, he was primarily a merchant. He simply studied thaumaturgy in private when he could find the time, to give himself a secret edge.

Yet one of his teachers had told him that any wizard had a chance of unmaking the mystical creation of any other, so long as he performed the banishment perfectly. Accordingly, the trader picked himself up, took a deep breath, and gave it his best effort, enunciating the words of power as clearly and sweeping his cane through the passes as crisply as possible.

It worked. Power groaned around him like a note from a giant's cello, until the air suddenly cleared. The small man felt a pang of delight in his own prowess, cut short by the realization that, with the fog gone, he was once more in danger of being recognized. He shielded his face with his cloak and scurried on toward the edge of the square and safety.

It was too late to block the battle-axe. Not even the Dark Father Abbott of Sefris's monastery could have managed it. She flung herself backward, and it saved her life. The mighty cut, which would otherwise have cleaved her shoulder and plunged on deep into her vitals, simply ripped flesh and tore free in a shower of blood.

It was a bad wound anyway, and Kesk realized it. Grunting like a maddened boar through his broken fangs, pressing the advantage, he drove in hard. The axe leaped at her again and again.

For a moment or two, as shock threatened to overwhelm her, it was difficult for Sefris to parry or dodge and almost impossible to strike back. Her training braced her, carried her to a place beyond pain, weakness, or fear, into a cold, clear state of mind vaguely suggestive of the perfect peace that would endure forever once all vile created things passed into nothingness. Strength and agility surged back into her limbs, and she hooked a punch into Kesk's side. A rib cracked. She was in too close for him to chop at her, so he lifted the axe high and rammed the end of the handle down at the top of her skull. She slipped the blow and whipped an elbow strike into his jaw.

The way the tanarukk's head sat atop his massive shoulders, he scarcely seemed to have a neck. Otherwise, the blow would probably have snapped it. As it was, the fire in his scarlet eyes seemed to dim, and when he tried to retreat and give himself room for another axe stroke, he stumbled. She leaped into the air and thrust-kicked him in the center of the chest. He fell on his back and lay motionless while she stamped on him.

That ought to have killed him, even as tough as he was. In other circumstances, she would have paused to make sure, but she wanted to start after Aeron without further delay. She didn't think he'd tried to lose her, not with his father still up a tree in the middle of the square, readily available for recapture, but she wasn't certain. The rogue was too tricky for her to feel confident of predicting his every move.

When she turned, her fog was gone. Though the wizard was nowhere to be seen, he'd evidently dispelled it before fleeing. A good many of the Red Axes had disappeared as well. They must have groped their way out of the square. Maybe they'd been afraid the mist would make them sick, like the poison vapor the magician had conjured back in the mansion, or perhaps they'd seen little point in stumbling around in the murk until the Gray Blades arrived in force, an event which was sure to happen eventually. In any case, even though Sefris would have taken a certain satisfaction in striking them out of her path, their departure ought to make life easier.

She sprinted toward the mouth of the alley where Aeron had promised to meet her. Up ahead in the darkness, a man cried out.

CHAPTER 18

Bow in hand and an arrow on the string, Miri crouched in the shadowy gap between two snarling gargoyles on the gabled roof of Griffingate House. She peered at the thick white fog in Laskalar's Square and the folk who periodically stumbled out of it and fled down the alley. She strained her ears in an essentially futile effort to interpret the confusion of shouts and other noises emanating from the midst of the cloud.

Where was Aeron? Her nerves were taut with waiting, and it seemed to her that it was taking him forever to appear. True, the mist had materialized as he'd said it would, which indicated a part of the plan had gone off properly, but it didn't necessarily mean he hadn't come to grief.

The vapor disappeared. She scowled in dismay until Aeron dashed down the passage. For a moment she imagined everything was all right, then a man and a limping orc came chasing after him. They'd apparently spotted him when the fog vanished, just scant seconds too soon.

Miri's fingers fairly itched with the urge to draw her bow, but Aeron had told her that no matter what happened, she wasn't to do anything that would reveal her presence prematurely. She was still hesitating when the human Red Axe whirled a sling and let the bullet fly. Aeron didn't duck or dodge, maybe hadn't even realized that the cutthroats were behind him. The lead pellet slammed into the back of his head with a thud audible even high above the ground, and he pitched forward onto his hands and knees.

When Aeron had first hatched the scheme of using Sefris to rescue his father, Miri had thought him insane, but gradually he'd talked her around. She still wasn't quite sure how, except that he was right about one thing. As a sorceress and expert practitioner of the Dark Moon's esoteric style of combat, Sefris possessed capabilities they lacked. Moreover, Kesk and his wizard partner wouldn't expect the monastic to join forces with Aeron, which gave her a good chance of taking them by surprise.

One difficulty with recruiting Sefris, however, was Aeron's alliance with Miri. It was inconceivable that the Shar worshiper would take anything the rogue said at face value if she believed the partnership was still in effect. An even bigger problem was what to do with her once she'd outlived her usefulness. Aeron and Miri were both able combatants with their respective weapons, but even so, they doubted they could defeat Sefris in anything even vaguely resembling a fair fight. The monastic simply outclassed them.

Aeron conceived a single ploy to solve both dilemmas. He contacted Melder, with whom he'd had some sort of shady dealings in the past, and bribed him to take part in the charade of Miri's capture and imprisonment. Despite her partner's assurances, she herself participated with considerable suspicion and reluctance, for after all, the innkeeper actually had sent the yuan-ti slavers after her. But Melder kept his part of the bargain, making no effort to molest her or detain her when it was time for her to go.

That left her free to climb to the top of Griffingate House and lie in wait for Sefris to appear. For all the Dark Moon agent's prowess, surely a well-aimed arrow could kill her if she never even saw it coming. Miri didn't much like the idea of striking down a sister human being in such a fashion, but she accepted that it was necessary. Sefris deserved extermination as much as any goblin or troll Miri had ever battled in the wild.

But Aeron was down, not quite unconscious but plainly stunned. The Red Axes were hurrying toward him, the human in the lead and the orc hobbling behind. They were going to capture or kill him unless Miri deviated from the plan and intervened.

She didn't see she had a choice. She loosed an arrow, which drove through the human Red Axe's torso. He cried out and collapsed.

The orc whirled, peered upward, and oriented on her. The night could do little to hamper its dark-adapted eyes. It thrust out its leather-gloved hands like a wizard throwing a spell.

She recoiled, and a spear of lightning sizzled past her. The magic didn't burn her, but the glare made her squinch her eyes shut.

It also shrank her pupils and carved a streak of afterimage across her vision, leaving her partly blind. She couldn't let that stop her. She had to kill the orc before it hurled any more lightning, either at Aeron or at her. She stared down, believed she glimpsed her adversary, and shot by instinct as much as sight.

It was good enough. The shaft took the orc in its upturned face, and it fell down on its back.

Miri sighed with relief—and something lashed around her, pinning her arms against her body. Blinking, thrashing uselessly, she perceived that the moon-cast shadow of one of the gargoyles had warped into a tentacle, reared up, and grabbed her.

In the mouth of the alley, Sefris looked up at the result of her spell. She'd evidently arrived while Miri was fighting the Red Axes, and waited to pick off the victor.

The monastic swirled her hand through a mystic pass. Almost invisible in the night, jagged black blades hurtled upward. Immobilized, Miri couldn't dodge. The magic pierced her flesh without breaking the skin, yet even so, the flare of pain was ghastly.

Dazed, Aeron noticed a curious thing. His wounded forearm and the back of his head were throbbing to the same beat. For a moment, he lingered on his hands and knees, hypnotized by that tempo of shock and pain, then remembered he was in danger. He dragged himself to his feet and lurched around—

—just in time to see Sefris savage Miri with bolts of darkness. The scout flailed, then dangled motionless in the coil of shadow that had caught her.

Smiling almost imperceptibly, Sefris stalked forward. Something had cut deep into her shoulder and soaked her robe with blood. Yet her movements flowed with the same sure grace as ever, and try as he might, Aeron could draw no hope from the fact of her injury. Somehow, it just made her seem all the more unstoppable and inhuman, as if she was Death itself come to claim him.

"Think about it," he panted. "Nothing's really changed. I still have *The Black Bouquet*. It will still be destroyed at sunrise if I don't retrieve it."

"My perspective has changed," Sefris replied, still gliding forward past the corpses of the Red Axes. "I'm done playing your games. You claimed you could hold up under torture for a long while, but now I'm going to put it to the test. We'll see if you can keep your secret while I mangle you one small piece at a time. Rest assured that if you do, after I finish with you, I'll hunt down Nicos and make him pay for your stubbornness."

Aeron backed away from her. He could feel the blood from his torn scalp on the nape of his neck.

"All right," he said, "you win. I'll take you to the book."

"It isn't that easy," Sefris said. "You've played too many tricks. I need to pluck an eye or cripple a limb, so you'll understand what truly lies in store for you. I need to hear you scream and beg. Maybe after that, I'll find it possible to believe what you say."

He lifted his weapons. For no reason, really, except that he preferred to go down fighting. He knew he had no chance, or at least that was what he assumed until he glimpsed a stirring at the uppermost edge of his vision.

Terrified as he was, he nearly jerked his head higher for a better look. If he had, Sefris would naturally have turned and peered, also. Fortunately, at the last possible instant, his instinct for stealth asserted itself, and he managed to glance surreptitiously upward without alerting her.

Miri was squirming inside the shadow tentacle. She must have played dead so Sefris wouldn't blast her with yet another spell. The monastic had turned her attention elsewhere, so the ranger was trying to free herself. If she succeeded, and Aeron stayed alive until she did, perhaps the plan could still work.

He retreated farther. Every second he could keep away from his pursuer was another moment for Miri to struggle free. Sefris broke into a sprint to close the distance. He wished he could think her reckless for rushing his long, sharp fighting knife that way, but knew she had no reason to fear it.

She leaped high, spun, and kicked at his head. Aeron

jumped back, and the attack fell short by inches. He slashed at her foot as it whizzed by, but he was too slow.

She touched down, and instantly, her stiffened hands chopped at him. He hopped back once more, faked a thrust with the Arthyn fang when she followed, and lashed the cudgel at her head in a true attack. She ignored the knife, blocked the club with her forearm, and smashed her leather-wrapped fist into his solar plexus.

All the strength went out of him. He would have collapsed if she hadn't caught him. Her fingertips dug into each of his wrists in turn. His hands spasmed, and he dropped his weapons. Still holding him upright, she manhandled him down the alley, no doubt seeking a dark spot where she could torture him undisturbed.

Sefris threw herself to the side, carrying him with her. An arrow from on high streaked past them. He didn't think she'd been looking upward, but somehow she'd sensed it coming.

A second shaft flew at once. Heedless of the danger to the man Sefris still clutched against her, Miri was shooting as fast as she could. Ironically, at that moment, it was the daughter of the Dark Moon who had the greater care for his safety. She flung him aside to smack down on the ground.

Unencumbered, Sefris shifted back and forth, her spinning arms a blur, either dodging the arrows or batting them aside. In a few moments at best, the wounded ranger's barrage must inevitably slow down, giving the sorceress the chance to cast another spell.

Which was to say that Sefris was still going to win the fight, and hurt as he was, Aeron had no idea how to change that. Even if he could muster the strength to find his fallen knife and attack, the monastic would just swat him down like a fly.

Unless . . .

He couldn't seem to catch his breath but forced himself

to crawl. It was easier than walking and less likely to attract Sefris's notice.

As he neared the dead orc, Sefris lashed lengths of black ribbon through the air. Up on the roof, a ragged bulb of shadow exploded into being. Caught in the dark flare, Miri wailed, lost her footing on the slanted tiles, fell on her rump, and slid. She plunged partway off the edge, then managed to snatch hold of something and catch herself. Her bow and most of the remaining arrows from her quiver tumbled toward the ground.

Aeron had to find the strength to rise. Otherwise, in just another second, Sefris would surely finish off the helplessly dangling ranger. He staggered up and charged the agent of the Dark Moon, shouting—or croaking . . . making noise, anyway—to divert her attention. She pivoted like a demonic dancer and lunged to meet him.

If the leather-and-copper gloves he'd removed from the orc's body had needed him to speak a trigger word or make some special mystic gesture to activate them, he couldn't have done it, but it turned out that the mere intent was enough. And if Sefris had been standing just a couple yards away, he was certain she could have dodged the magic. Fortunately, however, she herself was pouncing to close the distance, and the blaze of lightning caught her square in the middle of the chest. She shuddered and twitched, then fell. Aeron thought she clutched at him as she went down, but maybe it was just his imagination, for she didn't stir after she hit the ground. She simply lay inert, a contorted husk giving off a sickening stink of burned meat.

It certainly looked like death. But Aeron found the Arthyn fang and drove it into her heart anyway, just to make sure.

Only then did he look up. Miri had hauled herself back from the brink.

"Are you all right?" she wheezed.

"Better than I expected to be, certainly. What about you?"

"The same."

She knotted a rope around a gargoyle and used it to clamber to the ground, where she stood peering at Sefris's smoking body as if she too couldn't quite believe the Shar worshiper was dead.

"I think that if she hadn't already been wounded," Miri said, "we never could have beaten her, not even with the magic gloves."

"I think you're right."

"Thank the Forest Queen it's over."

He took a deep breath, preparing himself for further exertion, and said, "Not yet it isn't."

When Kesk staggered around the bend, he met three halflings slinking in the other direction. Lynxes, beyond a doubt. He would have known even if he hadn't encountered them in the Underways, where honest people had no business. It was obvious from their abundance of weapons and the hardness in their wary eyes.

He knew the small outlaws could tell plenty about him as well. They could scarcely miss his broken tusk and fangs, his pulped, bloody features, or the anguished way he hobbled along bent half double. Accordingly, he knew what they must be thinking. There was their chieftain's hated rival, alone, wounded, and ripe for the murdering at last.

Kesk had regained consciousness on the ground surprised to find himself still alive. Sefris must have rushed off somewhere in a hurry. Maybe she'd felt a need to chase after Aeron without further delay.

Thanks to her sneak attack, Kesk had lost the red-headed thief and Nicos, too. He was grievously hurt, as the agony in his vitals attested. The wizard had deserted him. Apparently off battling Sefris, pursuing the sar Randals, or simply blundering around lost in the conjured fog, none of his underlings were at hand to help him, either.

Still, he told himself, he was going to be all right. A priest of Mask could restore him to health. He just needed to return to the safety of his stronghold before the Gray Blades or any of his other countless ill-wishers found him in his current vulnerable condition. Accordingly, he rose and groped his way through the mist to the nearest entry to the tunnels.

To no avail, perhaps, for thanks to pure foul luck, the three Lynxes had discovered him anyway. He glared at them as ferociously as he'd ever glared in his life, and brandished his battle-axe, still wet with Sefris's gore, for good measure. The haft almost slipped through his numb fingers. He certainly didn't have the strength to swing the weapon.

"Do you think you can take me?" he snarled. "Me, Kesk Turnskull? Come on and try."

The halflings gazed back at him for what seemed like a long while.

Finally, when he was sure they were going to call his bluff, the one in the lead said, "Why dirty our hands? You're dead already, or so it looks to me."

The Lynxes edged around Kesk, giving him as wide a berth as possible, and prowled on.

Kesk started to laugh, but it hurt his chest like the jabbing of a knife, so he choked it off. Once the halflings disappeared around the turn, he too trudged onward.

The mansion is close . . . the mansion is close, he told himself over and over again, to keep one foot shuffling in front of the other.

Finally he spied a glowing scarlet lantern and realized the encouraging words had become true. He felt a swelling of relief, and naturally, as if some malicious god was having a joke at his expense, it was at that moment that a familiar voice spoke his name.

Kesk stumbled around. Aeron and the female archer had crept up behind him. Apparently the lone-wolf robber hadn't sold her to Melder after all. The report to the contrary must have been another trick.

It was immediately apparent from their level stares that Kesk had no hope of intimidating that pair of enemies. The woman was aiming an arrow. Aeron had his arms extended. After a moment—his eyes kept wavering in and out of focus—Kesk realized the red-haired rogue was wearing the lightning gloves that he himself had extorted from the wizard. It was quite possible that that same magic was going to kill him. The thought gave rise to a bitter mirth, and once again, he had to stifle a laugh.

"Track me, did you?" he asked.

"More or less," Aeron replied. "It was obvious where you'd try to go."

"Where's the other bitch?"

"We killed her." The human outlaw hesitated, then said, "If it was your axe that cut her shoulder, I guess the three of us did it together."

"I'm glad of that, anyway. Now I suppose it's my turn to die. Do it, then. But if you do, you'll never know who my partner was."

"I don't care who he was," Aeron replied. "You're the one I want."

Kesk centered his attention on the ranger. He knew she was his only hope.

"The wizard told me Dorn Heldeion wants to change how we live in Oeble," said the tanarukk, "by bringing in a new and lawful way to make coin."

She frowned at the mention of the name of her employer, a prominent member of the Council of Nine Merchants, chief deputies to the Faceless Master. Kesk realized that she must have kept the secret of the rich man's identity from Aeron, and he'd given it away. If the lanky thief was even interested, he didn't show it.

"I don't want to change Oeble," said Aeron, "except for erasing you from the middle of it."

"If you do want to make things different," said Kesk, still directing his words to the ranger, "you can't do it by killing me. Every city has somebody like me, and if you dispose of him, another just as bad pops up to take his place. The only chance to put Oeble on another path is for Master Heldeion's scheme to succeed."

"I told you," Aeron said, "I like Oeble fine the way it is."

"So does the wizard," Kesk replied. "He just wants to run it is all. In time, he will. He's clever and patient. He makes plans that take years to work themselves out. He's the one who sabotaged Master Heldeion's trading ventures and ran him into debt without Heldeion even understanding why everything was going wrong."

"Why did he bother?" the ranger asked.

"Dorn Heldeion has too much influence," said Kesk, clenching himself against another surge of pain. "When the magician has the Faceless Master assassinated, he wants to look like the only reasonable candidate to take over the job. That means ruining any potential rivals in advance. Though if Heldeion's gamble pays off, if he gets his hands on *The Black Bouquet*, he won't really be ruined. The coin-lenders will be happy to keep him afloat, knowing that in a couple years, the secrets in the book will rebuild his fortune many times over. So the wizard had to try to keep it away from him."

"He failed," Aeron said.

"At that scheme, yes," said Kesk, "but if you let him go free, he'll simply start over with a new one."

"He must be a prominent member of the Council of Nine himself," said the guide. "It would be useless to accuse him without evidence, or at least a witness more reputable than the leader of the Red Axes."

"I can tell you where to look for proof," said Kesk. "I can give you the name of the spy in Heldeion's house.

Squeeze him, and he's bound to sell out the wizard to save his own skin."

Aeron sneered and said, "Just like you."

"The coward betrayed me first," said Kesk, glaring back at the thief. "He ran out on me."

"As you betrayed Kerridi, Gavath, Dal, and me," Aeron replied. "And you know what, Pigface? I'm tired of hearing you oink."

Aeron extended his arms straighter. A blue spark popped on one of his knuckles, and the smell of ozone filled the air. Kesk held himself steady. They could kill him, but they'd never see him cringe.

"Aeron," the ranger said, her voice troubled.

"No," he said.

"If he's right, if we do need his help to give this sordid place a chance at a decent way of living . . ."

"Are you both deaf?" Aeron spat. "I said, I don't care about that. He tortured my father. He killed my friends."

"*I* killed your friends," said the ranger.

"I blame him, not you. Anyway, I don't dare let the vengeful bastard live. Father and I would never be safe."

"I vow by the War Maker," said Kesk, "that I won't come after either of you."

"Liar," Aeron said.

The ranger reached as if to take her companion by the arm, then, to Kesk's disgust, thought better of it.

"All right," she sighed, "I won't argue any further. It's your right to kill him if you want. In your place, I'd probably do the same thing."

"Of course you would." Aeron glared down the length of his leveled arms until Kesk's nerves positively screamed with the waiting, then made a sour face, lowered his hands, and said, "Damn you, Miri, why did you have to prattle at me? Now I can't do it, and I don't even know why. Maybe I'm just sick of killing."

Kesk felt lightheaded with relief. With nothing to lose

by trying, he'd argued for his life, but had never actually expected his foes to heed him.

Most likely the scout would never have cause to regret it. She'd vanish into the wilderness, never to return. Aeron, however, was a different matter. When the time was right, Kesk would avenge this humiliation on the lone-wolf rogue and his father, too. Surely offering up a pair of human hearts would appease the War Maker for a false oath sworn in his name.

CHAPTER 19

Miri was aching and bone-weary by the time she and Aeron reached the riverfront. Despite her rudimentary training in the mystic arts, she didn't truly understand how Sefris's bolts of darkness could cause genuine harm without breaking the skin, but it was obvious they had. Otherwise, she wouldn't feel so punchy and weak.

It didn't matter. The fighting was over, and the long search, nearly so. In another hour, she'd deliver *The Black Bouquet* to Master Heldeion, then she could return to Ilmater's house for healing and the use of a bed.

With his wounded arm and head, Aeron would benefit from the priests' attentions as well. She turned to tell him so, then gaped in horror. The rogue was no longer walking at her side.

She spun around. Except for herself, the narrow, trash-choked alley, foul with the stink of rotting fish and produce, was deserted. Aeron hadn't simply lagged a step or two behind. Somehow, he'd slipped away.

She cursed herself for a dunce. Once Nicos was safe, and Sefris dead, she should have known better than to take her eyes off Aeron for so much as an instant. But it was her nature to trust a comrade with whom she'd faced so much peril, and thanks to that gullibility, she'd probably lost the formulary forever.

She snatched an arrow from her quiver to hold ready in her hand, then started to run back the way they'd come. She knew how unlikely it was that she'd spot the liar skulking through the dark, but she had to try.

He called out to her, "Hold on."

She whirled back around, and Aeron stepped from the shadows.

"I'm right here," he said, "and so is this." He hefted a heavy, black-bound volume. "I kept it behind some loose bricks in a wall down thataway."

She peered at him quizzically and asked, "If you meant to give it to me, why did you disappear?"

"I don't know," he said with a smile. "A joke? Maybe I wanted you to know I'm turning it over because I want to, not because I'm afraid of your bow and sword. That I do keep my promises to the right people."

He placed the book in her hands.

When she opened the cover, a sweet scent wafted up. Holding the book close to her face, squinting against the gloom, she was just able to make out Courynn Dulsaer's handwriting. It was the real *Bouquet*, not simply another decoy. Aeron chuckled to see her check the book.

"I said you were learning to think like one of us Oeblar," he said.

"Thank you," she replied. "For the *Bouquet*, not that remark. It's still an insult."

He smiled a crooked smile and said, "From that retort, I take it you're still eager to go back to the woods.

I'll miss you . . . at least a little."

It seemed the perfect opening for Miri to propose the notion she'd been mulling over.

"You don't have to," she said. "You could come along. I'd sponsor you for membership in the Red Hart Guild, and train you, too."

"Now you're playing a joke on me."

"No. I've seen the better side of your nature, and you're too good a man to live out your days as a sneak thief in this wretched place."

"This wretched place is about to reform, or so I'm told."

"Over the course of years, maybe, if everything goes according to Master Heldeion's plan," Miri replied. "I'm offering you the certainty of a new life, a useful, honorable one, right here and now."

"I can't abandon my father."

"He can come, too. The guild provides a home for those of our kin who can't take care of themselves."

He stood mute for several heartbeats, seemingly pondering the offer.

At last he said, "Thank you. I'm flattered you asked, but no. I just don't see myself sleeping on the ground."

Though it was the response she'd expected, it disappointed her nonetheless.

"So be it, then," said the ranger. "I guess you'll have to settle for a bag of Master Heldeion's gold as a reward."

"For recovering *The Black Bouquet*?" Aeron said with a snort. "Not likely. Remember who lifted it in the first place, triggering disturbances across the city that even left some Gray Blades dead. You may have a high opinion of Heldeion, but I don't know him, and I don't trust him not to string me up. He's a merchant and one of the city fathers, in other words, an outlaw's natural enemy."

"Well, as you pointed out yourself, he doesn't ever have to see you or know your name. I promised you gold when we sealed our pact, and I'll fetch it to you."

"Again, thanks, but no. I only asked for a reward to persuade you to trust me. I took the same tack when I talked to Kesk in Slarvyn's Sword. People are usually inclined to believe you're speaking honestly when you say you want coin.

"The truth is, I don't take rewards from fat burghers for returning what's rightfully theirs. That's not my trade. If Heldeion gives you a bonus, keep it for yourself."

"Then you come out of this with nothing."

"I've got my father back, that's what matters, and these lightning gloves are worth having as well. Come on, I'll walk you to Heldeion's house before we go our separate ways. You may find it difficult to believe, but some people think the streets of Oeble are unsafe."

When the servant opened the door for him, Oriseus Forar stepped out onto the porch of his mansion, took a breath of crisp morning air, and tried to take pleasure in the start of a new day.

The gods knew, he had sufficient excuse for a glum mood. After his panicky flight from Laskalar's Square, his alliance with the Red Axes was surely at an end even if Kesk had survived his confrontation with Dark Sister Sefris. Oriseus still didn't have *The Black Bouquet* in his possession, and he doubted he ever would.

Yet the situation wasn't entirely bleak. As far as Oriseus knew, Dorn Heldeion didn't have the book, either, which meant the fool still faced ruin. Oriseus simply had to call in the debts his proxies had bought up. Even more importantly, neither Dorn nor anyone else of importance knew of Oriseus's criminal and treasonous designs. He'd emerged from the *Bouquet* debacle with his reputation unblemished, free to continue enjoying all the wealth and luxuries his station afforded while pursuing his clandestine efforts to bring the entire city under his sway.

Or so he assumed. But as he descended the marble steps toward his litter, a handsome, crimson-lacquered conveyance with appointments of real gold, he spied the Gray Blades. They'd apparently been waiting in the street, inconspicuous among the scurrying crowds, for Oriseus to emerge. Their expressions hard, they advanced on him, and Miri Buckman strode along with them.

Oriseus didn't know how it had happened, but he had no doubt the Faceless Master had ordered his arrest. He was equally certain of the grim fate awaiting him if he allowed himself to be taken. Struggling against terror, he told himself it needn't come to that. His magic would enable him to escape.

He began reciting a spell, lifted a hand to sketch an arcane symbol in the air, and a fierce pain stabbed into his palm. His arm jerked, spoiling the pass. Amazed, he turned his head to discover the source of his distress. He had an arrow sticking through his flesh, the bloody, razor-edged head protruding several inches beyond his knuckles. If only he'd worn his green cloak with its enchantment against missiles! Unfortunately, he'd been worried that people had noticed a suspicious character clad in such a garment fleeing the scene of the battle the night before, and accordingly had left it in his armoire.

He started conjuring with the other hand. Smiling, Miri shot an arrow through that one, too. He tried to finish the magic anyway, but fumbled. The Gray Blades grabbed him.

Once the lawmen laid hands on Oriseus Forar, Aeron decided he and Nicos had seen enough. Muffled in their cloaks and hoods, they turned away, then squirmed and dodged their way through the mass of gawkers who had, as if by magic, assembled to watch the wealthy and prominent—and accordingly, envied and despised—merchant's downfall.

Aeron's belly felt as hollow as a whore's flattery, and he was sure that after his ordeal, Nicos could use a hearty breakfast to rebuild his strength. He led the old man to an open-air food stand under a sagging, dilapidated awning. Behind the bar, eggs, battered bread, trout, and perch smoked and sizzled in cast iron frying pans, filling the air with appetizing aromas.

"I don't know why Miri didn't just shoot Forar in the vitals," Aeron said as they claimed a pair of stools. "I doubt either the Faceless Master or Dorn Heldeion would have minded."

Nicos smirked and replied, "She figured you were watching from somewhere close at hand, so she was showing off for you."

"I knew it had to happen sooner or later," said Aeron, shaking his head. "You're finally going senile."

"You could do worse than a lass like that."

"Right, a woman who likes to sleep out in the rain and snow and thinks the point of life is to risk your neck serving others. Plainly, she and I are a match decreed by the Morninglord himself."

"Well, when you put it that way. . . ."

A serving maid came to take their orders. After she finished, Aeron turned the conversation to more practical matters.

"What items do you need," he asked, "to undertake a journey?"

"A fresh supply of my medicines would be nice. Why, are we going somewhere?"

"Away. I don't care how many oaths Kesk swears. I've twisted his snout too many times, and if I linger within his reach, eventually he'll put an end to me."

"You don't seem too upset about needing to flee."

Aeron shrugged and asked, "What is there to hold me here? All my best friends have either died or betrayed me, and anyway, this whole town is nothing more than a black bouquet."

"What in the name of Baator does that mean?"

"I don't know, but I'm looking forward to finding out. Lately it's occurred to me that the world's a lot bigger than this one town. I've never even seen the Lake of Steam, and it's just over the next hill. Well, so to speak."

"Do we have the funds to pay for a journey?"

"We will once I lift a few purses. Afterward, we'll wander until we find a city that suits us. Someplace I can go back to thieving as a regular thing if I take a mind to."

"If you take a mind to . . ." Nicos chuckled. "If we want to eat, you may not have a choice."

"Well, as to that. . . ."

Aeron stealthily opened his tunic just long enough for his father to glimpse the old, brown sheets of parchment he carried inside, then fastened it up again.

Nicos lowered his rasping voice to a whisper and asked, "Pages from the formulary?"

"Slit neatly from the center. Dorn Heldeion has plenty of recipes left. He'll never miss these few. But if the whole book is worth a vast fortune, then even a piece of it should sell for a small one, once we get it authenticated. So you see, unless we develop a yen for golden ruby-studded chamber pots and similar extravagances, we're set for a long time to come."

Nicos grinned and said, "I always hoped to steer you toward an honest, upright manner of living. I'm starting to be glad it didn't work."

A Major

Event!

The Year of Rogue Dragons
Book I

The Rage

RICHARD LEE BYERS

An Excerpt

They shrugged off their packs and bedrolls—they didn't want the gear weighing them down in combat. Then they drank the elixirs intended to protect them from the acidic secretion slathering the dragon's hide. After that it was time for Pavel, brandishing his sun-shaped pendant, to work magic.

From past experience, Dorn knew the first prayer was a blessing to brace and invigorate the four of them. It cleansed the fleshly part of him of the aches and heaviness of fatigue even as it cleared and sharpened his mind. The second invocation engendered no such sensations, but in some subtle fashion he didn't pretend to understand, it would make it more difficult for the wyrm to strike them.

The third spell was for Dorn alone. The world fell utterly silent as Pavel shrouded him in stillness. In theory, the rest of his comrades might have benefited from the same treatment. But Will was too vain of his thief-craft to admit the magic might be of use to him, and neither Pavel nor Raryn wanted to dispense with their voices and thus their ability to recite incantations. The latter possessed his own store of cantrips, wilderness lore handed down from ranger to ranger, not as formidable or versatile as the cleric's divinely granted powers, but useful enough in certain situations.

After that, they were ready. Dorn nodded, signaling it was time to go.

They crept in single file, Will in the lead, Raryn second, Dorn third, and Pavel, the noisiest as well as the least adept with mundane weapons, bringing up the rear. Each kept several yards back from the hunter in front of him. Even if a dragon had no breath weapon—and if they were right about its species, the one they were stalking didn't—it was good tactics not to bunch up. That way, the creature couldn't rear up and fling itself down on the whole hunting party, pinning and crushing everyone with a single hop.

As he drew nearer to the quarry, Dorn's eyes started to water and sting. It hardly inspired confidence in the efficacy of the potion he'd just consumed. He wondered if old Firefingers had brewed up a weak batch.

He caught his first glimpse of the wyrm, hunkered down among the trees. They'd been correct, it was one of the bog-dwelling creatures called ooze drakes. Smeared with a vile-looking whitish slime, its dull green body was lanky and serpentine, and even the idiots who claimed to consider other breeds of dragon beautiful would have found nothing fair or graceful in its proportions. Its claws were gray, and Dorn knew that when he saw them, its fangs would be the same.

As usual, the sight of the thing gave him a pang of dread, but he reminded himself why he hated them, and he was all right. He knew his friends would be, too, for in all their years together, none of them had ever let him down.

The ooze drake jerked, and a stone rebounded from its flank, leaving a bloody pock behind. It seemed a miracle that such a small missile could penetrate the creature's scales. But Will was a master of the warsling, knew the spots where the dragon's hide was thinnest, and had hurled an enchanted missile. All in all, it was sufficient to give the beast a sting.

Far more quickly than such a huge creature ought to be able to move, the drake whirled in the direction of its attacker. Pale yellow eyes blazing, it opened its jaws. Roaring, surely, though Dorn couldn't hear it. Another stone caught it on the end of its snout, and it charged.

Dorn hastily drew back his composite longbow and sent an arrow streaking through the trees. He too knew where to aim, and the shaft plunged deep into the base of the dragon's neck. It stumbled, its sweeping tail obliterating a stand of blue-spotted mushrooms. The wyrm lurched around in the archer's direction. Will immediately hit it in the shoulder with another stone.

The ooze drake spread its batlike wings. If it took to the air, that might well give it a crucial advantage, even against foes who took care to remain beneath the sheltering trees. Or, if it was feeling timid, it could simply soar away and leave its attackers far behind. It was Raryn's job to keep that from happening. He scrambled out from behind a stand of brush and threw his harpoon. Trailing rope behind it, the lance drove into the wyrm's belly.

Most dragons were at least as intelligent as men. The ooze drake clearly had the wit to surmise that the white-bearded dwarf had knotted the other end of the line to a tree. Perhaps it even realized the harpoon was barbed, and that if it simply yanked it out, it risked giving itself a far more serious wound than it had taken hitherto. In any case, it made the right move. Twisting its neck, it reached to bite the rope.

If Dorn was lucky, he could prevent that, but not by sniping away with his bow. He dropped the missile weapon, gripped his bastard sword, and charged out into the open. Had it been possible, he would have shouted a war cry to attract the ooze drake's attention

Not that he needed to. The reptile could hardly miss such a hulk of a man, body half made of iron and long, straight blade in hand, sprinting to engage it. And it obviously realized that if it simply ignored him, he was likely to drive the sword into its eye while it chewed at the rope. The dragon swung around and pounced.

Dorn sprang aside, just avoiding the scaly foot and talons that would otherwise have eviscerated him. He cut at its foreleg, trying to cripple it, but scarcely nicked it. The creature spun around to face him.

When Dorn had nightmares, they were about dragons, and conducted in utter silence as it was, the duel that now commenced had something of the same eerie quality. Certainly, seen up close, the ooze drake was nightmare incarnate. Its gnashing, slate-colored teeth were like swords, while the citrine, slit-pupiled eyes shone with demonic rage. Its body, as long as a tree and as big as a house, coiled and struck with appalling speed. The wounds it had taken weren't slowing it at all.

Dorn fought as he generally did, the almost indestructible iron portion of his body forward to parry—or, when unavoidable, bear an enemy's attacks—and the soft, human half behind. The ooze drake caught his metal arm in its fangs, bore down, realized it couldn't bite through, and settled for whipping him up and down like a terrier breaking the back of a rat. Dorn was slammed to the ground.

The reptile raked at him. Dorn thrust, and the point of his sword drove into the flesh between two of the creature's claws. The wyrm snatched its foot back, away from the pain, and for an instant, the pressure of its jaws slackened. Fortunately, Dorn's artificial limbs had sensation of a sort, though it wasn't like a normal human's sense of touch. His master had seen no reason to make a tool meant purely for killing susceptible to pain. The half-golem felt the loosening and wrenched his grotesquely oversized fist free. The knuckle-spikes caught on one of the drake's lower fangs and ripped it from the gum. He heaved himself to his feet, and the reptile lunged at him once more.

As they fought, drops of the drake's corrosive slime, flung free by its exertions or his own strokes, spattered him. They stung his face, and he wondered again how well the potion was protecting him. Smoking and smoldering, the pasty stuff burned holes in his brigandine and even pitted the blade of the hand-and-a-half sword, enchanted though it was. Only the iron parts of him proved entirely resistant.

Finally, after what felt like an hour of frenzied struggle, even though it had only been a few seconds, Raryn charged in on the dragon's flank and chopped at it with his ice-axe. From that point forward, though his attention stayed focused on the wyrm, Dorn nonetheless caught glimpses of his comrades when the frenzied chaos of the battle brought them momentarily into view.

Raryn drove the axe into the creature's body. It pivoted, jerking the weapon from his grip, and clawed at him. Raryn jumped back, avoiding that attack, but the reptile wasn't done. It kept on turning, and its tail lashed the dwarf across his barrel chest. Raryn flew through the air and slammed down hard—hard enough, by the look of it, to break his bones—but scrambled up and grabbed for the hilt of his dagger.

Using his small size to good advantage, Will darted under the reptile's belly and jammed his curved sword through the scales, making a long incision as if he was gutting a deer. The wyrm slammed its stomach flat on the ground, sending a jolt through the earth. Its weight would have pulverized anyone caught beneath, but the halfling flung himself clear.

A translucent mace sprang into existence, and as if wielded by an invisible warrior, battered the ruff of jagged, bony plates behind the dragon's blazing eyes and snapping jaws. Having seen the trick before, Dorn knew Pavel had conjured the effect. A few seconds later, the priest himself advanced on the creature, the mace of steel and wood in his own fist shining like the sun.

Dorn did his best to stay in front of the drake and attack relentlessly, trying to keep the reptile's attention fixed on him while his friends hacked, bashed, and stabbed it from the sides and rear. He himself gradually cut its mask into a crosshatch of bloody gashes. Still, the wyrm wouldn't even falter, much less go down.

Eaten away by acid, the bastard sword snapped in two. As he fumbled for the shorter blade he carried as backup, or for fighting in close quarters, a column of dazzling yellow fire hurtled down from the darkening sky to strike the drake between the wings. Dorn knew Pavel wasn't sufficiently learned—or wise, or saintly . . . however it worked—to cast such a powerful spell from his own innate capabilities. He'd used a precious scroll, divine magic the arcanists of Thentia couldn't replace, because in his estimation it was the only way to put the dragon down.

The ooze drake convulsed, but only for a second. It rounded on the man it had plainly identified as the principal spellcaster among its opponents. Its head shot forward at the end of the long neck and caught Pavel in its jaws. Teeth gnashing, it reared high, on the brink of chewing him up and swallowing him down.

No time for the short sword. Dorn lunged in and ripped with his iron claws. Heedless of their own safety, Raryn and Will attacked just as furiously.

At last, reeking of burned flesh, the wyrm collapsed. The three hunters scrambled just as frantically backward to keep it from landing on top of them, then rushed to its head to determine if Pavel was still alive.

They couldn't tell until they pried the fangs apart and pulled him free. He was breathing shallowly, but might not be for long. His wounds were deep, bleeding profusely, and he was the healer. Who, then, would heal him?

The richness of Sembia yields stories within its bounds...and beyond.

LORD OF STORMWEATHER

Sembia

Dave Gross

Thamalon Uskevren II thinks he has a long time before he'll inherit Stormweather Towers and the responsibility such inheritance brings. When not only his father, but also his mother and mysterious servant Erevis Cale disappear, Tamlin will have to grow up fast. To save his family, he'll have to make peace with his brother and sister and face a truth about himself that he imagined only in his wildest dreams.

TWILIGHT FALLING

The Erevis Cale Trilogy, Book I

Paul S. Kemp

Erevis Cale has come to a fork in the road where he feels the pull of the god Mask and the weight of a life in the shadows. To find his own path, he must leave the city of Selgaunt. To save the world, he must sacrifice his own soul.

July 2003

The Hunter's Blades Trilogy

New York Times **best-selling author**
R.A. SALVATORE
takes fans behind enemy lines in this new trilogy about one of the most popular fantasy characters ever created.

THE LONE DROW

Book II

Chaos reigns in the Spine of the World. The city of Mirabar braces for invasion from without and civil war within. An orc king tests the limits of his power. And *The Lone Drow* fights for his life as this epic trilogy continues.

October 2003

Now available in paperback!

THE THOUSAND ORCS

Book I

A horde of savage orcs, led by a mysterious cabal of power-hungry warlords, floods across the North. When Drizzt Do'Urden and his companions are caught in the bloody tide, the dark elf ranger finds himself standing alone against *The Thousand Orcs.*

July 2003

R.A. Salvatore's War of the Spider Queen

Chaos has come to the Underdark like never before.

New in hardcover!

CONDEMNATION, Book III

Richard Baker

The search for answers to Lolth's silence uncovers only more complex questions. Doubt and frustration test the boundaries of already tenuous relationships as members of the drow expedition begin to turn on each other. Sensing the holes in the armor of Menzoberranzan, a new, dangerous threat steps in to test the resolve of the Jewel of the Underdark, and finds it lacking.

Now in paperback!

DISSOLUTION, Book I

Richard Lee Byers

When the Queen of the Demonweb Pits stops answering the prayers of her faithful, the delicate balance of power that sustains drow civilization crumbles. As the great Houses scramble for answers, Menzoberranzan herself begins to burn.

August 2003

INSURRECTION, Book II

Thomas M. Reid

The effects of Lolth's silence ripple through the Underdark and shake the drow city of Ched Nasad to its very foundations. Trapped in a city on the edge of oblivion, a small group of drow finds unlikely allies and a thousand new enemies.

October 2003

Starlight & Shadows

New York Times best-selling author Elaine Cunningham finally completes this stirring trilogy of dark elf Liriel Baenre's travels across Faerûn! All three titles feature stunning art from award-winning fantasy artist Todd Lockwood.

New paperback editions!

DAUGHTER OF THE DROW

Book 1

Liriel Baenre, a free-spirited drow princess, ventures beyond the dark halls of Menzoberranzan into the upper world. There, in the world of light, she finds friendship, magic, and battles that will test her body and soul.

TANGLED WEBS

Book 2

Liriel and Fyodor, her barbarian companion, walk the twisting streets of Skullport in search of adventure. But the dark hands of Liriel's past still reach out to clutch her and drag her back to the Underdark.

New in hardcover – the long-awaited finale!

WINDWALKER

Book 3

Their quest complete, Liriel and Fyodor set out for the barbarian's homeland to return the magical Windwalker amulet. Amid the witches of Rashemen, Liriel learns of new magic and love and finds danger everywhere.

The foremost tales of the Forgotten Realms® series, brought together in these two great collections!

LEGACY OF THE DROW COLLECTOR'S EDITION

R.A. Salvatore

Here are the four books that solidified both the reputation of *New York Times* best-selling author R.A. Salvatore as a master of fantasy, and his greatest creation Drizzt as one of the genre's most beloved characters. Spanning the depths of the Underdark and the sweeping vistas of Icewind Dale, Legacy of the Drow is epic fantasy at its best.

THE BEST OF THE REALMS

A Forgotten Realms anthology

Chosen from the pages of nine Forgotten Realms anthologies by readers like you, *The Best of the Realms* collects your favorite stories from the past decade. *New York Times* best-selling author R.A. Salvatore leads off the collection with an all-new story that will surely be among the best of the Realms!

November 2003